The MenD'lee

ZANN CORRIE KENNEDY

The MenD'lee

THE LEKTON CHRONICLES

TATE PUBLISHING & Enterprises

Published by Tate Publishing & Enterprises, LLC
127 E. Trade Center Terrace | Mustang, Oklahoma 73064 USA
1.888.361.9473 | www.tatepublishing.com

Tate Publishing is committed to excellence in the publishing industry. The company reflects the philosophy established by the founders, based on Psalm 68:11,
"The Lord gave the word and great was the company of those who published it."

Book design copyright © 2011 by Tate Publishing, LLC. All rights reserved.
Cover design by Amber Gulilat
Interior design by Chelsea Womble

Published in the United States of America

ISBN: 978-1-61739-625-0
1. Fiction / Science Fiction / General
2. Fiction / Romance / Fantasy
11.01.18

Dedicated to the memory of my loving parents,
Harley W. and Rosa Ryan Corrie

ACKNOWLEDGMENTS

My heartfelt thanks go to many wonderful people who have, literally, been my eyes. To my mentors, late author Mike McQuay and the late Dr. John Thompson—thanks for cheering. Domo arigatou to Sensei William Thurston and Sensei Jimmy Kennedy for their fascinating consultations on martial arts, and to Robert Puckett for his insights on law enforcement. Thanks also to my bro, Dr. Doug Corrie and my son, Sean Kennedy for technical research.

Grateful cannot describe my appreciation to Bert Hayling, Tessa Wilson, Diane Merrimon, Jeannie Kline, Teresa Crittenden, Paul Marek, and Angel Jones for tireless proofing again and again.

And a special thank you to Tate Publishing for believing in me and praying for my success. You are the best!

PROLOGUE

Excerpt from "Chronicles of Lekton:
An Historical Perspective, Part One"

It is my intent, as one born on Lekton and privileged to witness our world's rebirth, to create this chronicle for you, the people of Sol's third planet, Terra. To understand the significance of our small planet, Lekton, it's important to recognize our place in the galactic community. On June 10, 2080 (an approximation based on the Terran Standard Equivalent scale), Lekton became a member of the Confederation of Worlds, otherwise known as COAXIS. This new society, then barely twenty-five years old, included Venutia, a humanoid species like us, and two xenoid species, Xylonia and Tserias. COAXIS was created to share knowledge for the betterment of all, a lofty goal that Lekton embraced. With membership came gifts of transportation and communication technologies to facilitate interaction between worlds.

In addition, a COAXIS Institute was built on the southern shore of our sole, habitable continent. The five basic programs, called orders, include science technology, social services, diplomatic services, cultural studies and medical research. A team of professors from other worlds came to Lekton, trained our scholars, and then left the work to Lektonians.

As you might expect, these benefits revolutionized Lekton. COAXIS Sociologists worried that such rapid change would damage our culture or weaken our government. But our determination to retain what was intrinsically Lektonian in our nature spared us from corruption. To be honest, certain social changes might have benefited us, but our leaders maintained tight control. Overall, our experience with COAXIS was pleasant.

However, that wasn't so for your world. Twenty years later, COAXIS offered membership to Earth. Once again, the offer included the same technological gifts. While these were welcomed, the people of Earth suffered a profound xenophobia. They declined the offer to join the Confederation.

Some on Earth, though, favored membership. Political battles arose until the more progressive settlers of their moon colony claimed independence as a separate government called Luna. They accepted membership and let those of Earth refuse it.

Soon, Luna had a COAXIS Institute, and many of Earth's greatest scientists were lured to relocate there. A few weeks later, a mysterious virus infected personnel at Luna's Hilliard Research Station, causing a disease called DRA. Later, it was learned that Tserian scientists working there had stolen critical biofilters from a lab, inadvertently creating the virus. COAXIS decreed that Tserians would never again be allowed on any COAXIS world.

This treachery might have influenced Earth's leaders against membership. But fortunately, the Venutian's spectacular research abilities proved invaluable. They prevented a pandemic event and eliminated the virus. At last, Earth's United Nations recognized their need for membership. By June of 2121, the Earth formed a new, world government as Terra and became the sixth member of the Confederation. Their one provision was that no beings other than Terrans were to visit their world. No COAXIS Institute was built on Terra, and no COAXIS Embassy existed there to encourage interaction. So, Terrans interested in the educational opportunity attended the Institute on Luna.

Ironically, it was that Institute that trained several of the people who most influenced social growth on Lekton. This is their story.

THE MEND'LEE

To everyone comes a time to be born.
For some, that time isn't always childhood.
In deepest winter I was born,
far from the springtime
of blossoming and growing.
It was only by the wisdom of Time himself
that I was prevented from entering my springtime
as a child.

- Melenta Cha'atre -

CHAPTER 1

Lekton, 22 Zelonn, 2158 (December 21
Terran Standard Equivalent)

The still, cold air of darkest night pricked at her nerves. She stalked closer to yet another fateful encounter. Agent Dread checked her disguise once more in the mirrored door of the Moon Rising Club. The owner would recognize her solid, muscular form, perhaps, but the disguise would get her in and to a corner table. It was folly to meet here—too risky.

But risk, she mused to herself, *is why the Galactic Enforcement Agency pays me.* Closing her fingers on the chilled, metal handle, she pulled the door open and stepped inside.

As expected, the reek of stale bodies and even staler wine assailed her. The dim lights and too loud instrumentals hid all kinds of sins. *That's how I like it when I have to meet scum like "The Bruiser." Most agents turn down such sordid assignments. That's when the Commander calls me.*

Valiantly, she turned to her work. Feigning advanced age and a full night of drinking, she stumbled into a corner booth and ignored the sticky grit of the floor under the table. Across the room, her contact recognized her instantly. Digger, a poor krekk whom life had kicked down a few times too often, wore a brimmed hat to conceal his alien, Terran eyes. Beside him sat a hulk of a man, a bronze-skinned Lektonian who constantly shifted his gaze to every corner of the room.

This must be "The Bruiser."

The two men rose and wound between tables, coming directly to her. *Too obvious*, she thought. *Amateurs! Well, if I get this done quickly, I'll still make it to that appointment with the commander. The head of Lekton's GEA office hates to be kept waiting.*

The Lektonian brute slid into the booth across the table from her. Digger nodded to her and pulled a chair to her table. Reversing it, he straddled the chair and offered the standard greeting, "Jhendail."

It's odd to hear Fairday from a muck dweller like Digger, she thought, but she returned the greeting.

He asked, "Do you have the document?"

"Of course."

Digger's companion glared at her, wiped his hand across his moist forehead and grumbled, "Is this a krekking joke? She's a child!"

Her fingers curled into eager fists on the tabletop, ready to teach his mouth some manners.

But Digger waved a gesture of non-offense at her and whispered to the hulk, "You ludjit! She may be fourteen, but she's our best operative on this planet."

Her chin lifted with appropriate defiance. Her eyes narrowed to slits of warning until The Bruiser backed down.

Touching a finger to his forehead to gesture gaaro, he mumbled, "I ask your pardon, Miss... Miss?"

Melenta jumped, startled by the voice that had come from outside her daydream. Wistfully, she relinquished the mental reverie that made her feel significant in a way that her life didn't merit. Blinking, she remembered that she sat at a table in the school's library, where she waited to start her after-school tutoring session.

" Miss?" said the voice again.

Standing next to her chair and looking down at her was a boy her age, yet no one she knew. And he was not of her race. The dark-featured boy was most likely from the Sevenn Nation, judging by the squint of his eyes. He was strong and sure of himself. This made Melenta wish she looked more like Agent Dread instead of being so tall, gangly and unimposing.

It was rare in this Region of the Soloto Nation for fathers of the Barmaajian race to send their children to her school. *So, what's he doing here,* she wondered?

"Yes?" She sat straighter and stared at the stranger. She fought down the thought that he'd somehow discovered the contents of her daydream.

"I asked if you know a mentor named Ailman Brekket?"

"Sure. Ail. Brekket is my mentor."

Without permission, which was an infraction of no minor consequence, the boy sat across from her at the table. "My name is Tellik. I'm supposed to meet the mentor here after school. Have you seen him?"

Melenta eyed him warily. In her Nation, Familyheads maintained a pure lineage within the A'laantuvian race. Amid the typical blonds here, Tellik's black hair and dark, bronzed skin commanded immediate attention. She wasn't frightened but captivated by the difference.

Realizing she was staring, she hurried to identify herself. "I'm Melenta Cha'atre. I think you must be mistaken. Ail. Brekket is supposed to meet with me now."

To her surprise, he smiled and replied, "It's a last minute change, I think."

Tellik laid an unusual sack on the table. It was made from a hand-sewn fur pelt of soft brown and tied at the top with a silver cord. It looked strong and durable. He arranged it with such ceremony that it ignited her curiosity. Preoccupied with his mysterious bundle, she lost all thread of the conversation.

But Tellik went on. "My parents are migrant merchants. I'm registered at this school, but I study on the road. Father told me to set up testing to finish my lower school credits."

Melenta, who hailed from a wealthy family, was uncharacteristically envious. "You're testing out of school?"

He frowned. "It's not like I got out of studying. I've been doing the same work you have." Out of context, he asked, "Have you ever seen the Marble Palace in Sevenn Dunes?"

She was anxious to avoid the boy's boasting about the amazing places he'd seen instead of going to school. She clinched her jaw and admitted that she hadn't seen it.

But he didn't seem to realize her attitude. In a trivial tone, he responded, "Neither have I. If we sell our current stock, I'll get to go there." He smiled, and his humble offering of friendship charmed her. He had an unnerving way of disarming all her usual caution.

She pointed to his fur sack. "What's that?"

"Maybe I'll show you. It's a valuable treasure, and I'm in charge of it."

With effort, she hid her skepticism. *After all, I have my own fantasies that make me feel special. Who am I to demean his dreams?*

After a moment, Tellik seemed to make a decision and gestured for her to move closer. Fumbling with the knotted cord, he'd almost opened the sack when Ail. Brekket interrupted.

Like Melenta, Kendel Brekket was of pure A'laantuvian heritage, and he was young for a mentor. At twenty, fresh out of training at the COAXIS Institute on Luna, he'd returned home to begin teaching. His first assignment, a class of ten students who were all five seasons of age, had included Melenta. Under his mentorship, through ten levels, he'd watched those same small charges grow up.

As he approached, Brekket called out, "I assume you are Tellik Kaamzen?"

Promptly, the boy stood and performed the customary gestures of respect Tradition required. He bowed, keeping a lowered gaze as he stretched his hands before him, palm upward. "Yes, Ail. Brekket."

Melenta also rose and bowed to her mentor before he seemed to notice her. He said, "I'm going to skip a few of your tutoring sessions, Melenta. Before Tellik leaves town, I need to find time to give him the test for his credits." He turned to Tellik. "But for the next few moons, I'll help you review."

She felt slighted and wanted to stay. Before she thought, she broke in to ask, "Could I study with you? I'll be testing next mooncycle."

Tellik glanced aside at her. She noticed his shock at her boldness. Tradition frowned on interrupting a mentor.

But she wasn't worried. Her relationship with Brekket was a special one, and he understood her impulsive nature. He looked at Tellik for permission.

Tellik shrugged and waved his hand from side-to-side, the gesture bays for agreement.

Brekket smiled at her in a personal way. He whispered, "I suppose your father wouldn't object if we actually do study the curriculum he provides."

Despite surprise at his informality, she schooled herself not to react. She thought, *no one should know that the lessons we study aren't the ones Father approved. In front of this stranger, Kendel should have been more careful not to betray our friendship.*

It was an innocent relationship, but her father wouldn't like it.

Efficiently restoring his authority, the mentor called, "Let's get started."

Tellik smiled companionably as the three sat at the table. Melenta had never had any friend except her mentor, but she thought Tellik might be a candidate. Perhaps if she studied him, she'd figure out how he managed to be so confident of his place in the world.

Two cycles later when their lesson was finished, Tellik accompanied Melenta to the nearest transport station. They sat on benches and waited for their respective rail buses to take Melenta to North Road and Tellik to the San Durg Inn.

She was lost in thought, remembering how it had frightened her to walk through the lanes of her township with a boy of the dark race. Her father had always forbidden her to associate with them. Although no one especially noticed them, ingrained prejudices imposed reserve and formality. *Does he feel the same way,* she wondered?

She asked quietly, "Do you know many people from Soloto?" What she really meant was people who were of her race, but she was afraid asking that would offend him.

He smiled, taking no offense at all. "I know a lot of people from all five nations. Mostly, we travel between Soloto and Sevenn, but sometimes I've been to other places. How about you?"

Her instant response hinted at propriety. "Oh, I stay mostly in Soloto." Belatedly, she realized that had sounded judgmental. "But when I was a little girl, we use to visit my grandparents in Sumuru."

Tellik merely blinked at her in confusion.

That was stupid, Melenta. That's the other Nation populated exclusively by A'laantuvians. That was a poor example to prove your lack of racial bias.

She added, "Someday, I want to go to school on Luna and live with the Terrans."

"Really? Terrans? Great portals, Melenta! I'd be afraid to try that." Self-consciously, she glanced around to see that no one else had heard her and then murmured, "Well, it's a secret, so keep it to yourself."

He asked quietly, "What do you really study after school? I won't tell on you."

The frank stare of his dark, violet eyes warned her that dissembling was useless, so she answered truthfully. "Ail. Brekket is tutoring me for the COAXIS Institute's entrance exam. But don't tell anyone."

"Sure, but why? What's wrong with that?"

Apparently nothing, she thought bitterly, *if you're Barmaajian. Does he really know so little about the cultural restraints imposed on a family of pure lineage?*

But better manners prevailed. She explained it to Tellik. "You know that for both races, a Familyhead's decision is literally law. And Lukeniss Cha'atre is the most traditional Familyhead imaginable. He disapproves of COAXIS, so he won't let my mentor teach about it."

"And I thought my father was strict," Tellik said with sympathy. "I guess it does no good to complain?"

"No." She repressed her urgent longing to disavow the Law, for that, too, would do no good. Until The All Wise himself restructured Lekton's system of government, Lukeniss would hold true to the Law of Tradition.

But Melenta had other dreams. She told Tellik, "Fortunately, Ail. Brekket understands and helps me. The only reason Father hasn't found me a paying job after school is that my mentor insists that I need tutoring. We do study, but not what Father thinks we study."

This perplexed Tellik. "So, that's your dream? You want to go to the COAXIS Institute? Or are you only trying to get away from your father's rule?"

Put that way, she wasn't sure. *Tellik's perceptive,* she thought.

Her only goal for many seasons had been to find some sort of empowerment over her life. *Maybe Tellik's right and I'll have to go as far as Luna to have it.*

But now, she realized that what she actually longed for was a purpose for her life. Anyone could accomplish a meager existence, and some could even earn a wealthy lifestyle.

But I want—no, crave—a destiny that's significant.

Although explaining this to Tellik clarified her desire, she had no idea what difference she could make on her patriarchal world.

Tellik scratched his head. "I get why you want to break away from your father, Melenta, but... Luna?"

"Why not?"

He saw her concern and lifted one skeptical eyebrow. "Terrans, huh?"

"They're fascinating! Did you know that their hair is shiny? Can you imagine brown eyes? Or orange hair?"

Tellik laughed at her enthusiasm. "You're really obsessed, aren't you? I hear it's hard to get into those schools."

"Ail. Brekket has been tutoring me for seven seasons. I'll be qualified to enroll at a COAXIS Institute once I complete my lower school credits."

"But don't they require students to speak COAXIS Standard?"

"They do. I've learned it."

Tellik scowled. "Are you sure your work won't be for nothing? If your father is so against COAXIS, why would he let you go?"

Now might be a good time to dissemble. She said, "I'll think of something."

Melenta had a plan, but she didn't care to share it with Tellik. She'd be fifteen very soon, the first stage of maturity for Lektonians. At that age, women are expected to begin working for their family or enter an upper school for training. Otherwise, they must be given in betrothal.

Personally, she didn't mind leaving home as long as nothing prevented it. Betrothal would send her to live with her betrothal mate's family, subject to that Familyhead's rule. As long as she chose a betrothal mate who approved of a COAXIS education, success was assured. Lukeniss would have no say about it.

And best of all, it had been Kendel's idea. He'd made it sound easy although it had one flaw: Lukeniss would insist upon a betrothal by the old-fashioned, A'laantuvian custom of a Gift Rite ceremony. By that custom, her father would approve the men who would contend for her. Melenta would be expected to choose a mate from among those contenders.

However, Lukeniss would never approve any man to contend who favored COAXIS. *And he'd know. Oh, yes, Lukeniss would find out every detail about prospective contenders.*

She considered it for a moment and decided to tell Tellik the plan after all.

But then, her rail bus arrived at the station, and it was time for them to part ways.

As she stood to board her bus, Tellik told her, "My father says that if you want others to think you're important, first be important to them."

She boarded the bus and smiled through the window at her new friend. Taking a seat, she entered a code at the overhead panel and sat back to await the computer's signal that her stop was approaching. With spiteful satisfaction, she imagined reminding her father of how much better life has been since COAXIS upgraded their transportation system. *He certainly isn't averse to owning his own short-range shuttle—the hypocrite!*

"He doesn't know everything," she grumbled.

In fact, she'd seen today that his warning about the danger of getting acquainted with Barmaajians was baseless. She'd enjoyed Tellik's company.

And isn't it interesting that Lukeniss denies the value of different races interacting, and yet in the next breath, he might quote the philosophical concept of K'jhona K'trais.

The concept of amiable differences literally meant "my friend, my opposite." She'd found that the best relationships were usually people with opposite temperaments or abilities. *He praises variety in clothing, in furnishings for the home, even in foods. So, why not in people?*

Suddenly despairing, Melenta recalled Tellik's words. Maybe all her work would be for nothing. Time was growing short. The only man she knew who would allow her to attend the Institute was Kendel. She couldn't exactly bond with her mentor.

But she gave that some thought. *I wouldn't mind being betrothed to him. He comes from my race and Nation, which would definitely be the first prerequisite for Father's approval. Actually, Kendel's family could trace a pure lineage all the way back to the Old Ones who migrated here from the Koleeth continent.*

But would her father say that Kendel is too old for her? On Lekton, the ideal is a difference of ten seasons. *Kendel is only fifteen seasons older. That isn't too bad.*

As the bus glided the rails toward North Road, Melenta imagined Kendel claiming her hand in betrothal. Of course, that would have to wait. He shouldn't show personal favor until her credits were certified and he was no longer her mentor.

Both moons still painted the blue-violet sky as Melenta entered her gate around 2300. Her father owned a moderately large estate north of San Durg Township, the capitol of the Soloto Nation. He maintained a staff of servants who cared for the manor and grounds. Two were serving out a sentence as restitution for non-violent crimes.

The manor overseer, J'Mii, was a firm but good-hearted woman of middle age. Since the death of Melenta's mother four seasons earlier, she'd directed the workers, made all purchases and kept everything running smoothly. While the manor functioned well, it wasn't a home in Melenta's estimation. She could remember happier times.

Her happiest times were before the age of eight, when her older sister, Linnori was alive. She'd sneaked away to meet a Barmaajian man whom she loved and then died under suspicious circumstances.

After the girl's death at fifteen, one would have expected Lukeniss to dote on his remaining daughter. Instead, he pushed her away. Lukeniss had idolized Linnori, but he'd never seemed to love Melenta. That had always been the biggest mystery in her life.

Entering the manor, Melenta fingered a strand of woven twine braided to resemble flowers and strung over the doorway. Similar crafts her mother had made hung decoratively throughout the manor. Kamira's crafts were Melenta's favorite reminders of those happier times.

Her mother's death was the next tragedy in her life. Kamira had died giving birth to her younger brother, Cheelo.

As if on cue, the energetic child raced into the chamber and bounded into her arms. With cordial enthusiasm, he gave her a breathless recounting of his day. "I saw a bug today in the manor, and I wasn't going to touch it, but J'Mii thought I was, and she screamed, and then she ran outside. It was funny."

Melenta hugged him to her and tried not to laugh. J'Mii was easily flustered. She scolded, "When J'Mii is frightened, you shouldn't laugh, Cheelo."

"It was funny," he replied with an impish insistence. Wiggling out of her grasp, he was already bored with the topic. "I made you something." Running to his desk in a corner of their sitting chamber, he pulled out his small, computerized sketcher. On the screen, he'd written eight full rows of printed letters. He'd been practicing his name to please her.

Though only four and ineligible to attend school until next season, Cheelo had begun learning basic skills at home. She praised the effort, even though the last letter was not quite right. "You did this for me? That's really great."

A sly grin spread over his face. "Do you remember what you said?"

I guess I forgot something, she thought, *and it's obviously important.* All she could think to say was, "I'm still thinking about it."

"But you said," he whined as he pulled her by the hand toward another corner. There, a family shrine was displayed on a table. It contained holopics and mementos of the cherished departed of the Cha'atre family. Cheelo pointed to a picture. "You said if I did my schoolwork, you'd tell me about her."

A familiar anguish pierced her emotions, but she wouldn't let herself cry. She told her brother, "Mother loved us, but her health was very weak when you were born. What do you want me to tell you?"

The boy's lower lip quivered, pricking her heart further. "I want to know her."

Though Melenta's own loss still burned in her, she couldn't help agonizing over all the memories that Cheelo would never know. She sat down on a large floor pillow, the customary furnishings of a Lektonian home, and pulled Cheelo into her lap. "I play the games with you that mother played with me. I help you learn to read, and I sing learning songs for you. That's how Mother taught me. You can imagine that she was exactly like me. How's that?"

Her little brother relaxed against her without answering, but seemed content. Her explanation, however, lacked the comfort the young boy really needed. So she extended her hand to him, offering emotional support. When he slipped his hand into hers, there was no doubt about the love they shared. Truthfully, Melenta was

Cheelo's mother in all the ways that mattered. They both felt that way.

The Lektonian ability to sense others' emotions through touch was so complete that words conveyed merely a surface meaning. From the simplest meeting of one's public self to the deepest merging of personalities in a fulfilling, sexual union, emotional joining was a part of life. That simple act of holding hands and sharing emotions was integral to a child's normal development. Melenta knew the worth of such bonds in early years because Linnori and her mother had always provided that for her.

Tellik's words came to mind. She thought, *for others to think I'm important, I have to be important to them. I'm already important to Cheelo. So why doesn't that feel like it's enough? Why do I feel like the world has to need me, too?*

There was no doubt her brother needed her. She knew her father was incapable of providing Cheelo's emotional needs. Although their father spoiled his son, he never desired that relationship with her or with Cheelo. It was as if losing Linnori had blanched all love from his heart.

Gratefully, Melenta smiled, rejoicing at her brother's willingness to love her back. But unexpectedly, her thoughts strayed to old resentments and disappointment. She couldn't inspire her father's love, a failing in herself that she couldn't fathom. Lest she communicate those negative emotions to Cheelo, she blocked her feelings. Knowing when to shield emotions was as important as knowing how to share them.

When sharing wasn't desired, an organ called a deflector produced an energy field that deflected emotions. As she raised the emission of her deflector, she felt Cheelo's field rising to match it. She thought, *he shows no disappointment when I deny him my emotions. I hope he understands that joining is uncomfortable for me.*

Too soon, their father's shuttle landed outside, and she knew it must be Half-light. He was a very prominent man in their community—the township's principal banker. Steeling herself for an unpleasant reunion, she pushed Cheelo ahead of her to greet him at the door.

Lukeniss had a stately gait and moved always with a sense of purpose. Businesslike wasn't precisely the word for his attitude, though. It was dignified. By custom, each Familyhead picked one virtue that he wished to represent his family. He wore a symbol of that "credo" on a necklace that announced to all what he believed. A Familyhead is judged by how he portrays that virtue. His children also wear the same credoglyph necklace, but their behavior is accredited to their father for good or ill.

Lukeniss Cha'atre wore the credoglyph for Dignity.

Thus, when he came home, Cheelo waited respectfully to greet him. He never ran into his arms, bubbling over with too much to tell. He'd been instructed in formal, traditional behavior. Cheelo waited quietly, keeping his eyes lowered in denees, the gesture of respect.

When their father entered the door, Cheelo said with restrained decorum, "Welcome, Father."

Lukeniss smiled proudly at him and patted his head. "Thank you, son. Did you practice your numbers today?" To a banker, this was important.

The boy answered promptly, "Yes, sir."

"And you're writing?"

"Yes, sir. I showed it to Melenta."

Lukeniss gave a short nod of approval. "Good. See if J'Mii can use your help. I'm going to talk to your sister."

Melenta cringed. *As long as Tradition rules this manor, I'll never be important except to Cheelo. Maybe I should find my significance by changing that. Could I really stop the Law of Tradition?*

Abruptly, her course was realized; her goal was set.

CHAPTER 2

Once Cheelo left the chamber, Lukeniss turned to his daughter. "Melenta, I heard about a merchant who is looking for a woman to apprentice with him. He asked if you might consider it. You could work after school until you complete your credits and then begin apprenticing."

Here we go, thought Lukeniss. *She's going to disagree.*

Indicating a pillow, he told her to sit down while he sat on a taller floor pillow so that he gazed down on her. *What a pity I have to employ intimidation techniques with this independent child. She looks a lot like Kamira. I wish she'd gotten her mother's spirit of submission and duty. If not for my discipline, she'd never make a proper wife for anyone.*

That would be soon. It was his intention to see that she was betrothed as soon as she gained her majority, although in this matter Tradition wouldn't allow him to insist on it. Melenta would have to personally arrange for a Gift Rite ceremony, and he wasn't sure if he could get her to do it.

One thing is certain, though: I can see that she shows high moral character. To that end, I'll make her accept this plan.

He asked, "Is there any reason you can't work?"

With her gaze lowered, she replied, "I've been reviewing for my exam to complete my credits, and Ail. Brekket believes I need more study in two subjects."

Lukeniss considered her excuse, wondering if it were true or not. At least she didn't meet his eyes, and that pleased him. *I must keep reign on her willful nature.*

He asked, "And is the tutoring helping you?"

"Yes, sir. And I'm not the only student he tutors. If I'm going to take upper school training at a kaamestaat, I have to score in the highest third on my exam."

This is a surprise, he thought. *Or did she fabricate this only now because I mentioned a job? She's so contrary, wanting the opposite of whatever I decide.*

He'd assumed that suggesting a job would make her request betrothal simply to be oppositional. Now, he had to try a different tactic.

"So, you want to earn a degree? I thought you'd want to accept Gift Rite and find a mate. This has been Lekton's Tradition passed down by Familyheads for generations. You should attract a man of quality, given my station in our Region."

She hesitated slightly. "I suppose I could do that. But shouldn't I wait until after I finish the degree to choose a mate?"

Lukeniss had hoped to have her betrothed and off his hands long before that. He thought, *let her be the bane of some other Familyhead. But if she went away to school, well, she'd still be out of sight, at least.*

And then he realized that if she had a degree as a merchant, it would make her more valuable, more attractive to contenders. *Yes,* he thought, *that would be suitable.*

Artfully, he disguised his decision, knowing how stubbornly Melenta balked when she thought she wasn't getting her way. He said thoughtfully, "Some women earn a degree before accepting betrothal. Either choice is possible." He carefully avoided saying that either was acceptable to him.

Melenta betrayed only a slight smile that told him she thought she'd gotten her way. He must demonstrate how little power she truly had. "Tell me, what did your study group discuss after school today?"

Her answer came quickly and with a hint of confusion. "We reviewed the history of the Old Ones who lived on the other continent. We learned about the small group of families, the Travelers of the Great Trek, who crossed into our continent long ago. We ran out of time to discuss the volcanoes and quakes that destroyed Koleeth before those families could get home."

When he'd called Brekket this afternoon, he'd reported the same topic of discussion. With that, he rested his suspicion about Brekket's motive for spending so much time with his daughter.

He asked, "Isn't that rather elementary? You've learned the history of our ancestors all your life."

"We have a new student who is Barmaajian, so he's learning it for the first time."

Lukeniss thought it over. *If Brekket plans anything to keep Melenta from a proper future, he might betray himself in time. I'll contact my friend, Gruner. He's done a few jobs for me in the past, and I can have him follow Melenta. That would ensure complete disclosure.*

He told her, "Very well. You may continue to study after school. Try not to spend too much time with that boy of the dark race, Melenta. One never knows who is watching. I hope this Barmaaj doesn't hold you back from what you need to study."

His daughter bowed in respect, and he dismissed her.

While outwardly, Melenta maintained her dignity (for to slip in that would most assuredly ruin her day), inwardly, rage slithered through her veins like a poison. *His strategies are so predictable, and*

they're always aimed at controlling me. He makes a decision that I'd be sure to dislike, but it's never the real plan. He expects me to want whatever he doesn't want. Since he steered me away from betrothal, I know that's really what he wants me to choose.

Often, they battled back and forth this way until she let him believe she'd been forced into submission. Knowing her father's true intention gave her hope that her goals were still in reach. Discipline! She had to control her reactions, choke back the bitter retort that so easily leaped to her tongue.

Quickly, she sought the safety of her sleep chamber, the room she'd once shared with her late sister. It always soothed her moods. Opening her door, she glanced at her sister's fur-bed and smiled. A small lump could barely be noticed under the blanket. It moved until a tiny, black-furred face poked out from the edge of the cover. The gentle creature, a rushi named Teeka, had belonged to Linnori. After her death, Teeka had devoted all affection to Melenta.

Enfolding the animal into her arms, she smoothed her hand along the orange stripe that ran down its back from head to tail. She reached for the leash hanging by her fur-bed and whispered, "Sorry I'm late. Do you want to go out?"

Teeka hopped gracefully to the floor and struck a pose with her head and tail lifted. Melenta attached the leash to Teeka's collar and together, they left the manor for a long walk.

Melenta loved this time of day. The dim, lavender hues of Halflight always relaxed her. The weather had begun to cool once Bella, the larger moon, had set. Lekton's smaller moon, Tra'a, was almost in full phase and had a red-violet tinge to it tonight. Sometimes, that was a sign of rain coming.

Beyond her estate, there were few neighbors. Her father preferred living on the outskirts of town. North Road was secluded and quiet, save for a few haunting calls of night birds.

She wondered, *why did Father question what I studied today? Surely, if he knew anything, he'd punish me for it. He'd punish Kendel, too.*

Suddenly, she feared the consequences for her beloved mentor if they were caught. He could lose his mentor's license.

I can't take that risk. I'll tell Kendel tomorrow that the special lessons must stop. Anyway, maybe he'd rather give more time to other students, she thought.

San Durg Township, 23 Zelonn, 2158

Throughout the next day, Kendel noticed that Melenta wasn't concentrating. Of all his students, he believed she had the most potential, so he never allowed her ambition to wane.

Is she ill, he wondered? *Or perhaps she's distracted by a problem? In any event, she isn't in a mood to learn. And after the call I received from Lukeniss last night, her behavior is especially troubling.*

After school, Kendel dismissed the class, but he told her to stay. He wouldn't have much time since Tellik would be waiting for them in the library. Although he was alone with Melenta in the classroom, he carefully maintained professional behavior. Appearances would be important if someone looked inside the classroom.

Sitting at his desk, he whispered, "Did something happen at home last night? Why was your father checking on you?"

Thankfully, she had the good sense to keep a proper attitude of submission.

Her quiet voice carried urgency. "I don't know. I'm worried that he suspects what you've been teaching me."

His heart rate shot up. His eyes darted to the door, but saw no one watching. Forcing a casual tone, he asked, "Did he say that?"

"No. He was pressuring me to quit our tutoring sessions and take a job after school instead. But I think that was an excuse. Maybe we should stop."

He sighed. "I can't let you do that. You're close to your goal. We need to keep working."

Her answer was daring and personal. "We need to protect your mentor's license."

"No," he answered firmly. "After seven seasons of work, I can't let you quit now for my sake. You're almost ready for the entrance exam, but you have to be fluent in Standard."

Sounding hopeful, she said, "I heard about a translation chip that can be implanted in the brain so that you can speak in any language."

The suggestion irritated Kendel, as attempts to circumvent the hard work of learning always did. "You're talking about a TUP device, Melenta, and they're available only to diplomats and researchers. Besides that, it's very expensive. There's no substitute for hard work." Although he couldn't see her eyes, he was sure she was rolling them. *I guess I do stress that point a little too often.*

Patiently, he said, "You'll make it, even if your father makes you take a job after school. Don't doubt yourself."

Her huff of frustration explained her feelings, but she nodded the gesture of acknowledgment. She said with slow, measured words, "That's not really what Father wants. He wants me to be betrothed."

"What?" He'd spoken too harshly and glanced again at the door. "Didn't you say he's pushing you to take a job?"

"He proposed that so I'd rebel and demand betrothal instead. I barely convinced him that I should go to the kaamestaat first. He only consented because I'd be of more value to contenders if I have a degree. What if he changes his mind and insists on an immediate betrothal? What if I have to pick a contender who won't let me go to a COAXIS Institute?"

Kendel had considered that possibility. Raising his index finger to gesture keesla for silence, he nodded toward the door. He thought, *I wish I could ease her panic, but words seem so inadequate. I'd never join with a student, though. The poor girl is terrified.*

Tenderly, he whispered, "That won't happen. I'll contend for you myself if it's all ..."

Her head snapped up, daring to meet his eyes. "Your license!"

"It won't be a problem as long as you wait until you've earned your credits to announce Gift Rite. I won't be your mentor then." He couldn't touch her, but he was sure that she knew how much he wanted to express his feelings. *Surely, she knows. Doesn't she feel it, too?*

And then a brief flash of concern struck him. *Was she shocked by my interest? No, we've formed a friendship over many seasons.* Memories of sharing their mutual love of Terran culture quickly overcame that worry.

Still, their relationship had never been anything but appropriate. Had he offended her by his overemphasis on professionalism? When Melenta's face turned suddenly pale and grim, Kendel regretted his words.

Abruptly, she said, "Why does this world base its laws on a Familyhead's whims? Do you see that if I were a boy, I could petition the Elders of Soloto to head my own household and do what I please? But because I was born a woman, I have to be owned by a man!"

Her loud protest worried him. What if they were heard? Taking a risk, he grasped her hand and squeezed it. "No man can own you! Your husband may decree your choices, but you design your soul."

Self-consciously (and reluctantly, he thought), she dropped his hand. She uttered in a voice full of despair, "Can't someone do something to change the Law?"

"Who knows? Maybe The All Wise will decide to step in. It's his job to protect us, right?" He sat up straighter, moving further from her. Their quiet discussion was starting to appear too intimate.

Melenta jumped, surprised as much as he was at the appearance of impropriety. She asked, "Do you really believe those legends?" Then, mockingly, she quoted from the tales passed down over generations. "Destiny, daughter of The All Wise, will choose The MenD'lee, The Chosen One who will lead Lekton to a new era of prosperity and enlightenment." She gave a disdainful sound of disbelief. "Father's told me that my whole life."

"Nothing says your father has to be wrong about everything. Why couldn't it be true? The MenD'lee might be exactly what we need. Destiny probably has someone in mind already, so maybe Time will start the plan very soon."

His pupil glowered with resentment. "The only thing the son of The All Wise ever does is to interrupt my plans."

"Melenta!" He half-heartedly teased her for her outspoken blasphemy.

"Well, Time's never been very helpful." Passionately, she proclaimed to the universe, "Make me The MenD'lee, and I'll change things!"

But if the universe heard, no bolt of magic anointed her.

All of a sudden, her words embarrassed her, and she laughed. "Listen to me. I don't even know if there is an All Wise."

"Think of it this way," Kendel replied. "We've kept our study a secret for seven seasons. Someone must be slanting odds in our favor."

After the tutoring session, Melenta hoped to speak to Kendel alone. But then Tellik asked Kendel, "Do you have any experience in merchant craft?"

Melenta and her mentor were mutually wary. Brekket said, "I know the basics. Why?"

Reaching toward his feet, Tellik brought the brown, fur sack to the tabletop. "I'd like your advice about how to market this." Loosening the cord, he reached inside and produced a magnificent statue. The figure was made of grenva, a precious, golden metal. The figure, which was a little larger than his hand, depicted The All Wise. The majestic, robed image stood with outstretched arms, and from his hands, blessings trickled down like water to the base. Each drop of blessing was inset with a tra'adeen crystal in various colors.

Melenta gasped, "How beautiful!"

Brekket's expression brightened. "Tellik! Where did you get this?"

Tellik beamed proudly. "My mother designed it. She's a sculptor and jeweler."

"Exceptional," agreed Brekket. "Why are you carrying around something so valuable?"

"Mother made five of these statues. My father wants to get a merchant to commission a number of them. Then we could settle in one place. Traveling has become hard on his joints. Each of my four older brothers and I were given one to sell."

Melenta cautioned, "Don't let anyone know you're carrying this. You'll be robbed."

"I thought the same thing," said Brekket. "You need to show this only to merchants who might want to buy it."

"That's why I need your advice. I don't know how to find the right merchants."

Melenta said, "My father would know. I could show him a holopic of the piece and see where he'd recommend selling it."

Brekket laughed. "I have an even better idea. Melenta, since your father is so keen to have you be a merchant, let's make it an assignment. I want you to show the picture to an expert and ask how it would best be marketed."

Tellik complained, "But I don't have a holocamera."

"I do," the mentor replied. "It's in my desk. Take out your sketcher and let's create a marketing analysis."

Once their assignment was planned, Melenta and Tellik were dismissed. Together, they walked to the transport station. The late afternoon sky was beginning to fill with rolling clouds that threatened a storm.

But nothing diminished Melenta's spirits. She and Tellik had the hope of seeing their dreams come true. Even when they encountered a few furtive glances from Solotans of pure lineage, it didn't bother her.

Tellik said, "Won't your father be surprised when you show interest in merchant craft!"

Melenta knew that being a merchant was his ploy to get her to choose something else. Rather than return his excitement, she repeatedly chewed her lower lip.

He asked what bothered her.

"I wish fathers would let us choose our own goals for the future."

He chuckled. "All I ever wanted to do was study farming. I like watching a crop grow and know that I made that happen."

"Well," she teased, "you and the sun and rain." When he didn't laugh, she said, "I guess that isn't what your father wants you to do?"

"Oh, no. Father wants each of his five sons to franchise his business. But I might have one chance to get out of it. I have an uncle in Sevenn who never had children. He asked my father to send one of his sons to apprentice with him on his farm. Trouble is, all five of us want the job. So Father devised this competition between us. He gave us each an identical statue to sell. The one who gets the best selling price gets to work for my uncle."

Melenta stopped walking and Tellik turned back to look at her. She asked, "Do you know where your brothers will find buyers? It would save time if we avoid duplicating a sales pitch."

"I don't know. No one's going to tell his strategy."

His hopelessness spurred a devious streak in Melenta. "I bet that I can find out. I'm good at spying on people. At first, I was only a kid, pretending I was a GEA agent. But I learned a lot of tricks. I'll see what I can find out."

"What kind of tricks?" he quarreled.

She glanced casually around to see that no one was paying attention. From her daypack, she pulled out a text plate with no markings on it. "I ordered this three seasons ago, so I've studied it a long time."

He turned on his sketcher and inserted the text plate. He read the title page aloud. "What Every Girl Should Know About Etiquette." He grumbled incredulously.

She giggled. "It's a decoy title I included so Father won't bother me about reading it. It's a GEA training manual. It teaches investigation techniques. I'll start tomorrow."

At that moment, Melenta realized what it would mean to her if she could be The MenD'lee. She thought, *too many fathers make detestable choices for their children. Now, I know how to make a difference. With or without the help of Destiny, I intend to challenge the Law of Tradition.*

CHAPTER 3

At the Cha'atre manor, the children each had study desks in the family's sitting chamber. Presumably, this was for their use in doing homework within their father's view to prevent procrastination and laziness. However, Lukeniss rarely paid much attention. If Cheelo needed help, Melenta provided it while Lukeniss perused the day's news on computer. Through the Infocomm network he checked local community news, including market reports and pertinent legal rulings made by the Elders of Soloto, the five-man council who led their Nation.

Melenta looked up from her desk to watch him. Each day, her father faithfully reviewed every legal ruling to keep an ever-vigilant watch over the moral and ethical actions of his Council. Melenta thought to herself, *I'm convinced that he believes it's his responsibility to protect the Law of Tradition, single-handedly if necessary.*

Setting aside her hand-held compusketch (another piece of COAXIS technology which Lukeniss didn't object to using), she retrieved the holopic from her daypack. "Father?"

Without looking away from the Infocomm, he mumbled distractedly, "Yes?"

"If an artist had a product he wanted to market, would your company be an investor?"

Confused, he turned and gaped at her. "What are you talking about?"

"Ail. Brekket gave us an assignment. I'm supposed to tell how to build a business. This is the product." She handed the picture to him.

His eyes widened suddenly. "This looks valuable. Where did you get this picture?" He managed to make the question seem suspicious, as if she'd stolen it.

She pretended not to recognize the accusation in his voice. "My mentor gave it to me. The statue belongs to his friend."

Her father scrutinized the statue. "Ronjer Investments does finance production for several craft masters. To apply for that, you'd have to make certain information available before any decision could be made."

He didn't know it, but she'd called his firm after school and learned what information was needed. She showed him her sketcher. "Here are the production costs and projected yields."

For a brief moment, he raised one respecting eyebrow. Melenta had to admit that she enjoyed impressing him. It was nearly impossible to earn a gesture of his approval.

"Do you have adequate suppliers for the precious gems and metals?"

"Next page."

Lukeniss stabbed at the page selector button. "Well, that's convenient. Since the crafter already owns the rights to those mines, that's one legal matter settled. Who will be doing the mining if the craft master is busy making the statues?"

She didn't know that answer, so she made up a story. "Mining is their family business. The artist takes profits in the form of raw gems and processed grenva ore."

He continued to scour her notes. By his demeanor, it seemed he wanted to find her plan lacking. After a moment, he handed her the sketcher. "What's the purpose of the product?"

She gulped. "Umm, decoration?"

"Of course it's decorative. Statues don't serve a useful purpose." Punctuating each word, he sneered, "Who would want it?"

She pretended defeat until he was satisfied that he'd proven her unprepared. She said with great deference, "I'd hoped you could tell me. You're very accomplished at this, and I'm a beginner." For good measure, she bowed deeply, holding it longer than was actually expected.

That gesture of humility was the very thing he wanted. In the past, she'd watched her mother win all she wanted by appealing to her husband's ego.

Lifting his chin and smiling, he gave her a patronizing encouragement. "We're all beginners at one time. Statues of The All Wise are often displayed, but one this expensive would have a special use. It might decorate a family shrine, for example."

She hadn't thought of that. Melenta glanced toward the corner, eying the table that served as their family's shrine. There were no actual decorations among the pictures and mementos. She commented, "It would look very nice there. Would people purchase this, do you think?"

He thought carefully. "Considering the manufacturing costs, it would need to be marketed to elite families of title or station."

Suddenly, she remembered that their township was building a public shrine where families could purchase display cases. Her mind flew to images of statues adorning every case.

But Lukeniss warned her to be cautious. "I wouldn't invest in this without getting three jewel casters to estimate its value. Then, I'd want a market analysis that explained how well it had sold in the past. I'd wonder if the craft master has prospective buyers."

She nodded with real appreciation. "Thank you, Father."

He does know his business. But the prospect of learning to be a merchant, as he wishes doesn't *appeal to me. More than ever, I want a choice in my vocation.*

San Durg Township, 24 Zelonn, 2158

The following morning, Melenta left home earlier than usual to spy on Tellik's brothers. She caught the rail bus to the inn where the Kaamzen family lived. All she needed was a little luck, and she might follow one of them before school.

It was Half-light, when Tra'a provided a dim light for the indigo sky. Gradually, the larger moon would peek over the horizon and blend orchid and lavender against the deep blue of the early morning sky. By 0600, it would be Full-light, and businesses would open. School would begin then, too. Melenta had very little time to spare for this "mission."

So when she saw Tellik leave the inn, followed by four older young men who taunted him, she memorized their faces. Now, she'd recognize them.

Keeping her distance, she followed the oldest brother, Drus. Tellik had said he was his greatest competition. She could see why. His thick black hair, cut clean and neat, looked impressive with the gray leather suit he wore. He carried a fur-hide pouch that was identical to Tellik's, so he must have been going to look for a buyer.

Thrilled by her exploits, she followed him to the transport station and beyond to the Town Square. His choice of markets appeared to include the Council building, where the Elders and several officials of the Region worked. Because Drus was an adult, he'd meet with more success there than Tellik would.

She thought, *Drus might get a good price, but I'll find a way to entice the builders of that prestigious funeral shrine to commission a large quantity of statues.*

For now, though, she was due at school. She ran from the Square to the transport station. During her frequent adventures pretending to be a GEA agent, she'd discovered that she had a talent for running long distances. It proved handy today when she got to the station as her rail bus arrived.

This was her favorite time, when she practiced observation skills. Every day, she saw the same group of people here. An elderly man carried a cane that he wasn't afraid to use on anyone in his way. There were four children from her school who always rode with her, though she never spoke to them. She also saw the lady with long, blond hair who, each day, accompanied her young son to the station and put him on the rail bus that would stop at his school. Then she sat in the station again to read while she waited for the bus to return and take her home.

When the bus stopped at her school, she was eager to tell Kendel her idea to market the statue. But as she scanned the hallway, she noticed two of Tellik's brothers at the far end. She thought, *not only do they not belong there, but they aren't even good at looking inconspicuous.*

Raising the sketcher in her hand and pretending to read it, she looked over the top of it, and mumbled to herself, "Tellik won't be here until school is over, so what could his brothers be up to? I wonder if I should get closer to them to pick up some of their conversation?"

But her feet froze in place. The moment she considered skipping school to follow an adventure, a memory haunted the back of her mind. She felt as if her blood had hardened to ice, for the current situation too closely resembled the worst day of her life—the day her sister died.

Unwillingly, Melenta fell into a daydream.

San Durg Township, 1 Breel, 2152

Melenta's morning classes were at an end. The sun would soon rise for the four-cycle period of day called Full-sun. During this hot interlude, while all of Lekton took First-rest, she was supposed to sleep. As she was only eight seasons old, she took her rest at the children's dorm. Older students like her sister, Linnori, who was fifteen, went home to rest.

But today, Melenta told her sister there was no need to walk her to the dorm, and Linnori was glad to hurry on her way. Linnori started for home, unaware that Melenta was following her.

Yesterday, Melenta had heard two girls gossiping about Linnori, saying that she was seeing a man during First-rest. Melenta was sure it wasn't true since Linnori's Gift Rite ceremony was very soon, and girls weren't allowed to be alone with men before betrothal. Melenta wanted to follow her sister and disprove the lie. She pretended it was a mission for the GEA, a special job for Agent Dread.

Carefully, Melenta followed her through town and passed shops that were already locking their doors. Few people remained on the streets to notice one little girl who was out of place and unsupervised. Not even Linnori noticed when Melenta boarded the same rail bus that went to North Road.

But when Linnori got off at her usual stop, she bypassed their manor and strode quickly down a road that went away from San Durg. Melenta despaired of redeeming her sister's reputation then. As far as she knew, this road led only to places they shouldn't go.

Linnori might really be doing something wrong, after all, she thought, and it gave her a surge of thrill at catching her. With determination bolstering her courage, she followed at a discreet distance and ignored her pounding heartbeat.

Outside town, the landscape became boring. Only stubby, blue-green bushes cut the stark and barren slopes above the valley. Even the soil was gray and appeared lifeless. Added to the discomfort of the unbearable heat, it made for a miserable trip.

And it was rapidly getting hotter. The humid vapor steaming up from the soil clung to Melenta. She whispered to herself, "No one with a whole brain goes outside during Full-sun. Where is she going?"

Shortly, she got her answer. The road took them into the foothills of the Mountains of Sumer. Ail. Brekket had said that this place was beautiful long ago. When volcanic eruptions destroyed the other continent, the ruin also spilled across parts of Kolair's northern border. The dead-looking sand was littered with uneven shards of black rocks that crunched under her feet.

Bending to pick up a rock, she discovered it had sharp, brittle edges. She thought, *whatever made Linnori come out here had better be important, and it had better not be a man!*

Only yesterday, her father had explained that because of his renowned status throughout all the Solotan Regions, Linnori's Gift Rite would be an important event. If Linnori made the right choice of a mate, he'd be even more important.

A thought alarmed her. *What if I find out that Linnori is doing something bad? Maybe some man is making her meet him. If so, Linnori could be in trouble.*

Realizing what she might be about to discover made her legs suddenly go leaden, but her love for Linnori and her insatiable thirst for adventure kept her feet walking.

Ahead of them, large, glassy-black boulders stood to each side of the dirt road and provided hiding places. Suddenly, Melenta lost Linnori, who stepped off the road behind a boulder. She could barely hear the crunch of her sister's steps anymore.

Melenta reached the place where Linnori had left the main road, and she found the landscape was even more treacherous. A tremendous boulder sat watch there, and a glowering face had been carved into it to scare travelers away. Despite this looming discouragement, Melenta went on.

Behind the massive guardian, narrow paths made of rounded, flat granite angled away from the road. It looked dangerous. But then she saw Linnori far away and thoughts of her own safety vanished. A dark, Barmaajian man stood with her sister. Horrified, Melenta watched as he grabbed Linnori's wrists and pulled her close to him. Linnori began to cry.

Although Melenta was too far away to hear them, she saw more than she wanted to see. The man tenderly lifted Linnori's hand and formed a cup with her fingers, palm upward. Answering the gesture, he curled eager fingers downward into hers.

It was a gesture of intimate affection called Taam skla'a Kair, or Salute of Trust. It allowed a binding and intense intimacy. Through touch, they experienced each other's emotions directly. To allow the union, each would have to cut off the emission of their deflector. Without that organ generating an energy field to repel the other's emotions, they could join in the most personal way. The gesture represented surrender and sacrifice—a promise of lovers.

Without thinking, Melenta charged carelessly toward them, crying out, "Don't hurt her!"

Her sister screamed in outrage, "You followed me?"

Melenta's heroic resolve buckled as she reached them. Her limbs locked, but she fixed accusing eyes on the dark man who held Linnori.

Glaring at Linnori, he demanded, "You let your sister follow? How could you do that?"

"I didn't know about it!"

Linnori rushed to Melenta. Pulling her by the hand, she took her past the large stone and back to the safety of North Road. "What are you doing here?"

With an innocent shrug, Melenta hung her head. "I thought you were in trouble. He was going to hurt you."

Linnori hugged her. "Kellis would never hurt me, Little One. He loves me."

The child's eyes went wild with terror. "He's not A'laantuvian!"

Kellis appeared from behind the boulder. Keeping his distance, he kneeled, saying softly, "I'm not from your race, that's true. I know your parents want Linnori to choose someone of pure, A'laantuvian lineage, but I love her, and I'll be kind to her. Isn't that what matters most?"

Unafraid, Melenta countered, "I don't think it would matter to Father." Then, she looked at Linnori, asking, "Would it?"

"You know it wouldn't." Linnori winced at the prospect of her father's disapproval. Kellis snapped, "Do something about this, Lin. She's going to tell!"

"No, she won't. Will you, Mel?"

She considered Linnori's pleading eyes and thought, *I'll be the one in trouble if Father finds out I kept this secret from him. Still, Linnori has kept my secrets plenty of times.*

The confusion was agonizing, and she trembled with an overload of emotion.

Kellis stood and paced, mumbling a threat.

"Let her alone. You're scaring her," Linnori cautioned. "I'll handle it."

Defiantly, Melenta yelled, "But what about your Gift Rite?"

"I'm already betrothed to Kellis. He's the man I've chosen."

Melenta couldn't hide her disapproval. *Linnori's wrong,* she thought, *and Kellis is disgusting! He called her "Lin." It's rude for a person who isn't a family member to use a familiar name. Any child knows that.*

She whimpered to her sister, "How could you hurt us this way?"

Stung by her rejection, Linnori grimaced and turned away.

Kellis screamed, "See! Your family is all you care about! You never intended to leave them to be with me, did you?" Without waiting for an answer, he stomped off the road and out of sight behind the boulder.

Linnori cried in despair, "Mel, I love Kellis, and he loves me. Don't you think I ought to have a mate I want?"

Clenching her teeth, she responded with the perfect logic of a child. "Mother picked Father because he was from a pure family. They were betrothed and then she loved him."

Linnori held her in trembling arms. "It takes more than being betrothed to make people love each other. You know that Mother and Father aren't happy, even though they honored their fathers and obeyed Tradition."

Melenta denied that with stony silence.

Putting her hands on her hips, Linnori spoke firmly. "No more arguments, Mel. I've got to talk to Kellis, and then I'll take you back to school. Wait here."

Reluctantly, she nodded. Linnori hurried after Kellis and again circled the massive rock.

Melenta heard her call to him and then they began arguing. Kellis said harshly, "Take her then, but come back right away or I may not be here. I've waited for you to tell your father, but you won't. How much more do you expect of me?"

"Please, Kel," Linnori pleaded. "Wait a little longer. I don't want to hurt him."

Their conversation diminished with distance. But the last thing Melenta could make out was Kellis. He said, "I have commitments. I can't stay in San Durg much longer. I wish you'd worry more about hurting me than you do about hurting your father!"

Melenta squinted at the looming rock formation and gulped. Two deep indentions carved into the rock made it look like the eyes of a warrior standing guard. *I'm not so sure this mission was a good idea.*

Obediently, she waited until she realized that she no longer heard Linnori's voice. She told the guardian, "Since I'm already in trouble, would one more mistake matter? I have to follow Linnori and make her do the right thing!"

But when she rounded the boulder, her sister was nowhere to be found. *Linnori must have gone on one of those dangerous stepping-stone paths again.*

Suddenly, she remembered that this area was called the Skeel Pits. It was forbidden to come here. These pits were pools of volcanic acid disguised by a covering of sand. A path of round, flat stepping-stones skirted the edges, but clumsy feet would find death was merciful.

Her pulse quickened, and she dreaded further travel. Everywhere she looked, the dead, gray, sand-covered pits and black shards of knife-edged rock glared in sunlight.

Though perspiration drenched her and hunger made her feel weak, she carefully took a few steps and called out Linnori's name. With each call and each dreaded step, she grew more afraid because Linnori didn't answer.

Far ahead she at last saw Kellis and yelled, "Wait!"

He jerked around as he heard her. "Melenta? What are you doing? Stay there!" He retraced the path across the stepping-stones. "You should have stayed with Linnori."

"She went looking for you. Where is she?"

He had no answer. His face dissolved in anguish.

Slowly, they returned to North Road, where he ordered her to wait while he searched for Linnori. He looked desperately afraid, and that frightened her more, so she followed him.

He took every path through the Skeel Pits but found only a stone missing around the edge of a pit. Melenta watched terror creep over the man's face, and she knew what he feared.

She groaned, "Did she fall into a pit?"

"Why did you let her come after me?"

"She's oldest! I couldn't stop her. It's your fault!"

He gripped his head in both hands. "You're right."

Stumbling and torn with grief, Kellis still managed to take Melenta back to the road. He said, "You need to be safe," and he lifted her away from the last, dangerous pit to set her on even ground. Then, leaning against the boulder, the man collapsed into a squat. With his hands over his eyes, he screamed an impassioned plea into the air, "All Wise, bring her back!"

Shaking, Melenta accused, "You did this, not The All Wise. She should never have come here! She shouldn't have been betrothed to you!"

The dark man's eyes brimmed with tears, but he weakly stood and approached, reaching out to comfort her.

Immediately, she shrieked and recoiled from his dark arms. Then she ran home alone to deliver the distressing news.

Melenta broke out of the horrific memory of that day, though her pain never dimmed. She'd always blamed herself. Lukeniss blamed her, too. He'd never shown much interest in her anyway, but after that day, he seemed sorry that she hadn't been the one who died.

Again, she thought of Tellik's brothers, watching as they left the school. Despite her enjoyment of spy fantasies, she was too afraid to follow them.

A cycle passed, and she couldn't bear the shame of her cowardice. She changed her mind.

I'll skip class and do some discrete surveillance of Tellik's brothers. All I have to do is convince Kendel to let me go.

Once she'd written a note on her sketcher and asked to be excused. She placed it on Kendel's desk before him.

He read it quickly and looked her over with a critical eye. He whispered, "Are you ill?"

She added more to the note on her sketcher. It said, "I need to help Tellik. Please don't count me absent, and I'll explain later."

She could tell he wasn't pleased, but after a searching stare, the mentor asked, "Is this important?" At her gesture of affirmation, he took her sketcher and erased her request from the scene. In its place, he wrote a reply. "Go ahead, but talk to me soon."

Bowing, she erased his message. His trust meant everything to Melenta.

CHAPTER 4

Melenta made her way to the transport station, bound for the San Durg Inn and hoped to find Tellik's brothers.

Routinely, she scanned the crowds around her. This wasn't a time of day she ordinarily came here, so she was curious. Beginning a familiar game, she guessed the destinations of the citizens there, a very different task with no prior information about them.

But then, she recognized someone who shouldn't be there. It was the young mother with long, blond hair who escorted her son to his bus each morning.

Melenta thought, *I've always assumed that the woman sat down to wait for a bus to take her home. Surely, she didn't stay here all this time.*

But something else was wrong. The woman wore a baby's carry sling around her neck and cuddled an infant against her. This in itself wasn't unusual, except that Melenta didn't remember ever seeing her pregnant. Thinking that she was probably the baby's caretaker, Melenta dismissed the question.

Then a man approached the young woman's bench and said, "Jhendail, Taima! Congratulations! I heard your good news when I arrived in San Durg."

As Melenta watched, the man bent toward her and pulled back a fold of the carry sling to peek at the infant.

Melenta cocked her head. *I'd swear she hasn't been pregnant.*

Then the man did something suspicious. As he reached inside the sling to touch the child, she saw that he had a folded piece of paper in his hand. In one stealthy movement, he slipped the paper into the sling.

This mystery sparked immediate curiosity. What was this man up to that he didn't want others to know? She watched surreptitiously, but he didn't stay around. Wishing a blessing on her child, he went on his way.

Forgetting him, Melenta kept her eyes on the woman named Taima, who suddenly abandoned her wait for a bus. She left the station in the opposite direction as the man had gone.

To the casual observer, this meant nothing, but Agent Dread knew a handoff when she saw it. *Why were they being covert?*

She wasn't about to let nerves interrupt another opportunity for a spy adventure. Determined to pursue the mystery, she followed Taima and the note.

A short distance away, Taima turned into an alley between two businesses. Carefully, Melenta peeked around the corner in time to see the woman open a back door of one of the buildings. Melenta knew it to be a vacant shop.

Strolling casually into the alley, she moved into shadow and looked into a window near the door.

What she saw inside appalled her. Taima was removing the carry sling, callously peeling it off over her head. As shock crashed into Melenta, who feared for the baby, she realized that apparently, a doll had been sewn into the sling.

Taima briefly fanned her face with the sling before fishing inside it for the paper.

Feet shuffled suddenly in the street outside the alley. Concerned about being noticed, she alternated glances behind her with furtive peeks into the shop window.

Taima opened the folded paper and smiled. Quickly, she folded it again, replaced the sling around her neck and tucked the paper inside it. Without warning, Taima turned to leave.

Melenta scrambled from the alley to avoid being caught. She turned the corner onto the street, but halted. She thought, *since I can't get far before Taima sees me, it would be best to let her think I simply happen to be walking here.*

To be sure no one had noticed her, Melenta scanned the businesses and walkways. She tried to look as if she were hunting for a particular shop.

Then, crossing the street, she lingered there, waiting for Taima to come out and start walking. She'd follow her, but at a distance and from the opposite side of the street.

The thrill of a mystery filled Melenta's senses. *This is fun,* she thought. *Maybe Security wouldn't be a bad thing to study when I go to the Institute.*

Right away, she saw Taima leave the alley with the baby sling in place. She walked once more toward the transport station.

Staying on the opposite side of the street, Melenta followed, proud and relieved. *The techniques worked, just like the True Crime magazine said it would! As promised, it prepared me for when a mystery presented itself.*

Suddenly, the mystery branched in a whole new, dangerous direction. The white, folded piece of paper fell from the sling without notice, sailing quietly behind Taima into the street.

Melenta waited, expecting Taima to realize this and go back to retrieve it. But she didn't. This was her chance, despite the fact it wasn't her business.

She organized her plan. If she were caught picking it up, she'd claim to be returning it. She hesitated, though, afraid to get into trouble. Remembering her earlier cowardice, she lectured herself mentally to do it.

Waiting until Taima was well past her, Melenta crossed the street and walked the opposite direction until she could scoop up the paper. No one called attention to this, and Taima never looked back.

I did it! Immediately reversing direction, she kept walking to the transport station.

She didn't look at the paper until she was aboard a rail bus. Printed in neat type was a list of ten people's names. Centered as a heading at the top was the name, "Doctor Brelkaar."

Is this a list of his patients? Who would take such care to hide that? She smiled. *I'll have to find out.*

She began her investigation at one of San Durg's news diners, where an Infocomm on every table allowed customers to catch up on local events. After ordering a drink, she began her research on the names.

While she was acquainted with normal methods of searching on an Infocomm, it would only draw from posted legal notices or news articles about noteworthy individuals. As she expected, there was little helpful information.

Then, when she was about to give up, the computer signaled that a new posting had recently been added. *It's nothing,* she thought, and she decided to close the connection and leave.

But for reasons she couldn't understand, her finger hit a different key, one that would read the new posting. Before her appeared a name, Jareth Jenelonn, and she gasped. It was the first name on the list. The Council of Soloto had posted a decision to place a trustee over Jenelonn's assets for the duration of his life. The reason cited was diminished mental capacity.

While Melenta knew this wasn't an unusual practice where the elderly were concerned, something about the notice caught her attention with such force that she was helpless to ignore it.

Then, seeing why, she gave a yelp of surprise. The trustee named to administer Jenelonn's wealth was Dr. Pol Brelkaar!

She fought back chills. *I have to analyze this implication, sort out legitimate clues, if there are any. For the information to be posted this morning, this ruling must have been made yesterday during the Council's second session. What a coincidence that I was on Infocomm at the very moment the Scribe posted it.*

Coincidence?

She recalled her father teaching her that coincidence is an omen, a sign that The All Wise had a hand in something. Only she saw the list being secretly passed, and only she was on hand when it dropped. Now, an important clue to uncover the mystery had suddenly fallen into her hands!

This is evidence of my destiny to be a force for change on Lekton. If The All Wise sanctions it, surely Destiny approves of my self-appointed duty as The MenD'lee.

This changed everything. Armed with this knowledge, she'd visit Dr. Brelkaar's office instead of returning to school. She had to figure out the connection between Brelkaar and the people on this list.

Of course, never rule out the obvious, she told herself, quoting from her study manual. *The doctor could be a personal friend of Jenelonn who offered to help. But why the clandestine passing of the note?*

Maybe, she argued, *Brelkaar wants to help, but he doesn't want anyone to know.* But her counterpoint mind quipped, *it wasn't going to stay secret if it was posted to Infocomm.* This would take a bit more digging.

Melenta found the doctor's office in a reputable and long-established area of the township. The clinic offered opulent furnishings. *Business must be good.*

An attendant approached, a beautiful, young woman with the conspicuous, creamy brown skin tone of mixed, hybrid descent. She smiled with the patronizing manner one uses with a little child. "How can I assist you?"

Melenta struggled to appear confident. She didn't know what to say, which further embarrassed her. *Why didn't I plan this mission better before I jumped into it? 'Preparation isn't procrastination.'*

But the woman was kind. She prompted, "Did you want an appointment?"

"Yes, uh, I'd like to see the doctor." Glancing at a certificate displayed on the wall, she discovered that Dr. Brelkaar specialized in geriatrics. Quickly, she amended, "About my father."

Patiently, the Attendant explained that the doctor couldn't be of much help without seeing her father, but Melenta insisted on talking to him first. "I want to get information."

So, directed to sit down, she waited, though not long. Presently, a door to the inner offices opened, and several people entered the chamber. A girl nearly her age assisted an elderly man to walk. By the old gentleman's demeanor, he didn't appear to recognize his surroundings. The girl seemed accustomed to telling him what to do.

Behind them, a couple conversed together in agitated whispers too low to understand. But she heard one clear statement from the man. "This is simply another ploy for his money."

Melenta's ears strained for more.

The Attendant said, "Your father did well today. I'll call to remind you about his next appointment in three moons."

Melenta studied the pitiful man. *If this was doing well, what was he like before?*

Turning to the elderly man, the Attendant called, "We'll see you soon, Mr. Jhotolair."

Instantly, she recalled that Jhotolair was the second name on the list.

As the family left the office, the Attendant turned to Melenta, whose instincts told her that she'd get more information by following Nolan Jhotolair. She told the Attendant, "I'll have to come back some other time."

Leaving the office, she caught up to Nolan and his family, but maintaining a distance was necessary. The argument they'd begun in the office heated up.

The girl was directed to take her grandfather to their waiting shuttle. Once they were gone, Nolan's son said, "You don't know that this treatment Brelkaar is suggesting will make any difference. It will cost a fortune."

"Dresen, he's your father. You can't deny him any treatment he needs."

"Needs! That's the point. He can't reason or comprehend that his life is unpleasant. This doctor thinks his treatment would make him comfortable, but Father wouldn't know the difference."

The woman's voice quivered with pain. "He'll know! He isn't aware of us, but confusion frightens him. Hasn't this been helping him sleep without disturbing dreams? He deserves to be at peace."

Then, they went beyond Melenta's hearing. She asked herself, "What have I stumbled into? Does this doctor charge exorbitant prices for unnecessary treatments? Maybe Nolan's daughter-in-law has the right of it; maybe the treatments provide comfort to a feeble mind, but the son doesn't want to pay for it."

Of one thing she was sure: Dr. Brelkaar had been given the trusteeship of a patient's assets. This allowed the doctor to charge for whatever treatments he could justify.

And given the suspicious way that list of names was passed, Brelkaar wasn't the only person involved in this scheme.

Then, one more possibility occurred to Melenta. *Suppose this doctor is already under investigation? Could the note be information being given to Lektonian Security? If so, they wouldn't appreciate my interest in the case. It might even get back to Father.*

Melenta pondered what to do with this information. If an elderly person needed a trustee for his money, it made more sense to her that an investor, like Lukeniss, would be the more suitable choice. Putting his doctor in charge presented a conflict of interests. So how did the Council of Soloto let that happen?

At Late-meal that evening, after Cheelo had gone to sleep, Melenta considered asking her father for his opinion. While it seemed a good idea, Lukeniss had a tendency to find fault with her if she attempted to fix another's problems. He claimed that was arrogant and unseemly for a girl, and he always threw undignified into any criticism.

For another moment, she considered telling someone else. Kendel, maybe? But the truth still remained that she had no evidence of any crime. *Until I do, I shouldn't involve anyone else.*

Unfortunately, her distraction caught her father's attention. He'd been reading, but suddenly set aside his viewer and looked across the sitting chamber. Lukeniss gave her an intense look, as if he drilled into her mind with his vision. "Are you in some kind of trouble?"

Looking up from her desk, she masked her surprise and forced her expression into passivity. "No, I don't think so. Why?"

"Something is bothering you, and you seem afraid to bring it up to me."

Irritably, she thought, *of course, the first thing he'd think is that I've done something wrong.*

He continued, "Your expressions are easily read."

If so, I have to work on my acting. Meekly, she pretended a resigned change of heart, because he wouldn't give up until he'd proven he was right. She told him, "I've been worried about a friend at school. Her parents are considering some advice that would affect her grandfather's life, and maybe not for the better. My friend doesn't want them to do it."

He sighed with exaggerated weariness. "Why would someone else's problem concern you? It's not your business."

"No, sir, of course not. But someday, it might happen to me. That's why I'm upset."

He relaxed and offered her a way to save honor. "Young people shouldn't dwell on possible trouble, although, I suppose, there are times that we can learn from other's plights. What bothers you?"

Melenta didn't intend to explain the truth, but she wanted to know if her father would disagree with the Council's decision. She made up a story. "If one day, my husband became ill, so ill that he couldn't think and reason clearly, should I petition our Council to make me trustee of his money?"

Lukeniss waved the matter aside and returned to reading. "Trustee? No. As spouse, you'd inherit his money anyway. You'd be made Head of Household to protect your family."

"As I understand the Law," she returned. "If there isn't a spouse, his oldest child would take charge because he's heir. Right?"

Annoyed, he dropped his viewer again. "Why would you question that?"

"I don't, but someone outside the family became the trustee for my friend's grandfather, even though his eldest son is living."

"This was done legally, by Council ruling?"

Finally, I've got his interest! She gestured agreement.

Again, he dismissed the matter with a glare of dissatisfaction. "If the Elders ruled on it, I'm sure there was a reason. We have no right to question it."

She hadn't considered that. Even if she discovered that Dr. Brelkaar was doing something underhanded, her father wouldn't be proud of her for uncovering the deceit. Doing so would prove the Elders had made a mistake. Once again, after countless rejections, she accepted that nothing she did would make Lukeniss love her.

Excusing herself, she went to her sleep chamber and dropped onto her fur-bed. She stared at the twine flowers adorning the walls and cried in despair.

Teeka curled up beside her, and eventually, she slept. Her recurring nightmare about Linnori haunted her.

San Durg Township, 2 Breel, 2152

The moons were gone, lost in Full-dark. The child of eight seasons had gone home from the Skeel Pits and exclaimed to her mother the sad news about her sister's death. Mother had sent her to hide in her sleep chamber, for they both knew that Lukeniss would take out his grief on her. Cycles later, she still cringed in a corner, hiding from him.

The manor was very quiet once her parents went searching for Linnori. But then, through swollen eyes, she saw the door creeping open, and she was terrified. When her mother entered, Melenta ran to her, seeking comfort.

But instead of holding her, Kamira paced around the chamber. She said, "Your father has returned. Most of the township helped to look for Linnori. They found the place where a stepping-stone was missing around one of the pits. Kellis had written a cowardly message in the sand, claiming that he caused Linnori's death. He said that he didn't want to live without her, so he'd let the Skeel Pits punish him."

"They're both gone?"

Her mother nodded. "Lukeniss is deeply hurt. Oh, how he'll miss that girl!"

Mother didn't have to say the rest—Father wouldn't be grieving if his younger daughter had died.

Melenta wailed, "I tried to stop her from going there, Maata, but she wouldn't listen to me." Even as she said the words, she knew she'd never believe them. She'd always believe she could have convinced Linnori to come home if she'd tried harder.

At last, her mother turned to look at her. "I know, Little One. I don't blame you."

Again, unsaid words screamed in her mind, *but Father does!*

Wringing her hands, Kamira asked, "Why would Linnori go there to meet Kellis? Did he force her to go?"

Melenta gestured the up-and-down hand gesture for "no" and turned away. *How could Linnori leave me the job of explaining this?* She answered, "Kellis said he loved her."

"Kellis Paara seriously thought he could contend for betrothal? He isn't A'laantuvian! That doesn't make sense! Linnori knew her father wanted her to choose Derris Linifee."

"Linnori didn't want to choose a mate by Gift Rite. She wanted Kellis."

Kamira shook her shoulders. "Never tell your father that!" she ordered. "If he knew that his beautiful daughter intended to defy him, it would destroy him."

"Don't you understand? She didn't love Derris. She didn't want to be betrothed to someone she didn't love, even if Father chose him."

But logic didn't seem to matter. Kamira couldn't think beyond what society dictated. She asked Melenta, "How could she be unhappy with honoring her father? This is scandalous!"

"Please, don't yell at me!" Melenta's fingers clung to her mother's sleeves.

Kamira took a deep breath to calm down. "You told me the truth. I'm not angry with you. If I'd given Lukeniss a daughter worthy of the Linifee family, I'd have won his heart at last!" She spoke evenly, but her voice still cracked and tears glistened in her eyes.

Again, her mother paced the room, planning and speaking to herself. "When we were betrothed, Lukeniss said I was valued for the prestige my family's station brought him. Then, I gave him a beautiful heir. I'll be of no value to him, now."

Melenta slumped into her fur-bed. Somehow, this was her fault. She thought, *is Mother going to feel differently about me now?*

Suddenly, Kamira stopped pacing and whirled around. "I know what to do. Your father will find no more pleasure in life unless I can give him a son. Melenta, I want you to go to the garden and bring your father to me. He's gone there to grieve."

This plan had no appeal to Melenta. "I don't know what to say."

"You're young, but you can understand. Grief is hard for a Lektonian man to bear, especially when his credo is Dignity. Do you remember when the school caught fire last season? You went into trauma-shock because you were so afraid. That kind of shock is what your father feels. You could share his grief, Melenta, and he'd be proud of you."

The pride she might win interested her most, but this sounded frightening.

"Go to him and lower your deflector completely so that you can share his grief."

"That's all?"

"Hold his hand and help him to feel better. I'll wait here."

Solemnly, the little girl agreed.

Kamira hugged her with a desperate intensity. Melenta felt her joy in knowing that her "Little One" had lived. She also felt her mother's insecurity. *She's afraid of Father, too,* thought Melenta. *But isn't that what marriage is like? The husband commands his wife to do things he wants, and she has to do it?*

Although her mother always seemed happy to please him, sometimes, like now, she was afraid to find out what he wanted.

In the darkness of late evening, with only lamplight to illuminate her way, Melenta followed the path that led around the manor to the garden. The promise that, for the first time, her gesture of help would make her father proud of her was all that kept her walking.

In the garden she saw her father on his knees, his arms enfolding his chest as if he held his lost child. Shaking with sobs, he silently swayed rocking the invisible child.

She gasped at the sight of her tall, dynamic father's emotional and undignified display. His behavior truly frightened Melenta more than the help she came to offer.

Inching closer, she called him. He didn't respond. Gathering courage, she cut off her deflector emission and slipped her fingers over his hand. In less than a heartbeat, waves of distress slammed into Melenta's mind and washed over her like a flash flood. Her own identity perished as his grief overpowered her mind in joining. They were united in pain, but even more, she was his pain. Her identity was gone, and she was pain.

A last, fleeting thought entered her mind before she fell unconscious on the ground at her father's feet: *Did I help him? Did he know?*

From within his pain, Lukeniss recognized that someone else's emotions had joined with his. When his sight cleared, he found his younger daughter had taken pity on him. She'd made a personal sacrifice on his behalf.

And so renewed, he smiled at the small moon that brought the Half-light of the new morning. He touched Melenta's small, blond head to awaken her.

She looked up at him with expectant eyes. He thought to himself, *I refuse to offer her praise for this. No child should be rewarded for giving a service when it's owed. Melenta let Linnori die, so a sacrifice is due from her.*

Renewed, Lukeniss strode briskly to the path that led to the manor. His daughter trotted behind him.

Kamira waited at the door with outstretched arms. "Come to me, my husband, and I'll give you sons."

Melenta watched her parents go inside together. She longed for her mother's welcoming arms, too, but the welcome was for her father alone. Unsure what to do, she waited at the door of their manor.

"No, dear," her mother said, stopping her outside the door. "You'll be staying with your grandmother for a few moons. She's on her way to get you."

The door closed.

Melenta watched, thinking, *they'll change their minds and come back to include me in our family's sorrow.*

But the door didn't move, and she couldn't go in once it was forbidden.

She wondered, *why doesn't someone offer me a hand to share my suffering? Maybe that's not appropriate if I'm the one who caused it. Knowing Father, it must violate some rule of Tradition.*

Mostly, she wished for the comfort of the chamber she'd shared with Linnori. She longed to rest on her sister's soft fur-bed and smell her fragrance. She wanted to watch the moonlight shining on the twine flowers that Linnori had strung across the walls. Instead, she huddled on the step, sank to the chilled stones of the porch and fell asleep waiting for her Neena.

CHAPTER 5

San Durg Township, 25 Zelonn, 2158

After school the next day, Melenta fully intended to tell her mentor the truth when he asked why she'd skipped school yesterday. Facing him now, though, she wondered, *can I do it?*

When the last of the students left for the day, Kendel said sternly, "Melenta, you're not a child. If you have something to do, I understand. But you'd tell me if you were in any trouble, wouldn't you?"

She smiled at him fondly. "I wouldn't ask you to lie for me and then get into trouble. Can I ask you a personal question?"

Kendel indicated a chair beside his desk and sat down to talk. Childishly, he said, "I'll answer your question if you'll answer mine."

She giggled at the shrewd glint in his eyes. "Do you believe coincidence is evidence of The All Wise working?"

Surprised, he jumped. It wasn't at all what he expected to hear. "I suppose it depends on the situation. Sometimes, coincidence is exactly what it seems to be."

She made up her mind quickly. Tellik would be waiting for them in the school's library. She said, "Let's say there's a crime committed, and you happen to be present at the right time to witness it. Did The All Wise create that coincidence because he wants you to expose the crime?"

With a deep sigh, Kendel gave the question thought and then answered, "If he created the opportunity to expose the crime and a way to do it safely, then I'd say yes, that's The All Wise."

She was pleased. "So in that situation, doesn't that person have to act?"

He tilted his head. "That's up to one's conscience, don't you think?"

"What if you don't act? What would The All Wise do?"

He reached his hand toward hers, but quickly withdrew it. "Melenta, if you aren't sure, give it time. The All Wise will create the opportunity again if you're needed."

That made sense. She decided to wait and see if The All Wise gave her another opportunity to stop Brelkaar. She felt confusion and worry drift away.

Kendel said, "Now, I want to know where you went yesterday. You promised."

"Right." She stalled, looking for a way out. "But that wasn't a question."

By coincidence, (and she was sure The All Wise arranged it to help her), Tellik entered the classroom and interrupted. "Are we still going to study?"

Melenta laughed. "Just in time, Tellik. I have an idea about how to sell your statue."

Kendel scowled at her playfully. "You still owe me an answer."

San Durg Township, 28 Zelonn, 2158

After three moons of planning, they were ready to sell the statue. After school, Tellik and Melenta walked to the Market Place. The stores were still called market booths, a holdover from a more primitive era when traders traveled in wagons and set up tents to display their wares. Even in modern times, some traders still transported their wares by wagon—a kind of gypsy life she knew nothing about until she met Tellik.

Melenta followed Tellik into a booth called, "Ancestral Memories." Located in the heart of the most elite section of the Market, it sold various items for home shrines, everything from modest pillars to entire walls of carved granite to proclaim the merits of the beloved departed. Melenta's research had determined that it was a family-owned business. That meant purchasing decisions could be approved locally. Their plan counted on the owner making a snap decision.

At the door, a fragrance of rainbow lilies wafted to them, inspiring a deep inhalation of pleasure. The carpet was a pale blue, plush fiber that absorbed sound. Faint musical crystal chimes and a wistful mooka flute drifted throughout the chamber as if on the wind.

A little over dramatic, thought Melenta, *but I can see how it would feel comforting.*

Tellik smiled appreciatively. He whispered, "It's a first-rate place. Thank you."

An elderly, white-haired man appeared through an indigo, velveteen curtain. His smile as he greeted his customers was painted on with professional style. But when he saw the two young people, he dropped his reverent bearing. "Welcome. I'm Trennis Meelo. Can I be of service?"

Tellik introduced himself. By custom, it wasn't polite to introduce a woman. She'd do that if she wished. Today, she only stepped behind her friend and kept quiet.

"I'm Tellik Kaamzen. Perhaps you're familiar with my mother's art craft, known as Leethin Crafts? Her work has been very popular among funerary businesses in Sevenn."

Meelo clasped fingers across his chest, appearing to consider how polite he had to be with children. At last, he opted to accept Tellik's statement. "I've not had the pleasure."

Bowing to the gentleman in deep respect, Tellik placed the fur pouch on a nearby pedestal, one of the carved granite displays used to mount statues. With care, he slowly removed the statue, implying value and honor in his handling of the piece.

Squinting, the merchant reached into a tunic pocket to bring out a pair of magnified jeweler's lenses. After a close examination of the statue, he abruptly stepped away and gave an involuntary gasp. "This is quite exquisite. Where did you get this, boy?"

Melenta frowned. *Is he implying it might be stolen?*

The question didn't surprise Tellik, who crossed wrists, palms down to gesture kaalsoto, the Oath of Truth. To offer this gesture without honesty would dishonor his family. "My mother creates these lovely images of The All Wise, and our family sells them. I wished to offer you an opportunity to commission her work for sale in your market booth."

Throughout this discussion, Melenta had been standing with her hands clasped behind her back in the friendly gesture of J'la'a. Her back was to the front windows of the building. At Tellik's offer, she wiggled two fingers to signal a third accomplice who waited outside.

On cue, the door opened. Meelo turned a sidelong glance at Tellik, whispering, "Stay here." He repeated his warm, reverent greeting to the customer. "How may I serve you, sir?"

Kendel wore an expensive set of clothing that Melenta hadn't seen. It was fashionable, amber leather enhanced with expensive golden clasps. His credoglyph necklace, which Kendel didn't often display at school, coordinated with amber gems.

She watched Meelo glance at the glyph and register that his credo was Responsibility. The businessman's immediate reaction aligned with that credo, adjusting to treat Kendel as a customer with much to do and little time. He said succinctly, "I'm at your service."

Maintaining an air of dignity that would have made Lukeniss proud, Kendel said, "I'm designing a family shrine. I need a number of matching decorations, but so far, I'm dissatisfied with the selection I've found in San Durg."

"I'm sure I can help," crooned Meelo as he fingered his own credoglyph for Reliability. Bowing slightly, he nodded twice to indicate that Kendel should follow him.

Kendel did so, but made sure to turn toward the pedestal displaying Tellik's statue. With an abrupt halt, he gasped and said, "This is fine work!" He approached the statue reverently, allowing a greedy gleam to show on his face.

Tellik remarked, "I ask your pardon, sir. This is ..."

"It is my finest piece," interrupted Meelo. "I've recently purchased it. You said you need a number of matching pieces?"

"Yes. How many do you have in stock?"

The merchant glanced behind Kendel at Tellik, stalling as if remembering a figure.

Tellik held up five fingers.

"I have five at this time," Meelo supplied. "I can, of course, commission more, I'm sure."

Tellik nodded eagerly.

Kendal smiled with satisfaction. "I'll discuss this with my uncle. He's purchasing a number of displays at the new public shrine being built here. You know of it, of course?"

"Of course."

Kendel told him, "I think the builders should see this. They might wish to adorn each display case with this image of The All Wise."

There was no doubt in Melenta's mind of the avarice flowing through the merchant's veins as he contemplated a sale of that magnitude. He asked Kendel, "May I reserve these lovely statues for you today?"

Kendel betrayed no obvious decision. "I'd like to see a jewel caster's statement of value."

Behind Kendel's back, Tellik slipped an appraisal card under the statue.

Bowing, Meelo smiled. "I can provide that." He retrieved the document, read it quickly and then handed it to his customer. "For you, I'll offer this lovely piece at only ten percent over this estimated value."

Kendel tapped a hand on his heart in a gesture of gratitude. "I'll try to return with my uncle and have a decision in three moons." Handing back the card, he left the shop.

Tellik said, "My mother can replicate two statues within five moons. Did you wish to inquire of the builders of the new shrine? Because if you don't, I think I do."

"I think I shall speak to them," Meelo inserted defensively. "The tip was given to me, and ethically, that gives me first right."

Tellik bowed. "That's why I asked."

Satisfied that he wasn't being cheated, Meelo told him, "I can offer you 50 percent of value for the five statues."

According to production reports, Melenta knew that his mother spent 50 percent of the stated value in production costs. That would give her no profit.

Tellik glared and told Meelo, "I wouldn't sell it for less than eighty. And without this piece, you'd have a difficult time making your pitch to the shrine builders."

"Young man," argued Meelo, "the point of business is to make a profit for both crafter and merchant."

"My father is a licensed merchant, too," answered Tellik shrewdly. "He could as easily contact the shrine builders and arrange sale for full, estimated value—without markup—and make a better profit."

He's right, thought Melenta. *But it would mean adding a sales force to their business, which at this time, Tellik said his father didn't want to do. They need a vendor.*

At that, the older man lowered his voice in a growl, "Except that you didn't secure that information—I did. Stealing the idea isn't ethical, and your father's honor in this town would be at stake if I tell other merchants. That may work in Sevenn, but it's not how we trade here."

"But you don't own this statue, Trennis. You have nothing to show the shrine builders, so your hot tip is useless to you. However, I'll agree not to approach them if you purchase this statue today for full, estimated value. I'll offer eighty percent for the remaining four statues I have in stock. Then, if you agree to commission future statues, I can agree on 70 percent of value, with jewel crafter certification for every piece."

Meelo gave no answer, but seemed to consider it.

"Oh, and as for how we do business in Sevenn, I think you've under priced the statue to that customer. These sell easily for a 20 percent markup in Sevenn."

Melenta spoke for the first time. "His mother does design the statue, sir. She also deserves a decent profit."

Tellik added, "I think my 20 percent discount plus your 20 percent markup is a decent profit margin and more than fair for someone who only has to open a carton and set it on a display shelf."

The merchant decided he was right.

San Durg Township, 30 Zelonn, 2158

Half-light, the first six cycles of the Lektonian day, is commonly slow-paced and relaxed. Tra'a provides a twilight effect that adds to the solemnity of the morning. By 0600, Bella rises and brightens the sky to light blue, tinged with a lavender hue. This time period,

Full-light, announces the opening of businesses and the start of the school day.

Until then, families enjoy First-meal together. Fathers instruct their domestic help of their needs, while mothers prepare the children for school. That was a typical morning.

However, in the Cha'atre manor, typical days were rare, and this one was no exception.

While J'Mii scolded the cook for taking too long to serve the meal, she fussed over Cheelo's attire until it was spotless and fit to present to Lukeniss.

But Melenta usually stayed in her chamber until after Lukeniss left for work at 0430.

However today, once her father left the manor, she planned to use his computer to search for any new information about the people on Dr. Brelkaar's list. Lately, she'd been preoccupied with helping Tellik. Having completed their sale two moons ago, she again felt the compulsive pull toward her earlier mission.

At 0445, she entered the living area, but her father was still home. She tried to sneak quietly past him and into the kitchen for a meal, but he heard her.

"Melenta, bring your meal to the garden. I want to speak to you."

Inwardly, she ran the list of possible infractions he might have discovered, but nothing came to mind. *I left school a few moons ago, but Kendel said he didn't report that. And I've been very careful about investigating Brelkaar, too. But Father has a way of finding things out.*

"Cheelo may need me soon."

"Cheelo and J'Mii went shopping in town. I'll meet you in the garden."

Filling a plate with fruit and pastries, she started toward the back door. But her father was still inside, and she heard him speaking to someone on telecomm. She crept closer to the doorway and listened.

Though he used a remote ear link so that she heard only his side of the conversation, it was soon evident that he was speaking to his assistant at Ronjer Investments. He said, "Brenner, check on the status of an account for Jareth Jenelonn. File a claim against his estate for the balance of his loan."

The name grabbed Melenta's attention. That was the first name on the list she was investigating.

Then, her father snapped, "Of course, the full balance. This morning the Infocomm reported his death."

Melenta dropped her plate. Dr. Brelkaar had become trustee of Jenelonn's assets, and now the man was dead. *Won't that ruin the doctor's scheme, now that he can't charge him for any more treatments!*

While she cleaned up the spilled food, she heard her father say, "I don't care who is in charge of his money. Whoever it is must reply to our request for fulfillment of Jenelonn's contract. I'll be in the office later."

Her mind raced through multiple possibilities about how the doctor might profit from his patient's death.

Another thought occurred to her. *Could I be in trouble for having the list? Did Lektonian Security investigate the doctor and somehow learn I found the evidence? Did they tell Father?*

After a rapid analysis of these implications, she realized that the patient's death wasn't in Brelkaar's best interest. His chances to pad his bill would be over. *Unless,* she thought, *someone suspected him. Then, Jenelonn's death while Brelkaar still controlled his assets would be convenient.*

She believed that all the names on the list were sick, elderly people with money to steal before they died. How long could the doctor do this before someone noticed that his patients were getting no benefit from his treatments?

As she reached that conclusion, Lukeniss entered the kitchen and complained bitterly, "Why are you standing there? I nearly ran over you. Go to the garden, girl!"

Obediently, she followed him to the garden without getting a meal.

CHAPTER 6

Her father sat at a low, stone table, sipping a mug of hot jittra. Getting immediately to the point, he said, "You test for your credits in twelve moons. What are your plans after that?"

His frank stare was meant to show authority and intimidation, and it almost felt obscene. Steadying her nerves, she replied, "I'm going to apply to the kaamestaat in San Durg."

"The business program at Remuel Cove has a better reputation."

She didn't doubt that he mostly preferred it because it was out of town. "Yes, sir. I might think about that."

"If you want a serious profession, get a serious education. Contact the director at Remuel Cove and enter your application."

She knew there would be no choice in this. Although she'd regret it, she pushed her opinion. "Father, I couldn't start classes at the kaamestaat until after my fifteenth naming day. That's three mooncycles away. I have more time to consider my options."

He gave her assertiveness no regard but barreled on with his decrees about her future. "You can apply before you're fifteen. I don't want you to go anywhere else. It would be a pointless waste of money. Take care of it this afternoon."

And just like that, her life was planned for her. Details were set into motion and taken out of her control. *As long as I'm part of his household, I'll never be allowed choices of my own. In fact, I'm sure that he'll deny me anything I've planned, even if he agreed with it, in order to prove his dominance.*

In that instant of awareness, she realized that betrothal offered the only chance for her dreams to come true. But now that she'd stated a desire to attend upper school, changing her mind would only seem like childish rebellion against his rule. And then, betrothal would be the last thing he'd approve.

What she needed was a realistic reason to change her mind, something he'd favor. Only one idea made sense.

She caught his arm as he rose to leave the garden. "Wait, Father. What about betrothal? I don't want to be betrothed in Remuel Cove. I don't know anyone there."

"What does that have to do with it?"

Incredulously, she gasped, "Please! At least allow me to choose from men I know. I deserve that much consideration."

Lukeniss smiled in uncharacteristic sympathy. "Well, I suppose I can't find fault with that. The best families of our Nation are in San Durg, after all."

"Yes, they are," she agreed, wondering at that unique situation. They rarely agreed on anything.

"Very well." He was convinced and his mood brightened. "You may arrange for entrance to the kaamestaat in Remuel Cove Region or petition Elder Bolaith to preside at your Gift Rite. Either of those options will be accomplished by your fifteenth naming day." He hesitated, waiting for her response.

"I understand," she mumbled.

This only angered him. "Have I not taught you to respond with the Litany when you're given instructions?"

Humbly, she lowered her head and repeated the Litany of Tradition. "Tradition is Truth. I will honor my father as I honor truth."

Lukeniss was satisfied. "I'm going to work. Don't forget your homework," he called amiably.

She was left with the belief that Lukeniss had gotten his way, even though it was what she wanted and betrothal to Kendel was now possible.

She whispered, "Destiny, in three mooncycles, I'll have my Gift Rite, and all my dreams will work out. Please keep things on track."

In the meantime, I'll do something about Dr. Brelkaar, starting with a background search about his reputation as a physician.

After school that day, she stayed behind, waiting for the other students to leave. Before her tutoring session, she wanted to discuss Tellik. She told Kendel, "Tellik called me last night. Trennis Meelo purchased all five statues, and he commissioned a dozen more to be made."

"He won the contest?" asked Kendel brightly.

"Absolutely. His family is thrilled about settling in San Durg."

"He also earned his lower school certificate today. I signed it this afternoon. He said he'd be on his way to Sevenn tonight."

"Oh. I guess I won't get to say goodbye." She looked away sadly. "Do you think we'll ever see him again?"

Under the table, she felt his hand touch hers with a sympathetic pat, and he whispered, "Maybe, if it isn't too far away. Where is his uncle's farm?"

"You know, he never told me. Well, it's back to the two of us again. Is there somewhere we can speak without being heard? I have to tell you something."

Kendel closed the classroom door. Although it was clear glass to ensure they were always in view of someone passing in the hallway at least they could speak privately.

Being careful of appearances, Kendel indicated a chair that wasn't too near his desk, and she sat down. He sat behind his desk, placed his folded hands on the desk and appeared to be doling out a lecture. In COAXIS Standard, he asked, "What's concerning you, Melenta?"

Lowering her eyes, she gave a wry smile. Kendel was determined to get a lesson in today. Classes at all COAXIS Institutes, even the one on Lekton, were taught in Standard. Soon enough, she'd be glad for his insistence on fluency.

Her mind made the linguistic switch. "Father cornered me into a commitment this morning. By my naming day on 29 Jaila, I have to move to a kaamestaat in Remuel Cove. My only alternative is a Gift Rite ceremony on that day. Either way, I have to be out of his manor."

Kendel was careful to look professional. "He said that? What did you agree to do?"

"I told him I didn't want to hold Gift Rite in Remuel Cove where I don't know anyone. I think I'll have to be betrothed." She watched his eyes for a clue of his feelings about this.

He remained carefully reticent. "I see. You should announce your intention soon to give plenty of notice to the young men of station. You want the best possible selection of contenders."

Her heart whispered internally, *but I want you.*

Then it hit her that Kendel had only agreed to contend if no suitable partner came forward who would support her desire to get a COAXIS degree. *I guess I was hoping he'd promise to contend,* she thought.

But he maintained his relationship as her mentor.

Of course, she thought suddenly. *He has to do that. Someone could be looking at us through the door.* She chided herself for expecting anything else. Glumly, she said, "Would you like to start studying now?"

"I think we should."

"May I ask something before we go to the library? Do you know how to check on a particular doctor's reputation?"

He raised an eyebrow, and it was obvious even with her head lowered. He said tentatively, "I know how to find out if any charges or complaints of misconduct have been brought against him."

"That will do fine," she replied cryptically. She immediately composed a cover story in case he asked why she wanted the information. When he didn't ask, she was relieved. She'd rather not have to lie to him.

San Durg Township, 1 Chaith, 2159

On the following morning, the new season began. The Assistant in Dr. Brelkaar's office took a final glance to be sure no one was in the waiting area before making a call. She spoke softly to someone on telecom. "Are you there now? We should move swiftly. Nolan Jhotolair's son won't allow any more treatments, and Nolan is failing. The doctor says to go ahead."

In San Durg's Town Square, a man in his early fifties took the call on his pocket comm. He was a handsome and impressive figure, a typical Solotan with blond hair and blue eyes. He responded, "I'll make an appointment with the Elder this morning. Thank you for calling."

Casually, he placed the comm into a pocket of his elegant, brown jacket. Assuming a proud bearing, he mounted the steps of the Council building.

Inside the marble entryway, lines of people waited to petition their Elders. They stepped aside deferentially and bowed to him as he moved to the Attendant and said, "I wish to petition the Arbiter on behalf of a client."

The Attendant, who was new, had served less than a mooncycle in his position, so he didn't recognize him. But noticing how citizens treated the man, he inquired uncomfortably, "I ask pardon, but may I have your name, sir? I haven't been here long enough to recognize every legal servant."

A man who was apparently training him rushed to interrupt. "Traan, this is Representative Cha'atre from Woodlake Region. Always allow him to petition next."

Traan gestured gaaro with a finger to his forehead. "Pardon my oversight, Representative. Did you say Cha'atre? Not the banker, I assume."

The gentleman smiled tolerantly. "Lukeniss is my brother. I'm Loris Cha'atre."

"I see." Traan consulted his computer. "The Elder is free. I'll have the Council Page escort you if you wish."

But at a curious half-smile from Loris, he ducked his head submissively and said, "But you know the way. I'm the one who is new here."

Kindly, the Representative said, "Don't worry. Everyone is new once."

In moments, Loris entered the Council Arbiter's office. His assistant announced him, and Loris was directed into the Elder's private, inner office chamber.

Elder Rees Sa'abree, a slight man of sixty was unusually tall. A quiet and unassuming man by nature, he was nevertheless renowned as a fierce champion of rights. It was his duty for the Council to be the final judge of civil disputes in his Nation. Known for neutrality, the Elder rarely took sides, even with other Elders of his Council.

Loris bowed. "Jhendail, Elder Sa'abree."

"Loris! The Representatives aren't meeting, are they? What brings you to San Durg?"

"I'm here as legal servant this time. I wish to petition on behalf of an elderly man whose son is neglecting him."

Sa'abree nodded soberly. "I'll call for the Scribe and we'll see what we can do. Let's go to the Council Chamber."

In San Durg Township

Melenta didn't go to her tutoring session after school. She was determined to continue her investigation of Dr. Brelkaar until she found evidence against him. At Kendel's suggestion, she consulted the Library of Records at the town hall.

A small Solotan woman directed her to a computer station where public records were available, and Melenta went to work. But to her disappointment, there were no reports about Brelkaar, neither good nor bad ones.

As she prepared to leave, the librarian asked, "Did you find what you wanted?"

Melenta bowed to her. "Not really. I was researching a certain physician to find out if his practice is well respected before I see him."

"A wise precaution." The librarian gestured for Melenta to follow her to her desk. "What is the specialty?"

"Geriatrics." Then Melenta realized she'd said the doctor was for her.

"Trying to find the right physician for a grandparent?"

My grandparents are deceased, she thought, *but she doesn't know that.* Melenta said, "That's right. My Neena is a proud woman, you know. Thinks she's able to make decisions, but I don't know if I can trust this doctor."

The librarian whispered back. "I had a Neena like that. What's the doctor's name?"

"Pol Brelkaar."

The woman's fingers routed through several files on her computer screen. "He's licensed, I see, and specializes in neurological disorders. Last season, he was certified to test a treatment program for dementia and similar age-related illnesses."

"No disputes or complaints about the value of his treatments?"

After making further inquiries, she stated, "At the time he filed application with the Physicians Board to certify the treatments, it says three of ten specialists doubted the usefulness of his procedure. If there'd been anything harmful, though, I'm sure it wouldn't have been certified."

"I'm sure. Thank you for your time."

Melenta couldn't be sure yet, but something about that doctor felt wrong to her. His treatments were apparently costly, but they might be helpful. It didn't seem likely that the Elders would let the doctor take legal action against a family without prior success with his treatments. She needed more information.

She said, "Since I don't have to be home for a while, I'm going to find Brelkaar's manor."

Shortly, a rail bus dropped her near the address. As she'd expected, the doctor's manor was expensive and well kept. At the gate to the estate, a young woman rushing from the manor suddenly knocked Melenta down. Slowing only briefly, the woman glanced at her.

Wondering at the woman's agitation, Melenta asked, "Are you hurt?"

The woman stopped and took a deep breath. "I ask pardon. I didn't see you. If you're here to apply for the housekeeping job, don't do it. You'll never be paid enough for what he expects, that's if you're ever paid at all." Saying nothing else, the woman hurried toward town.

Melenta smiled. *So, Dr. Brelkaar has problems paying his help? A need for more income could motivate him to make himself trustee of his patient's wealth.*

"I'm finally getting evidence!"

San Durg Township, 3 Chaith, 2159

Within two moons, the Infocomm reported that at Jareth Jenelonn's death, the Council amended the trusteeship and returned control of the assets to the man's heirs. Melenta was delighted that the Elders had discovered the doctor's deceitful scheme.

But then, a day later, her faith in the Council dissolved when they approved a new petition by Dr. Brelkaar to seize Nolan Jhotolair's assets.

Determined to stop this evil plot before every name on the list was bankrupt, Melenta went to the offices of San Durg's Lektonian Security.

While the office didn't appear outstandingly busy, no one had time to talk to her. A form was thrust at her, along with an offer to "follow up later on her report."

Melenta seethed at the condescending treatment. To get someone's attention, she wrote only one sentence on the form, under a section entitled, "What did you witness?" She wrote, "I saw a murder being planned." Handing back the form, she disdainfully took a seat to wait.

The officer coughed, choking on his surprise. "I'll show this to the Chief."

She imagined another desk that would become the final resting place of her concise report. She asked, "The Chief? I suppose he's also going to give it to someone higher up."

The Defender shook his hand, denouncing her statement. "Chief of the Watch. Today, that's Unit Commander Baireen. You'd better be sure about this. A false crime report is grounds to be called before the Council."

She recognized this tactic. "I'll wait here."

Resigned, he left the room.

Very soon, he returned, gesturing for her to follow him. Melenta was taken to a large office chamber. Behind a massive desk a uniformed man stood to meet her. Commander Baireen wasn't as old as she'd expected. He had the look of someone of blended races. Solotans of pure lineage most discriminated against those whose ancestors broke the vow to protect their race. The products of those unacceptable unions often drew criticism from Familyheads like her father.

Will Commander Baireen expect mistreatment from me and ignore me?

With this in mind, she faced him without lowering her eyes. *I hope he* doesn't *know my father directly.* Careful to show respect, she introduced herself. "My name is Melenta. I wanted to tell someone what I've found out. I may have overstated the part about murder."

He frowned.

"But I do have information about a crime," she hurried to say.

The vestige of a smile that had almost graced his expression disappeared. "Are you aware that a false crime report is grounds to be called before the Council?"

She thought, *is this how they always treat reports?* She humbly lowered her gaze and responded weakly, "So I've heard. I only wanted that Defender to listen and take me seriously. He wasn't."

Baireen sternly gestured to a bench across from his desk. "I'll listen, but no more games. Tell me why you're here, Melenta."

In a nearly panicked burst, she outlined the story, from the list she'd found to the Council order that named Brelkaar trustee for the first patient on that list. "And when Jareth Jenelonn died, the same ruling was made for the next name on the list. I met Nolan Jhotolair's family, and they didn't want him to have the treatments."

Baireen waited through her barrage of facts and then signaled her to quit. He asked, "You actually have no direct evidence of a crime, only your suspicions?"

She knew her cheeks were flushed. "What if Nolan dies?"

He lost patience. "He's an old man, Melenta, and very ill. If he's seeing a neurologist, he's probably not clear-minded, either. Maybe someone needs to make decisions for him."

"But the doctor is having money problems. I forgot to tell you that part. I talked to his housekeeper, who said he didn't pay her. He needs money."

"We all need money. No crime in that. And you can't take the word of a disgruntled employee without checking in more depth. What if he withheld her pay because she was a poor worker? Maybe she breaks things, and he's taking the replacement value from her salary. I appreciate your interest in security work, but you aren't properly trained. Leave it to us."

Melenta glared at him with fury. "You don't believe me?"

"I didn't say I wasn't interested in the matter. If you'll leave this to me and stop trying to investigate on your own, I'll look into the doctor's dealings."

It wasn't what she'd hoped for, but with regret and a touch of humiliation, she realized that it was the best answer she'd get. She rose to leave.

Baireen said, "Can you bring me that list?"

She thought, *what if he loses it? Then, I'd have no proof when the third name becomes a victim.* She lied. "I lost it. I memorized the first two names."

"You lost your evidence?" he chided incredulously.

"Well, it blew out of my hand."

He hustled her out the door while cautioning stiffly, "If you interfere with our work again, I'll bring your father in to answer for it."

That prospect sobered her. "Please, don't do that. I'll stay out of it."

She fled the enforcement station with mixed feelings. *This should have been the right thing to do. The All Wise wouldn't have led me to the list unless it was my destiny to help. If no one believes me, I'll take care of it myself.*

San Durg Township, 5 Chaith, 2159

Melenta had succeeded in keeping her investigation from Kendel. However, after two moons, her mentor decided that he needed answers. Before school he asked her, "Why did you miss another study session after school?"

"I'll be there today."

Sternly, he gave her a glare that said she'd better keep her word.

And she meant to keep it, she really did. But something unexpected happened. After school, while she waited in the library for Kendel to come, she started a new computer search. It produced a home address for Mezla Krenn, the third name on the list. That piece of information had eluded her until now.

"I'll have to apologize to Kendel tomorrow." Her feet carried her to the transport station.

This manor was also in a wealthy area of town. She grumbled, "I'd be surprised if the doctor wastes time on anyone who isn't wealthy."

Ringing a chime at the estate's gate, she waited for a servant to come out. She was surprised to see a young man, barely older than she, exit the manor and approach. "Yes? You have a delivery?"

"No. Does Mezla Krenn live here?"

The boy answered cautiously, "That's right. He doesn't take visitors, though."

She took a chance. "Well, of course. I suppose he wouldn't really know if someone visited him."

The boy relaxed and smiled with gentle sorrow. "Not much."

She gestured to her credoglyph necklace, the symbol for Dignity. "And I certainly wouldn't wish to embarrass him. I wanted to speak to someone who takes care of him or makes decisions about his estate."

The boy looked immediately suspicious, now. Melenta realized that it sounded as if she wanted to sell something. Quickly, she amended her approach. "I think that came out wrong. I wanted advice. I'm about to take in my grandmother, who has the same condition as Mezla Krenn."

His suspicions died, but determined resistance replaced it. "His daughter, my mother, is in charge of his business. She's very busy. Perhaps you ought to consult a doctor."

Glad for an opening, she broke in abruptly. "What about Dr. Brelkaar? Do you like him?"

"Who?"

His genuine confusion hit Melenta hard. "Isn't that your grandfather's doctor? I wondered if you'd recommend him."

The boy didn't resist helping her, but sincerely he replied, "I don't know that name. His condition doesn't require a doctor's care. Nothing can be done for him. Now, I really must get back to my duties."

She stepped in front of him and asked, "But haven't you consulted Dr. Brelkaar about his new treatments?"

The young man was through being interviewed. He sidestepped Melenta and closed the gate between them. "Never heard of him."

Melenta watched the boy return to working in the garden, wondering if there was any possibility he was lying. But why would he? If Dr. Brelkaar had victimized this family, he wouldn't protect the doctor.

There seemed to be nothing else that could be done to stop Brelkaar from taking advantage of unfortunate, mind-sick people.

But as a final effort, she yelled to the boy, "Tell your mother she shouldn't trust Dr. Brelkaar!"

Then, a new idea suddenly changed her ambitions. *Now that I've learned how to trace the names on the list I can locate each of the families and warn them.*

Gruner Bennis watched Melenta leave the wealthy estate. Per orders from Lukeniss, he watched to see if the girl's reputation was being compromised by the attentions of a man. The boy she'd spoken to at the gate hadn't seemed especially friendly to her.

So, he resumed his station, following her at a distance.

CHAPTER 7

San Durg Township, 7 Chaith, 2159

The planning had taken two moons and plenty of ingenuity. But at last, Melenta was ready to warn the remaining families away from Brelkaar. This time, she'd need a little more time than the two cycles she was allowed after school.

And so, one cycle before the end of class, while the students quietly read their lessons or did homework, she approached her mentor privately.

He looked at her so sternly that Melenta almost backed down. She'd disappointed him several times by skipping her tutoring or ducking out of class. And so far, she'd given him no explanation for that.

Timidly, she whispered, "May I be excused early, Ail. Brekket?"

His eyes narrowed with a shrewd, calculating appraisal. He whispered, "You still owe me explanations for the last two times, Melenta."

"Yes, sir, I know."

"Well, I want them. Now."

She wished he'd blink. "I'm doing an errand for my father," she lied.

Kendel knew her too well, though. "Then, I'll ask him why his errands are more important than your education."

She sighed. "I'd rather you didn't. I don't have time to explain now. I need to leave. Please?"

He spoke louder, ordering her, "Come outside the classroom." He left the room.

Her classmates snickered and teased her about getting in trouble. She followed Kendel to the hall, closing the classroom door. There were no eyes watching now, and no one could hear.

He said, "Don't lie to me again. It's dishonorable."

Lowering her gaze and apologizing with a gesture, she replied, "Yes, sir."

"And don't call me sir. I'm much too… invested… in you for that. I'm your friend. If you're in trouble, I want to help you."

She dared to look up. "I know, and I'm glad. I'm not in trouble, Kendel, I promise. It's simply personal business." *Maybe that will stop his interest,* she thought.

But Kendel only prompted, "What kind of personal business?"

I need an excuse that would be embarrassing to talk about so my refusal is believable. Then, she thought of something and pretended to give in. "Oh, fine, I'll tell you. I'm not feeling well. I've been having some… female problems. I'm going to see if I can find a doctor to see me today."

He breathed deeply, and she saw his anger fade into only worry for her. "You should have told me. I hope these absences won't continue."

She fought an impulse that was totally new to her, one that also surprised her: She wanted to embrace him. Instead, she answered, "No, it won't. I miss our lessons." The tenderness in her voice shocked her.

But it warmed Kendel, and he smiled. "So do I. Go, then."

Melenta retrieved her daypack from the classroom. Formally, she bowed to the mentor and, for the benefit of other classmates, said, "I'll finish my assignment at home, after my appointment."

She'd prepared a route that allowed her to stop at each of the seven manors in the least amount of time. However, in her planning she didn't account for the amount of time it would take to actually get a face-to-face meeting. If these wealthy people were anything like her father, they were rarely home. They would avoid being approached by strangers and would be unwilling to listen to a girl. Nevertheless, she'd try.

Halfway through her mission, she realized how late she'd get home. Her father wouldn't go easy on her. Despite the consequences, she decided to complete her mission rather than ask Kendel to let her off once more.

It had been worth the trouble, because at least she got her message across to someone at each manor. But she had one other problem. Perhaps it was a case of nerves for doing something she shouldn't and lying to her mentor to do it. Perhaps it was her natural aptitude for observation. Whatever the reason, it seemed like someone was following her.

Almost four cycles after school, she walked into her manor having determined that even her father's anger wouldn't take away her sense of satisfaction. Lukeniss met her at the door. "Give me an explanation, and tell me that I'm not going to receive a summons from the Council to answer for any of your mischief."

Had someone she'd visited recognized her and reported her to her father? Forcing her expression to remain placid and innocent, she told him, "I wasn't doing anything to be reported, Father. Don't worry."

He didn't appear mollified. "You didn't go to your tutoring session. I know because I sent someone to the school to give you a message. He spoke to your mentor and found out you'd left school early."

He made the last word sound sinister, and she had to force a quiet gesture of acknowledgment. "You sent someone to the school? What message?"

He glared at her attempts to side step. "I wanted you to run an errand after school, but it doesn't matter now. Why did you leave school?"

I'll use the same excuse. It had worked on Kendel. And anyway, it's always best to be consistent with my stories. She answered, "Didn't my mentor tell you I wasn't feeling well? I've been having some female problems. I wanted to talk to a doctor."

This changed his mind. Relaxing somewhat, he gave her the benefit of the doubt. "That's where you've been? You saw a physician?"

The way was growing slippery, now. The next thing he'd ask was a doctor's name. Carefully, she fumbled for the right excuse. With him, the best idea was always to admit to incompetence, since he'd expect that of her.

She told him, "I waited to see her, but she had a full schedule. I'm supposed to call tomorrow for an appointment."

Giving her one of his best glares, he pronounced, "Don't you know you can't expect to see a doctor without an appointment? Tell J'Mii when you'll be late. Don't take that kind of liberty again, Melenta."

I got off! Unbelievable! But she had to cap her performance with humility. She bowed to him, and he walked out of the chamber.

She'd avoided trouble this time, but now, she'd have to make a doctor's appointment. If she thought about it, she could find a way to avoid that, too.

Just when her nerves had settled, her father suddenly reappeared and asked, "Are you still planning to accept Gift Rite when you turn fifteen?"

Suspicion and dread rose in her mind. She thought, *I get in trouble, and he wonders when he's getting rid of me.* Humbly, she lowered her gaze and gestured agreement.

"You should have your intention announced to the community right away to give plenty of time for the right families to hear of it. I'll dismiss you from school tomorrow so that you can go to the Council building and petition Elder Bolaith."

A multitude of thoughts rocketed through her mind at once. Everything she wanted was falling into place, but it depended on several factors succeeding in order. Her dream of attending the COAXIS Institute would depend fully on having a betrothal mate who would allow it.

She outlined the steps in her mind. Once Kendel certified her final credits, he could contend for her hand. She'd choose him at the ceremony, of course and then he'd be her Familyhead.

Perhaps, she thought, *when we move to Luna, he'll teach at the Institute.*

But the reality was that if her father knew how much it meant to her, he'd refuse Kendel's gift. He stood before her, waiting for an answer. Making a show of acting nervous and uncertain, she stammered, "I ... I have to announce it so soon?"

"Soon? You turn fifteen in two mooncycles. Is there any reason you don't want to give plenty of notice to contenders?"

She pretended submission to placate his ego. It always made him back down. With her agreement, he smiled and left the chamber.

San Durg Township, 8 Chaith, 2159

With Lukeniss Cha'atre as the director, Ronjer Investment Firm had become prosperous. As sole owner, Lukeniss had a vested interest in seeing that loans made were loans paid on time and with the full interest allowed by the Council of Soloto.

Today, as every day, Lukeniss began the business day by reviewing a list of clients who were late on their payments. Those who were more than two payments behind would be summoned to his office to account for their delinquency.

A knock at the door interrupted him. Brenner Dolenn, his assistant, entered and announced the arrival of one of the summoned clients.

Lukeniss called, "Thank you Brenner. Have him enter."

A young man pushed the door open and immediately bowed to Lukeniss. The man wasn't as old as his weathered skin indicated. Certainly, he wasn't the age of most of Ronjer's clients. Then, Lukeniss remembered that this was the client's son. "I believe I summoned Jhonn Chemis regarding his loan?"

The young man maintained denees and clasped his hands respectfully behind his back. He spoke in polite whispers. "Yes, sir. My father is taken ill. I'm Maiken, his eldest. He asked me to explain that I have taken work to help catch up our loan on the manor. Next mooncycle, I should be able to make an extra payment."

"Should be? I can't operate a business on possibilities."

The young man nervously gripped the bottom edge of his tunic. "I will, sir. I mean … be able to pay."

Turning to his computer, Lukeniss pulled up the account. The family was behind four payments. But Lukeniss was wealthy and successful because he knew how to be creative. He said, "Where do you work?"

"I'm Repair Master for San Durg Lower Schools, sir."

Melenta's school? This was the kind of opportunity he called "creative collections." He gestured to a chair before the desk. "Be at ease, Maiken. Your father has always been a good client of Ronjer. You can do a service for me, and I'll bring all your payments current so that your manor isn't jeopardized."

Amazed, Maiken uttered a relieved gasp. "That would be so good of you, sir."

Leaning over his desk, he lowered his voice. "You see my daughter will test for her credits in only a few moons. She's about to arrange Gift Rite, but I'm concerned that her mentor has been pressuring her to make unwise decisions. Oh, I haven't been able to observe anything directly, you understand. You work at her school, so you could observe for me and get near enough to hear what they discuss at their tutoring sessions after school."

"I'm happy to be of service! I'm a man of my word, sir. If that mentor is up to no good, I'll find out."

Lukeniss sat back in his chair. "Excellent!"

In San Durg Township

When the Council of Soloto opened session that morning, Melenta learned that to see Elder Bolaith, she'd have to petition him during a Council session. Her name was placed on a list, and she waited.

Elder Leeth Bolaith was the oldest member of the Council of Soloto. As Minister, he presided at ceremonies and legal functions. Though Melenta had never met him, Lukeniss spoke often of this Elder as if he, alone, rivaled her father's reputation for strict, Traditional beliefs.

Soon, she was taken to two heavy, wooden doors that were artfully carved with the crest of Soloto. The page took a step inside, announced her, and she silently followed him inside.

Although she'd learned much about the Council in school, she'd never had reason to petition them. It was quite intimidating. The Council Chamber was grand and elegant, all that the seat of power for a Nation should be. It seemed dreadfully quiet to Melenta, and it smelled of must and oiled leather.

Facing her at the rear of the immense chamber was a long, marble dais. On that, extending almost the length of the dais, sat a wooden table with panels enclosing three sides. The front panel displayed intricately carved artwork of Soloto's crest.

And at that Bench presided five men, the Council of Soloto. Each Elder was dressed in formal robes of various colors that differentiated the man's role for the Council. Over the robes, a long mantle of white rested around the neck, extending down the front of the robe. Each mantle was embroidered with the Elder's credo in lieu of wearing a credoglyph necklace.

Impressed beyond measure, she took in these sights quickly and then lowered her eyes. She walked hesitantly forward, shaking slightly, and bowed in deep reverence.

Memorize this moment, she told herself, *my first appearance before the Council. It's incredibly humbling. These are Elders, the men who have ultimate authority over an entire Nation of people.*

Tradition gave them the duty to judge her behavior. If she disobeyed her father in any way or dishonored his credo, she'd answer to this Council. Every day, the weight of that knowledge forced her to carefully choose her words.

A voice called, "You may come closer. What do you petition?"

To make legal petition, she kneeled on one knee and said, "I'm Melenta Cha'atre, daughter of Lukeniss Cha'atre. I petition to accept betrothal through Gift Rite."

She couldn't lift her gaze to see who spoke, but she knew it would be the Minister, the Elder in violet robes. He said, "You're descended from a family of pure, A'laantuvian heritage, so you may request that Rite. When is your fifteenth naming day?"

"It is 29 Jaila, Elder."

"Do you willingly request that I preside at your Gift Rite ceremony, and will you pledge to make your vow of betrothal on that day?"

With both hands on her heart, she replied, "I pledge."

"At your ceremony, you may choose from any contender whom your father approves by accepting a gift. Once I bless your betrothal, do you pledge to be united to that family, dwelling honorably with them and maintaining pure heritage for his line?"

"I pledge," replied Melenta.

The Leader of the Council, who wore robes of white spoke, then. "Your petition is approved, Melenta. The Scribe will post notice tomorrow on Infocomm. May The All Wise bless your choice and grant you happiness."

She thought, *that's it? I'm dismissed? It seemed too simple.*

Rising, she bowed again, turned and walked quickly from the chamber. Although Lukeniss hadn't required it, she'd return to finish out the school day. She was anxious to tell Kendel her news.

After school that day, Melenta lingered in the classroom. Ordinarily, she'd wait for her mentor in the library, but there was so little privacy there, and she wanted no one else to hear.

When the last student left, she whispered, "I petitioned for my Gift Rite this morning." He seemed surprised. "Didn't my father call you to excuse my absence?"

"He only told me you wouldn't be at school today. Since you went home ill yesterday, I assumed that was why you were absent."

Melenta found she disliked deceiving this friend. "Actually, I lied about being ill. I'd like to tell you what really happened, though."

Sitting across from her, Kendel listened as Melenta recounted her suspicions about Dr. Brelkaar. But he wasn't pleased that she'd warned the families. For the first time she could remember, her mentor reprimanded her, and it hurt her.

He said, "Don't you know that the doctor could bring charges against you for ruining his practice? Melenta, you have no real proof that his treatments are either harmful or unnecessary."

She looked into Kendel's eyes with determined faith in everything she'd done. "If he wasn't doing anything wrong, why would that woman hide a list of names?"

A momentary doubt crossed his expression. "I don't know. But you don't know, either," he scolded.

Suddenly, Kendel glanced at the door to his classroom. Melenta turned to follow his gaze and saw the school's Repair Master sweeping floors outside the door.

Her mentor rose and dragged her quickly to a small supply area off the classroom. He had her stand outside the small closet with her back to the classroom door, maintaining propriety.

Careful to hide his face, Kendel whispered, "You'll risk all you've worked for if you get into a legal mess over this. Seven seasons, Melenta! You're about to test for your credits and be betrothed. Leave this alone."

He's right, thought Melenta. *Now that I've warned the people about Brelkaar, if they get hurt, it won't be my fault.* Smiling, she waved her hand in the gesture of agreement. "I'm going to pass that entrance exam for the Institute and make you proud. When I finally get my Specialty degree, it will be because you helped me defy Father's restriction against teaching me about COAXIS."

"And I'll be proud, Melenta. Wait and see. All our work for seven seasons will be worthwhile if this stays a secret."

From a classroom next door, Maiken listened. Mentors often forgot that the walls of the supply areas off their classrooms weren't solid. He smiled and murmured softly, "Thank you, Melenta. You just saved my manor."

Lukeniss heard the knock at his office door. Expecting Brenner, he answered without looking away from his computer. "Enter."

"I ask pardon, sir?"

It wasn't Brenner. Lukeniss looked up with a start. The young Chemis man was back. Annoyed, for he'd only assigned the man his task this morning, he responded, "Was there something else you needed, Maiken?"

The door was quietly closed behind his back before Maiken replied, "No. I have something you need. I think it's worth more than a few delinquent payments."

Lukeniss felt a surge of power supercharge his blood. "You heard something to incriminate the mentor?"

"For the four back payments we owe, I can tell you what he said and what he did. For a little extra consideration, I can tell you what your daughter has been doing behind your back."

Lukeniss positively glowed with eagerness. "By all means, Maiken, tell me. Tell me everything!"

"After class was dismissed, she stayed behind in his classroom. They were in full view of the doorway, and I couldn't see anything I'd call improper. They were speaking so softly that I couldn't hear, but the mentor seemed to be disciplining her."

Lukeniss huffed and sat back in his chair. "She's usually defiant. I'm not surprised. That isn't very important."

"No, but when the mentor saw that I was outside his door, he pulled your daughter to a supply closet with him. He hid inside, so I couldn't see what he was doing. She stood in front of the closet, but still in the classroom."

Furiously, Lukeniss envisioned an immoral implication. "Are you saying that you saw them touching?"

Maiken considered what to answer. Lukeniss impatiently pounded his desk. At last, the young man said evasively, "I'm not so sure what I saw. Maybe I might remember later."

Lukeniss pressed him for an answer. "Did you hear anything they said in the closet, then?"

"That I did. Your daughter said the mentor had been helping her to defy your restrictions about her curriculum. I gather you never authorized her to learn about COAXIS? Well, from her own mouth, I heard her say she'd been studying to go to a COAXIS Institute. The mentor has been helping her prepare for it."

Lukeniss lost the last tenuous hold on his temper. Leaping to his feet, he threw back his chair, which formed a serious dent in the wall behind him. "I knew it! I knew something was going on these last few mooncycles."

Maiken calmly completed his report, sure of his success now. "No, sir, I heard him say they've been at this for seven seasons."

"He will pay!"

With an evil laugh, Maiken added more spice to the story. "Sounded to me as if they've gotten too close. I wouldn't be surprised if he isn't planning to contend at her Gift Rite, too."

Lukeniss joined in a raucous hoot. "I can spoil that but good. I merely need a solid witness to that impropriety."

"If it's worth it, financially, I mean, I'd say I saw something naughty going on."

This brought a scowl and a brisk retort. "I don't falsify evidence, Maiken, and I don't break the law." He suddenly stared away, thoughtfully. "Unless..."

Maiken raised his eyebrows.

With a lilt in his voice, Lukeniss crooned, "You said Brekket pulled her toward the supply closet? Wouldn't that mean he was holding her hand?"

The greedy young man beamed wickedly. "And honestly, with her back to me, I couldn't see if she ever dropped his hand."

The plan solidified in his head, brilliant in its simplicity. He gave Maiken a steady, knowing look and made his pitch. "If you'll testify to this before the Council, I think your ailing father deserves to have his entire debt forgiven. After all, he's suffering an unfortunate hardship."

Maiken bowed to him. "Oh, I'm good for my word, sir. I heard it all."

San Durg Township, 11 Chaith, 2159

Three moons later, Kendel proudly administered a test to his class of twenty students. It was very satisfying to see these students, most of whom he'd taught since the age of five, earn their credits for lower school. Teaching the same students from five through fifteen marked an accomplishment, his first completed rotation as a mentor.

Two opportunities were open to him after his rotation contract was fulfilled. He could make a new contract with the Headmaster of Schools. He could also take two seasons off to return to school and upgrade his skills. Neither of these opportunities appealed to him.

Knowing that he'd prepared Melenta for something few students even attempt gave him great satisfaction. *I've never known a person so hungry to learn and so determined to meet a goal. I'd like to teach a dozen more like her.*

He'd thought about teaching privately and guiding a few more young minds toward a COAXIS education. Between Melenta's zeal for making significant progress for Lekton and her uncommon drive to overcome all obstacles, he expected her to achieve something important. *If preparing that girl for greatness is all I ever achieve, I'll be proud. No mentor could ask for a greater legacy.*

Kendel had never allowed their relationship to be obvious. With testing over, he was free to treat each of his students as if they were equals. He hoped to angle that into a friendship with her, one he could openly acknowledge.

Outside the test chamber, parents of his charges waited to honor him, and their praises made him blush. Suddenly, he found Lukeniss Cha'atre before him. He inquired, "When will I receive Melenta's certificate of lower school completion?"

"I'm not allowed to grade my student's tests. By evening, the scores will be ready, and I'll sign certificates. It will be sent to your manor within the next few moons."

"I'd like to avoid delay. If you sign it this evening, I'd like to pick it up myself."

Why the hurry, Kendel wondered? *Melenta wasn't applying to a kaamestaat.* But he graciously gestured agreement.

As Melenta and her father walked away, she glanced back at him and smiled. He couldn't help reacting and smiled back, showing her how proud he was of her.

CHAPTER 8

San Durg Township, 12 Chaith, 2159

A soft, overnight rain chilled the early morning air as Melenta rose and dressed. The rain brought scents of freshness, the fragrance of blossoms, and it reminded her to appreciate her surroundings. For so long, mornings had only been a busy time for her. Rush to get ready and then rush to get somewhere. With lower school behind her, she planned to start enjoying the day. Maybe she'd start running every morning.

But today, J'Mii would be going to San Durg to shop, and Melenta hoped to go along. She went to the kitchen for First-meal and discovered that J'Mii had already left. Her father and Cheelo sat quietly eating their meal. Melenta asked, "Father, may I go shopping today?"

He turned a cold look on her. "Shopping?" he asked. "Or were you intending to visit your mentor? No need. I picked up your certificate last night."

This surprised her at first, but anxiety replaced it almost immediately. Something was wrong. She lowered her eyes in respect. "It's not that. I've saved back my royalties from Mother's crafts to buy new clothes."

Decisively, he said, "J'Mii will be away all day. You are to stay here and watch Cheelo."

"Yes, sir," she told him, smiling at Cheelo. Melenta never minded watching her brother. Soon, she'd be living elsewhere, so she cherished every moment with him.

Having nothing more to say, her father rose and left for work.

She let Teeka out of the bedroom, scooping the rushi into her arms to cuddle her. Following Cheelo to his sleep chamber, she sat with him to watch him play. The boy's attention was divided between listening and playing with a model of an Interplanetary Communal Traveler, one of the large, luxury shuttles used by COAXIS. Again, she marveled that their father could so intensely dislike COAXIS and yet welcome the marvels of technology the Confederation provided.

She asked him, "Did Father tell you about my Gift Rite?"

The child busily piled assorted toys across his floor to represent the many worlds his ship would visit. He answered, "No. What's that?"

She wasn't happy that the explanation was left to her. Setting Teeka on the floor, she told him, "Please set your toys down for a moment and listen to me." She pulled him closer so that she could hold his hands. Effortlessly and with complete trust, he joined to her emotions. Melenta regretted what she must say, regardless of her own excitement over prospects for a happy future; Cheelo would miss her.

She told him, "I finished school, and I'm almost fifteen. It's time for me to be betrothed." She thought, *he's taking this too well. Maybe he doesn't understand.* "I'll choose a mate and then go to live with his family." She felt his heart breaking right along with hers.

"You can't leave," he cried earnestly, as if proclaiming that made it so.

"I'll be in San Durg. I'll still see you all the time, but I'll live somewhere else."

Through their joining, he knew that she meant it, although it wasn't much comfort to a child of four seasons. "But I'll miss you," he whined morosely.

His touching complaint stirred a deep loneliness in her. "Sometimes. But you're about to turn five and start school. Once you make friends and get busy, you won't notice I'm gone."

"Could I come to live with you, then?"

She hugged him to her. "If it was my decision, I'd do it. But that would be Father's decision. I don't think he'd agree. Do you?"

He laughed at the idea. "I don't think so." He took her hand, enjoying their close bond.

And Melenta could only dwell on how much she'd miss sharing emotions with her little brother. Would joining with a betrothal mate ever be this fulfilling?

In San Durg Township

Kendel worked at home today finalizing reports about his completed rotation. He also started letters of recommendation for some of his students who wanted to find employment. For others, he'd complete forms to certify them for continuing education. He was only barely distracted when the wind chime outside his door was pulled, announcing a visitor. Setting aside the work, he opened the door to find two uniformed Defenders from Lektonian Security standing before him.

One Defender asked, "Are you Kendel Brekket?"

"Yes," he replied politely. He couldn't imagine what they wanted. Was it about his parents? Had something happened to them?

"You're summoned to appear before the Council of Soloto to answer charges."

His first impulse to laugh was thankfully overcome by confusion. Their words seemed to stick in his mind, and yet meant nothing. *I must not have heard correctly.*

Then, his mind leaped to a better conclusion. *They're looking for someone else. It's a mistake. Maybe they only want my help to locate some neighbor.*

Kendel shook his head, smiling. "I don't understand. Who are you looking for?"

Again, the Defender replied, "You're Kendel Brekket? Please, come with us. The Council has summoned you to answer charges."

At last, the words sank in. "What charges? I'm not going anywhere without an explanation." It was a feeble protest to his own ears, but his mind was falling victim to panic.

"The Elders will explain."

Turning back into his apartment, Kendel fumbled on a shelf for his identification and then followed the two men outside. Nothing felt real about this summons. All the way to the Council building, he continued to ask for information, but none was offered.

Until the very moment that he entered the Council Chamber, Kendel still expected to learn that a mistake had been made. He believed it right up to the point where he saw the Elders sitting at the Bench, and Lukeniss Cha'atre stood before them.

Fear crashed into Kendel's soul, and his heart was instantly racing. Meanwhile, his mind ran through all the possibilities that the word "charges" implied.

Robed in white, Jonik Garthrik, the Council Leader called, "Are you Kendel Brekket?"

He bowed to the Elders and humbly approached. "That's right."

"We've summoned you to reply to a number of charges." He read from a computer screen in front of him. "On 11 Chaith, you were observed having a private conversation with Melenta Cha'atre.

A witness gave testimony today that you took this minor's hand and forced her to follow you into a secluded closet off your classroom."

Kendel gasped. Of all the things that might have been reported about him, this he hadn't expected. He took a moment to frantically recall that day. Did he grab her hand and pull her into the supply room? He couldn't remember.

Garthrik continued. "Concerned that a minor was being coerced into an inappropriate situation, the observer found a location nearby to listen to a conversation between you and Melenta."

At this, terror trickled with the sweat going down Kendel's back. He couldn't entirely recall the conversation, but he was sure that none of it should have been overheard.

Garthrik added, "The witness also stated that you verbally admitted to teaching Melenta information expressly forbidden by her Familyhead." Then, the Elder read directly from the testimony. "Melenta thanked her mentor for helping her to defy her father's restrictions on curriculum for seven seasons."

The trickle of terror had seeped into his bones, now. Kendel knew he was completely and thoroughly doomed, and apparently, so was Melenta.

Garthrik continued, "Furthermore..."

Kendel moaned. *There's a furthermore?*

"Furthermore, you were heard offering to contend at this girl's Gift Rite so that you could continue to support her in this forbidden education."

Kendel froze, thinking, *I could swear that nothing like that was said that day. I'll deny that.* He looked up. But seeing the Elder's expressions, he held no hope for a defense. He couldn't lift his eyes from the floor, and his legs felt like fire circulated within them.

Elder Garthrik called, "Lukeniss, as Melenta's Familyhead, what charges do you make?"

Lukeniss stood apart from him, nearer to the Bench. With clear and harsh conviction, he answered, "I charge you with corrupting my daughter's education. I charge you with willfully disobeying my expressed restrictions on her curriculum."

Garthrik called, "The charge will be professional misconduct. We will give you time to consult a legal servant before you answer the charge."

Kendel considered fighting it. There was only the proof of one witness, who admittedly wasn't with them. Maybe there was room to prove a misunderstanding.

But then, Lukeniss told the Elders, "That wasn't my only charge. Summon Melenta here and question her. Have her swear paan kaal-soto with joining to assure the truth. We'll learn all that was going on in that closet."

The image this sent to Kendel's mind sickened him. He loved Melenta dearly and would never defile her. Uncontrolled, he screamed, "Elder, I'll answer the charges, but I take full responsibility. I don't want any of this to harm Melenta's reputation."

"Then you admit she's defiled?" yelled Lukeniss.

"Nothing happened!"

Garthrik sat straighter and silenced them. "As Melenta is a minor, I'll allow Kendel to bear full responsibility. She won't be charged."

"She defied me!" Lukeniss bellowed.

Garthrik replied firmly, "She was coerced and misled by an authority figure whom she respected. She won't be charged."

Devoutly grateful for that, Kendel bowed. He knew what he'd have to do. "I don't want a legal servant, Elder. If Melenta is left free, I'll answer the charge right now."

Garthrik told him softly, "When you're ready, the Scribe will record your statement."

Kendel glanced at the young Elder in bronze robes who sat beside Garthrik. His fingers keyed settings on his computer, and he nodded that the recording device was ready to make Kendel's words a matter of legal history. Patiently, the Elder nodded in support.

With a deep breath to steady his nerves, Kendel began. "I did teach Melenta information that I had been ordered not to teach. I want it known that the forbidden subjects were nothing more than the material about COAXIS that I taught the rest of her class. I did not force her, either. Melenta was eager to learn it. That was my mistake. I don't think she should be punished for being curious."

Lukeniss shouted, "Mistake? That's what you call it? You cannot take back seven seasons of corrupt training, mentor!"

Inwardly, Kendel hid his smug reaction. *No, it can't be taken back, you old fool!* And his silence infuriated Lukeniss even more.

The Scribe spoke to Garthrik beside him, "I can't get a clean recording if Lukeniss interrupts. Please ask him to leave."

"We don't dare let him out of our sight. You'd better type his statement."

Meanwhile, Lukeniss challenged Kendel again, charging toward him and demanding, "And what immoral payment did you require of Melenta in exchange for your extra lessons?"

Kendel reeled to face the accusation, yelling vehemently, "That is untrue!"

Instantly, two Defenders stepped between them.

Garthrik demanded silence, and the chamber fell into a hush, trailed by echoing voices. He asked Kendel, "Do you deny that she addressed you by your familiar name?"

Kendel wondered, *how much more despair can I take?* He admitted freely, "She has been known to use my proper name upon occasion, but not my familiar name. I think it's only because she trusts me."

Garthrik pressed further. "Do you admit to joining with Melenta?"

"Never!" Kendel pronounced defiantly. "I have never joined emotions with a minor—not Melenta or any other child."

Lukeniss laughed cruelly. "You were seen, Brekket. You can't deny it."

"Enough!" The Council Leader demanded. "Kendel Brekket, by your admission, you have violated the directives of your mentor's license. You have admitted to a longstanding history of violating rules of ethics in your profession. By this, you aided a minor to defy them as well. I'm revoking your license to teach. Do you understand this ruling?"

Kendel expected it. Dutifully, he responded, "Yes, Elder."

By the Law of Tradition, the victim of a crime decided when justice had been met. Another Elder dressed in the green robe of an Arbiter asked Lukeniss, "Does this satisfy your honor, Lukeniss?"

Ominously, he replied, "Barely, Elder Sa'abree. This man has taught harmful, deceitful practices to my daughter. A change of careers keeps future children safe, but it hardly pays restitution for seven seasons of immoral conduct."

"I agree," called Elder Bolaith, the Council's Minister and guardian of morals.

Elder Garthrik looked to Elder Rameeth, the Advocate, whose job in such cases included assuring fair justice to both accuser and defendant. He said, "In the future, Melenta won't likely hold the beliefs and values her father intended. Deciding those values is a Familyhead's right. A mentor's role in shaping young lives must be held to high standards."

Kendel had no more to say. He knew further punishment was coming, and it would set an example for every mentor.

The Council Leader announced, "Your citizenship in this Nation is revoked. You are ordered to surrender all valuable possessions to be sold and returned to the school system for reparation. You are banished from all Solotan Regions. You may reside in an amnesty zone at the border of either Sevenn or Sumuru. Do you understand this ruling?"

Kendel never knew if he answered. His mind was in shock as the Defenders escorted him out. They followed him home, where he was allowed to pack clothing and personal needs. He asked to take his holopic album of family pictures, but was denied any comfort or luxury. He was told it would be returned to his parents.

As they left, locking his apartment behind him, the Defenders asked only which border he preferred. His entire family lived in Solotan Regions, and they'd be forbidden even to speak to him again. He picked the Sevenn border.

Lektonian Security flew him to the amnesty zone between Soloto and Sevenn and dropped him off. It was a small, unadorned settlement of people who, like him, had been cast out of their homelands for any but violent offenses. It was foul and fit only for the destitute. He thought, *under no circumstances could I live with that lawless lot of criminals.*

Then, Kendel remembered that Tellik had moved to Sevenn. *I'll look for him. Hopefully, my previous assistance to the Kaamzen family will be remembered, and he'll offer me sanctuary.*

In despair, he cried, "All Wise, please protect Melenta from her father's wrath, because he's undoubtedly going straight away to inform her of his deed."

In San Durg Township

Long before First-rest, Melenta and Cheelo heard their father's shuttle arriving outside the gate. He came to them in the garden, where Cheelo greeted him with enthusiasm. "See my garden, Father?"

"I see," he answered proudly. "Cheelo, go inside, please, and get a bath. Change your clothes, too. You and I will spend the day together." Cheerfully, he ruffled his son's hair and gave him a friendly push toward the manor.

Melenta, sitting on the ground beside the flowerbed, looked up at him. *Father is in a good mood. I wonder why?* She asked him politely, "That's nice. Are you doing something special together?"

The scowl he gave her was all the warning she was to have. "Your defiance is over, Melenta. I've discovered your little plot with Brekket. You'll never see the inside of any COAXIS Institute. And don't expect him to show up for your Gift Rite, either."

Melenta screamed, "No! Where is he? Please!"

He smirked at her pain. "He's been escorted to the border, banished from our Nation in disgrace. Kendel Brekket won't be teaching you or anyone ever again."

Her cheeks started burning, and crippling horror gripped her lungs until she feared she'd quit breathing. Only the tears stinging her lips reached her senses and kept her mind present in this moment.

Without warning, he bent over and grasped her arms, jerking her to her feet. With joyful disdain, he declared, "Go hide in your chamber to whimper like a rushi. If I have a moment of trouble from you before your Gift Rite, I won't hesitate to disown you. Do not cross me, or Cheelo will be out of your life."

Nothing could hurt her more, and he knew it. Her love for Cheelo would be his bargaining tool. As he pushed her away, she faced the reality of her broken dreams. Someone else had to be the hope of Lekton, for Melenta Cha'atre expected only a loveless betrothal that boasted a single advantage: She'd no longer live under the tyrannical rule of Lukeniss Cha'atre.

San Durg Township, 13 Chaith, 2159

Even by the next day, Melenta didn't leave her sleep chamber. Cheelo thought she was ill, which was partly true. Exposure to this horrible depression would do him no good. Besides that, he'd try to cheer her up. She didn't deserve it, and she couldn't allow it.

Near the end of the evening, J'Mii knocked softly at her door. She called, "Mel, let me give you a meal, child."

"No, thank you." She reached for Teeka, her sole consolation. Her pet sensed her pain and wouldn't leave her side.

Then through the door, she heard, "You must eat a few bites."

She looked at Teeka, who cocked her head and winked her dark, beady eyes. Melenta whispered, "If I take the tray, she'll go away. I could give the food to you."

So, she rose from her fur-bed and opened the door. J'Mii sighed in relief. "Please, try to at least drink the broth."

She nodded agreement.

J'Mii glanced behind her, as if assuring that she wasn't watched. From a pocket of her dress she pulled an envelope and whispered, "It was delivered for you today. Your father doesn't know about it, and I don't suppose he needs to know." She hurried away.

Closing the door securely, Melenta sat again on her bed and placed the tray on the floor beside her. The broth did smell enticing, but first, she'd see what was in the envelope.

The letter was brief. She looked to the end to find a signature. It was from Tellik's mother, Brutha Kaamzen. She read slowly, taking in the message.

"Melenta, I heard from Tellik this morning. He asked me to call you. I tried, but your father refused my call. Tellik wants you to know that your mentor is safe and staying with him instead of going to an amnesty zone. Kendel believes in your goals and asks that you preserve your future by letting the damage fall to him alone. As long as you don't sacrifice your chances by defending him, you can succeed. You will honor him best by living up to your potential."

Through another torrent of tears, she whispered, "I will honor you, Kendel. My goals might be delayed, but they aren't demolished. I'll make a new plan. I will be The MenD'lee!"

Looking again to the future, a betrothal mate would have to be part of that plan because she'd sworn to the Elders to go through with her Gift Rite ceremony. She'd choose someone—anyone—and then do the best she could.

I'll have to do it, thought Melenta. *I can't accomplish anything for Lekton if I'm disowned. If I get my family name stripped from me and get thrown out of my Nation, I won't even be able to find a job. I have to be betrothed!*

San Durg Township, 29 Jhaila, 9

The crisp Half-light morning of Melenta's fifteenth naming day came at last, the Lektonian age of first majority. Until she was twenty, she'd still be considered a minor for most legal matters. This was, though, the age to make her first important decision for her life. Today, Melenta would choose a betrothal mate.

Fifteen was also the age her sister had been when she died. Without realizing it, this caused her to feel a subconscious connection between death and betrothal. Thus, while she waited in a small room off the Council Chamber for her ceremony to begin, nothing seemed right. She could hardly bear the outrageously formal ceremonial gown her father had insisted that she wear. As was customary, it was one of the colors seen in Lekton's sky. Her gown was deep violet and trimmed with elegant, gold stitching. Her credoglyph necklace had been so richly upgraded with tra'adeen jewels that it almost defeated the purpose of wearing it. A display of such wealth didn't seem dignified.

Soon, she expected to hear the trio of le'era harp, pakkis drum and mooka flute announce the beginning of the ceremony. Her father would come for her, and she'd be taken to stand before Elder Bolaith, who would ask her to choose a betrothal mate. This should be a happy occasion, but she harbored a desperate desire to escape.

Peeking through a thin, brown curtain that covered the only window of the stark dressing chamber, she whispered, "Why am I doing this?"

In the Council Chamber, she saw a hundred of the finest families of Soloto waiting to witness her Gift Rite. Five men, sons of wealthy, prominent families waited to contend for her. Melenta didn't want any of them. They were strangers to her.

She remembered, then, the excuse she'd used to keep her father from sending her to Remuel Cove—she wanted to know the men who would contend for her. The truth was, she'd never known any men except her brother and her father … and Kendel.

Memories remained of her mentor and friend, the only person who had helped her rebuild her life after Linnori's death. When she heard he was with Tellik in the Sevenn Nation, sometimes she entertained daydreams about running away to find him.

Will he look on Infocomm today, wondering whom I've chosen? If he shows up today, I'll gladly run away with him.

But Kendel wouldn't do that. He wanted her to follow her dream and help Lekton out of the stagnant mire known as the Law of Tradition. To her regret, she admitted that his ruined reputation gave her that chance.

Most of all, she regretted that her mother hadn't lived to see this important day in Melenta's life. After Linnori's death, Kamira gave birth to three sons. Miklii, Nerris and Jhonn were conceived in quick succession, but each was miscarried. The reconciliation with Lukeniss that she hoped for drifted further away with each son's death.

After that, Kamira's doctor said her health was too fragile to survive another pregnancy. She insisted that Lukeniss wouldn't survive unless she gave him a son to continue his family line. Soon, she conceived another child, enduring her pregnancy in complete rest to be certain that her frail health would get her through delivery. Unfortunately, Kamira didn't survive the birth, but her son did.

Cheelo was born in Melenta's tenth season. And now, almost five seasons later, Cheelo was here to watch his sister choose a mate.

That is, if her father let her choose. As she recalled, Lukeniss provided contenders for Linnori; though all along, he'd told her she had to choose Derris Linifee to settle a business debt. It was no wonder Linnori wanted to run away.

"At least this time," said Melenta. "I'll do the choosing."

Those words were barely spoken when Lukeniss entered the chamber. Melenta asked, "Where's Cheelo?"

"He's outside with the Elder. He asked to be a contender. I don't think he'll understand when you choose someone else."

It warmed her to imagine the small child trying to coerce the Elder. It was good to know that Cheelo loved her and felt secure because of her affection. She worried that leaving him now would take away that security. He was losing the only mother he'd ever known.

"Are you ready to go in?" her father asked.

Melenta swallowed hard, driving back a wave of nausea. In no way was she ready.

CHAPTER 9

Sighing, Melenta offered a gesture of indecision. Extending a fist in front of her, thumb upward, she gently opened her hand and told her father, "I'll do as you want and choose a mate, but I really don't know any of these men. How can I know whom I'll like?"

"I suppose you hope Brekket will come to your rescue. He's too cowardly to show his devotion openly. He deals with his needs in closets."

Bile rose in her throat. Her father got a perverse pleasure from shaming her. She thought, *I'll be so relieved to get away from you that any man will do!*

Offhandedly, he remarked, "If you don't have a preference, it doesn't matter. I'll make it an easy decision. Choose Derris Linifee."

She cringed at the name. Bitterness and intense disrespect for her father smothered her mind. Rudely, she answered him, "Derris isn't a contender at this Gift Rite."

"Oh, yes, he's always been a contender. He's eligible, from a good family, and his credo is Honesty. That's a good glyph for you to pledge, I'd say."

"But he's over twice my age, and he isn't even here!"

"He is. I told him to come. The arrangement was made long ago. I made a contract with the Linifee family when their son was born. He's to be betrothed to my firstborn daughter. His father fulfilled a business debt with that contract. If I fail to let him keep it, I'll dishonor his credo. Linnori would have fulfilled that agreement, but now you can."

Melenta bit her lower lip but couldn't contain the rage spilling out. "You want me to fulfill a pledge made for Linnori? You never treat me like a person. I'm your daughter, not a bargaining chit in your business!"

His face darkened. "Don't be disrespectful to me! You said you didn't care whom you pick. A Familyhead has the right to suggest someone."

She waved her hand like a bird in flight. "Suggest away, but I don't have to take your advice."

He bellowed, "I want you to choose Derris, and so you will."

"I will not!" The words slipped from her mouth before she could stop them, and she marveled at the satisfaction the declaration brought her.

She paced away from him thinking, *Mother and Linnori both died, and I've lost the only man I ever cared for, all because of his tyrannical domination! I won't back down this time. If it robs him of the satisfaction of controlling me, as well, I'll take this one spiteful act of defiance to my grave.*

Lukeniss only glared at her. "You won't defy your father."

"Watch me!"

Curiously, he smiled. "What did you say?"

"I won't choose a mate. I've decided to remain unmarried."

Staring at her in disbelief, he gripped the credoglyph around her neck with both hands, jerking her closer. "How can you dishonor this? Does Dignity mean so little to you after all I've done for you?"

She daringly returned his cold stare.

His grip tightened on the necklace and slipped upward until the chain bit into her neck. Through clenched teeth, he said, "So, my independent little viper, you've made your decision? All of your life you've defied me. Now, you'll pay for it. I'll call the Elder and disown you."

Her fingers couldn't pry off his hands around the chain. Somehow, she rasped a reply. "Disown me! I don't care!"

"First, you'll hear what I have to say. You can choose to disobey, but you can't control your decision about a mate. Women have only one fate to depend upon in life: They always submit to a man. Your mother should have given you training in such matters."

She tried to ground her fingernails into his fists but couldn't free his grasp on the necklace. She whispered, "I won't listen!"

He laughed at her, a raucous, evil laugh. "A time will come when you will be physically attracted to a man. As hard as you try—and I'm sure you will—you won't be able to drive off the passion. The man only has to touch you when you feel that passion, and it will control you. You won't resist him. You won't want to resist him. That's what it is to be a woman of Lekton!"

Desperate to defend herself, Melenta punched him in the stomach as hard as she could. His grip loosened enough to let her gasp a breath.

But he took control again, pushing her backward into the wall and pressing her against it with his weight. He grasped her wrists, pinning her hands to her side while his fingers dug into her skin.

With each bitter word he said, the pain seemed worse. "Let me go!"

"I'm done with you!" Lukeniss whirled around, pulling her with him and flinging her across the chamber. He showed no concern when her head slammed against the opposite wall. She bounced off the wall in an uncontrolled plunge to the floor.

Though her thoughts were fuzzy, she heard him leave the chamber. The door slammed behind him, reverberating in her aching ears. The blow on the head wasn't serious, but it clouded her mind long enough for Lukeniss to bring Elder Bolaith to her. She'd missed her chance to run.

The Elder glowered at her and asked, "What's this, Melenta? Did you say that you wouldn't accept Gift Rite today?"

"Not today or any day," cried Melenta. She fumbled behind her to gain a purchase against the wall. Rubbing her aching left shoulder that had taken the biggest force in her fall, she faced Elder Bolaith. "If I can't make my own choice, I don't want a mate."

The Elder looked inquiringly at Lukeniss, who stammered, "She said that she had no preference, so I suggested one."

"Suggested?" Melenta argued.

Bolaith silenced her with a stern look. "If you have no preference, could you not honor your father by accepting his suggestion?"

How could she explain this? She was in serious trouble, and she knew it. "The Law says I can choose. I choose not to have a mate."

Her father huffed and paced the chamber. "She didn't tell me this until we were ready to begin the ceremony, Elder. She knew it would dishonor me and humiliate me before my Nation!"

Bolaith said, "Melenta, you petitioned me to preside at your betrothal. If you intended to remain unbetrothed, why did you arrange for me to be here? You pledged to abide by your decision at Gift Rite."

Spitefully, Lukeniss growled, "You won't tarnish my name by your disrespect. I'll remove my name from you."

"Don't be hasty, Lukeniss," called Bolaith.

Melenta felt her legs buckle, and she thought she'd faint.

Her father called in firm, decisive words, "I am not your father. Before this witness, you are disowned."

Melenta shielded her fear with a false show of pride. "I'm glad! I don't want to live with you anymore. I won't let you make me into a dependent, insecure woman like my mother. You killed her with your possessiveness!"

Lukeniss took a threatening step toward her, but stopped when he remembered the Elder was watching.

Rubbing her sore shoulder, she retorted, "No man will ever brutalize me again. The next time we meet, I'll know how to defend myself!" She glanced meaningfully at the Elder, who cocked a suspicious look at Lukeniss. She saw that she'd get no help from him.

She broke the clasp on her expensive necklace. Throwing her father's credoglyph to the floor, she stomped on it as Lukeniss watched in horror. She said, "That's my opinion of your dignity." Then, she stumbled out the door.

Closing her eyes against the pain in her head, she tried but failed to ignore the final words shouted from behind her. "Remember what I said. Prepare to be dominated because you can't escape what you are. Someday, you'll be attracted to a man. He will possess you with a touch!"

In blind rage, she ran north, out of town, heedless of stares at the woman running away from the Council building in a ceremonial gown.

She took out her frustration in the exertion, despite the wrong kind of footwear, and she refused to acknowledge pain. She risked going into trauma-shock, but the physical exertion and her anger eased the emotional overload. It kept her conscious.

And maybe that's no blessing, she thought as memory of the morning plagued her.

All her thoughts fastened on escaping the township. She was glad to be free of her father's abuse. Yet, if what he told her were true, remaining unmarried wouldn't ultimately protect her from submitting to a man's domination. Somewhere in her future, there would be a man—one man—and she'd want him if he touched her.

Melenta had little experience with relationships. She knew nothing about marriage except what she learned from her parents' example. Many times, she'd seen her mother respond to her father's wishes when Melenta knew it wasn't what her mother had intended to do. Was that because she couldn't resist his domination?

Believing what Lukeniss told her, she was more determined than ever to let no man into her life. "No one can make me accept a mate, not even The All Wise!"

She immediately regretted her words. She wasn't exactly in a position right now to annoy The All Wise. Looking upward to the universe to say, "But if you want to help, make Time leave me alone so I can be The MenD'lee. I'll change the Law of Tradition and protect women from brutes like Lukeniss Cha'atre."

Fueled by her anger, she ran for a solid cycle, noting how the vegetation diminished outside San Durg. She passed North Road and continued into the foothills of the Mountains of Sumer, where trees thrived in stream-fed valleys. There weren't many manors in this rural Region, only a few, scattered farms.

Glad to be free of crowds, Melenta enjoyed the solitude. It gave her the opportunity to rip several layers of the fancy gown off her body until only the thin, comfortable lining covered her like a short dress. She kept the violet, satin belt from the dress, though. Discarding the finery with zest, she was able to run once more.

But soon, Full-sun would come, and she'd need shelter from the unbearably hot part of the day. And she'd need food. So far, she'd found neither.

I have to go forward, though, she told herself. *There's no way to go back. By the time my disowning is posted on Infocomm, I'd only be welcome in an amnesty zone.* Like Kendel, she rejected that option.

Finally, the road began a steeper climb, and she slowed to a walk, going ever farther into the mountains. For the first time, she wondered, *has even The All Wise deserted me? I'm finding no shelter.*

The sky grew steadily lighter. Melenta had no idea how long she'd been walking. She was nearly asleep on her feet when, in the next Region, she found an abandoned cottage. The one-room place had little in furnishings and no stored food, but a thick layer of dust covering every surface convinced her that no owner would evict her.

Opening the door and window, she left the cottage to air out and went exploring for food before it became too miserably hot outside. Behind the cottage, she found an overgrown garden. Loving hands had planted it and tended it not long ago. Digging with a stick, she found a few vegetables remaining. "I can boil the praat tubers and eat the other vegetables raw."

Nearby, a stream flowed downhill, and she washed the vegetables, scrubbing them with a sharp stone. As she devoured a few red-orange klet roots, she saw that the stream held fish.

"When I'm rested, I might try to rig a way to catch fish. A jokka fish or two would taste good, especially if I find any herbs to season it."

This sounded good until it occurred to city-bred Melenta that she'd never cleaned fish. She'd never caught one, either. The prickly fins of a jokka could be difficult.

She discovered a bush on one side of the cottage. Surprisingly, it was full of sweet jenreel berries. *Why haven't the birds feasted on this fruit*, she wondered?

"Tell the birds thank you, All Wise," she called aloud. It was enough to soothe her immediate hunger.

But her head and muscles ached. On impulse, she shed the makeshift dress and plunged into the stream. Though the sun was rising, the water from the mountains felt cool. By the time she'd soaked her bruises a while, she made her way back to the waiting cottage.

After one more look around the small interior, she realized there was no fur-bed. "I'm not sure I'd want to use it if there were one. I saw a thick patch of tall grass along the stream, though. I'll make a proper mattress."

Once again, she went to the stream, picked armloads of grass and then returned to the cottage. Piling the grass in a corner, she pulled the curtain from the window and considered it dubiously. "Too filthy. I'll wash it after I sleep."

She spread her thin, semi-clean dress over the grass and lay down to rest. It wasn't ideal, but it would do for now.

With more comfort and ease to enjoy her freedom, the stress of her ordeal dribbled by bits into her mind. Mostly, she thought of Cheelo. How would he feel about her now? Lukeniss wouldn't tell him the truth, of course. Her brother would have to take comfort in Teeka, even as her little pet had seen her through the grief of losing Linnori.

Despite missing her brother, she was glad to be rid of Lukeniss. But what if she couldn't find a way to take care of herself? "What was I thinking? If I'd stayed at the Council building, the Elders would have arranged some support, since I'm technically still a minor. Running away was foolish. I was lucky to find this cottage and food for one meal."

With a start, she realized how unlikely it had been for her to find exactly what she needed. *The cottage … by a stream full of fish … a garden with mature vegetables … the bush full of berries—that's some coincidence that I happened to find what I needed and all conveniently before First-rest.*

It was a sure sign of The All Wise at work. Time, son of The All Wise, must be helping, too, since she arrived here by First-rest. *So, isn't it possible that Destiny has chosen me to be Lekton's champion?*

San Durg Township, 30 Jhaila, 2159

Lukeniss Cha'atre smiled at the bright, new morning, his first morning without the headache of dealing with Melenta. Even though the day began with a summons from the Council of Soloto, nothing would dull his spirits.

Walking through his township toward the Town Square, he held his head high. Occasionally, he got nods of respect from other Familyheads. At his insistence, news of his daughter's disowning had been posted on Infocomm immediately. Posting would dispel rumors and prove him guiltless in her spontaneous cancellation of the ceremony.

He told himself, *by standing firm to protect Tradition, all of Soloto profited. I'm confident that the Elder's summons will be a routine matter. Though I won't say so to the Elders, I plan to see that no Solotan gave that defiant little vixen aid or comfort, wherever she was.*

But when he entered the Council Chamber, the Elders appeared troubled, and his confidence wavered. He bowed to the Council, noting they weren't smiling.

The Leader addressed him formally. "We have summoned you to finalize the disowning of your daughter and heir. Ordinarily, we prefer to follow procedure. It's unfortunate that Melenta ran away before we talked with her."

Lukeniss hushed the worries leaping to his mind. He refused to allow anything to interfere with restoring his honor. He replied, "She chose that, Elder Garthrik. No one told her to run away. I followed the Law strictly, and Elder Bolaith witnessed that."

Elder Bolaith nodded, but Garthrik didn't look at him. He looked straight at Lukeniss, letting his next words interrupt with a decisive, raised pitch. "There's no dispute about the ruling. The disowning has been approved and announced. I know you're aware that a disowned heir deserves safe passage away from our Nation. Do you know where she is now?"

"Of course not! She knows enough to find an amnesty zone to take her in."

The Arbiter, Elder Sa'abree called, "That doesn't satisfy our responsibility. Because of her age, she's eligible for subsistence payments from this Nation for one season. It provides her needs while she finds work within an amnesty zone. However, neither zone on our border has received her. I understand that you don't care about helping her, Lukeniss, but we must."

Lukeniss said coldly, "After the way she treated me, I owe her nothing."

Garthrik understood. "We'll make an effort to locate her and fulfill our obligation. You are ordered to inform us if you learn where she's living."

The Scribe, Elder Chonaira, added, "In other words, Law says that the ruling isn't finalized until this Council has made a fair attempt to locate her. But I'm sure you don't want to be remembered for being remiss in the Law or uncooperative to the Council."

Indeed, he did not. Lukeniss bowed very deeply and replied with a kinder tone, "I'll be sure to contact you if I learn her whereabouts."

Inwardly, he sighed, thinking, *and I'll probably do it. An Elder's order is to be obeyed.*

In the Sumer Mountains Region

Melenta expected this second day at the cottage to be relaxing. But although she had met her immediate needs for shelter, water, and a little food, the morning brought other needs.

She'd eaten the last of the vegetables from the garden and saved the berries. Eventually, she could find seeds and plant a new garden. Until then, she'd have to go back on the road and find a meal.

"What about clothes? This won't do," she said, fingering the material of the shift that had lined her gown. She regretted ruining it now, because she might have sold it. She tried not to admit it to herself, but she was a little sad to know she'd never wear a dress like it again.

"Move on," she commanded herself.

Only now did she allow herself to think about making her way to an amnesty zone. Everyone there would be disowned or shunned.

But she scolded herself for considering it since the zone boss was always a man. "Trusting a man to help me is the last thing I need to do."

Having no other option, she dressed in the shift and wrapped the worn, green curtain around her waist. Holding it on with the violet, satin sash from her ceremonial gown, it made a passable skirt. She laughed at the comical combination. "Well, at least it will stay on."

With a quick wash of her face at the stream, she set out into the early Half-light. She knew only scant details about this place. Sumer Stream was a Solotan Region in the rugged foothills that bordered the Sumuru Nation. The Mount of Sumer supported a few families who farmed or raised livestock. Her best hope was to locate anyone who had a garden she could raid.

I might even locate better clothing. She made a promise to herself to take only one need from any one family. She wouldn't rob the needy.

After a cycle, she noticed a small manor beside a stream. She stayed in hiding, watching as an A'laantuvian man and woman made several trips between the manor and a barn. They loaded a wagon with baskets of grain. While the man hitched two sturdy traag oxen to the wagon, the woman called for two small children. A boy and girl left the manor, climbed into the wagon with their parents, and the family drove away.

Melenta made sure they were far down the road before she sprinted quietly to the manor. Finding a window open, she climbed inside.

It didn't feel right to steal. She thought about taking a set of clothes. But by the time she'd looked around for items of food that she could take, she felt too guilty to steal clothes, too.

In a corner of the children's sleep chamber, she saw that the little girl's bed was a stack of several folded pieces of cloth. Melenta swiped the thinnest, which barely provided any padding. And behind the mother's clothing box, she noticed an old, worn scarf that had gotten lost. She took it with her.

She was especially grateful when a trip to the barn yielded an assortment of seeds. This farmer would know how many packets he had, but he wouldn't count the seeds inside them. Carefully, she took five seeds from each packet and resealed them. She tied the seeds she'd keep in the old scarf and tucked it into her belt.

She also found a few hand tools that would be useful for gardening, but she resisted the temptation to take more than one.

She thought, *there must be only one missing item from the barn. I might have to raid this place again, but not soon. I'll try to find other farms.* She was amazed at the number of items she'd taken away that wouldn't be missed.

Before the sun rose for First-rest, she'd managed to plant her garden. She'd bathed in the stream and hung her clothing to dry while she rested. Now, the thin cloth from the little girl's bed became the mattress cover over a fresh collection of grasses.

Once again, her needs were met. She wondered, w*hat if I can't find food? How soon will I be forced to be a bandit, robbing strangers on the road?*

Amid her worries, it occurred to her to call upon The All Wise to bless her with the ability to care for herself legally. Lukeniss had told her that The All Wise protects those who live honorable lives. Conversely, then, would a dishonorable life produce the opposite of blessings?

"Maybe I shouldn't attract the attention of The All Wise at the moment. I guess it's doubtful that Destiny would choose a thief to bring prosperity and enlightenment to the world. But I can still attend a COAXIS Institute on Luna. I'd find work and attend school, too."

She laughed at herself for thinking the government would ever give her a travel certificate. As dreams go, that one was pitifully out of reach. Desperately, though, she clung to that dream as the only treasure she owned. Sleepily, she murmured, "I don't have much, but I have me. And I don't have a Familyhead."

CHAPTER 10

Sumer Mountains, 19 Breel, 2159

After almost two, full tendays had passed, Melenta was settled in the cottage and living a comfortable but meager existence. She'd discovered only two farms within a day's walk of her cottage. She knew pilfering from these families wouldn't see her through a season. Yet somehow, she managed not to be caught.

It wasn't until the seasonal storms began that she realized the struggles ahead. Rain and gale winds sometimes forced her to stay inside for several moons. She kept a guarded watch on the stream behind her cottage, too, although she'd seen no signs that the cottage had ever flooded.

When she could get out, she used her ability to run long distances to harvest a few crops from a field or orchard. She'd mastered fishing, and cooking them. She'd scavenged at a dumpsite downstream, one of those places where folks illegally throw away things they shouldn't. That had equipped her with a dish or two, a cooking pot, and several other useful tools. She'd only raided the two nearby farms once more, and this time, she took a blanket from one, a set of worn clothing, and an extra pair of warm boots.

One evening, after she'd garnered a few days' worth of rations, she sat outside the cottage to watch the two moons set behind a peak. It had a name, but she didn't know it. She called it Stealer's Peak. A sudden gust of chill wind whipped through trees with vengeance.

Worried, she turned into the wind and saw dark clouds looming. The wind was flinging debris ahead of the storm and lightning traced the edges of black billows, as it grew ever closer.

But then, far down the road, she saw a man driving a team of traag oxen from the top of a huge wagon. She didn't doubt there might be others inside the structure, for it was the sturdy kind of building on wheels used by migrant traders. Shortly, it would arrive at her cottage. Very likely, it would stop for shelter.

Hustling inside, she closed the door behind her, thinking, *what if this cottage belongs to the traders and they're returning home from a season on the road? And if he's not the owner, what if he knows the owner?*

Outside, she heard the braying beasts and the rattle of wagon wheels against the clatter of rain and thunder. As she'd feared, these sounds halted outside the cottage.

A man's voice bellowed from outside, "Hail the manor! If any be present, we mean no harm. I've young children aboard who could use a dry roof until the storm passes."

He could have walked in, she thought, *but didn't. He's being respectful.*

Thinking of Cheelo, she defiantly wiped away a trickle of tears. Racing to the door, she opened it.

A middle-aged, Barmaajian man stood on the porch, humbly bowing to her. "I ask pardon, Miss. Can we beg shelter for a time, 'til the rain stops?"

She beckoned him in with the gesture gleenay, a double nod of the head that meant come.

A woman and two boys of about eight and ten emerged from the wagon in rain covers. They helped their mother from the wagon.

Automatically, every member of the family turned to a chore, unloading two large trunks and pulling out feed sacks to strap to the oxen.

Meanwhile, the man unfastened a large, heavy cook pot from the back of the wagon and carried it to the porch along with the trunks. The boys took towels from a trunk and dried everything before it went into the cottage.

Melenta was terrified. Did these people expect her to feed them?

From the porch, the woman must have noticed her reaction. She quickly explained, "We caught a fair-sized kreen hen earlier. I've all the ingredients for a stew, if you'll be willing to share it."

Relaxing, Melenta smiled.

The woman turned to her sons and instructed, "Dry off and leave your wet gear on the porch. Joza, help your father clean the game. Dellis, can you build up the fire?"

"Can I get dry stockings?" he asked.

His mother smiled. "Sure. Fire first."

Melenta stood in confused wonder as all four of her guests prepared a meal. She began to feel as if she were the unexpected visitor in the storm. When she saw the woman pull knives from her chest and begin to clean and cut vegetables, Melenta retrieved her own knife to help.

The dark woman was remarkable. Neither storm nor hardship diminished her enthusiasm. It was as if her current circumstances were no more than mere inconveniences. She said, "Pardon. I should have introduced myself. I'm Loreeth, and this is my husband, Jeme'el Rozair. I haven't seen you in this cottage before. Are you taking shelter for a while?"

Melenta swallowed hard. "I thought no one lived here."

Loreeth smiled brightly. "Oh, no one does. Hasn't been a permanent resident in four seasons. Once and again, we've seen travelers stop here. It's fine that you're here. Whoever needs it is welcome, it seems."

Melenta was relieved. "I was traveling, but I needed some rest."

Loreeth smiled at her, but it was patronizing. She didn't believe Melenta but said only, "I see. You poor dear. For your kindness, I'll give you some clothes and a pair of warm shoes. Clothing is our trade."

Wonderful! I'd love a new set of clean, proper clothes. But I can't show too much gratitude and betray how destitute I really am.

So, she told her, "I appreciate it. My name is Mel."

"I am honored, Mel. In the morning, we'll move on. We want to go to San Durg and try to meet a few of the merchants. Usually, we trade north of here. Do you know anything about that township?"

"Some," she replied, devoting herself to slicing the last of the vegetables.

Jeme'el brought bits of the chopped meat he'd prepared, adding them to the pot. He asked no questions. "Mel, if you want to ride along, we can take you south. You'll need better shelter than this when winter comes."

"I've got family in Sevenn. I'm hoping to work my way that direction."

He gave her a measuring look. "We go that direction in a mooncycle. How would it be if we hire you to help us at markets?"

She panicked. *It won't do for me to be caught in San Durg in violation of the Council's ruling.*

Knowing her fear was branded across her face, she made up a reason not to accept his offer. "I couldn't! I'm very afraid of crowds. That's why I live out here."

Loreeth leaned closer, whispering, "That's fine, dear. We'd be grateful if you could stay inside our wagon while we're working at market. We've been robbed several times when the wagon wasn't guarded."

She could do that. "I'm a pretty good guard. I can cook and help with the children, too. I used to teach my little brother."

This brought Jeme'el to his feet in excitement. "Really? You've got your credits? We never finished school. If you could teach the boys to read, I'll trade that for your needs. Food, shelter, clothing, everything."

As if the deal was set, the youngest boy asked her, "Can you read to me?"

Tears appeared in Loreeth's eyes.

Melenta made up her mind. She told the child, "Sure. I can help all of you learn to read."

The parents exchanged hopeful looks. "Tomorrow," said Jeme'el, "we go to San Durg!"

However, Melenta feared returning to the township where so many people might recognize her. *But I know the merchants very well. By telling Jeme'el the best merchants to meet, we can leave town before the Rozairs learn that I'm disowned. If they know that, they'll have to report me in order to protect their business.*

Sumer Mountains, 20 Breel, 2159

First Moonrise the next day was crisp and cool, but the rain had moved into the mountains. As the Rozair family prepared to leave, Melenta again marveled at how industriously each person worked at their chores. The boys knew their duties, and needed no supervision. While that alone impressed her, it struck her that Lukeniss wouldn't have handled his children's responsibilities that way.

Once the wagon was ready and Loreeth had prepared a meal of fry bread and fruit to take along, Jeme'el called everyone together for instructions.

Melenta admired his natural style of leadership that was as different from Lukeniss as a man could be. He said, "Mel, we have a custom in our family. When I see The All Wise at work, I point it out to the boys so that they'll learn to recognize it. What did you see, boys?"

Joza, who was eight, quickly responded, "He took us to shelter."

Dellis rolled his eyes at the obvious answer. "And he showed us that kreen fallen from her nest. It was a good meal."

"Very good," their father praised. "When we need help, we're granted it, and what does that mean?"

They replied in unison, "We pass that help to others."

Loreeth smiled at them. "We'll each leave the cottage a blessing for the next weary traveler who is stranded. I'll donate my old window covering. I have no need for it."

Jeme'el stated, "I could donate our two oldest sleeping furs. I'm going to buy new ones in San Durg anyway."

Melenta grinned. "I can testify that it would be a blessing. I've already made one donation by planting the garden. When I arrived, I salvaged the last foods. I'll water it well before we leave." She looked at Jeme'el for approval.

"That's very good, Mel. The All Wise will see that someone comes along occasionally to tend the garden. What about you, Dellis?"

The boy of ten seasons appeared confident. "I noticed that the door wasn't closing properly. In winter, drafts would come in. I adjusted the brackets and filled in a notch hole with some of my clay."

Melenta asked, "The notch hole where one looks out to see who is at the door?"

Confidently, he replied, "I'd rather keep the cold out than know who's coming."

But the youngest boy couldn't think of a gift. Loreeth suggested that he load firewood in the hearth for the next resident.

Soon, they climbed into the wagon and set off. Feeling satisfied and protected for the moment, Melenta knew it was only temporary.

Determined to protect the family, she rehearsed in her mind every situation she could conceive of, any outcome that would put her at risk. It was the best she could do to be prepared.

Meanwhile, she settled back to enjoy the trip. The wagon, hitched to the two oxen, was more of a small house mounted on a flatbed rig. A seat outside the house gave Jeme'el an elevated advantage for viewing the way ahead. He held two long quirts to tap the beasts and direct turns. A stick braking system beside him allowed him to lock the wheels. *Technology could revolutionize this family,* thought Melenta. But she knew they enjoyed their life.

Sitting inside, she heard him call out guttural utterances directing the oxen ahead. They were on their way.

The house was no more than a room, but space was carefully arranged. The boys could play in different corners without annoying each other and still keep out of their mother's way. On both sides, boarded shutters lifted and latched to allow airflow and light to enter. When Loreeth raised the shutters, though, Melenta tensed. She hadn't expected to be visible while inside the wagon.

Loreeth didn't notice but asked cheerfully, "Have you been thinking about how you'll teach the boys? I don't know what materials you'll need, but I've set aside a few kerrig. I can purchase what you need."

Glad for experience to draw upon, she still had a different task here. Lukeniss had spared no expense to provide her with equipment and curriculum for Cheelo. She told Loreeth, "To begin, I think two sketchers would be important."

"Sketchers?"

"Compusketch? Hand-held computers with touch recognition. I'll download a curriculum and set up files to let the boys practice writing and reading."

But still, Loreeth looked puzzled.

"Don't you use something like that to keep your accounts?"

"We've always used the Tra'an system." She opened a compartment beneath the bench where she sat and pulled out a long, deep box. Removing the security locks on the lid, she showed Melenta her record-keeping system.

The box had five rows of six, deep-set compartments, each containing a few colored stones. She explained, "Each sale is recorded on the day of the mooncycle by adding a stone. Red is the highest payment, green is next and … don't you understand?"

My grandparents would. I wouldn't want to offend Loreeth. Since the woman can't read, I suppose this antiquated system would be the best way to manage her records.

Melenta told her, "If you want to buy a third sketcher, I can help you set up a way to keep accounts as the merchants in town do it. You don't object to COAXIS methods, do you? I should ask you that before I begin teaching your sons."

Loreeth wasn't angry or hurt. Self-consciously, she glanced at her sons.

Maybe I shouldn't have asked in front of her children, thought Melenta. *Jeme'el might not favor new methods and outworld ways.* Like Lukeniss, many parents disagreed with introducing too many alien ideas into society. To Melenta, such resistance contributed to Lekton's backward laws.

After a pause, Loreeth said, "I'll discuss this with their father. When my boys are grown and have businesses of their own, do you think they'll have to use COAXIS methods?"

Melenta thought, *Great Portals of The All Wise, I hope so.* Gently, she replied, "Yes, Loreeth, I do. While they're young, they can adapt to new ways far easier than in adulthood."

She took only a moment to decide. "Jeme'el must determine if you should teach them about COAXIS. But in any event, they absolutely must read and write."

Melenta agreed. "Sketchers would be enough for now, then. I can teach with learning songs and one curriculum text plate."

Eagerly, the mother pulled open a drawer secreted below the box of stones and retrieved several coins of large tender. She offered them to Melenta. "Then, I'll let you purchase what you need when we get to San Durg."

Oh, no! There's no way that I could enter a market booth in that township!

Seeing her fright, Loreeth patted her shoulder maternally. "That's all right, Mel. I forgot about your fear of crowds. If you can write a list of what to buy, I'll take care of it."

Though grateful for the woman's understanding, she was unaccustomed to her feelings being considered. Without warning, Melenta burst into tears.

Loreeth reached for her in concern, but Melenta couldn't tolerate it. Her mind recoiled from the idea of sharing her emotions with anyone.

Willing fear under control, she declared, "Let's get to those learning songs."

In San Durg Township

Loris Cha'atre was in San Durg for a meeting of all the Regional Representatives of Soloto. Although this was his birthplace, he'd moved to a different Region after he'd achieved his degree in law. While Woodlake Region and the township of Kaanotok had become home many seasons ago, San Durg still stirred deep memories for Loris.

When he checked into an inn, he had a message waiting for him. He wondered if it was from Lukeniss. They weren't close, but his brother was the last living member of his family. Since Lukeniss had suffered a recent heartache, he might try to make contact.

I never heard the entire story about the disowning, thought Loris, *but I'm sure he'd be eager to share his ordeal with me.*

However, the message wasn't from his brother. It was an official summons to appear before the Council, who asked to visit with them prior to his meeting.

He hurried to answer the summons, but he knew he wasn't in trouble. His best friend, who was the Scribe for the Council, would have warned him of that.

Confidently, Loris entered the Council Chamber, where five men in different colors of ceremonial robes sat at a carved table on a raised dais. Loris bowed to the Elders and then waited with his eyes lowered in denees.

Council Leader Garthrik, dressed in white robes, called cheerfully, "Fairday, Loris. I ask pardon for calling you here. I know your meeting is soon, so I'll explain. I'm sure you heard about your niece's disowning?"

Loris looked up slightly, a concession to protocol that was allowed because of his station. He answered, "Yes, of course. Is there a problem?"

"Only a concern. Melenta ran away before we could offer her assistance during her relocation. Has she contacted you?"

"No, not at all. She ran away? Lukeniss hasn't told me anything. He must be devastated."

Elder Sa'abree, wearing green robes, was critical. "I don't think it mattered to him. She hasn't registered at any amnesty zone. Do you know anywhere we should look, or any friends she might go to for help?"

"Actually, I don't know her very well. I'll certainly tell you if I learn anything."

Garthrik thanked him with a heavy sigh. Loris knew him to be a fair and caring man and also a father himself.

Loris was dismissed, but his friend, Donni, dressed in the bronze robes of the Scribe, excused himself from the bench and followed him to the door. Softly, he whispered, "We need to find her, Loris. She's made a mess of our project."

"Melenta? What did she do?"

With his back to the Council Bench, Donni answered, "Lektonian Security told me she was the one who contacted the families and warned them against trusting Dr. Brelkaar. No one will speak to him."

Loris faked a smile, for the benefit of the other Elders who might be looking. "The little sneak!"

"Find her soon! I may not be able to undo her interference, but I'll talk to a few families."

Grasping his friend's forearm in a Comrade's Grip, Loris said louder, "I'd be happy to help. Call me later and tell me what they have to say."

Donni whispered, "I'll have to wait until I'm home. The tele-comm here isn't secure."

Loris flashed a sardonic smile. "Get a pocket comm, Donni. What are you waiting for? It's helpful."

But Donni only glowered with stubborn insistence. "No, thank you."

En Route to San Durg Township

Melenta wiped the back of her hand across her brow, mopping away perspiration. As midday approached, the morning grew warmer inside the confined wagon. Lekton's two moons lit the sky with a soft haze that provided complete illumination without glare. But the sun would rise in less than a cycle, and the brilliance and heat would be unbearable.

Earlier than Melenta would have expected, Jeme'el pulled the wagon into a grove of trees in preparation for Full-sun. Gratefully, the travelers climbed from the wagon to stretch journey-weary muscles. Jeme'el and the boys saw to the needs of the traag, while Loreeth prepared a simple meal.

Melenta asked Jeme'el, "Can I help?"

He handed her a basket and pointed to a stand of bushes nearby. "You could pick some berries for us. It makes a good treat on the road."

Smiling, she took the basket, which looked very much like a craft her mother made long ago. With a smile that no one else comprehended, she began to harvest the fruit.

Once, she glanced back and saw the boys struggling with one of the oxen that wanted to grab both feedbags from Dellis. But Jeme'el and Loreeth didn't notice. They'd climbed inside the wagon.

Instinctively, Melenta returned to their camp, ready to hold the beast if Dellis needed help. But as she neared the wagon, she heard Jeme'el talking about her. Although she hadn't meant to listen, Melenta caught Loreeth whispering back, "Give me a bit of time alone with our new mentor. I'll try to find out."

Melenta peeked around the side of the wagon and discovered that Dellis had the problem under control. Silently, she crept away from the wagon and returned to picking berries.

But her mind was on the conversation in the wagon. *Did I give something away,* she wondered. *Are they suspicious of me? I need to find out.*

When her basket was half-full, she returned to the wagon. Jeme'el and Loreeth were coming outside again. Melenta asked Loreeth, "How can I help with the meal?"

She gestured beside her to a lawn pillow. "You don't have to do anything, dear. Can I ask you about the family you have in Sevenn?"

"Family?"

"You said you wanted to get to Sevenn to find your family. Pardon my curiosity, but it's unusual for Solotans to relocate to southern Nations."

Melenta smiled and shrugged to hide her anxiety. If she didn't come up with a convincing story and stick to it, she'd invite more suspicion. *It's time for another lie.*

Short notice didn't permit her to devise anything elaborate. She told herself, *if I make the story tragic, their suspicions would be transformed to empathy. I'll invent a crisis in my past to explain my solitary nature, though not the true one, of course. And the drama shouldn't unfold effortlessly. I'll allow Loreeth to pull it from me with difficulty.*

So, with much cajoling and compassion, Loreeth finally got an answer from her. "I'm betrothed, and I think we're very compatible. I love him already. I went to live with my betrothal mate's family."

"That's always helpful. What is his name?"

A name escaped so easily that even Melenta was surprised. "Kendel. He works for his father, and he's due to take over the business within ten seasons. But Kendel also has an uncle near his age, and his father often threatens to give the business to his brother if Kendel doesn't obey his wishes. So he defers to his father in everything. But he must, you see?" She let her emotions feel the pain she described.

Loreeth listened, smiling sadly and waiting for more.

Swallowing hard, Melenta said, "Sometimes, his father's plans for our life aren't what we want, but we have to obey." She knew this created images of servitude or worse. Melenta let her wonder a while.

Loreeth said, "Most women of my age earned their right to one day supervise their own manor by serving a mate's mother. It may seem difficult for a while, but when your mate inherits the business, you'll be rewarded."

Now, Melenta thought, *the drama needs to be embellished.* Since Loreeth didn't read, Melenta decided to borrow from Lektonian literature that she'd studied in school. "Koren's Fight" was a classic tale of a young couple's struggle against an unyielding and dictatorial Familyhead.

Adding a sniffle for effect, she said, "Kendel is used to accepting his father's authority, but he knows I struggle with it. One day, his father found out that Kendel lets me do what I like when his father isn't around. His father sent Kendel to Sevenn to oversee his business there. I was required to stay behind and live with his parents. When I'm molded into submission, he'll let Kendel return."

Loreeth's face dissolved in pain. "He separated the two of you after betrothal? That's so cruel. You must miss him terribly."

Honest tears accompanied her reply. "I miss Kendel so much I can't stand it, Loreeth."

"It's not wise to keep you apart. Betrothal is supposed to be a time for getting acquainted and for adjusting to joining. Delaying that will postpone your eventual marriage. I can't see how he'd think that helps you."

With a flare, Melenta wiped a tear and dropped her face into her hands. "He doesn't care! It's so unfair! I ran away to look for Kendel and tell him that I'll do without the wealth of his inheritance if he'll petition the Elders to head his own household. Then, we can be together."

Loreeth accepted the story and agreed with her intentions. "Where does he live? Do you know the township?"

"I only know that it's in the Sevenn Nation. I do know that he works with Tellik Kaamzen, whose mother lives in San Durg. I thought I'd ask her where Tellik lives. Do you think Jeme'el would be willing to find her when we get to San Durg?"

"I can find her and help you speak to her."

New wrinkle, thought Melenta. She shuddered in furious denial. "No! I can't be seen in town! Someone might tell Kendel's father."

Loreeth was startled. "Dearest All Wise."

Meekly, Melenta requested, "If you can find Tellik's mother, I'll send her a note asking what I need to know. She can write a reply."

Loreeth's expression wasn't encouraging. "Do you think she'll tell you?"

"Tellik and I were friends in school. She won't mind."

When Loreeth consented to help, a great weight left Melenta's heart. Now that she and Kendel were both shunned by their Nation, they could be together.

As the sun rose, Melenta and the Rozair family settled on furs to rest. For the first time in a long time, Melenta slept peacefully.

CHAPTER 11

In San Durg Township

In the township, First-rest was over and Second Moonrise had begun. Near the Town Square, Loris Cha'atre entered a dining hall that was frequented by staff working at the Council building. Loris knew exactly which private room he needed and went directly there.

Opening the door, Loris bowed to the Elder and closed the door. The room was small but elegant, so he felt better about his friend dining at such a common, public dining hall.

Donni Chonaira, who was distinguished as the youngest man ever to be ordained an Elder of any Nation, greeted him warmly. "Come in and take a meal. Thank you for coming on short notice."

Loris relaxed. "Sure. I've never had an Elder summon me to a dining hall before. I didn't know you took meals here, Donni. I'm not sure I approve of one of my Elders eating among common people."

"Please," he replied with mock disdain. "Not you, too." He frequently mentioned how he relished the few chances he had to bypass formality. "This is near my office. I couldn't think of a more private way to meet with you where we won't be overheard."

"You're sure about this place?" Loris asked with disdain.

The Elder smiled confidently. "Very sure. Dr. Brelkaar has identified two more people to put in treatment."

Loris filled his plate from the selection of dishes on the table. "I don't know if we should try it. Melenta left town, but what if she told someone else about her suspicions?"

"The doctor wants to try, but I think we'd better use a different legal servant this time. I know a few people to approach. On another topic, did you learn anything about your niece?"

Loris sighed. "I had a lead. Someone saw her walking on a road in the Sumer Mountains. So far, I haven't found where she's hiding." He saw Donni's face fall and asked, "Why? What's happened?"

"After you left the Chamber this morning, Jonik told us he's putting a deadline on finding her. After three moons, we can't legally offer her subsidy. If she continues to take care of herself, it shows she doesn't need any assistance."

Loris groaned, "Three moons? Can't you get him to extend that?"

"Maybe so, since you have a lead." Suddenly, Donni gasped. "Did you say she was seen in the Sumer Mountains?"

"In the foothills."

Donni smiled. "Lektonian Security told me that a couple of families in that area reported break-ins and robberies at their farms. Nothing valuable was taken, only food and old clothing. That sounds like Melenta."

Loris agreed. "It's promising. I'll look into that."

"Good. Find her, Loris. I want you to be the one with influence over her. If she owes you her livelihood, she'll be more likely to work for us."

Loris grinned at his friend. "You're a devious man...for an Elder."

En Route to San Durg

Melenta enjoyed teaching, she discovered. It was rewarding to watch the boys grasp a new concept. While the wagon rolled its way along the road, she didn't notice the landscape outside. When she finally looked out and realized that they were on North Road, she became anxious and couldn't continue teaching.

She glanced outside so often that Loreeth commented on it. "Is something wrong, Mel?"

Embarrassed, she drew her thoughts back. "I ask pardon. I think this is the road that passes the Skeel Pits."

"We've always turned south before now, but I'm sure we're safe. Our distributor wants us to open new markets in San Durg, and he said the road is safe. It is, isn't it?"

Melenta waved her hand from side to side and answered, "Oh, yes. Don't worry." But inwardly, she felt a dread too horrible to bear. The wagon would soon pass the Cha'atre manor, and this was a danger she must keep to herself.

With a steel effort, she pretended to relax, never looking outside as she waited to know that the wagon had moved past her estate.

But too soon, she felt the wagon coming to a stop. She thought, *we shouldn't be in town yet! This wagon must be in view of the manor! What if Cheelo sees? Or J'Mii? Oh, galaxies, what if Lukeniss stayed home this afternoon?*

Terrified, she shouted to Jeme'el, "Why are we stopping here?"

Loreeth exclaimed in surprise, "Great All Wise, girl. What's wrong?"

"You can't stop here!" she implored.

Jeme'el's voice called from outside, "We have to camp outside any township. This seems like a pleasant location with plenty of shade."

Melenta began to tremble, and her distress couldn't be overlooked. Loreeth asked her, "Isn't this far enough away from San Durg that no one would see you?"

Her mind raced to a convenient solution. She said truthfully, "The Cityhead's office is very strict about migrant traders camping near their township. There's a specified campground for traders on the south end of San Durg. As long as you stay there, the Cityhead won't charge you a fine."

"Calm down, dear," Loreeth soothed. She called out the window, "Did you hear what she said, Jem?"

"I heard. We'll keep going, then. Thank you, Mel."

Sure, now that it was safe, and she wouldn't be on her father's doorstep, Melenta collapsed in relief. But the prospect of a trip through San Durg frayed her nerves. She asked to rest and found a corner of the wagon where she wasn't likely to be seen through the window.

Loreeth seemed tolerant. "That's fine. The boys wouldn't be in a mood to study now that there's town sights to watch."

Melenta laughed when the boys immediately planted themselves in a window, anticipating new marvels.

By the second cycle of Half-light, Jeme'el pulled his wagon into an area identified on a sign near the entrance as "Trader's Field." A camp manager greeted Jeme'el and explained that he could stay tonight, but in the morning, he must either register with the Cityhead's office or move on.

A youth, probably the manager's son, showed him where to stake the wagon. He indicated an adjoining, fenced field that would accommodate the oxen. Jeme'el was glad to let them graze and save his herd feed for the road.

Inside the wagon, Loreeth was finding it difficult to repress her son's desires to take off and explore the camp. She ordered, "Wait until your father knows the rules here, boys."

Melenta didn't share their curiosity. She told Loreeth, "I'll be perfectly happy to stay inside the wagon and rest if you'd like to go meet people."

But Loreeth insisted. "Mel, no one would understand if you hide in the wagon after a long trip. Don't you think it might cause more suspicion?"

"Say I'm sick," she suggested.

"No! The last thing we need is to cause concern that we've brought an illness into camp. Kendel's family won't be lingering in a migrant trader's camp."

"Please, don't say his name here," urged Melenta. "Any of these people might trade with his father. No one can see me."

"I guess that's true," she finally agreed. "Well, I'll do the best I can to help you hide, but staying trapped in this small wagon the entire time we're here? Mel, that won't be pleasant."

Melenta reminded her, "Not long ago, I was living in the woods with no safety or comfort. This isn't so hard to bear for a short while."

San Durg Township, 21 Breel, 2159

By the start of the next business day, Jeme'el found out that another trader in camp, a man named Belva, was on his way to the Cityhead's office. Belva said, "In a new town, it's always best to find a guide."

Jeme'el was grateful for the help, but he wasn't surprised by it. An ancient legend told of a traveler, The Herald of The All Wise, who rewarded those who helped travelers. The Herald granted special blessings. Traders believed those blessings are financial ones. So, while they could be fiercely competitive in the markets, traders helped anyone who made their living on the road. Jeme'el thought, *you never know when the man you help could be The Herald.*

Belva, who traded in commodities and not clothing, could afford to be especially helpful. Jeme'el told him, "I'll give you a discount on any of my stock if you like."

"Done," agreed Belva's wife, who loved to buy clothes.

The two traders crossed town to a building that sat adjacent to the Square and the far more distinguished edifice where the Council of Soloto presided. Jeme'el found that Town Squares everywhere were similar. In the center of the district, a statue of The All Wise stood within a decorative pool. Reverently, Belva and Jeme'el bowed to it and crossed to the Cityhead's office.

There, they were directed to a particular man behind a desk. Jeme'el clasped his hands behind him, bobbed a slight bow and bid him Fairday. "Jhendail. I'm a clothing trader. I wish to purchase a license to trade in San Durg, please."

Behind the half-circle desk, the man nodded and asked politely, "Do you read?"

Many traders had been unprepared for the deluge of technology introduced by COAXIS a little more than two generations past. Jeme'el had never faced discrimination for that. With some trepidation, he replied, "I do not."

Then, he was respectfully directed to a different corner and another man behind a desk. However, this man had no legs. He sat before a computer terminal and greeted him warmly. "You wish to register?"

"Yes, but I'm at a disadvantage. I can't read."

With no malice, the man answered, "Your disadvantage produces my occupation. Please sit down." He gestured to a chair in front of him. "Tell me about your trade."

Jeme'el relaxed. "I'm Jeme'el Rozair. I represent D'Laani House of Sumuru. We have markets between Sumuru and Sevenn, but I haven't yet called on merchants in San Durg."

The assistant recorded these details for him and asked other particulars of his craft. Then he asked, "Who is in your household living with you at camp?"

"My wife, Loreeth and two sons, Dellis and Joza. I recently hired a tutor for the children, and she travels with us, too." Suddenly, he realized that he didn't know her last name. He thought, *it might appear suspicious. I'll look incompetent for not asking or it might appear she was disowned if she wouldn't tell us her family name. Maybe* he *won't ask.*

But he did. "The name?" he asked, hands poised at a keyboard to record it.

Jeme'el used his wife's family name. "Mel Morin, my wife's cousin."

Promptly, Jeme'el was granted a trader's license and provided with a list of all other traders currently working in San Durg. The list included each trader's line of work as well as any items they wished to barter or buy. He could ask Mel to study the list for him, but he had one question now. "Belva, is there a trader on the list named Kaamzen?"

Belva scanned the sheet, but the assistant interrupted. "They're no longer traders. They've settled here as merchants. I believe you can find them living at one of the inns."

Belva asked, "How about a list of local merchants?"

The assistant smiled and printed one more list. "It notes which market booths welcome new trade and which don't. Watch that column carefully, because some exclusive merchants expressly request no contact. On the last page, you'll find a map describing how to find each merchant."

Jeme'el gestured alay with a hand tap on the chest and added a slight bow to lend sincerity to his gesture of gratitude.

The assistant asked, "Could you wait for one moment? I'm remembering a notice placed for clothing traders. Let me find it." He browsed through advertisements on infocomm and found the notice he wanted. "Yes, here it is. A local businessman posted a request to talk to clothing traders who come to San Durg." He printed off the ad, handed it to Belva and pointed to a name.

Belva nodded. "I know the place."

Jeme'el smiled. "I'll call on him right away. What is his name?"

"Lukeniss Cha'atre."

A Half-cycle later, Jeme'el entered Ronjer Investments and was asked to wait in a beautiful, richly appointed office chamber. Soon, an assistant escorted him to meet the Financial Director, Lukeniss Cha'atre.

A tall man of late middle age greeted him. By the man's dignified bearing, Jeme'el knew who he must be. If the man's style of dress were an indication, he'd gladly spend a fortune on clothing. *Maybe he's simply too busy to shop and prefers to purchase his wardrobe this way.*

Jeme'el gave a short bow as to one of higher station.

Lukeniss nodded. "Jhendail, and thank you for answering my notice. Are you familiar with a clothing line from Kedii House?"

Straight to the point, thought Jeme'el, *so it must be important. Well, I'm up to the test.* He replied, "Of course, sir. It is one of the most elegant clothing manufactures on the planet. My line is similar. May I show you?" He indicated a catalog tucked under his arm.

But the man ignored his offer and instead, waved him to a chair near his desk. "Recently, I purchased a wardrobe of fifteen outfits from a Kedii distributor in San Durg. It was for my daughter's betrothal, as we anticipated she'd join a prominent family of station."

Jeme'el only listened, wondering what any of this had to do with him.

Opening a drawer of his desk, Lukeniss handed him a stack of receipts as he explained, "The outfits were never worn. The ungrateful girl decided not to honor her obligations and had to be disowned. Because of her disgrace, the merchant won't accept return of the clothing. He said resale in this community would be impossible. I'd like to sell them to a trader who can find a buyer outside Solotan Regions."

"I see." *Now,* thought Jeme'el, *I understand why this man of high station is treating me as an equal.*

Nevertheless, he looked more carefully at the receipts, although he couldn't read a word of it. He knew the value of the merchandise, however. "I'll pay you 70 percent of the original sale price. I might make only 10 percent profit, but I'm glad to be of service."

Lukeniss computed the figure in his mind and said aloud, "Three ketikerrigs?"

Accounts were Loreeth's specialty, so Jeme'el couldn't say if the figure were right or not. As usual, he bluffed. "That matches what I've figured. I'll arrange a draft on my business account now."

"My assistant will help you arrange it," Lukeniss replied, pleased with the transaction. "How may I bring the clothing to you?"

Jeme'el put on an air of importance to reply. It was as if being in the Director's presence somehow required that. "I'll be calling upon merchants today, I'm afraid. But my wife is at our wagon. Could you have someone deliver the clothing to Trader's Field south of town?"

Lukeniss didn't flinch. "I'll call J'Mii, my house manager and arrange it. How can she find your wife?"

"Ask anyone there for the Rozair wagon." Quietly, he left.

Lukeniss sat at his desk and touched a button that was preset to dial his home. As a face appeared on the screen, he interrupted the normal, polite greeting. "J'Mii, I found a buyer for those Kedii clothes. I need you to gather everything and deliver it to the Trader's Field. Bring back a signed receipt of delivery. You know where it is, don't you? South of town?"

J'Mii nodded. "What about Cheelo? Should he go with me?"

The thought of his son running around among the filthy traveling class irked him. He didn't need his son—and now his only heir—learning unwholesome interests. He told J'Mii, "You'd better bring him to me. I'll let him play on the computer again. He always likes that."

As he closed the link, Lukeniss reconsidered setting Cheelo free with a computer. He called one of the programmers, a young man who had only been with Ronjer a few mooncycles. He told the young man, "I have a unique request. My son, who is five, will be visiting me shortly. It would be a thrill for him if you'd show him a few things on the computer that he might do. Entertaining my son isn't exactly why you were hired, I know."

The programmer was gracious. "That's fine. Maybe it will give him an interest in studying computers one day."

Lukeniss felt worry slinking through his veins. "That's taught at a Lektonian kaamestaat, isn't it?"

"Yes, sir," the man replied with a note of bewilderment.

It had settled Lukeniss, though. *The last thing I need is for Cheelo to start insisting on a COAXIS education.*

At Trader's Field

Melenta hid inside the wagon, even though most residents in the camp liked to gather outside for meals. While she sipped an excellent cup of jittra and sampled more than her share of sweet rolls, she considered a teaching plan. Joza and Dellis were very behind, and the rudimentary subjects they needed would be unappealing for the boys. She needed a way to sweeten it.

The door of the wagon suddenly opened, throwing Melenta into instant alarm.

Loreeth raised both eyebrows in surprise. "Don't be afraid, dear. We always lock the door behind us. The only people coming through this door will be family."

Embarrassed, Melenta laughed at herself. "I'll get over my nervous habits as soon as we clear this township. I've been thinking about how to begin lessons."

Behind Loreeth, the two boys entered the wagon in time to hear that pronouncement, whining as if it predicted torture.

Behind them, their father climbed into the wagon. "None of that, boys," he said in a stern voice. "If you don't want to be migrant traders like your Maata and Dai, you need to learn better skills."

"And COAXIS ways," Melenta added. "Lekton's progress will be tied to technology. We have to know how to use it."

Jeme'el handed her a list. "I could use your help planning my visits to the merchants. That paper is supposed to tell me the ones to see."

She studied it. "At the very least, it says the ones to avoid, who won't want to see you."

"Would you help me mark a dot on the map where merchants will talk to me? Underline locations that might not want to see me, but who don't forbid it."

While Melenta prepared the map, Jeme'el ate another hearty meal. He'd walk great distances today.

Loreeth, though, was more interested in the list of traders. She asked "Could this list tell us where to find the Kaamzens?"

Her husband replied, "The assistant at the Cityhead Office told me they've settled here as merchants. He said they live at one of the inns in town."

Melenta looked hopefully at Loreeth. "I know which one it is. Could you take my letter to Brutha Kaamzen?"

Loreeth softened at the anxious look Melenta gave her. "Oh, of course. I want to go into town to shop for those sketchers. Write your letter, and I'll run it to her. Maybe she'll send a note back telling you what you need to know."

"You're leaving?" Jeme'el asked in surprise.

"Yes. Mel will be tutoring the boys. Why?"

"I purchased some goods from a fellow in town. He's having a servant bring them here."

"I'll be here," Melenta offered. "If all you need is someone to accept it."

They stared at her until Loreeth finally asked, "Are you sure?"

"I'm sure, Loreeth. I don't think anyone's servant will recognize me."

In San Durg Township

Loreeth couldn't help feeling envious of the Kaamzen family when she entered the San Durg Inn. Most migrant traders dreamed of a day when they could afford to establish a business in one location and live in splendor like this.

She'd walked from the street into a huge entry chamber. The floors were an expensive marble. If it was imitation, she couldn't tell. In a corner of the chamber, tremendous, fluffy pillows in muted, sky colors invited weary travelers to relax.

Opposite the lounge stood an elegant registration desk. Behind it, a gentleman in fine clothing greeted her.

Loreeth said, "I have a message for Brutha Kaamzen."

The young, fair-haired gentleman looked up with interest until he saw that she was a common worker. He relaxed his intention to go out of his way to serve her. "Thank you. I'll see that the message is delivered." He held out his hand.

Loreeth was accustomed to being treated as if she was unimportant, but she carefully withheld any evidence of insult. Experience told her it would only make the man defensive. "I ask pardon, but I'm to deliver the message myself and wait for a reply."

The innkeeper notified Brutha. Loreeth didn't wait long before a tall, beautiful Sevenn woman came into the entry chamber. With a smile, Brutha came nearer.

Loreeth saw no discrimination in her eyes for their dissimilar stations. Reminding herself not to expect mistreatment, Loreeth smiled back.

"I'm Brutha," she told Loreeth. "You have a message for me?"

Loreeth handed her Mel's letter. "I'll be happy to wait for you to write a response."

Brutha looked at the paper and stared, reading it again.

Is something wrong, wondered Loreeth? *I think the letter upset her. Maybe*, she thought, *Mel didn't make her need clear.*

But then, Brutha's reaction went from puzzled to something Loreeth thought was fear. She said, "Come to my suite, if you don't mind, and I'll get the information you need."

Loreeth was puzzled, too. *She might be offering to give the next day's weather report for all the importance she's giving this.*

Loreeth followed her, saying nothing. Once she entered the suite, Brutha gently closed the door and whirled to face her. "It was dangerous to bring this here. Is she well, though?"

Loreeth smiled, grateful for the opportunity to discuss her mission openly. "She's quite well. My husband and I are migrant traders. We've taken her into our household as mentor to our two sons. We'll see she gets to Kendel if you can tell us where he is."

Brutha gasped, absolutely horror-stricken. "You shouldn't have done that. Tellik helped Kendel at first, but only out of debt. He said that Kendel found work and left. Tellik doesn't know where he is now."

Loreeth's heart sank. *I'd so wanted to see the betrothal mates reunited. Why do I get the feeling Brutha doesn't?*

Brutha's expression darkened as she firmly said, "I owe her a debt of gratitude for helping our business, but I can't allow her disgrace to jeopardize my family."

"Disgrace?" Loreeth bit her lower lip. In panic, she thought, *what have I done?* After a moment, she said defensively, "Mel has been victimized. I hardly see how it's her disgrace."

"Didn't you know?" asked Brutha, astonished. "Kendel was shunned by Soloto. Melenta was disowned, and her family is of high station in San Durg. You must get her away from you before you lose your trader's license!"

Loreeth felt her face flush with embarrassment. She mumbled an apology for bringing trouble to her door and hurried from the suite.

Bitterly, Loreeth chastised herself for being taken in. For as long as she could remember, The All Wise had repaid her for helping strangers. *I was so sure that I was supposed to help this girl,* she thought. *How could she endanger us when all I did was show her my compassion? I don't know if I can fix this and keep my family safe, but I have to try.*

Loreeth raced home to her wagon to throw Mel out.

CHAPTER 12

Melenta had collected a few scraps of paper to begin teaching Joza and Dellis to write. With a boy on each side of her, she sat on the floor of the wagon and demonstrated how to write their names. She had the boys trace a finger along the characters as they recited its name.

Joza enjoyed the task, but Dellis didn't. He whined, "I feel like a total ludjit doing these childish tutorials. Boys half my age study this way."

"Don't worry. In no time, you'll be able to write and read, and no one will ever know that you got a late start at learning it. Trace them again a few more times."

What she didn't tell the boys was that these childish methods were unpleasant for her, too. This was how she'd taught Cheelo, which made her miss him so much more.

Dellis asked her, "Do mentors teach like this in school?"

His question drew her mind back to the present. "Absolutely, but they use sketchers instead of paper. Your mother is purchasing your sketchers right now. By Second Moonrise, when we start our studies again, we'll have proper teaching tools."

Joza whined, "You mean we have to do lessons in the afternoon, too?"

Suddenly, outside the window of the wagon, she heard a call from a neighboring wagon, "Visitor in the camp!"

Melenta had heard the camp manager use that signal once before. It alerted traders to a possible customer. Nothing was expected of her, but she kept listening in case it was the delivery Jeme'el expected.

She tried to return to the lesson. "We'll study four cycles, Joza, morning and afternoon. But it will be other subjects, too."

"Like what?" they both asked.

"Geography. We'll read about all the Nations and learn to find them on a map."

Suddenly, though, she snapped to attention. Outside, a woman's voice asked the camp manager. "Did you say the Rozair wagon is at the end of the row?"

Terror like a sword thrust through her, terror like she'd never known. It gripped her so firmly that she stopped breathing. *I know that voice!*

The boys saw her reaction. "Something wrong?" asked Dellis.

Melenta jumped to her feet, laboring to make her shocked mind choose a way to deal with the crisis. If J'Mii came to this wagon, she'd be caught violating the Council's ruling of banishment.

They'll send me to the asteroid mines on Pandeera Station, that's for sure!

Most of all, she realized the horrible consequences Jeme'el and Loreeth would suffer for giving her shelter and aid. Above all, she must avoid that.

Quietly, she commanded, "Dellis, a woman is coming to this wagon. No matter what, you must not tell her about me. Do you understand?"

"Why?"

"There's no time to explain! Keeping that secret will protect your parents' lives. This is very serious." She paused while the shock slowly registered on the young faces.

She could spare no more time to be sure the boys would obey her. Abruptly, she said, "I have to leave."

Unlocking the door of the wagon, she flung it wide so that the door hit the wagon with a boom. In the same instant, she burst from the wagon at a run, for running was her only chance. She could run farther and faster than anyone. It was as if all her seasons of running for fun had designed her for this day.

She thought, *I'll storm through the camp so fast it will startle J'Mii. She's easily frightened. Hopefully, that nervous old woman won't have the presence of mind to recognize me.*

So, Melenta fled, head down and looking at no one. Other residents of the camp called out alerts. "Thief in the camp! Thief in the camp!"

But she ignored everything and simply ran.

Then, a single word reached her through the confusion of outcries. She heard J'Mii scream, "Melenta?"

Though crying, she continued to race away. There was no hope left that the Rozair family could avoid punishment. She ran from the camp and didn't look back, while behind her, J'Mii was screaming, "Disowned! Disowned!"

When she looked back, the camp manager and three other traders had begun a pursuit, but they were no match for her.

She leaped obstacles and avoided any route that would slow her down until she escaped to safety outside the camp boundary. On open road, now, she knew the exhilaration of certain freedom. Her mind operated on several levels, simultaneously.

She thought, *I was irresponsible for coming to San Durg, but I'd better plot the safest route now and decide how to stay hidden.*

Running north would take her toward town, the place she should most avoid. Continuing south toward the border of Soloto and Sevenn was her best bet, even though it was far away. *If only I could have delayed leaving until Loreeth had returned with the information about how to find Tellik and Kendel.*

Up to now, she'd been running along the road because the well-cleared and paved street gave her the best chance for speed. But she imagined traders were, even now, hitching up wagons to follow and punish her. It was time to vary her escape route again.

Ahead, she saw a thick stand of trees off the road. Instinct told her it would make a good place to hide and rest. Choosing a place deep enough in the woods to give cover, and yet near enough to watch the road, Melenta sank to the ground, stretching out flat.

Her heartbeat hadn't slowed since the moment she'd heard J'Mii speak. She willed her body to rest, but she wouldn't feel safe until she'd made it out of this Region. Woodlake Region would still be part of the Soloto Nation, but at least she wasn't known there.

Except for the unfortunate fact that Lukeniss has a brother who lives in that Region. If Lukeniss warns him, would Uncle Loris hunt me down? As a Representative, he'd have connections to the Council. I'd better give this more thought.

She gave it thought. Since her uncle had stopped visiting them long ago, he hardly knew her. Would he be as strict about honoring the Law as his brother? Even if he weren't, he wouldn't jeopardize his political position on her account. He'd be sure to require punishment.

Right now, her more immediate worry was the approach of Full-sun. She needed a safe place to sleep in the shade. Standing, she walked deeper into the woods.

It wasn't long before she found an improvised shelter where several trees had fallen seasons ago. Once she'd taken that moment to rest, a powerlessness she'd never known crept over her like fog. She couldn't stop a torrent of tears that washed grief from her heart. She cried out, "What will I do?"

Behind her came an answer she never expected. A fierce growl brought her swiftly to her feet to face a half-starved gaarig. The canine, often domesticated as a pet, might be guarding someone's property. But this animal looked abandoned. It had gone feral, and she sensed no reason or trust from it now.

Melenta ran again. She wasn't sure if the animal would chase her, but she didn't wonder long. Behind her, she heard the rhythmic crunch of trampled leaves as a ferocious snarl at her heels sent her mind into turmoil.

Though already tired, the peril behind her added fuel to her flight. A moment at a time, she gained a lead only because the beast was starved and weakened. *How long before I'm starving and weakened, too?*

At the edge of the woods, where the paved road into town was visible, the gaarig dropped pursuit. Experience had taught it to fear civilization, she supposed.

Melenta collapsed in sullen defeat, for although she'd escaped being devoured by a wild animal, she was once again trapped on the road to San Durg. In desperation, she raged aloud, "All Wise, why are you doing this? Let me alone!"

Instead of a solution for her problem, she saw more trouble on the road ahead. Coming toward her from San Durg was a flatbed wagon pulled by two traag oxen. Several people rode in the back. It was driven at a slow pace, though, so she doubted that they were looking for her. She decided to sit quietly and allow the wagon to pass. However, the tactic would only work if she appeared harmless to them.

Staying seated, she hailed the driver as he approached. "Beware ahead. There's a mad gaarig chasing people entering the woods."

The driver, a young man near her age, gestured alay. He called a warning behind him to his companions.

The wagon passed her. *I dodged exposure this time, but I have to get off the road soon.*

Watching the back of the departing wagon, she saw a woman stare at her. Again, Melenta feared she'd been recognized. She thought, *this is the life I'll face from now on—always running from people, always wondering if this will be my last moment of peace and freedom.*

For now, she saw no one else coming from the direction of San Durg. If she was going to be chased away from town, no one was in a hurry. They'd probably assumed she was halfway to the next Region by now. Would they call ahead to warn Lektonian Security in Woodlake to hunt for her?

Any way she looked at her options, safety was most important. So was food. She weighed the risk of sneaking into the trader's camp for food, perhaps during First-rest.

Then, the decision became moot. She heard the commotion of several wagons rolling in from the south. At a distance, she heard them calling out, "There she is!"

Once more, she leaped to her feet to run, but where would she go? She couldn't outrun teams of wagons or the starving gaarig. Fleeing off the road across farmlands wouldn't get her very far before fences barred her way.

A man in an approaching wagon screamed at her, "Get from our border. Soloto Valley warned us you'd be looking for shelter. Woodlake won't take in the disowned. Go back!"

The wagons were loaded with people, most of them children who were throwing something, and from the bite of the sharp pellet that struck her leg, she guessed it was barb berries. The hard, thorny seeds were weapons farmers used with slingshots to drive predators away from their stock.

As Full-sun loomed closer, Melenta was forced down the road at a run. Though overheated and parched, each time she attempted to slow down or deviate off the main road, a hail of biting barbs assaulted her.

On she went, past Trader's Field and toward the center of San Durg. She limped painfully and endured several welts on her arms and legs.

Her relentless pursuers drove her directly to the Town Square. Of all places she should avoid, this was the greatest danger. She was about to drop when, before her, a booming, male voice screamed, "Leave her alone!"

Melenta crumbled to the ground in exhaustion. When she looked up, her pursuers were coming to a halt.

She thought, *if that voice belongs to a Defender from Lektonian Security and he's come to arrest me, it wouldn't be an improvement in circumstances, but at least he won't hurl sharp weapons.*

Squinting upward, she saw a very tall man silhouetted against the rising sun. The bright light blinded her vision. But although she was afraid, she forced herself to stand. Only then did she recognize the features of her uncle, Loris Cha'atre.

Ironically, her first thought was, *that's the handsomest man I've ever seen!*

Loris told her softly, "I've been looking for you, dear!"

His voice was kind, but he was, after all, her father's brother. Her uncle must want revenge for his brother's dishonor. As an elected official of Soloto, he had the obligation and the authority to make her pay, so why wouldn't he do it?

Again, Melenta turned to run.

Loris raced after her. "No, wait, Melenta!" He caught her arm and held her securely. "I want to help you."

"Why would you help me? You're his brother."

"Being born brothers doesn't make men friends. One of the Elders contacted me about challenging your disowning."

Melenta relaxed her guard and studied her uncle. He was tall, like Lukeniss, and both men had a thick pate of white-gold hair and blue eyes. Beyond that, they shared no resemblance.

Melenta fought to free herself and was surprised when he released her. She stood still and, crossing her wrists, covered her face with her hands outward. It was the request for mercy called J'lek seen.

Loris pulled her hands away. "I won't hurt you."

She whimpered, "You can't really believe that the Elders would let you challenge my father? He has friends in San Durg who respect his name. One of them is Elder Bolaith. No one will cross Lukeniss."

"Am I not a Cha'atre, too? Whatever respect he's given for his family name will also be granted to me. And one of the Elders is my friend, too. As for any other influence he has here, it's no match for my skill and training in law. Believe me, I'll be heard."

Maybe he's right, she thought. *He has a very commanding presence about him. But unlike Lukeniss, his charisma is natural, not assumed by wealth or station. It* isn't *a pretense of Dignity, either.*

She replied cautiously, "I mean no dishonor to you, but I'd rather not challenge my disowning. Now that I'm not his daughter, I don't have to be dominated anymore."

"What can you do without a name?"

"I can take care of myself!" Her current appearance must belie that, she knew.

He smiled patiently. "No one would employ you."

Does he mean to be patronizing, she wondered. "I don't have to stay here. I'll move away."

"No man will ever be allowed to bring you into his family."

Muttering a cynical curse under her breath, she replied bitterly, "Like I'd gretching care! You live alone. Is it so bad?"

Loris mockingly scolded her profanity and defiance. "That's not becoming. And for your information, being unmarried isn't bad. However, I'm grown and not disowned by my family. Do you intend to turn down assistance if the Council provides it? You might get tired of fishing and picking berries. And I wouldn't go back to stealing from farms, if I were you."

Embarrassed, she ducked her head. "I suppose if the Elders want to give me a subsidy to care for myself, I'd agree to that."

"I thought so." There was a twinkle in his pale, blue eyes. "You're a smart girl, Melenta. I think Lukeniss taught you a few valuable lessons, although I'm sure he never intended to."

Weakly, her lips curled in appreciation.

"Why don't you come inside the Council building with me, and I'll do what I can to help you." He started pulling her with him.

She squirmed free of his grasp. "The sun is rising. The Council won't be in session."

He pointed to the steps of the building where two Elders waited. Nodding at Melenta, they went inside.

Loris whispered, "The Advocate will extend the session for us."

Looking up at him, she said, "I'm going to hope you're a blessing from The All Wise."

Planning strategy as he went, Loris firmly grasped Melenta's hand and pulled her with him into the building. As the morning session had ended a half-cycle ago, only one guard was around, but he expected them.

Loris tried to pull her into the Chamber, but she was too afraid and wouldn't move. *Of course,* he thought. *She doesn't understand that my anger is put on for effect. How could she know that I'm actually in control of every word and gesture?*

Willing himself to more patience, he turned to reassure her. "Please, trust me. I'm going to help you."

"Don't send me back to him. Please!"

His heart melted. He leaned closer to speak privately to her. Gently touching her shoulder, he asked, "Do you detest Lukeniss that much?"

The girl glanced warily at the guard to see if he'd heard the question.

Loris hated that he'd scared her. She was conditioned to expect retribution for voicing disrespect for her Familyhead. He whispered, "Your silence is more than he deserves." He hugged her affectionately.

Right away, his frightened niece withdrew, refusing to let him hold her. Though he made no comment about her aversion to his touch, inwardly he promised to heal all the emotional damage his brother had caused this child.

Taking her hand against her will, Loris dragged Melenta into the Chamber. Their footsteps echoed across tile floors and walls of alabaster.

From the back of the Chamber, her vision went immediately to the carved, polished wood of the long Council Bench. At that seat of authority sat five men in official vestments and ceremonial robes. They waited impatiently as Loris forced Melenta nearer and issued reproving stares at their unorthodox entrance.

Once Loris and Melenta stood before them, he glanced at his niece to be sure she understood what was expected of her. He needn't have worried. Her eyes were lowered, and she looked utterly defeated. When he bowed to the Council, she followed suit. Only then did he drop her hand.

Taking one step forward, he tapped his hand on his heart and said, "It was kind of you to wait for me. I've come as legal servant for this young woman."

As expected, the Elders exchanged astonished looks. Loris imagined them thinking that she wouldn't need a legal servant unless she planned to challenge her disowning.

I'll bet, thought Loris, *they're wondering why I'd defend my brother's disowned heir. If I can successfully bend things to my liking this morning, they'll soon understand.*

He kneeled on one knee in the formal posture required to initiate a legal petition. In his best courtly voice, he called, "It doesn't serve justice to deny Melenta the necessities of life. She's of age to be betrothed or to take employment and support herself, but now cannot. Disowning doesn't mean she should starve; only that Lukeniss isn't responsible to support her. Therefore, we petition the Council to provide her needs for one season, according to her rights under the Law."

That was, of course, why the Council had wanted her found. But Elder Bolaith, who wore the violet robes of Minister, seemed to believe some pretense of earning the subsidy was in order. He said stiffly, "She has the amnesty zone to provide her needs. And since she's fed herself without help for an entire mooncycle, I believe she can adequately do so after this."

Inwardly, Loris groaned to himself, *Bolaith knows full well that the Council has agreed to help her. This foolish old man only wants her disowning to hurt as much as possible.*

But for now, Loris wouldn't get into a debate on what constitutes "adequate care." He told Bolaith, "If that's your position, I challenge my brother's charges against her. Lukeniss denied my niece her lawful right to refuse Gift Rite."

Bolaith rose from the Bench to point a knotted finger at Loris. "I know you to be a just man. As a boy, you vowed your credo of Justice to me. But you'll serve no justice until you know the full truth about this case."

Melenta whispered, "Uncle, he came to my Gift Rite and witnessed my disowning."

Bolaith declared, "Melenta wasn't denied a chance to refuse. In fact, she requested that I preside at her ceremony and pledged to me that she'd abide by her choice. However, once the time had come to honor her pledge, she refused to obey Tradition. She dishonored her father before the Familyheads of Soloto. Do you understand the shame he endured by having to give back all the gifts to men who came to contend?"

Slowly, Loris stood, placing an arm around Melenta's shoulder so that the difference in their size would make her seem especially young and vulnerable. "The Law allows Gift Rite to be cancelled before the ceremony. She had not entered the Council Chamber when this alleged dishonor took place. Therefore, it was still a legal cancellation."

The Leader, Elder Garthrik whispered to Elder Bolaith, who reluctantly verified that Loris had accurately presented the facts. Promptly, Bolaith sat down.

"Further," Loris continued, "Lukeniss had not told Melenta until they were about to enter the Chamber that he'd insist on choosing her betrothal mate. It was that knowledge that made her wish to stop the ceremony. I submit that my brother withheld that knowledge until a point when it seemed like she was bound by her pledge. This implies that he intentionally denied his daughter a lawful chance to refuse Gift Rite."

Melenta stared up at him in wonder, but Loris didn't have time to explain how he knew so many details about that day.

Garthrik stood. A short man of commanding presence in his white robes, he smiled at Melenta. His kind demeanor seemed to sincerely wish Melenta well. "There's no more we can do. As you know, the entire Council reviews the ruling when it concerns disowning. Lukeniss only suggested a choice after Melenta stated that she had no preference. By refusing his choice, she meant to humiliate and dishonor her Familyhead."

Again, Loris kneeled on one knee to ask, "Please reconsider, Elder Garthrik. It was Lukeniss who chose to make that suggestion at a moment that would embarrass him."

Garthrik placed his palms firmly on the Bench, a declaration of his authority. "Our ruling is given, and it shall stand. I see no reason to reopen the case for challenge."

Humbly, Loris rose and bowed and gave the proper response of agreement to an Elder's ruling. "J'maari Lesto." Then, lowering his eyes sadly, he looked down at his niece and touched his finger to his forehead in apology. The Elders didn't see that he winked, allowing her to see that his remorse was faked for the Elder's benefit.

Again, he addressed the Council. "I accept your ruling. Will you also give a ruling to provide for her care? Must one so young be condemned to an amnesty zone? Couldn't someone be assigned to provide for her basic support?"

Suddenly, Melenta jumped, and he saw her stifle a smile. She'd figured out that he never expected to reopen her case at all. Assisting in the charade, she pleaded, "Uncle, please, don't let them send me to a zone to live with murderers!"

Elder Garthrik asked Loris, "Would you care for her yourself?"

He feigned surprise. "Me? But I'm unmarried, and I travel often."

Garthrik frowned, but through the wrinkled brow, Loris sensed resignation. The Elder would be deemed unjust if he refused to make provision for a disowned minor. Loris counted on him to realize that no one else would offer to help. It was time to pour on the pathos.

Frantically, Loris argued, "She isn't my legal ward. I'd have no rights to even arrange for her needs while I'm away."

Hastily, Garthrik snapped, "Then, I make her your legal ward."

He gulped audibly. "Now, Elder?" Loris arched his pitch in fear. "Do you mean right away?" He hoped by appearing to withdraw his assistance, it would force Garthrik to a swift, reflexive reply.

Garthrik sighed in irritation. "It is done! She is your ward."

Hastily, Loris kneeled. "Then, as legal guardian of the girl once called Melenta Cha'atre, who was denied right to a family name, I claim my right to adopt my legal ward and give her my family name. By my right, I claim her as my daughter, Melenta Cha'atre."

Standing again, Loris removed his credoglyph necklace, the symbol for Justice. With great pageantry, he placed it around Melenta's neck.

Suddenly, it was clear to the Council that Loris Cha'atre had outwitted the Law. Essentially, he'd devised a way to render her disowning void.

Grinning at her uncle in awe, Melenta stroked her new credoglyph. *I'm someone again!*

An Elder wearing a bronze robe rose from the Bench. He was significantly younger than any of the others. He began to chuckle and shake his head in wonder. Each of his fellows glared at him reprovingly. By his age, she knew that this was the man she'd learned about in school, Elder Chonaira.

The young Elder said, "It is so witnessed and will be posted." That was the only requirement to make the Council's ruling official. "Are there any personal items you want from your manor, Melenta?"

It seemed strange that he'd offer that. But she noticed that the credoglyph stitched onto his vestments was Compassion. She thought of asking for her rushi, Teeka. But Cheelo would need her furry friend now.

Smiling shyly at the Elder and admiring how his bronze raiment matched his dark blond hair so well, she answered, "No, thank you, Elder."

With lowered eyes, she still saw that he smiled back at her. She lowered her head further, hoping no one saw how she blushed.

Loris thanked the Elders and then, bowing, they left the Chamber together—a new family.

Outside the door of the Council Chamber, her uncle asked, "How do you feel about this?"

Because she didn't know him well, she was afraid to look directly at him, to show the gratitude in her eyes. She honored him with a big grin. "I feel satisfied ... vindicated."

"Justice was served." With one finger, he lifted her chin, asking, "Will you look at me, please?"

She tried to comply but found it difficult to do. Lukeniss had so instilled the requirement of denees that she felt guilty to do otherwise.

"Melenta, I don't require or even want you to practice denees with me, unless there's reason to show an unusual amount of respect. You can lift your eyes and face the world."

With effort, she did, and found that his eyes were twinkling.

Her uncle placed a large arm around her shoulders, leading her outside the building. She stepped into the bright sunlight and yawned. "What happened, exactly? It was so fast."

"I know you're confused. There wasn't time to let you in on my intentions. You've been given back your name, the name that should never have been taken from you. The Law of Tradition took your name, and the Law returned it—that's only just."

"Just." She fingered the golden, credoglyph necklace she wore. It sparkled with purple tra'adeen gems. "Justice is my credo now?"

"It's mine, so now it's yours."

"This can't be real. Someone will change this ruling."

Loris stopped by the statue of The All Wise that stood in the Square. Sunlight glinted on the jewels inlaid in the base. "I'll explain it to you when we're alone. Right now, understand that the Law of Tradition is sometimes unjust. When a law is wrong, it can be undone."

Melenta stared up at The All Wise. Inwardly, she asked, *are you real? Will I still be The MenD'lee, the Chosen One?*

Taking a deep breath, she looked around her. Time had been cheated again of his plot to ruin her life! No one waited to chase her away. She told her uncle frankly, "I wish I felt accepted, but I don't."

He seemed to understand. "I expect you feel betrayed and rejected. Remember that our people honor the Law of Tradition, and by the Law, you're my daughter. You have a name. When the Scribe posts notice of the ruling on Infocomm, the people will accept you."

For now, the answer was enough for her.

CHAPTER 13

Melenta and her uncle walked through quiet streets. She asked, "The Elder in bronze, the Scribe? That's Elder Chonaira, isn't it?"

"Yes. He notified me about your unjust treatment so that I could help you."

"Where are we going?" she asked, thinking of how much she needed to sleep.

"We'll go to the inn where I'm staying. As soon as I complete my business in San Durg, we'll leave for my manor in Kaanotok Township. I want to speak to Elder Chonaira after he's been to see Lukeniss."

This alarmed her. *Is Lukeniss supposed to have some veto power over this ruling?* She asked fearfully, "Why does the Elder have to see him?"

"Don't worry, dear. You'll never have to see him again. As Scribe, the Elder must notify him of the ruling that provided for your care. I'm curious to know what he'll say."

"I'm not." She had other things on her mind. The image of the smile she'd exchanged with Elder Chonaira teased her and embarrassed her all over again. "Why did the Elder laugh when you changed the Council's ruling?"

Thinking of the scene, he laughed, too. "Donni is as convinced of the injustice of the Law as I am."

"If he doesn't believe in laws, why is he an Elder?"

"Oh, he believes in the need for laws, but not the Law of Tradition. Being an Elder gives him plenty of opportunities to, shall we say, bend the rules a little."

That's what Brelkaar does. He takes advantage of the Law to get what he wants. I don't think manipulating things that way is the answer. Lekton needs a clearly defined set of rules like the Terrans have. Changing the laws completely is the best way.

She said, "It's not so hard to get around the Law. People commit crimes, and no one can punish them. I know of a certain man who cheats people and steals their money, and he does it all legally."

He didn't look at her, but casually glanced around them as if he were worried about being overheard. "Keep it to yourself for now, and we'll talk about it later."

"But I think…"

"And I'll listen to you. Later. We'll discuss Dr. Brelkaar, but not here. All right?"

How did he know? What does he know? Fearing she was in trouble, she braved one more comment. "I wanted to help."

Her uncle's voice sounded stern. "You don't know how much I lost when you wrecked that deal. In the future, talk to me before you try to fix something."

Holy Portals! My uncle is in on it with Brelkaar! I've gone from being the daughter of a tyrant to being the daughter of a criminal. I'd better act willing to be submissive.

She lowered her head, gestured agreement to surrender, at least for the moment. With a family name, she could return to her original goal to be The MenD'lee.

Unless, of course, my new Familyhead also disapproves of COAXIS. She asked, "Do you object to COAXIS?"

He relaxed his shoulders and sighed, obviously glad to change the subject.

"I got my Specialty and Command degrees from the Institute. Why?"

"I only wondered." She sighed with pleasure and her mind churned with plans. She thought, *I might have a thief for a father, but I'll go off world as soon as possible and get free of implication.*

They arrived at a very nice inn, where her uncle asked to change to a two-room suite. Alone in her own chamber, she finally crawled into a soft fur and slept.

Some time later, Melenta rolled over in her sleep. Elements of her surroundings blended with the images of her dream. She felt something very soft under her face. *My grass mattress at the cottage certainly isn't this soft.*

Slowly, more reality intruded, and the dream faded. *Oh, right. It's not the cottage. I'm in the trader's wagon. But that bed definitely isn't soft.*

At last, the incongruity pierced the last veils of sleep. She opened her eyes to see the gentle rays of afternoon out the window. She was in a sleep chamber at the inn, and the softness she enjoyed was the most luxurious fur-bed she'd ever seen. This wasn't just any inn. The San Durg Inn was nice, but this place made it seem no better than the rustic cottage she'd left.

"No, I'm in the Laampeer D'Lair, the Divine Summershade Inn. It's an exclusive lodging for those of high station. Visiting Elders stay here! Do I rate something like this?"

In the next room, she heard a sound. "Uncle Loris must be awake." But she didn't want to leave the solitude of her splendid room. Smiling, she settled back in her fur and thought, *what a remarkable day it's been!*

She reflected on all the coincidences involved in this morning's events. *Jeme'el happened to buy my clothing from Lukeniss, so that J'Mii would be sent to Trader's Field. I just happened to arrive at the*

Town Square when my uncle was there. Then, the Council happened to be available, even though morning session had ended.

She whispered, "All Wise, have I finally noticed your hand at work in my life?"

She heard tapping sounds beyond her chamber door and then heard the door to the suite opening. Someone was here. Careful to stay quiet, she tiptoed across the room, put an ear to the latch and listened.

"How are you?" her uncle said in greeting.

A man's voice replied, "Better now. I talked to Lukeniss."

Melenta realized that it must be the Elder! More than ever, she wanted to hear their conversation.

Loris said softly, "Come to the serving chamber. Melenta is still sleeping."

As the voices faded away, she heard the Elder's final comment. "Poor woman. She must be totally exhausted."

Woman? He called me a woman, not a girl. Isn't that interesting?

She softly touched the latch sensor, hoping a place so fancy had quiet locks. The door whispered open, allowing her to creep outside into the empty sitting chamber.

A separate serving chamber for meals was around the corner, though not visible to her. She moved closer, allowing the wall to hide her.

Around the corner, Loris was saying, "So, we can stop worrying about Lukeniss?"

"I think so. What a problem we'd have with him if he knew what we've done. He's such a strong fighter for Tradition."

Melenta clamped her hand over her mouth, afraid that she'd cry out. The Elder was helping Brelkaar, too!

Loris replied, "Don't think about it. We have to figure out what to tell Melenta. I only hinted that she should stop interfering with the doctor's work until she talks to me. I'll convince her to cooperate, I'm sure."

"I hope so. She could ruin the whole project."

Melenta lifted her chin and clamped her lips into a rigid line. *We'll see about that,* she thought. *This is getting dangerous. Maybe I can sneak out and ask Tellik's mother where Tellik lives. I'll run away and find Kendel.*

She looked at the door to the suite. Could she make it without being seen?

From around the corner, the Elder said, "You'd better wake her, Loris. I can't stay very long."

Uttering a mental curse, she hurried back to her sleep chamber. There wasn't time to close the door, so instead, she yawned loudly and came out of the room as Loris rounded the corner. She made her speech fuzzy and squinted her eyes.

"Jhenbonay. You slept all afternoon. Come to the serving chamber and have a meal. Elder Chonaira is here."

She followed him. The Elder stood to greet her, hands clasped behind his back in a gesture of friendly greeting.

Melenta bowed to him. In his presence, she found it hard not to feel intimidated, despite the fact that he deserved no honor for what he was doing with Brelkaar. In truth, this was a powerful man who had ultimate authority over her life.

The Elder said, "Sit with me, Melenta. Loris will get your meal, and we can talk."

She tried to overcome her trepidation, but his proximity was an overpowering pressure. She felt herself shaking.

Immediately, he changed his manner. "Oh, don't be scared. You aren't in trouble, I promise. Loris and I are very good friends, so you'll be seeing a lot of me. I can't bear to think of you quaking around me all the time. I get tired of being an authority figure, a subject of awe. I appreciate your uncle because he lets me be merely Donni. Understand?"

She absolutely couldn't look up. The protocols of respect for an Elder were firmly drilled into her. She barely knew it when a saucer of fruits and grain rolls appeared before her.

"Here, dear. What would you like to drink? I didn't know if you like jittra or not."

She couldn't decide. Her mind didn't function. *Is the Elder staring at me?*

Loris ignored her discomfort, sparing her embarrassment. He asked, "Donni, would you like something?"

"Jittra would be fine. Thank you."

"Melenta?" he asked again.

She only nodded and then greedily enjoyed the food. No amount of fear would assuage starvation.

Loris set a steaming cup in front of each of them and sat down.

The Elder told her, "I want to ask you something. I really want your truthful feelings on the matter. In exchange, you can ask me something, too. Ask anything you want, and I'll tell you the truth."

She wondered, *does he really mean that? I can ask anything at all?* She looked at her uncle, who smiled and gestured, yes. She wasn't sure what to ask, but said timidly, "I know that your name is Done'el. Why do you let people use your familiar name?"

"That's it?" he laughed in surprise. "I give you permission to ask me anything you want with a guaranteed, truthful answer, and that's what you want to know?"

Melenta felt her muscles release their knots. He had a refreshing laugh. She answered, "I was taught that only a relative could do that."

"All right," he told her as they both sipped at their drinks. "You see, I'm named after my father. Since everyone calls him Done'el, it's less confusing to use something else for my name. I've always been called Donni."

She let her crooked smile and one squinted eye communicate her feelings. It wasn't such a spectacular answer after all.

Laughing, Loris teased, "He told you it was a waste of a good question."

Lowering his voice to a conspiratorial tone, the Elder told her, "I'll let you ask me another question some day."

She thought, *he thinks I'm a ludjit.* She hid her embarrassment by again lifting her cup to her lips.

"Now, it's my turn. Are you ready?"

Setting down her cup, she stared at her lap and replied formally, "Yes, Elder."

"Call me Donni," he said without much emphasis. "Now, this is what I want to know: If you could do away with the Law of Tradition, would you?"

Alarmed, she snapped to attention. Her eyes shot straight to his face. This was a trap, a trick to get her in trouble. *What do I do?*

Steadily, he returned her daring stare, frankly returning this challenge with no sign of offense or judgment. "That's what I said. Would you, Melenta?"

She swallowed. "Would I do away with the Law?" She tried to make her voice reflect incredulity and absolute shock.

But Donni Chonaira (somehow not Elder Chonaira) gazed back at her with lavender eyes that held no contempt. "Your truthful feelings on the matter?"

She knew that she shouldn't betray herself so blatantly, but she also couldn't lie—not to him. Without a blink, she said, "Before you could breathe twice."

A smile slowly swept across his features. She wasn't in trouble. He said, "If I could tell you a way to do that, would you want to hear it?"

Her thoughts exploded into rivulets of possible futures. Every path, every answer to that question took her beyond any dream she'd ever conceived. "Do away with the Law? On a world so traditional and patriarchal as Lekton? It can't be done. Impossible."

"Is it?"

She turned to Loris, who had the same direct, confrontational look in his eyes. There was a touch of hope, as well. She closed her eyes and considered this amazing but improbable idea. *Maybe they aren't crooks. They said do away with the Law and not go around it.*

She opened her eyes, maybe for the first time in her life, and turned back to the Elder. "Tell me!"

He released the breath he'd been holding and grinned at her. "Welcome to the Revolution," said Donni.

Her mouth became suddenly dry. "Revolution?"

"The Quiet Revolution," Loris added. "We secretly repair injustices caused by loopholes in the Law. I think you can appreciate how important the work is, since your disowning was our most recent case."

Melenta was certain there was more to this explanation. She faced the Elder. "Really? But you did that legally."

"Of course." He seemed confused at first, but then abruptly, his features showed insult because she suspected him of wrongdoing. "It's always legal," he declared.

She turned to her uncle. "Why, then, would you help someone like Dr. Brelkaar to swindle helpless old people?"

At that accusation, the two men seemed to re-evaluate the decision to be honest with her. The Elder sent an angry glare at Loris. He'd guaranteed that she would cooperate and Chonaira was not happy.

Loris raised four fingers to Donni in the gesture beknees. He said, "Wait." Turning on her, he asked, "Exactly what do you think I've been doing?"

For these two men trained in law, she'd have to deal in facts. "I saw the ruling that made Dr. Brelkaar trustee for Jareth Jenelonn's money. But the man died before the doctor could charge him for his phony treatments. Maybe you aren't aware of Brelkaar's real intentions. I researched those treatments. Did you know that other doctors think they're worthless? I happen to know that he tried to convince Nolan Jhotolair's family to allow them. When they didn't agree, he got someone else to take custody of Nolan's money. I'm sure he'll approve treatments. It's a scam, Uncle Loris, and you should do something about it."

"You did research?" asked Loris skeptically.

"That's right."

Elder Chonaira asked, "Did you tell anyone about this?"

"I tried," she admitted. "Lektonian Security didn't believe me, but that's because I'm young. If you talked to them…"

"Melenta!" Loris stopped her. "Please listen. We know that you talked to eight families, warning them not to trust Dr. Brelkaar. I need to know how you learned those names. Did someone tell you?"

She studied the men, wondering at the intense looks they gave her. Puzzled, she replied slowly, "Well, no. No one told me. I saw one of Brelkaar's accomplices passing a list."

"The list!" cried both men in relief.

She looked from one to the other. "Someone dropped it."

The Elder laughed. "You picked it up and started to investigate."

"I don't think you understand. What they're doing is illegal." She thought an Elder of Soloto ought to be more concerned about that.

But he spoke to Loris and ignored her. "We don't have a leak after all. I'll pass that message on. Meanwhile, you can make sure your new daughter is trained properly."

Melenta was livid. She wanted to throw the plate of food. Instead, she huffed and looked at her lap.

"I ask pardon, Melenta," said the Elder. "I did hear what you said, and I'm proud of you for wanting to help when you saw a problem. I want you to listen and let your father explain. There's more to this story than you know. Will you let me handle it?"

From the beginning, she'd wondered if she was blundering into a covert investigation. Contritely, she lowered her eyes and uttered, "Yes, Elder."

He gestured his gratitude. "Loris, I think you should consider her for a Messenger position. I have to get to the Council building. I'll talk to you later."

Melenta stood and bowed to him, but it only amused him. With a long-suffering sigh, he repeated, "I really like being Donni sometimes."

Loris escorted him to the door and she watched him leave. Immediately, her uncle turned to her and gave her "the look."

She knew what it meant because Lukeniss used it on her whenever she tried to be assertive. It meant, time to take control. She asked herself, *how much trouble do you want to start? Is it worth it? Can one be disowned twice in one day?*

Firmly, he said, "Now, young woman, we're going to have a talk."

She stared, boldly and replied, "I guess that look is something your father used when you were in trouble. Lukeniss does the same thing, and it doesn't work when he does it, either."

He pressed his lips together and glared. "It is my household you've joined. I'll never be the tyrant my brother is, but I will be in charge of my daughter, adopted or not. I ask pardon if my declaration sounded disrespectful. It wasn't my intention."

He apologized to me, she thought with shock. *Oh my, this is… different.* "I ask pardon for offending. I just… well…"

"I understand, perhaps more than you know. Lukeniss was my older brother, and he tried to control me, too. I've worked diligently to learn skills to negotiate with others without bullying them." He waved toward the serving chamber and her unfinished meal. "Let's start over. While you eat, I have a lot to explain to you."

She smiled, glad to allow civility into their conversation again.

CHAPTER 14

Loris refilled his jittra mug and sat with her, saying, "I'll tell you everything, and truthfully, I promise. I'm the one who helped Dr. Brelkaar become trustee. It's true that some doctors think his treatments are worthless, but did you learn why?"

"Why? Why they're worthless?"

"Why other doctors think they are. Did you study the reports written by doctors who approve?"

"There weren't any positive remarks in the file I read."

Carefully, he asked, "You read only one? Could that have been the one written by a competitor, as opposed to the thirty written by independent researchers who praised the treatments?"

Her meal was suddenly unappealing. He was right.

Loris continued, "I'll pull the information on computer for you to read. You shouldn't take my word for it, either. You'll find that Dr. Brelkaar's treatment for end-stage dementia has been criticized because it doesn't cure the condition. What it does, though, is beneficial in another way. It restores the patient's mind to clarity for a short time, just before death. That blessing of dignity in death is important. So is the final chance to speak to family and friends. It also allows one to give instructions about how to settle financial affairs."

Ashamed, she thought, *how could I have jumped to so many assumptions? I rushed through the investigation, seeing what I wanted and ignoring the rest.*

She wished for a way to redeem herself, and then something occurred to her. She asked, "But Uncle Loris, even if the intent was noble, Brelkaar still didn't have the right to steal from these people. He did this to make profit because he has financial problems."

Loris smiled patiently. "Oh, I didn't know that. You saw his financial records for his business? You sneaked a look at his household budget?"

She couldn't say that she'd talked to a disgruntled servant whom she should have known would say nothing nice.

He told her, "Let me tell you what my investigation uncovered. The ten names on that list are people who are incompetent due to their illness. They have adult sons or daughters who have assumed responsibility for them, yet they've received little to no care for dementia. These children have control of their parents' money and can afford to see a doctor. They spend the money on themselves."

Melenta was horrified. "Are you saying that these people are withholding treatment to keep their parents incompetent? You're sure?"

"Donni is sure. He has the authority to find out things I can't. Dr. Brelkaar came to me, a Solotan Representative, to get help for those elderly people. I contacted Donni. This is what we do in the Quiet Revolution. We watch for opportunities to bend the Law of Tradition so that justice prevails. We call ourselves Lawbenders."

"You and Elder Chonaira?" She suspected something larger in scope was in play.

"There are Lawbenders throughout every Nation, Melenta. We're organized and networked through a blind chain. Each Lawbender knows only the person up-chain (the one who recruited him or her,) the person he recruits (who is down-chain) and a Leader in their Region. It's safer that way."

The Elder's caution made sense. This sounded dangerous. "Why haven't I heard of this?"

He simply blinked. "Quiet Revolution, remember?"

"But if there are so many, why don't you make it known? Elder Chonaira could ask the Councils to consider reforming the Law."

He nodded wisely. "One day, when there is enough support, that's probably what the Leaders at top-chain will do. At least, that's what Donni thinks."

That would take a long time. Melenta couldn't stand the thought of waiting when something should be done now. "How long has it been going on?" She asked.

"I don't know. Donni recruited me toward the end of 2147."

"I was three seasons then!"

He laughed. "Donni was only sixteen. He was in law school, and I hired him to work a few cycles in my legal office. After he taught me about the Lawbenders, I became a Leader. That means a lot of messages go through me to Donni. Each Region has a Leader who can contact me directly when an urgent need is discovered."

"So you're different. You know a lot more Lawbenders."

He shook his head. "Not a lot, only the few other Leaders who make contact. And Donni, of course."

She thought of something the Elder had said earlier. "What did the Elder mean about making me a messenger?"

He hesitated, and she thought he seemed afraid to answer. Then, he seemed to make a decision. "It was a recommendation. I guess you could say he meant it to be his approval on it, but I'm leaving it up to you. It's impractical if you're planning to go to the COAXIS Institute."

A longing, deep in her heart, pulled at her soul. For seven seasons, that had been her greatest desire. To fulfill that dream would honor the sacrifice Kendel had made. She did want that. She asked carefully, "You'll let me do that?"

His smile was tender. "Let you? I'd be happy to help you do whatever you want to do."

Hopefully, she said, "I can't afford it."

"I can. That isn't a problem. I only want you to have options for your life. Whether it's the Institute, working for the Lawbenders or betrothal, it's your choice."

"It won't be betrothal. I'll never marry. Never!" She knew her tone was too sharp.

"School, then. That's fine."

Up to now, choices had been only shams, illusions that Lukeniss manipulated until everything went his way. Because of what she'd learned today, her goals changed. The reason to get a COAXIS degree had been to someday reform the Law. But others had already begun that goal. Being a Lawbender could be the best way to accomplish her dreams.

She asked, "What do Messengers do?"

"They pass messages. Leaders get hundreds of them each season. What I receive, I pass on to Donni. As a Messenger, I'd have you take my messages to him. For your protection and that of our cause, you must know only me and my direct contacts on the chain."

She sat straight in her chair. *If he trusts me with important jobs, I'll accomplish more than I ever would alone.*

She told him, "I'd like that."

Her uncle extended his hand to grasp hers. It might have been a simple gesture of appreciation or maybe one of affection. Whatever the motive, it sent her into a desperate panic. She twisted away from him before he'd ever touched her.

That startled him. "I ask pardon, dear. I mean no harm."

Why did I do that? She tried to analyze it, but she discerned only dread. Embarrassed, she told him, "I didn't mean to ... I don't like to be touched, that's all."

Loris smiled gently. "I'll remember next time. You've been through such trauma lately, so you're bound to be nervous. I'm glad you're with me now, Melenta. If you're ready, I'll take you to your new home in Kaanotok. We're going to accomplish so much for Lekton!"

And she believed him.

Kaanotok Township, 23 Breel, 2159

After two moons, Melenta had learned enough about the Lawbenders to feel confident of her future. Her uncle's knowledge amazed her. He could sway conversations to preferred topics. He could influence people to accept as truth nearly anything he said. When she really thought about it, the power that the Lawbenders exerted on the public was frightening. The right information in these hands was inspiring, but a trained Lawbender with false motivation could harm the world, too. Power, he'd told her, can have two outlets, and integrity decides its direction.

Gratefully, though, she'd never have to worry about wielding power. She'd be happy to run messages and leave the leadership to those trained in law.

And so, faithfully, Melenta memorized codes and keywords to be hidden in messages so that it sounded conversational. For example, when approaching someone to deliver a message, the word "news" was to be used in the sentence along with the name of a township. And if she suspected that someone she spoke to might be a Lawbender, she was to use the name "Oberonn" in the conversation. It could be used as a street name, a person, a town, or anything else. Any Lawbender would verify identity by agreeing that he or she had a relative by that name. The name itself was quite rare.

Late that day, she'd rehearsed the codes and keywords while she jogged through the rows of trees in her uncle's orchard, for running was now a firmly established routine in her day. As Half-light wore on, she stood in the kitchen, preparing a special meal for them. She gathered fresh vegetables from the garden and started a stew.

Sighing with satisfaction, Loris entered the kitchen. "That smells wonderful. I hope it isn't ready now."

She cocked her head and turned to him. "You hope it isn't?"

"We have a visitor. Of course, we could invite him to Late-meal, if you have plenty."

Melenta knew she did, but saying so might depend on who was visiting.

Sensing her inner debate, he told her, "Donni's shuttle is landing at my shuttle pad."

Her heart began to thud in her ears. *Oh, krek! Did the Council reconsider my adoption? Had the Rozairs demanded restitution? Or the farmers in the mountains whom I robbed? I wouldn't put it past Lukeniss… or Bolaith… to find a way to undo everything.*

Then, another thought took over. She'd been running and cooking. Elder Chonaira mustn't find her messy and disheveled, as if her new father wasn't taking proper care of her. Lowering the heat to allow the stew to stay warm, she raced to a reflection glass to inspect her appearance.

Loris chuckled at her primping. "You really should stop acting as if he's The All Wise, Melenta. He doesn't like it."

But she ignored him and went to the manor's entry hall to greet him, as the lady of a manor would do. *I'll show him I belong here,* she thought.

She opened the door, and at his approach, she bowed reverently.

He called, "Fairday. I have something to tell you both. Am I interrupting your meal?"

Over her shoulder, Loris called, "Not at all, Donni. Please come in."

Donni smiled warmly at her and teased, "Loris, would you tell her she doesn't have to bow to me here?"

"I've tried, believe me."

Blushing, she tried to look at his face, but couldn't quite handle it.

"If you don't mind," Donni continued to Loris, "I need to discuss something privately with Melenta first."

She tensed, sure that this meant something had gone wrong.

Her uncle, guessing her thoughts, rested a hand on her shoulder, squeezing the tense muscle and whispering to her, "It's all right." He responded to Donni, "Would you like to go to the garden? I'll watch the stew."

"With your permission," said Donni to Loris. "I thought I'd ask her to walk with me along the lane."

Melenta felt terror would be lurking along that lane. What did he want to say that he couldn't say with Loris listening? *Surely,* she thought, *Uncle Loris would want to hear what he said if this was some legal problem.*

But her uncle didn't object, although maybe he wouldn't refuse an Elder's request. It really told her nothing about his feelings one way or the other.

He said only, "I think my daughter is certainly safe with you."

Donni motioned for her to follow him as he walked back to the gate of the estate. Trying not to tremble, she followed him.

They walked away from the manor along the paved lane. She wondered, *is Uncle Loris watching us? Lukeniss would.* She quickly reconsidered that. *No, he never would have let me leave in the company of a man at all, not even an Elder. Uncle Loris must truly trust his friend.*

That was somewhat reassuring. Once again, the difference between Lukeniss and her uncle was astounding.

To keep from prolonging this walk, she asked, "What did you want to tell me, Elder?"

He gave an exaggerated sigh. "First of all, no one will care if you call me Donni."

She didn't respond.

He stopped. "Come on, say it. Say Donni."

She stopped, too. Tilting her head up, looking skyward, anywhere but at him, she muttered, "The clouds in the east are my favorite color right now."

He sighed again, but she heard mirth in it. "Fine. If you want me to be an Elder to tell you this, I will. But remember that it was your idea. We can change that whenever you want—just call me Donni."

She turned to him in fright. Whatever he came to say, it apparently wasn't pleasant. "Am I in trouble again?"

"Let's walk." And he did. When Melenta caught up to him, he began to explain. "I made sure that the Rozair family wasn't harmed for helping you by issuing a statement of the Council's gratitude for finding you and bringing you to us."

Relief flooded her. They could have been shunned for giving her aid. Tears came unbidden as she gestured her sincere thanks.

Softly, he replied, "I thought you'd want to know. And Loreeth asked me to give this to you." Pulling an envelope from a pocket of his tunic, he handed it to her.

She was shaking as she took the letter out of the envelope and read it.

"Greetings, Mel. One of the traders is helping me write this. Jeme'el and I are glad to hear you're safe with your uncle. I talked to Brutha for you about your betrothal mate. She said Kendel was living in Vennua Township with her son. But he met someone who was willing to give him private employment as a mentor, so he left without saying where he was going. I'm very sorry to have no better information. The All Wise bless you, Loreeth."

As these words imprinted in her heart, she couldn't hold back her tears. Kendel was gone forever. Gulping in a breath between sobs, she suddenly realized that the Elder might know the contents of the letter. Gathering courage, she asked, "Do you know what it says?"

"The letter is addressed to you, Melenta. I didn't read it," he assured her. "But to be honest, when Loreeth handed it to me, she told me it was about your betrothal mate. She said she'd asked about him, but he'd already left town."

This was why he'd said she didn't want him to speak to her as her Elder, for Elders were responsible to correct a citizen's morals. *What must he be thinking? Is he wondering if the accusations against Kendel had been true, and we'd secretly been betrothed?*

She decided to convince him that Loreeth had misunderstood her. She could always claim that she made it up as a cover story for why she avoided San Durg. That was actually true.

Squarely, the Elder faced her and made it clear that he wouldn't allow her to run from an explanation.

Moistening her lips and taking a deep breath to get control of her emotions, she said, "I lied to the Rozairs about why I'd left San Durg. I told them that I was looking for my betrothal mate because his father had separated us. I used it as an excuse for why I couldn't be seen in San Durg. I said his father lived there. I guess Loreeth decided to look for him to help me."

He wasn't angry. "I thought as much. I have no problem with the lie."

She looked up. "Really?"

"I understand that you couldn't tell the truth. You were taking care of yourself, as anyone in that situation would do."

Again, she dropped her head. "Thank you."

"But..." he began.

She squeezed her eyes shut, forcing the last of her tears down her face. "But?"

"Either your Elder or your new friend needs to know why Loreeth referred to an actual person. She must have known a name. One of us needs to know who that is—it's your choice."

She knew what he meant. "I'd rather answer Donni."

"Good!" he said, brightening. "He'd rather hear it. Friends can keep secrets that Elders can't."

She saw his point. "I was talking about Kendel Brekket."

He jumped. "Oh! That worries me."

"He never did what Lukeniss said, I promise. Kendel was never more than a mentor around me." She looked into his eyes.

Donni tapped his hand over his heart in gratitude. "I believe you. But he did teach a forbidden curriculum to you, right?"

She nodded. "We'd talked about having him contend at my Gift Rite." She thought about how that sounded, quickly amending it. "But that was only so I'd be able to attend the COAXIS Institute." Studying him, he didn't seem to believe that.

Awkwardly, he glanced away, embarrassed. "I hope you don't run away again, Melenta. You may not realize it, but Loris loves you. It would crush him if you go looking for Kendel."

"It doesn't matter," she replied, waving the letter. "Loreeth said Kendel left, and no one knows where he went. I don't think I'll see him again."

"I'm sorry that hurts you, but associating with someone who is banished would compromise your work with the Lawbenders. I'd hate to see that happen."

She shrugged, conceding the point.

"And I have to say that I'm glad you're not betrothed." He smiled.

She wasn't sure, but she thought she saw Donni blush. Timidly, she smiled back.

Loris was terribly curious. Donni never told him what he'd discussed with his daughter. When they returned to the manor, Donni joined him in the garden while Melenta brought out a pitcher of fruit juice and three glasses. She served the stew, and they all enjoyed the meal in companionship.

Once their meal was finished, Donni told him, "I got an interesting message this morning. Lekton's COAXIS Ambassador will be submitting his resignation at the end of this mooncycle."

Loris shrugged. "At his age, I guess that's expected."

Donni grinned at him. "That message came down-chain to me. Loris, the Lawbenders at top-chain want you to replace him as Ambassador."

Melenta cried, "Uncle Loris, you'd be a wonderful Ambassador!"

Donni agreed. "Your COAXIS degree in Diplomatic Services qualifies you."

"It's only my Specialty degree."

"But your Command degree in law makes it stronger. Top-chain thinks you'd be in an ideal position as Ambassador to propose reform."

Loris rose and paced the garden. "I'm not so sure about that. The COAXIS charter restricts an Ambassador from any action that influences the government."

"Well," Donni commented slyly, "directly, anyway. Think of what you could do behind the scenes."

Melenta was delighted. "Does that mean we would get to move to the Embassy in Lukree?"

He bristled, feeling control of his life being ripped from him. "I wouldn't want to move. I'm accomplishing my leadership of the Lawbenders by staying in Kaanotok where other Leaders can reach me. Moving to Lukree would ruin that."

Donni suggested, "Could you arrange to divide your time between the two places, Loris? At the very least, we can see that a Lawbender Leader is placed in your position as Representative."

Stomping a foot, Loris tried one last argument. "But my orchards!"

Melenta countered that one. "You told me last night that the couple who helps you with the orchards and the manor have lost their lease. You could let Brees and Netta Benjonn live here as caretakers, and we could move to Lukree."

Donni added, "And you could hire Melenta as a Diplomatic Aide."

Seeing her excitement at that prospect, Loris relented. "Very well. I guess we're going to Lukree."

"Yes!" cheered Melenta. She turned to Donni, congratulating him on their teamwork.

Donni instinctively extended his arm and grasped hers, offering a Comrade's Grip. She returned his grasp without the slightest self-conscious fear of his touch. The Comrade's Grip was exchanged between equals. *What happened on that walk*, he wondered?

Loris stared at them, and a smile drifted slowly to his lips. He knew something they didn't know. They were growing close, becoming friends.

CHAPTER 15

Kaanotok Township, 30 Lairees, 2160 (September 1 TSE)

"Time can be wasted, time can be spent and time can be lost. No doubt about it, English is a strange language."

On this quiet, Half-light morning, Melenta sat alone in the garden. It had become her favorite place in the twelve mooncycles since she'd lived here. She understood, now, why her father hadn't wanted to leave Kaanotok. True to his word, he'd found a way to be Lekton's COAXIS Ambassador and yet live at home.

Sitting beneath the spreading kalpus tree, a compusketch in her lap, she thumbed the page selector switch and continued reciting aloud from the English lesson. "Time can be killed..." She stared at the page. *Is that what it says? Time means something different to Terrans,* she reminded herself.

On Lekton, Time is a deity, a supernatural entity who governs the implementation of events planned by his sister, Destiny. And as Melenta well knew, their father, The All Wise, didn't realize how often Time upset those plans.

"Time is no friend of mine," she grumbled. "Time can be killed." With wicked enthusiasm, she remarked, "Oh, really?"

"Melenta!"

Startled by her father's stunned exclamation, she looked up. He stood before her, and by his frown, she knew he'd heard her uncharitable comments. Raising her head, she called contritely into the air, "I ask pardon, All Wise." For good measure, she gestured gaaro.

But her apology didn't satisfy her father, who scolded, "What if The All Wise noticed what you said about his son?"

She returned a weak smile. "He knows what a ludjit I am. Besides, Time gets in the way of every krekking thing I try to do. Does The All Wise notice that?"

"Your foul mood doesn't excuse immoral language, Melenta. Cease that. How does Time get in your way?"

She covered her avoidance by readjusting the tie that gathered her long, honey-blond hair at her neck. She thought, *how can I explain to anyone else that I know I'm supposed to become The MenD'lee and Time won't let me?*

To her, the facts proved it. A multiplicity of coincidences after her disowning arranged her adoption and restoration of a family name. Since then, plentiful opportunities to help Lekton had fallen into her hands, both as a Lawbender and as a Diplomatic Aide for her father. All these opportunities set her up to be The MenD'lee.

But as surely as she knew it was true, she knew that Time was sabotaging her chances for success.

No, her father was asking how Time got in her way, but he'd never believe the truth. Instead, she replied, "I've been a Lawbender for over a season, as well as your Aide. But Time didn't put me in those positions as a grown, educated person of status, someone others would take seriously. I'm useless!"

He gave her that paternal smile that she so hated, the one that was supposed to entreat her to patience but achieved the opposite. "How are you useless when you work so hard?"

"Never mind," she said and then changed the subject. "I found this text plate about Terran English in your office. Did you learn English, Father?"

"No, since COAXIS Standard was more helpful. Now, you answer my question."

She set aside the sketcher and crossed the garden to sit beside him at the low table. "Nothing I do impacts the Law. Time is against me, I tell you!"

"What about those messages that you deliver to Donni? Each one provides an opportunity to bend an unjust decision made under the Law. Maybe it's true that the words of an Elder or an Ambassador carry more influence, but you help us achieve it. And if you didn't help by drafting all my status reports for the Embassy, I'd get nothing done for the Lawbenders. Doesn't that help Lekton?"

She wanted to argue, but that wouldn't be respectful. *He deserves no less for all he does for me. He certainly loves me. I wish I felt more comfortable with returning his affection.*

Calming herself, she told him, "I pass messages from you to Donni so that Donni can make a difference. I fill out COAXIS forms about what you do for Lekton."

"You also arrange my schedules, remind me when to file those reports, manage my finances, and plan my travel itineraries. Because you do all those things, I have the freedom to travel throughout the Regions to advertise the Embassy's services. I'd say you make a very important contribution. Even the Embassy's Chief Aide doesn't help me as much as you do."

She didn't say it, but that was probably because Bronn, the Chief Aide was too busy handling business the Ambassador should handle. Previous Ambassadors always lived at the Embassy and reported there for work every day.

But not her father. He lived at home and only went to the Embassy once every tenday. Granted, the trip from Kaanotok to

Lukree in northern Soloto Valley Region took two cycles, but all the more reason he ought to be living there.

At her silence, Loris sighed. "Sometimes, you accompany me and speak to people, too. Remember the Sumuruan farmer who had obsolete farming equipment? You helped him apply for upgrades that saved his crop."

She shrugged.

"And what about that family in Selii who struggled to recover after storms destroyed their home? It was you who found them. Word is spreading that COAXIS can help in cases where local government or Elderships have no resources. You're part of that effort."

She gave an unconvincing smile. Maybe traveling was a valuable use of an Ambassador's time, but for her, it was ineffective in accomplishing broad, sweeping change in the Law.

Loris lifted a suspicious eyebrow, knowing her thoughts. He said firmly, "Rapid change doesn't last, so we have to be patient. And before you say it, moving to Lukree wouldn't improve your opportunities to contribute. Traveling as I do allows me to be a Lawbender Leader, and I get more done that way."

It was a tired argument that she expected to lose. Disappointed nonetheless, she realized that he couldn't understand her driving mission to change Lekton, one assigned by Destiny. It was up to her to find specific, direct ways to combat Tradition.

To begin with, thought Melenta, *I could pay more attention to my surroundings and watch for coincidences. That will tell me what The All Wise wants me to do. After all, if he wants enlightenment, and wants me to inspire it, he should show me a way to do it. Maybe he's been trying to do that, but I'm not paying attention.*

A plan developed in her mind, but to throw off her father's suspicions, she laughed at herself. "You're right, I guess. Patience isn't easy for me."

His concern evaporated. "Yes, I've noticed. I'm going to the Embassy today, and I'd like you to deliver some messages to Donni in San Durg. Do you have my travel itinerary for next mooncycle?"

"It's on your desk. Don't forget it this time or the Chief Aide will be angry."

Teasing back, Loris assumed a superior pose and replied stiffly, "Bronn works for me, not the other way around. We'll take the flyer, and I can stop in San Durg to drop you off."

She grinned. "Or you could take the shuttle, and I could take the flyer." She never passed up a chance to pilot his new, fashionable two-seater.

Playfully, he rolled his eyes and complained, "But my trip would take longer in the shuttle."

Cunningly, she pointed out that if they both rode in the flyer, he'd still lose time in dropping her in San Durg. Then, he'd wait for clearance to take off again, probably causing the same amount of delay.

He gave in. "Fine, but mind the lane laws."

"Yes, sir!"

When her father reached out to affectionately pat her back, she evaded his touch. As always, affection made her uncomfortable, and that pricked his heart. She used to wonder why it bothered her so badly. Now, she'd forgotten the reason for that unknown dread that seemed to overwhelm her.

Love, she thought, *simply isn't in me. If I'm meant to be alone, that's fine with me.*

In San Durg

Since her disowning, San Durg had lost any appeal to Melenta, especially after Lukeniss prohibited her from seeing her younger brother. She hadn't been allowed to say goodbye or explain why she couldn't see him. That had dissolved her feelings for the township of her birth.

She wasn't sure if Cheelo wanted to see her. Most likely, he wasn't told that his father had lied to create a legal reason to disown her. Whatever he believed, though, she wouldn't have been able to see him once she was disowned.

And then, miraculously, her name was restored. Donni made sure her rights were enforced, ruling that she could visit Cheelo once a season on his naming day. But last season, Lukeniss planned a trip out of town and kept them apart. As long as she didn't violate the Council's restriction, she might get her chance next season.

So whenever she was in San Durg to give Donni his messages, Melenta protected her rights. She carefully avoided her old manor or Cheelo's school. She also stayed clear of Ronjer Investment Firm, the company Lukeniss owned. Donni had warned her that Cheelo played on the computers there after school each day.

With all these restrictions firmly in mind, she watched the skyline of San Durg appear a cycle later. Since this smaller craft didn't have to use the Skyport, she flew to a public landing pad near the Town Square. The gentle hum of the engines cut back automatically as the flyer made its descent and touched down. The craft shut down and the translucent hatch above her head slid into the rear hull.

Smiling, Melenta inhaled the familiar, sweet fragrance of a fresh breeze. Unlocking her gravbelt, she retrieved her daypack and slipped it onto her back. Energetically, she leaped to the paved landing pad, ready for an adventure.

An attendant approached her with a data pad in his hand. He checked in the flyer and logged her plans to leave San Durg at 2500, which would let her get home as Half-light was beginning. That way, her father wouldn't worry about her.

Although she was supposed to go to the Council building to talk to Donni, it was too early. Right now, the Elders would be in morning session. So, remembering her decision to spend more time in public to watch for directions from The All Wise, Melenta took a stroll.

As a child, she enjoyed walking through the business district. She still had fond memories of the market booth that her mother's parents owned then. Long ago, the business had closed when her grandparents died, but being here made her feel close to them even still.

She hadn't gone far when she saw a delightful sight. Along the doorframe of an interior decorator's shop, she saw her mother's craftwork hanging. It was a long strand of braided, twine flowers painted in pastels and laced with bright beads. As always, she enjoyed an exhilarating sense of her mother's legacy being preserved. Melenta still remembered how to work the famous Kaantina'a weave of complicated knots.

At the end of that long strip of businesses called the Market Place, another familiar shop owned by friends tugged at her heart. Ordinarily, she stopped there to visit Brutha Kaamzen and ask if Tellik had ever heard from Kendel again. She asked, even though the answer was depressing each time.

Today, though, her heart couldn't bear the disappointment. Of all men she'd ever met, only Kendel Brekket might have made marriage an option. And although she missed him, she couldn't fulfill her mission for The All Wise if she were with him. No one had redeemed his name as Loris had done for her. To be The MenD'lee, she must protect her reputation and let him go.

So turning around, she entered a side lane that took her into a new section of San Durg. Ahead, she saw a school that she'd never seen before. She panicked, wondering, *what if, by chance, Cheelo has transferred to it?*

But before she could turn to leave, something caught her eye. A man rushed out of the school, roughly pulling a young boy of seven or eight by one arm. *He looks terrified,* she thought. *Probably anticipating punishment for misbehaving at school.*

To her, though, the man's attitude was far too aggressive for such a young child. Unless it wasn't his child. But the school wouldn't release a child to anyone other than his parent. Even if this was a parent treating the boy so cruelly, a problem still existed. In that instant, Melenta recognized the coincidence of her presence to witness a Familyhead's abuse of power.

While she considered what to do, she recognized the possible danger she faced. "Father was right," she whispered to herself. "If I interfere directly, I could get hurt. Even if I call for help, it would call attention to me, and that could jeopardize the Lawbenders."

Suddenly, she heard the boy yelp in pain. She had to take action. Daringly, she charged the man, shouting, "Sir, may I speak to you?"

The man only glanced at her before moving on and telling his son to follow.

Melenta refused to be ignored. She ran ahead and stepped between them, blocking the child's path. While the father continued walking, she spared a moment to look down into the boy's large, frightened eyes and asked, "Do you know this man?"

Trembling, the boy gestured that he did.

The man's footsteps stopped, and she faced him. His eyes hot with anger, he growled, "Of course he does. I'm his father."

Behind Melenta, the boy peeked around her but stayed shielded by her body.

Instinctively, she looked at the father's chest and saw that his credoglyph was Diligence. This told her that he was someone who wouldn't back down from what he believed was his duty.

Calmly, she stated, "He looked frightened, so I wanted to be sure."

As she had done, the man glanced at her credoglyph and learned that Justice would rule her behavior. Understanding her purpose, now, he explained. "My son has misbehaved, and I'm taking him home as discipline." Believing he'd offered a just reason for his actions, he went around her, grabbed his son's arm and pulled him once again down the road.

She wanted desperately to stop him. *But how? Should I call Lektonian Security, even though it might take a long time for someone to respond?* Automatically, she followed them, drawn to the compelling terror on the boy's face.

But then, the child twisted back to look at her, and his expression jolted her senses. Rather than begging her to rescue him, he gestured kos with his free hand, telling her no. He mouthed, "Go away."

Melenta froze in place. Didn't he know she wanted to help him? As she watched, the boy followed his father obediently, and the rough treatment ended.

Despite her good intentions, Melenta felt ashamed for not doing more to protect him. Why hadn't the school's Headmaster or his mentor intervened?

Shaking and worried, she walked back to the school and entered. She saw an office near the door that would be the best place to start an inquiry. But nearing the door, she heard a woman's voice. "Headmaster, this is the fourth time he's called Deevin out of class for this foolishness."

Melenta flattened against the wall outside the door and listened.

A man's voice replied, "His father says Deevin uses school as an excuse to shirk his chores at their farm, leaving the work to his pregnant mother. His father is teaching him to be responsible."

"But Deevin is seven seasons, Headmaster! He shouldn't have to do that kind of labor under any circumstances. His father could hire help or accept a few field workers who are working off legal sentences."

With a mental nod of appreciation for the mentor's outrage, Melenta agreed.

But the Headmaster believed otherwise. He raised his voice and insisted, "It's not our business to tell him how to head his family."

"Even when this child is absent four times?"

"You know that he's allowed to be absent four times before I can talk to the Solotan Representative about truancy. I realize that he's taking advantage of the Law, but you can be sure Jai Renzdaal won't give me a reason to charge him. Right now, there's nothing I can do."

Melenta thought, *maybe the Headmaster can't do anything legally, but I can unofficially report this to Donni. Finally, I have something important to contribute to the Quiet Revolution.*

The Attendant at the Council building knew Melenta was a courier, so he didn't question her errand. She crossed from the entry to the hallway containing private offices and turned into the second office on the left.

Elder Chonaira's assistant, a soft-spoken woman of sixty named Noree, greeted her warmly from an outer office. "Melenta, it's nice to see you."

She offered a customary bow to gesture respect for her position. "Fairday. I have papers Father wanted me to deliver personally."

"The Elder is in session, but you're welcome to wait." Noree smiled and indicated a bench against one wall.

While time passed, Melenta planned what she'd tell Donni. The more she remembered the bullying she'd witnessed, the more she regretted that she hadn't known how to fight. Mentally, she fantasized being the bully who dragged Jai Renzdaal through the streets while Deevin watched.

Fortunately, session ended earlier than usual. Dressed in his formal bronze robe and official vestments, Donni soon entered the office in a hurry. Without noticing Melenta, he handed Noree the transcription plate from his morning session, saying, "Please check over my session notes. I may have missed a few designations of protocol. I have a horrible headache."

Noree bowed her head. "I'm glad to help. Can I get something for you? I have medication in my desk."

He shut his eyes and pinched the bridge of his nose. "Thank you, but I think it's because I haven't eaten today. I skipped First-meal." He opened his eyes and at last looked in Melenta's direction.

She stood and formally bowed. "Fairday, Elder Chonaira."

He smiled, and his aching head seemed to be forgotten. "Melenta? Oh, that's right. Loris told me you'd be bringing some papers to sign. Please, come in." He indicated his inner office behind Noree's desk. Entering after Melenta, he quietly closed the door.

By unspoken agreement over the last season, both dropped their formality once they were alone. She said, "If you don't feel well, I won't stay long."

His lavender eyes softened. "No, please stay."

She pulled the daypack from her back, took out a data disk and handed it to Donni. Although the forms included on the disk each time were merely props to provide a cover for her visits, they were true, legal documents. Donni always affixed a digital signature to them, and Melenta always returned them to her father. Should anyone ever suspect deceit and demand to see them, they were legitimate forms that requested an Elder's signature of witness. It was irrelevant that they were always newly dated copies of the same set of documents.

She sat down on the visitor's soft bench to wait.

Ordinarily, he sat behind his desk and pretended to read the phony forms. But today, he sat beside her. Comfortable with her company, he settled back and asked in a low voice, "What's your news?" He was asking for her Lawbender messages.

Remembering his headache, she asked, "Are you sure you wouldn't rather I came back later after you've had a meal?"

"I have a better idea. Why don't we share a meal while we talk?"

Her reaction surprised her. She and her father had shared meals with him often, both at her home and his. But this invitation unnerved her, and it had been a long time since she'd felt so awkward with Donni.

He laughed. "Stop it. It's only a meal."

"But doesn't it attract attention?"

Donni gave a long-suffering groan. "Elders eat, you know."

"Not with me!" she protested. "At least not in public."

He smiled tolerantly and muttered into the air, "When will this young woman relax and stop worrying so much about my attention?" Then, he stood and opened his door to call, "Noree, would you please ask Greeva's Dining Hall to deliver two meals? See if they have more of the fresh pairkin and praat. If not, any seafood will do. Thank you."

Shutting the door, he returned to sit beside Melenta again. "Now, I'm ready for those messages."

She stared at him, horrified. *He told Noree we'd be dining alone together!*

"What's wrong?" he asked innocently.

But he knew. She tested her words internally before saying, "What will Noree think about this, and who will she tell?"

"Nothing and no one. She knows we're friends. We're having Midday-meal in my office, not sneaking off to the inn. No one, especially Noree, would accuse an Elder of misconduct inside the Council building, much less with his assistant in the next chamber. Would you relax, please?"

Reluctantly, she did. "I'll have to trust you on that."

"Good! About time you trusted me. Messages?"

Closing her eyes to concentrate, she repeated two messages she'd memorized. The Lawbenders had great success with oral transmission of messages. It was a matter of great pride for those who delivered them to be precise.

Listening, he took notes on the first message to work on later. The second one was easily addressed with a telecomm call. Although the heart of the issue wasn't his jurisdiction, he was able to get word to a Representative in that Nation.

As he finished his call, Noree knocked at the door. Their food had arrived. Opening the door, he took the tray of food. "Thank you, Noree. Enjoy First-rest." Quietly, he closed the door. But then, he saw that Melenta was staring. He asked her, "Would you feel better if I leave my door open?"

That's precisely what she wanted, but she answered, "I have one more report, so maybe you'd better leave it closed."

"One more? I thought Loris said there were two."

As they ate, she described what she'd seen that morning. She reported Jai Renzdaal and made a point to stress that the child was afraid.

Donni was as angry about Deevin's mistreatment as she was. He promised to call the man before Elder Rameeth, the Council's Advocate, who'd make him answer for it. "The Headmaster may have no cause to report him, but I know our Advocate. Marlonn Rameeth hates child abuse. He'll demand to know why a child so young is asked to do farm labor, and he'll charge him if necessary."

Hope lifted her heart. "So then, it was all right that I told you?"

He gestured gratitude and then tenderly added, "You can tell me anything."

Feeling a stab of conscience, she lowered her head and whispered, "I wanted to hurt that man today, Donni."

He reached out and caught her hand in his before she could snatch it away. But his deflector didn't fall. It was a supportive gesture. He said firmly, "If you'd done that, Renzdaal would be bringing you before the Council on charges. You did exactly the right thing, Melenta." With a last squeeze, he dropped her hand.

But that simple touch had frightened her so much that his words of praise were lost. Her mind blared unconscious alarms to warn her that touching Donni made her powerless. She recognized her reaction but not why she'd feel that way.

Donni watched her lavender gaze dissolve into terror. His simple gesture of affection was apparently misunderstood. He thought, *but how could it be? I'm sure that over the last season, I've convinced her I wouldn't hurt her.*

Then, a sentimental memory came to him. From the moment she'd been brought to Council, dirty, frightened and disowned, she'd captured his heart. She'd seemed so small beside Loris, so vulnerable. Without knowing it, he'd smiled at Melenta, and her answering smile had sent electric currents through him.

Now, he watched her shrink away from him and thought, *something truly horrible must have happened to her in the past. What else would make her so afraid to be loved? I believed her when she said Kendel never touched her. Who else could it be? Since she confessed her desire to hurt Renzdaal, maybe she'll tell me her fears one day, too.*

CHAPTER 16

Kaanotok Township, 16 Zelonn, 2163

Loris returned home after a trip to the Valley of Sevenn and decided to unpack later. First, he poured two cups of hot jittra and started looking for Melenta. After working for him four seasons, he knew where to find her.

He went to his office, a converted sleep chamber that held two desks and a telecomm station. As he'd expected, she was working at a desk that was cluttered with machines that wrote, read and filed data disks. He laughed. "Melenta, after all these seasons, I should have known you'd have your nose buried in work."

Melenta looked up. "It keeps me amused. Welcome home, Father." She held a stack of travel receipts to post, but laid them aside when she saw the cups in his hands. Gesturing alay, she took one of the cups. "Besides, if I stopped to rest very often, you'd hire someone else to be your aide."

"No, dear one, I'm very happy with your work. I need to consult my schedule for today."

"Certainly." Melenta called up the scheduler on her computer.

"I called the Council office at San Durg to ask for Donni. His assistant said he'd flown to Kaanotok for a Late-meal conference. Did I forget an appointment?"

Puzzled, she skimmed urgently through entries. "There's nothing here, Father."

"Really? I checked my favorite dining hall for reservations. There's a table reserved for Chonaira and Cha'atre. You're sure I'm not supposed to meet him?"

"I'm sure. Donni must have forgotten to invite you but thought he did."

With a conniving gleam in his eyes, he whispered, "Or, perhaps he's meeting the other Cha'atre for Late-meal?"

"Don't be ridiculous. An Elder of Soloto has a reason to see the COAXIS Ambassador. Maybe he's coming to discuss Lawbender business."

Pulling his desk chair, he sat near hers and said, "There's more to life than business, dear. You're much closer to his age and much nicer to look at than I am. See if I'm not right. Donni will call you. If you do see him, I have a message for you to send up-chain. Yesterday, a Lawbender in Vela Nua'a had to resign from the Cityhead post. There was too much controversy over his appointment. Donni may want to draw attention away from him until the situation is resolved."

She seemed to suspect something else was on his mind. Uncertainly, she replied, "I suppose I'll see him, then. Was there something else?"

Actually, he'd been waiting for the right opportunity to discuss something. "I'm wondering about your education plans. Are you still going to apply to the Woodlake Kaamestaat?"

Suddenly, his daughter relaxed, as if relieved this was the topic he'd been reluctant to discuss. She told him, "I've applied. I'm not sure when I'll start."

He nodded. "I'll need time to hire another aide. You told me once that you've also considered going to school on Luna. If you do that, I'll need to replace you as Messenger for the Lawbenders."

She looked away and seemed nervous. She said, "I don't know yet. I can't decide."

"I don't mean to pressure you. You've enjoyed living with me these last four seasons, haven't you? And Donni's been a good friend. Would it be so bad to stay here?"

"I love living in Kaanotok with you, Father, and I like being your liaison for the Lawbenders. As for Donni, well, we're friends, and that's nice. But living away from Lekton would be a good experience. My mentor went to school there, and he told me about it."

Across the room, the telecomm's silvery jingle interrupted. Since protocol required his aide to respond first, she crossed to the station and checked the caller identity display.

By her reaction, Loris knew it must read Council of Soloto, but he pretended curiosity when she turned to look at him. With a hint of suspicion in her eyes, she clicked a switch for vid response.

On the screen, Donni's pleasant, smiling features greeted them. He wore his official robe, and in the background, Loris recognized the Elder's private office.

Melenta bowed and greeted him, "Fairday, Elder Chonaira." Through long agreement, they maintained formality and protocol when he was in official vestments.

"Fairday. How are you, Melenta?"

"I'm well, Elder. Father is right here." She started to step aside.

But Donni interrupted. "Wait! I don't need to speak to him. I'm calling you."

Loris covered his mouth and pretended to cough. Obviously, he hid a smile.

Melenta ignored her father's teasing. "You're calling me? Is something wrong?"

"Not at all. I'll be in Kaanotok tonight to conduct Council business. I'd like to invite you to have Late-meal with me afterward. I'd enjoy your company."

Company? Did he mean as his social companion?

Her voice came out in a squeak. "You want to have Late-meal with me? Well, it would give me a chance to tell you news from Kaanotok, I suppose." She thought frantically, *that sounded like I expect this to be business, right?*

Donni didn't acknowledge the code, but he understood. Smiling in that charming way she always liked, he put her at ease. "Good. May I come for you at Half-light? About 2600?"

She forgot to take insult that he'd made reservations before inviting her. "That's fine. I'll be ready." The telecomm darkened on Donni's satisfied smile.

Melenta knew her father was staring at her. Turning away from him, she paced nervously to the window. Outside, the sun was beginning to rise. She called over her shoulder, "I've never gone out as anyone's companion. Why do you think he wants to see me? I didn't hear any code about a Lawbender message. Did you?"

She felt her father behind her. He squeezed her shoulder momentarily but quickly released her before she could object. He'd developed her trust by only touching her briefly.

Gently, she heard him say, "There wasn't a code, but I know why he's coming. Donni asked my permission to speak to you about betrothal."

She whirled to face him. "Betrothal? Donni Chonaira wants… me?"

"I wasn't surprised. Why are you?"

"I'm not surprised at his interest, exactly, but I can't believe he's spoken to you about it. He knows I've vowed never to marry."

"Vows sometimes change. You made that decision four seasons ago, and under emotional distress. Donni hopes you've seen that he can be trusted."

His patience didn't soften her anger. "I've discussed this with him before. He knows my plans for the future don't include marriage."

Loris reached for her hands. "Give him a chance."

She broke free immediately and backed away. "You'd make me obey?"

"Certainly not!" His body became rigid. "Why would you say that when the Quiet Revolution labors to grant you the justice of making your own choices?"

His eyes burned through her. Instinctively, her finger touched her forehead, and she lowered her head in shame. She wondered, *why did I say that? Father is nothing like Lukeniss.*

He sighed. "Donni would never want that for you, either. I only ask that you consider his offer as an option."

Her slender frame, taller with the last seasons of healthy life, trembled with trauma she didn't understand. Again, he reached out to help her avoid emotional overload.

Embarrassed by his concern, she closed her eyes. *I've offended him by refusing his help, but I can't let him believe I reject his love, too.*

So, lowering her deflector, she took his hands and allowed joining to steady her emotions. This wasn't the first joining they'd shared, but they were few. Though she'd hurt him, his warm, loving emotions flowed gently in, blending with hers in unconditional acceptance.

As they joined, Loris marveled at the depth of fear that assaulted him. Gathering her into his arms, he concentrated on the relief he meant to feel rather than what she suffered. It didn't disturb him that she wasn't returning his embrace. To be honest, Loris was amazed that she wasn't fleeing from his affection.

While relishing the moment he'd longed for, he felt her withdrawing, reaching to be separate beings again. Gradually, he controlled the release and let her pull out of his mind. He opened his arms and she ran from the room.

But she realized that her reaction was impolite and called back to him, "I'll consider all my options."

Loris let himself weep quietly. *What did he do to you, Mel?*

That evening as Melenta fastened the strap of her second sandal, she heard Donni's voice in the entry hall. Taking one more glance in the mirror, she hurried to greet him.

But before she entered the living area, she heard her father say to Donni, "I can't say for sure, but I doubt she'll accept."

Then, he heard her footsteps and changed his tone. "Forgive me if she's not ready. I've kept her so busy that she didn't have time to prepare properly to be companion for an Elder."

Then, Donni saw her. His eyes glowed with admiration. "No apology is necessary, I assure you."

Her father caught his reaction and turned to look.

Not since her father's investiture as Ambassador had Melenta found occasion to wear a formal gown. Tonight, she wore a light blue, lacy gown with opalescent beads studding the bodice. Her honey-colored hair, usually gathered in a long braid down her back, was pulled upward into twined flowers. She smiled, embarrassed by the men's stares.

Donni smiled back. "You honor me by the vision you've created on short notice. I'm properly chastised for rushing you."

She laughed. "You're being silly, but thank you. Isn't it risky to meet you in public like this, and on social terms instead of business?"

"I have social intentions, Melenta. And there's more to life than business."

She gave her father a withering look. "So I've been reminded. People who know me will suspect something if I'm companion to an Elder. Won't we be conspicuous?"

Her father said, "All they could suspect is that he invited you. Elders go out. They take companions. Nothing wrong with that."

Confidently, Donni told her, "Shall we go?"

Despite his efforts, Donni's confidence waned. Her father's warning had made him more nervous. But he opened the door to the manor, and they stepped outside into the twilight.

As he closed the door behind him, he lingered on the steps to take in the beauty of the Cha'atre estate. The air was cool and quiet, and the single, smaller moon that lit the sky was a delicate violet color. With an instinctive, guiding hand, he reached toward Melenta and was startled to find she was trembling! Had she changed her mind about going? Softly, he asked, "Is something wrong?"

She looked down. "This is new to me. I never go out in public except with Father. I'm not sure I know how to be a social companion."

He noticed her blush. "I don't go out, either. I haven't chosen a companion since my time at the Remuel Cove Kaamestaat. The last thing I want to do is frighten you."

He backed up the stair steps to stand in the shadow of the doorway. Taking her hand and pulling her up the steps to him, he teased, "Mel, this is me, Donni. I'm the same man who's visited your manor for over four seasons. You can't be afraid of me, are you? I'd never hurt you." As evidence of that, he dropped her hand.

She didn't look at him, but at least she laughed.

He said, "I've let you know me in a way no other woman ever has. I could find plenty of companions simply by waving my professional title." The truth was, he wouldn't even have to wave it. As Loris had also learned, women approached unmarried men of title all the time.

She whispered, "That's true. So then, why me?"

"Only Melenta Cha'atre really knows me. With you, I'm just Donni, a lonely man too long without a mate. I'm the one who should be nervous. I have to count on you to appreciate my company without relying on prestige of my title. It doesn't impress you anymore."

"Yes, it does! Don't you know how intimidating it is to be companion to an Elder?"

"Believe me, the man with you now doesn't plan to be an Elder tonight. Good thing, too. I don't think I could manage much objectivity and concentration as I admire you across a table." He was relieved when his self-deprecating humor charmed her.

Finally, she smiled back at his flattery. "You're exaggerating."

"I'm being honest." Tentatively, he laced his fingers with hers, never giving in to the temptation to lower his deflector. "Friends tonight? No official titles or business formalities?"

"Yes, Donni," she laughed and squeezed his hand once in return. Awkwardly, then, she released it.

They left the estate and stepped into his steel-gray shuttle to relax in the craft's control section for the short flight into Kaanotok.

But an awkward silence possessed those first moments. Anxiously, he thought, *All Wise, please don't let her turn me down.*

When he could no longer stand the silence, he commented, "I can't believe that in the privacy of a moving shuttle, you're still nervous with me. You haven't been this uneasy since the day I met you." Suddenly, he knew why. "Oh, I understand. Your father told you about our discussion. Well, I'm encouraged that you agreed to come, knowing my motives."

Pain struck her expression abruptly.

Hesitantly, he continued, "But I suppose you'd still see me to decline my offer." The vulnerability of the moment terrified Donni. His mind was saying, *admit it, man. Her refusal will rip your heart apart.*

A soft beep drew his attention. Turning his eyes back to the control panel, he discovered they'd arrived at the dining hall. Glad for the diversion, he landed and completed the shutdown procedures. But he stayed in the seat, afraid to move.

Melenta's instincts were telling her to run away as fast as possible. But she, too, couldn't move. *How could I hurt this kind friend who so obviously adores me?* With a shaking voice, she told him, "Above anything else, I don't want to hurt you."

"No!" Donni interrupted. "No, don't… please don't. I'd rather forget my suggestion. Forget the whole subject. I don't think I'd survive hearing your refusal."

She couldn't do that. "We're good friends—the best! I'm honored to know how you feel, and I dearly wish I felt as much for you. But I'm not sure I could ever love any man."

"I'm not asking for love. Don't you feel enough, my lady, to share a life together?" The eagerness in his eyes pierced soul-deep.

For the briefest moment, she considered that. Many couples paired for companionship, for convenience, or to consolidate family alliances. Couples often learned to love each other over time. More than any man on Lekton, she trusted this one not to hurt her.

So, could I do it? Couldn't I try? What's wrong with me?

But though her heart worked to convince her, her mind wouldn't consider it. She said softly, "Donni, I might feel enough to share my life with you if I knew how to share anything. You aren't the one who hurt me, but others did. My faith in relationships was destroyed long ago. That's the reason I vowed never to marry. I ask pardon if that hurts you."

His eyes implored her to reconsider. He pleaded, "I know how deeply your childhood tragedies have damaged your trust and kept you from accepting love. Right now, you don't know how to allow a man in your future. But if you think of me as a trusted friend instead of as a man, maybe I could help you learn."

Pressure built in her chest. His words seemed so logical, yet her mind screamed that she was in imminent danger. She couldn't stand another heart-felt entreaty. To avoid it, she leaped into a rash decision that would free her. "No amount of trust would make a difference. And besides that, I've decided to leave Lekton for a few seasons. I've been accepted at the COAXIS Institute on Luna. I'll enter next mooncycle."

His face paled as Donni slumped into the shuttle seat. "Do you have to go so far away? There's an Institute on Lekton. And if you stay, you still have a chance to see Cheelo occasionally."

At that point, all her reserves of strength buckled, and panic crashed in on her. Defiantly, she insisted, "I can't grow here! Lekton's rigid laws and traditions smother me!"

"Then, stay and help me change them!"

The pain reflected in his eyes tore away pieces of her determination. She almost saw them like flakes floating in the air around them. Urgently, she replied, "I can't stay! I have to leave Lekton while there's something left of me that this world hasn't corrupted. Maybe when I return, I'll know how to be happy living here."

Barely whispering, Donni asked, "But will you return to me?"

His soul-ripping plea drained away her resolve and left her hollow with guilt. With no will to resist, she let herself be drawn into Donni's arms.

Even though both kept their deflector raised to guard against sensing each other's emotions, she recognized the intensity of his feelings as he trailed the back of his index finger along her jaw.

Abruptly, she realized that Donni was trembling. She thought, *oh, great portals! His emotions are overloading, and it's my fault!*

Amazed, she realized that she cared so much for her friend that she didn't mind holding and comforting him. But then, the hand that had been stroking her face slowly lowered and extended to her in invitation. Reflexively, she tracked the movement and saw his fingers curl into the up-turned cup gesture of Taam skla'a Kair. He was asking her to release her deflector and join with his emotions.

With that gesture, her tender concern for him collapsed and caution flared in her mind. The truth became unmistakably clear—she had to leave Lekton.

Melenta pulled slowly away from the warmth and love of Donni's embrace. She ignored the inviting gesture, but clasped his opposite hand, pointedly offering comfort rather than the emotional union he requested.

Disappointed, he clung to her and begged, "Join with me, Mel. See if loving me is so beyond your ability. If you can't enjoy it, then I'll believe you."

But the peace that comes from a firm decision made and the absence of regret braced her determination. As gently as she knew how, she told him, "I can't join with you. Until now, I didn't exactly understand why. I've never joined with any man, and I won't. That... is... what I have left of me. When I give that away, I don't exist."

Unrestrained tears framed Donni's eyes. As he stiffened and disentangled his arms from the embrace, his sad expression resolved into a rueful smile. "Since the only thing you can't give me is the only thing I need, I guess it's settled."

Melenta was relieved. She told herself, *this is the right thing to do.* It felt right because she had control of her future. She felt guilt, not for her decision but for his pain. She told him, "We can still be friends."

Until she said that, he thought he might survive the sorrow. Angry, he turned away from her and thought, *I'll walk out of her life and show her what misery feels like.*

But he knew he wouldn't be able to do it. *No, I couldn't hurt her for any reason. And what if, after a change of scenery, she realizes that she's missed me? I should preserve our friendship and keep doors open.*

With that in mind, he smiled, pretending the resigned acceptance she wanted him to feel. Feigning cheerfulness, he told her. "We'll always be friends. Why don't we go enjoy a meal and you can tell me about your plans."

But throughout the evening, Donni tried to think of one more idea that would make Melenta trust him. Meanwhile, he'd wait. She'd figure it out eventually.

CHAPTER 17

Kaanotok Township, 17 Zelonn, 2163

Loris awoke with a catch in his back. He hadn't slept well. Last night, he'd been disappointed when his daughter returned home without Donni. He'd hoped to hear an announcement that they were intended. Instead, Melenta announced that she was leaving Lekton. She'd be attending school on Luna next mooncycle.

He'd gone to sleep thinking, *maybe such plans can't be arranged that quickly, and she'll have to stay home another half-season.* That would give Donni time to change her mind.

But the morning brought more disappointment. Loris found her in her sleep chamber, and she was packing everything. Standing outside the doorway, he asked, "Packing a little soon, aren't you? You don't even know if there's time to arrange enrollment."

Melenta didn't look up. "I was accepted last season under a deferred enrollment status. I can start whenever I'm ready."

"You never told me that," he said with justifiable insult.

"I ask your pardon."

Suddenly, his mind didn't feel very steady, and apparently, she wasn't concentrating very well, either. Frequently, she'd finish packing a bag, remember something she'd forgotten and then have to repack it. *Why is she so preoccupied,* Loris wondered?

He asked, "Are you worried about your flight to Luna? When I went there for the last Interworld Conference, the big Xylonian ICT was a very safe and comfortable craft."

She nodded.

He tried again. "I hope you aren't worried about me?" But in a way, he hoped she was.

"No."

Her blunt answer didn't dissuade him. "Is it leaving Lekton? I know you'll have to adjust to new customs and use a different language. I suppose you'll even need a different style of clothing." He was beginning to ramble.

At last, she paused her activity and looked at him. "I admire Terran culture, remember? It will be fun to learn their customs and change my lifestyle."

Loris went to her. "You'll do very well. You've mastered COAXIS Standard as fluently as anyone on Luna. Won't you please tell me what's bothering you? I'm used to being involved in your life, and you're making me a spectator." He reached to her cheek to brush upward strokes with the back of his fingers. Ordinarily, she could accept this affectionate gesture because it requires no reply. But today, for some reason, jhaarteel seemed to frighten her. Now, especially since his daughter would be leaving home, he wished she'd find courage enough to return his affection. He couldn't hide his disappointment.

At first, she looked away, uneasy with his reaction. Then, she turned and faced him, resolutely looking into his eyes. Firmly taking his hand between hers, she told him, "Thank you for being so patient with me."

He felt her deflector disappearing and gratefully lowered his own. Their joining was superficial, as it always was, but that didn't matter.

Loris sighed deeply, his eyes gently closing to enjoy her touch. "It doesn't take patience to love my daughter. Are you upset about leaving Donni?" He knew at once that he'd said the wrong thing. Through their joining, her immediate fear told him so.

The request to confide her feelings for Donni sent Melenta back to packing her bags, but she answered, "After you've given me shelter and care for these four-and-a-half seasons, you may not like my answer."

"Nothing would hurt me unless, after these four-and-a-half seasons you say that you aren't my daughter as much as if I'd fathered you."

Melenta put aside her work and sat down on a floor pillow, folding her hands in her lap. "You're my father. I wish you'd been my father for the other fifteen seasons of my life. Then, I wouldn't have suffered so much rejection from Lukeniss."

Loris looked away, ashamed of how his brother had treated her.

"I guess I'm worried about Cheelo. One day, he might decide to leave Lukeniss. Since I've only seen him once when he was six, he might not think of calling me. But when I'm so far away, it would be even harder for me to help."

Encouraged by her candor, he pulled another floor pillow close and sat beside her. "Donni watches over your brother. Lukeniss appears to be kind but strict with him. Cheelo's a strong-willed boy, often pushing his limits, so a strict, firm hand is best. But if Lukeniss gets out of hand, Donnie will report him to the Advocate, I assure you."

That relieved her mind. Softly, she confessed, "I was also thinking about Mother."

Kamira's death when Cheelo was born had been a great loss, he knew. It had happened a season after Melenta lost her sister, Linnori in a freak accident. It was, of course, normal to think of a departed loved one during important stages of ones life. But he got the impression that Melenta had another reason for missing her mother.

"Why?" he asked her.

"As a child, I used to dream about what it would be like to grow up and leave home. I expected Maata would wish me all the happiness that she'd never found."

"I regret she isn't here to tell you, but you know she wished that for you. So do I."

"I may be nineteen, but I wish I could hear her call me by my child name once more." Melenta dropped her head and smiled. "I was called, 'Little One.' I never knew why she gave me that particular name because I was always tall for my age."

"She didn't choose it randomly," Loris remarked casually. Then, he froze, thinking, *would my knowledge of the subject seem odd? Maybe she'll ignore it.*

But she looked up at him, amused bewilderment pinching her face. "Oh?"

Offhandedly, he issued a hurried explanation. "She told me it was a traditional gift that each woman in the Kaantina'a lineage bestows upon a daughter. She said that she'd told Linnori so that the tradition would be carried on, but she gave you the name because she loved you."

But Melenta wouldn't let this answer be sufficient. In a hushed voice, she gasped, "She told that to you, her husband's brother, but not to me? Why?"

Can't she let it drop? I never intended to carry her curiosity so far, but I thought she should understand the significance of that tradition. She deserves the truth.

However, Loris wasn't that brave. Shrugging, he stood and contrived to end the conversation. "I guess we'll never know why she didn't tell you." He sipped his drink.

She jumped to her feet. "No, you have to explain this."

Defensively, he argued back, "Melenta, I can't explain it. Perhaps she thought you were too young to appreciate the gift of a traditional child name. I'm sure she expected to live to explain it when you were older."

"I was ten seasons at her death. I'd have understood. Are you saying she told you before she died so that you could explain it to me later?"

The direction of this conversation frightened Loris, who couldn't dishonor her with a lie. "No, you were a baby when she told me. We were good friends. You know Lukeniss and Kamira didn't have an ideal marriage. Since Lukeniss had no time for her, she talked about her feelings with other people, and I was one of them. She said that Linnori was the child she gave Lukeniss, but you were the child she gave herself. No one else could have been Little One."

It made sense. She remembered how her mother often called her "my Little One." She still thought it odd that he knew so much. "Why didn't you tell me before?" she accused.

"Dear, I never realized she hadn't told you, or I'd have told you sooner."

Melenta's mind was filled with disturbing, conflicting thoughts. Her father's sudden admission of knowledge meant he might know more. *Do I really want to ask him the biggest question that's hurt me so long—why Lukeniss hates me? What if he does know? That would mean that he's known all along and didn't tell me.*

Distressed and hurt, she shielded her suspicions in denial. She told herself, *Father would never do anything to hurt me. He seems to want the matter to drop, so maybe I should let it.*

He asked, "Have I said something wrong?" There was alarm in his voice.

Finally, a need for answers pushed away fear. Melenta blurted out, "How could you have been such a close friend to my mother when you hardly ever visited us?"

A future he'd always dreaded was at hand, and Loris was terrified. He'd perpetually assigned the duty of giving this explanation to that ambiguous point in time called "someday." Someday had come, summoned by her suspicion.

So that his silence didn't seem like evasion, he took a deep breath and faced her. "There were visits you never knew about. Aren't you glad she had someone to talk to?"

"Of course. I know she was lonely. Lukeniss treated Mother like a possession to store away and enjoy at his leisure. She spent a lot of time alone."

Loris swallowed the lump in his throat and nodded.

"Father, tell me the truth: Did Lukeniss know about those visits?"

"Not always." His heart sank—*she knows!*

Inhaling deeply, she extended her hands before him, wrists crossed upon each other with open palms upward. The gesture asked him to swear kaalsoto. Lying while answering that gesture would dishonor both of them. In a culture so devoted to honor, that simply wasn't done.

Calmly, she asked, "Did Lukeniss ever know about those visits?"

Though fearing her reaction, he lifted his head, locked his gaze on hers and replied, "No."

"Am I to understand that Lukeniss had a good reason for never loving me? And you've known that all this time?"

"What do you want me to say? Do you want to hear that I'm sorry? I am! I've always been sorry, and I'm sure I always will be."

"Don't give me apologies! You've taught me your mediation tactics, and I resent having them used on me. What's your answer?"

"If you must have one, then yes. Lukeniss didn't love you because he didn't want you."

"That wasn't what I asked! Am I his daughter?"

He crossed his wrists, palms downward. His tone was direct and dispassionate. "No."

It was the hardest, single word Loris Cha'atre had ever uttered.

Melenta dropped her hands to her side and fought to keep composure. There was so much she still needed to know, and yet, this small piece of the puzzle told so much. Then, she saw her father's undisguised humiliation, and it provoked her. *Does he think I'll feel sorry for him, the man who's credo is Justice? He's getting his justice now.*

She screamed, "If Lukeniss knew the baby wasn't his, why didn't he have you both shunned? He disgraced Kendel before the entire Nation for much less. Didn't he hate you?"

His head bowed in shame, and he buried his face in his hands. "Lukeniss didn't report her to the Elders, but not because he loved her or wanted to win her back. He'd married into a prestigious family, and he had Linnori, a beautiful heir. Those honors were his happiness. As for me, he never wanted to know how Kamira came to bear you, and she never implicated me. He still doesn't know."

These revelations explained Melenta's doubts and settled the mysteries of her life. Loris had protected his reputation by sacrificing his daughter's self-esteem. He'd allowed her to grow up believing that Lukeniss didn't love her because she was unlovable.

Now I know the truth, she thought. *By withholding the key to my insecurities, Father betrayed me, just as Mother, Lukeniss and even Donni did. There really is no one who can be trusted.*

She stormed toward him, yelling, "Do you know how much suffering I'd have avoided if you'd told me the truth long ago?"

She didn't wait for an answer. With an angry snap, she closed her last bag.

For Loris, there was no escape from this shame. He'd wanted to confess the truth shortly after Kamira learned she was pregnant. Then, if Lukeniss had them shunned and banished from the Nation, Loris would have cared for Kamira and their baby within an amnesty zone. It wouldn't have been a good life, but they'd have been together.

But Kamira wouldn't allow him to tell Lukeniss. There was no need. Lukeniss knew Kamira carried another man's child because he never wanted relations with her. Instead of reporting her to the Council, though, Lukeniss used the shame against her. Kamira was compelled to obey him at all times under threat of ruining her life and taking her children away from her.

So, she kept her secret, submitted to Lukeniss and forced Loris to stay away. He did as she asked, believing that protected the reputations of Kamira and his daughter.

Seeing his daughter's reaction now, he knew he'd done the wrong thing. Helplessly, he watched as she strapped a daypack on her back and grabbed luggage in each hand. She strode to the door without a word.

"Don't leave, Melenta. I've tried for so long to teach you to be open with people and to let others love you. You'd almost broken down the barrier for me. If that trust is gone, please don't shut out everyone else. Don't build more walls and make it impossible for anyone else to have your love."

"How dare you lecture me about trust and love! What right do you have to wear the glyph of Justice? Was it just to deny responsibility for your actions and let Lukeniss punish Mother?"

He blocked the door. "Wait! You're right. If I lose you, that's just punishment, but please don't throw away the progress you've made. That would only punish you."

Defiantly, she snapped, "No one will punish me ever again, Loris. You can be sure I won't punish myself. My life will be on my terms. You were the one who deserved punishment, but you got out of it, didn't you, Ambassador?"

He was trembling badly now. Inside, he wailed, *Oh, Great All Wise, make her listen to me.* Forbidding himself to cry, he told her, "My sweet girl, I've been punished more than you could imagine. For these nineteen seasons, I've loved you because you were mine, blood of my blood, but I couldn't claim you. That hurt me, but no pain is as cruel as hearing you call me Loris again instead of Father."

With an expression like stone, she pushed him aside and walked to the front door. Without looking back, she called, "I'll leave your shuttle at the San Durg Skyport. Have someone fly it home for you."

Melenta looked forward, maybe for the first time in her life. She said to no one at all, "No more mysteries of my past. No more obligations to anyone else."

As she lifted the shuttle into the air, she avoided looking down at the manor, the orchards—all the places she'd thought were home. "No, home is where my foot steps down. A wise, Terran poet once said that."

She was in for a long journey. From San Durg, it would take two moons to get to the Xylonian Transit Authority's Spaceport. When she arrived, she'd spend the last of her savings on passage to Luna by standard freighter, which would take fourteen moons more. There was still another two-moon flight from the XTA Spaceport orbiting Mars to reach Luna.

"The semester will begin before I get there, but it can't be helped. I'll ask to start late."

Her only regret was in leaving Cheelo, and once again, without seeing him to say good-bye. *But no tears*, she told herself firmly. *When you set foot on Luna, it will be home … forever.*

In San Durg Township

A cycle later, she reached the San Durg Skyport and berthed the shuttle in a storage section. An attendant, a boy of fifteen who was probably apprenticing there, asked, "When will you be back for it?"

"Ambassador Loris Cha'atre will reclaim the shuttle when he can. I'm moving to Luna to attend the Institute." Saying it aloud made it finally seam real in her mind.

The young man's eyes lit with enthusiasm. "Really? What'll you study?"

She almost said Law. For so long, she'd planned to prepare for her work as The MenD'lee. But like so often in the past, those plans were useless, too.

She told him, "Maybe I'll study to be a Galactic Enforcement Agent. One thing is sure: The next few seasons will be busy, fulfilling to my needs and as devoid of relationships as I can manage."

Ignoring the boy's shocked stare, she picked up her daypack and bags and headed to the Off-world ticket counter.

There, a pleasant woman in a light blue XTA uniform greeted her.

"I'm going to Luna." Melenta handed over her currency card and fished in her daypack for her COAXIS I.D. If her work for the Embassy hadn't required one, there would have been a significant delay to order it.

"Your name?"

"Melenta Cha'atre." She presented her I.D.

The ticket agent said, "Yes, your passage has been arranged by the Embassy. Your ICT flight will board in a half-cycle at the Red Gate. I'll have your luggage loaded for you." She reached for the luggage.

Melenta said quickly, "I can't afford the interplanetary crafts."

The agent smiled, saying once more, "There's no charge. The COAXIS Ambassador called and arranged everything. You'll be on Luna in four moons. Enjoy your flight."

Four moons, not eighteen? It occurred to Melenta to be offended by her father's preemptory planning of her life. But it was nice to know she'd arrive before classes began. And she'd fly in comfort, a benefit of his diplomatic status.

I think I have to accept this last gesture from Loris. Maybe I'll even send one last letter to thank him. I'll insist that he do nothing else for me, though. From now on, I'm on my own.

That was both exhilarating and terrifying.

CHAPTER 18

Luna, Center City, December 17, 2163 (20 Zelonn TSE)

This had been Melenta's first flight aboard an Interplanetary Communal Traveler, the fastest and most luxurious Xylonian craft. By ICT, travel to Lekton's transport station outside the solar system had taken two days. Then, using the Xylonian Doorway, the ICT had jumped in a matter of minutes to a corresponding XTA Station near Mars. After two more day's journey, Melenta had arrived on Luna. In sharp contrast, an ordinary freighter would've taken two weeks to complete a journey to a Confederation world.

Now, as she walked down the ramp of the ICT into the Spaceport terminal, her thoughts were on her mentor and friend, Kendel Brekket, who'd helped her prepare to attend the Institute. Since he'd graduated from this particular Institute, he'd been able to alert her to problems she'd likely face in adjusting to an alien lifestyle.

In wonder, she thought, *Oh, Kendel, I'm standing on a new world for the first time, and you made it happen.* She hadn't realized how much she'd miss him. *For his sake, I'll do my best to adjust.*

Immediately, she saw one disturbing adjustment that Kendel had mentioned. Within the domed environment, the artificial light was intended to resemble normal sunlight on Terra. But for Melenta, who had grown up under a different light gradient, one that was also slightly purple rather than yellow, the daylight seemed intense. She convinced herself she was fortunate not to be actually on Terra, where there were no filters to ease natural glare.

Next, she noticed the difference in the gravity, which was only slightly lower than on Lekton. *I won't mind a little extra ease to my step,* she mused.

But the smell of this place is a problem. The odor of soil, grass, and trees was remarkably more potent than on Lekton. While not exactly unpleasant, it wasn't as fragrant as the flowery scent of Lekton. Kendel had said that she'd adjust to that eventually, but it would be one of the hardest adjustments. She grimaced and thought, *I hope you're right, Kendel.*

Along the walls of the terminal, lighted displays in four languages, Lektonese included, instructed new students to go to the green desk for processing at the Institute.

It wasn't difficult to find. Behind the desk, a young, Terran man greeted her in Lektonese. "Jhendail. K'preen taamalaa?"

"Hello," Melenta said, demonstrating that she could speak Standard.

The man asked, "You're a new student?"

"That's right. I'm Melenta Cha'atre." She presented her COAXIS identity card.

He consulted a computer in front of him. "Yes, we've been expecting you."

He handed her a packet of information. "This will help you find your dorm assignment." He pointed out a map of the campus, saying, "You'll want to keep this handy."

Melenta sorted through five booklets titled, Science Technology, Social Services, Diplomatic Services, Cultural Studies, and Medical Research.

Seeing her confusion, he asked, "Have you chosen which degree you'd like to study?"

She hesitated, thinking, *would he laugh at a woman wanting to go into Security?* Anticipating a scoffing reaction, she answered, "Maybe Security Investigations."

But he didn't react in any negative way. "That's under the Social Services Order." He indicated the book with a red cover. "The information about the orientation meeting in your field is listed inside. Don't worry if you decide on a different program later. Choose something you like in order to get started."

Another form was placed in her hand. The man said, "And here's your dorm assignment voucher."

As she placed the voucher in her packet, a single page fell from it. Bending over to pick it up, she noticed bold letters across the top that said, "Learning to Adjust on Luna". "What's this?"

"It gives some tips for non-Terrans to help them get used to a new lifestyle here. For example, it's best to speak only Standard from the beginning of your stay. You might consider changing your name to a Terran version if it's difficult to pronounce."

This caught her interest. "I can do that?"

"Sure. If you want, you can fill out the form now. I'll enter your Terranized name in the city's personnel files as an alias. That way, no one will have to relearn what to call you."

With the help of a special linguistics application, she created a Terran alias. "I'll be Melantha Chatrey."

He added the correction to the computer. "I'm reprinting your dorm voucher with the right name." They exchanged the forms. "Welcome to Luna, Melantha."

After claiming her luggage (and that turned out to be far more involved than registering for school had been,) she left the terminal to find the bus that would take her to the Institute.

Outdoors, she took in the landscape, and it gave her mixed feelings. There were a few differences in colors—much more green, much less purple. And she found that she didn't appreciate the architectural styles that tended to consist of either ovals or sharply angled boxes. "Not much variety," she mumbled in disappointment.

Finally, she located the bus, a railcar system similar to the Xylonian technology on Lekton. Stepping aboard, she stowed her luggage in an overhead rack. Everyone else on the bus was Terran. She wondered, *how many other Lektonians live here? I don't want to stick out.*

As the bus moved on, an elderly man stood at the front and began to tell the passengers about Luna. "Center City consists of a central dome surrounded by four domes called Quadrants. It has a surface area equivalent to that of Great Britain. The center dome holds mostly apartments and many businesses, restaurants and entertainment facilities. The COAXIS Institute and the Embassy are also there. While Center City has its own hospital, medical research companies and a research hospital are located in East Quad. Our North Quad are primarily mining and industrial facilities. Property in South Quad is dedicated to organic farms. I'm afraid West Quad is rather boring for any scenic tour, unless machine storage flies your flag. Then, I'd find you boring."

Several new visitors laughed. As she didn't understand the joke, she felt self-conscious. She suddenly knew that living here would be the hardest thing she'd ever done.

Their arrival at the Institute was chaotic, with students calling out questions and trying to keep their belongings together. Following the map, she found her dorm.

The building was a four-story, common-looking structure made of brown stone. Metal trim had been painted blue in an attempt to adorn its unimaginative style. But she reminded herself, *no one said it would look like home.*

Soon she located her room, which was small but adequate. However, little else seemed to go well. Though she'd opted for Terran furnishings on her application, she'd never counted on there being so much of it in the tiny room. There seemed to be two of everything.

And that was another issue. She thought, *didn't I request a private room? I don't want roommates.*

Melantha glanced at the two, stacked beds and wondered, *will I even be able to sleep on Luna? Why didn't I pack my fur-bed?*

Behind her, there was a knock at the door. Opening it, she found a Terran woman dressed in a familiar COAXIS Embassy field uniform—gold jacket with maroon trim over black, pressed slacks. The presence of one, round pin on her collar indicated that she was an aide to a COAXIS Ambassador.

Smiling warmly, the woman said, "Welcome to Luna. I'm Gretta Dunn. Ambassador Cha'atre told us you were coming. I came to see if you'd like any assistance to get settled."

Embarrassed, Melantha thought, *Loris has no right to interfere in my life anymore. But this aide is graciously following instructions and probably disliked being assigned to pamper an Ambassador's daughter. I won't take it out on her.*

So she held back an unkind remark.

But before Melantha could utter a self-righteous dismissal, Gretta exclaimed, "And it's a good thing I came. This isn't satisfactory."

"I'm sorry?" asked Melantha.

"You requested a private dorm assignment, didn't you? There must be a mistake. If I may see your dorm voucher, I'll take care of this. If you'd like to leave your belongings here, I'll have everything transferred to the correct room for you. You can take a walk and get to know the campus. When you come back, there will be a note for you at the supervisor's desk telling you your new apartment number."

Then, Gretta looked at her voucher. "I see they've also misspelled your name. I'll have that fixed for you."

"No, don't correct it," Melantha protested. "I've Terranized my name. Look, I appreciate the offer, but I can take care of myself."

Gretta suddenly changed her manner and adopted a Lektonian posture of respect by clasping her hands behind her. "We won't impose. Maybe I should tell you that I was sent to the Embassy on Lekton during my last season in school. I have some insight into how hard it can be to transfer between our two cultures." She placed one hand on her heart and gave a half bow, gesturing that she meant no offense. "I know you don't need help."

The sentiment eased Melantha's stubborn independence. "I suppose I do need a different apartment, if you know how to do that. Thank you, Gretta."

Relaxing her formal stance, Gretta said, "Is there anything you'd like to change? More furniture, less furniture…a fur-bed?" She glared at the impersonal bunk.

This endeared her to Melantha. "Yes, that would be wonderful. I like the furniture, but less of it. Maybe a mirror?"

Gretta seemed pleased to be allowed to help. "I'll take care of everything." From the inside pocket of her jacket, she took a card and handed it to Melantha. "This is how you can reach me. I won't hover the way I'm sure your father would prefer, but if you need anything or have a question, call me."

Melantha bowed to her and took the card. "I'll take my map and start finding my way around campus."

First, Melantha set out to find the buildings listed in the red Social Services booklet. Most of all, she wanted to see the gymnasium.

It wasn't hard to find, as it was the largest building in that section of campus. Pulling open a door, she walked inside.

Classes hadn't begun, so she wasn't worried about disturbing anyone. Sounds from ahead of her caught her attention. She stared at a set of double doors. "That sounds like a fight." Melantha pushed one door slightly open and peeked inside.

She saw eight Terran men dressed similarly in black workout apparel, and they were fighting each other in pairs! But it was a most unusual form of fighting. Surprisingly, the men were smiling or laughing.

She thought, *is this martial arts? I've heard about this. I'm glad there's padded mats on the floor.*

Although each man was Terran, their coloring indicated a variety of races. Two seemed significantly older than the other six, making Melantha wonder if they were instructing the other men. But it didn't take long to understand that every one of them were professionals in Security.

From the lobby behind her, a man's voice said, "You can go in, if you want."

She jumped, whirling around to see a young student carrying a gym bag. He stood at the glass door that went outside. Grinning, he said, "New here? They don't mind if students go in and watch." He exited the building.

Once her heart rate returned to normal, she opened the door and entered the gym.

The pair of men nearest to the door noticed her, but then they returned to their workout. Assured that she truly was welcome, she sat against a wall to watch.

After twenty minutes, one of the oldest men left the center of the floor for a break. He had a tanned complexion and very short, gray hair. Melantha guessed about fifty-five, but his body was muscled and strong. Going to a bag near the wall where Melantha sat, he took out a bottle of water. After a long drink, he pulled out a towel and wiped his face.

Melantha was trying not to look at him, but he approached her and said, "I haven't seen you here before. I'm the Program Director, Commander Black Horse. Are you one of my new Security students?"

Immediately, she stood and lowered her gaze. Reminding herself to speak Standard, she replied, "I hope to be. I arrived today."

Another much younger, black-haired man came closer, calling to her, "Investigation or Defense?"

"Investigation," she answered.

He seemed disappointed. Turning to one of the other men across the gym, he called out something she didn't understand. Until that moment, he'd been speaking Standard. It made her nervous.

The other older man walked up to her. By his skin color, darker than anyone she'd ever seen before, he was obviously of a different race. His hair and eyes were even black. In a deep, rumbling voice, he said, "I'm Commander Greg Baxter. You're going to study Investigation?"

Greatly relieved that he'd spoken Standard, Melantha gave him a low bow. "I'm glad to meet you. My name is Melantha Chatrey."

"Lektonian? We don't have many from that planet who study Security here. Have you had any training before this?"

She thought to herself, *none I can tell you about.* But she simply shook her head.

He surveyed her critically. "What about fighting skills? Have you taken any classes?"

She almost laughed. "Not in fighting. I like reasoning out a problem. I prefer Investigations so that I don't have to fight. I'm too thin and lightweight to be any good at that."

Commander Baxter cocked his head. "You'd be surprised. Security Investigations also requires a good ability to defend yourself. Stand closer, would you? I'd like to show you something."

Eager to learn, she brightened and moved nearer to him.

He began, "There are benefits to having strength and bulk, but it's sometimes an advantage to be lean and agile. It lets you move faster. Having less weight to lift also gives you better reflexes and endurance."

One of the other men added, "And since you're Lektonian, you're in a lower gravity here." To the others, he said, "She might be hard to catch."

Melantha responded, "I'm a very good runner."

This caught Commander Baxter's interest. "Really? Let me try something." He motioned to his workout partner to step closer and demonstrate a block.

As Melantha watched, Commander Baxter pulled one arm over his head and brought it down in a chopping motion toward his partner's head. The move was so quick, she barely saw it. Amazed, she saw that his opponent had lifted his arm at a perpendicular level just in time to stop the arm lowering down on him. They repeated several other attacks and blocks from differing angles.

Melantha was mesmerized.

Baxter turned back to her. "Could you try it? I'll move slowly, and I won't hit you, of course. Let's see what kind of reflexes you have."

Without warning, he lifted his hand toward the side of her face. Her wrist went instantly in place to protect her ear.

"Very good," Baxter praised. "You'll learn not to block with your joints, though. Make sure it's the broader, fleshy part of your arm that blocks the blow. One more time, but a little faster?"

Repeatedly, the Commander tested her at various strike points, and she was always ready with a block. Faster and faster, he came at her, but she was always ready.

After a few minutes, he stepped away and regarded her. In fact, the rest of the instructors had gathered around and were staring at her in surprise.

She looked from one to another and asked, "What?"

Commander Black Horse chuckled and uttered a comment that the others found humorous.

There's that other language again, thought Melantha irritably. "I only speak Standard," she admonished.

Black Horse moistened his lips. "Sorry, of course you do. I was saying that I find it hard to believe you haven't learned this before."

Instinctively, Melantha thought she'd been accused of lying. *On Lekton, I'd swear kaalsoto and they'd believe me. How is it done on Luna,* she wondered? Hoping her promise would be enough, she said, "I don't lie."

A smile spread over Baxter's dark features. "I believe you." He signaled to someone else, and a very tall, younger man came to her. His hair was an unusual reddish color. She'd heard about auburn hair, but it was the first time she'd actually seen it.

The man told her "I'm Commander Blake O'Connell. If you don't mind my saying so, you'd be a much better Defender."

Her reply was a squeak. "Me?"

The instructors laughed, but Blake scolded them, "Knock it off. She's a natural, but she's green."

She wasn't sure what he'd meant, but his tone obviously defended her, so she felt better.

To Melantha, he said proudly, "Commander Baxter did his best to surprise you, and you always anticipated his move. For a beginner with no experience, that's exceptionally rare. Believe me, you'll be a Defense major. And I'd like you to train for the Keplar competitions."

"What is that?"

"A competition between the best amateur defense artists in the Confederation."

Another instructor stepped closer. It was the tanned man with the unusual accent who had seemed disappointed that she wasn't seeking a Defense degree. He said, "I'm Guillermo Ruiz, one of the Defense Instructors here, and I'm also the Keplar coach. If you'll give me two years to train you, I'll have you competing!"

Commander Black Horse interrupted, drawing her aside. "Before my defense masters get too out of control with their enthusiasm," he said, glaring teasingly at Ruiz and O'Connell, "let me explain something. Security majors have to be defense masters, regardless of their field of specialization. You'll learn these defense techniques in the normal, four-year program. But without prior training of any kind, you'll have to take extra courses."

"How many extra courses?"

"Don't let it discourage you. If you train with Ruiz, you won't be able to take as many courses each semester, so it usually takes an additional two years. But these gentlemen are right about your potential. And you won't regret the extra training. Keplar competitors are in high demand by employers. Think about it for a while."

She didn't have to think long. *If I'm not going to be The MenD'lee, I'll need new goals and a way to support myself without relying on my father. Being able to defend myself would be a plus. I'll never allow someone to assault me the way Lukeniss did.*

Melantha never wanted to feel that helpless again. And although she didn't consciously think about it, somewhere in her deepest thoughts was the realization that if she were busy studying for her degree and using her free time to train for the Keplar, she'd never have time for relationships.

"I'm going to do it," she told Ruiz.

CHAPTER 19

Lekton, San Durg Township, 31 Jhaila, 2164 (May 3 TSE)

It was raining as Loris stepped out of his aircar in front of the Laampeer D'Lair Inn. He struggled to push away the memory that bruised his soul, but even the miserable weather didn't distract him.

His daughter's first semester at school was ending, and he'd asked her to come home for a visit. Melenta had returned the letter to him, unread. *How long will she hate me,* wondered Loris?

An attendant at the door instantly bowed and called, "Welcome, Ambassador." He offered his rain shield, a tented acrylic covering to hold overhead.

Waving away the shield, Loris gave a brisk order, indicating his aircar should be sheltered for the night.

There was no need for Loris to ask if Donni had arrived, since it was he who was late to their appointment. He went directly to the private dining floor and was met once more by an attendant giving a cheerful greeting. Giving no reply, Loris handed over his cloak and opened a door to the private dining suite.

Donni rose from the floor pillows generously arranged around a table only a bit above the carpeted floor. He started to approach until he saw Loris' mood. "Have you had a hard day?" Donni grasped his forearm.

Loris sighed heavily, returned the gesture and made an effort to temper his answer. "A hard tenday. I'm glad you invited me to Latemeal tonight. Since my Chief Aide's mother died and he's been away, I've been forced to stay in Lukree. I needed this diversion."

At his words, a young member of the serving staff appeared and placed a glass of wine before him. Without imposing further, the staff silently left the chamber.

Donni patted his friend's shoulder in concern. "Relax, then, and let these good people care for you tonight. I've ordered our meal." Donni returned to the table and reclined again on the cushions. "As I remember, you were holding interviews for a new Attendant, too. How did that go?"

"Not as I'd hoped. There's a very capable man from Sumuru whom I'd like to place in the position." He took a sip of his wine and cleared his throat. "However, Bronn doesn't agree. He invited a Terran woman, Kathryn Blair from Luna to apply. I don't think she's appropriate to greet visitors to the Embassy, but COAXIS loved the idea."

Donni leaned forward, "That's your problem?" He gestured his worry, touching the first two fingers of his left hand to those of his right, the gesture teepaa.

Loris smiled. "How smart would I be as an Ambassador to challenge my Chief Aide's hiring practices? Especially one who already disapproves of how I do my job? Statistically, the Chief Aide will replace me when I retire."

Donni mockingly scolded, "That won't be for some time. Is Bronn really the problem you're worrying about?"

"No, Melenta is my problem."

"Ah!" Donni fell back on the pillows and sighed. "I take it she isn't coming home during the break between semesters?"

But Loris didn't answer. He grabbed a cord beside the table. When a server opened the door and bowed, Loris said wearily, "We're ready to be served."

When they were alone again, Donni asked, "What did she say?"

"She didn't say anything because she still won't return my calls. I spoke to Gretta, the aide at the Embassy on Luna. She said Melenta is excelling at her studies and doing very well."

Proudly, Donni nodded. "I knew she would."

"When Gretta offered to arrange passage to Lekton, Melenta replied, 'Why would I do that?' Apparently, my daughter has become proficient in her fighting skills and wishes to use her extra time practicing. Oh, and I'm not to call her Melenta anymore."

Donni raised his eyebrows.

"She's Terranized her name to Melantha Chatrey."

Donni closed his eyes. "She's defining herself, Loris, you know that. Everyone does in upper school. Give it time."

Loris fell on his back, rubbing his hands over his face. "How am I not supposed to feel offended that she refuses to use my name?"

More softly, Donni answered, "I know you miss her. I do, too. Give her time to find her dreams. Lekton is a part of her, so she'll come back one of these moons."

Loris examined his young friend, both admiring and pitying him for his faith. "I can't dwell on this anymore. Tell me some good news."

"Good news?" His optimism failed him. "I wish I knew some. The last three reports passed to me have been situations I couldn't bend. The other Elders on my Council can be so infuriatingly Traditional, especially Leeth Bolaith. How about you? Any positive reports to cheer me up?"

Loris gave a derisive, guttural moan. "Not long ago, I witnessed a man dragging his daughter away from a physician's appointment. While the girl cried, her mother followed them, begging him to let their daughter stay because she was ill. The father made her go back to school anyway. If he'd hurt either of them, I was prepared to call Security myself."

Donni's eyes flashed with indignation. "Where was this?"

"In Sevenn. Knowing that the Representative in that Region wouldn't get involved, I contacted a Lawbender Leader. He promised to assign someone to watch the family closely."

Their conversation was interrupted when servers began delivering their food. But once they were alone, Donni whispered, "What concerns me is that although our numbers are still growing, I see no change in public attitudes, even though, for a while, I did. The cases coming before our Council are increasingly more violent, too. I've spoken to the Scribes of the other Nations about it, and Loris, violent crimes are rising everywhere. What's happening to our world? Since Melenta left, it's like the planet gave up hope."

Suddenly, Loris broke into laughter.

Staring with undisguised disapproval, he asked, "You find that amusing?"

"Melenta used to complain that she made no personal contribution of any consequence. It strikes me as ironic that you mentioned it." With difficulty, he sobered again because the Elder was in no mood for levity. Dropping his head sadly, he said, "Change isn't pretty, my friend. What will the Councils do about it? I'll bet they believe the decline of moral values requires stricter adherence to the Law of Tradition." He punched a pillow beside him.

Donni lowered his head. "Not exactly."

Loris turned pale. "It's worse?"

"I'll try to counteract it, but I should warn you that Bolaith is vigorously campaigning to blame this on our cooperation with COAXIS. It seems your daughter and our planet are both rebelling against growing up."

For a long while, they ate in silence. But when Donni suggested Loris should go to his suite and rest, Loris didn't resist.

Donni said, "I regret how she's hurt you so much on my account. I never should have proposed betrothal."

With a jolt, Loris realized his mistake in not telling his friend the entire truth. "You're not to blame. That's not why she ran away."

"Of course it was. It must be."

He raised his face and quietly murmured, "All Wise, help me."

"Loris?"

He couldn't look at Donni. "Can you come to my suite with me? I think I should make something right with an Elder."

"An Elder?" his friend repeated as if the word were an insult.

"As my friend, I can't let you go on thinking you're responsible for Melenta being angry with me. And as my Elder, you deserve to know why I'm to blame."

Donni groaned. "I won't like this, will I? Shouldn't you talk to a different Elder?"

It would be easier, he thought, *to see the disappointment on someone else's face. But I shouldn't take that way out.* This Elder's forgiveness mattered most to him.

"No. If I don't tell you what I did to drive Melenta away, I couldn't face you again." He pointed to his credoglyph. "I hope you'll forgive me. By avoiding punishment, I disgraced my credo." With great remorse, he expressed shel gaaro, holding his flat palm on his forehead.

Donni grasped his own necklace, as much for reinforcement as for a visual promise, for his credo was Compassion. "Always. Let's go talk."

Luna, COAXIS Institute, May 17, 2167

Each May, the COAXIS Institute on Luna hosted a premier sports event second only to the Olympics held on Terra. This was the

Keplar Competition. Melantha hadn't believed the students who told her how popular the event would be until she attended her first competition. She'd been a spectator at three competitions in the past, but today, she'd be a competitor.

By 17:00, the seats in Shepard Arena were packed with Embassy employees and the students and staff of the Institute. Visitors who hadn't realized they should arrive early were hunting for seats. Journalists and photographers circulated to gather sights and sounds to send home. Although they were pleased with whatever they could get, the story of the day was Melantha Chatrey.

It was something of a rarity that a Lektonian was competing, but one who competed on behalf of Luna was unprecedented. It was unheard of, in fact, that one would attempt to compete after only two-and-a-half years of training.

However, Melantha was doing it, despite the fact that many of the judges, instructors, and martial arts masters in attendance doubted the wisdom of it. But the two Lunaran judges who'd seen her workouts knew there was something exceptional and unique about Melantha's talent. Her Defense Instructors were sure of it, especially her trainer, Specialist Guillermo Ruiz.

Ruiz, who had won a Keplar medal in his last year at the Institute, had carefully groomed her for this day. He'd seen her through the preliminary rounds and into the final rounds of competition. She surprised even him by making it to the last round.

Now, to prevent a journalistic feeding frenzy, he stayed inside the arena to dazzle the press with background information about his famous student. He knew that after today, it would be his last moment in the spotlight.

Inside the locker room at the arena, Melantha heard Ruiz draw the attention of the crowd outside the door with a comment. "Right away, I recognized the treasure in my hands. Patiently, I perfected her abilities, and I'll tell you how." His voice trailed away, and she heard the crowd follow him away from her door.

Melantha smiled at the man beside her, the Institute's Defense Chair, Commander Blake O'Connell.

"Nervous?" O'Connell asked her.

She shook her head. "Excited. Can you believe how many people are here?"

"It's always like this." He was checking her drill suit for tears.

Suddenly, the door burst open, and they were jolted by the eruption of noise coming from the arena. Shoving reporters aside, Commander Elijah Black Horse slipped into the room, pushing the door closed and locking it behind him. "I didn't know I'd be taking my life in my hands to come back and wish you luck."

Confidently, she quipped, "Don't need it."

Black Horse smirked. "I know. This is the last match, Melantha, all or nothing. Samuel Sumatra has muscled his way to the top. You can't forget he won this medal last year. Fight smart, remember what we've taught you, and don't take chances."

Melantha nodded politely. She turned to O'Connell to hear his final recommendations.

The cocky Irishman cursed and told her, "He's a fat, overconfident razorback with more muscle than brains. He hasn't given a single thought to strategy, because he thinks he'll squash you in the first minute. Here's my advice, lass: Sumatra is fast. Be faster. Now you know why, on the day we met, I was so excited to know you're a runner."

Black Horse raised a fist in the air to lead them in their school's victory cry. Melantha and O'Connell raised their fists and with a wicked grin cried in unison, "Conquer!"

Outside the locker room, she heard the accented, Latin voice of Ruiz announce on microphone, "Esteemed guests, turn your attention to ramp B. From the Solotan Nation on Lekton, competitor Melantha Chatrey!"

Outside her door, she heard the exasperated cries of a multitude of reporters who'd thought they were waiting at the right place. "Ramp B? Get out there, hurry!"

Black Horse laughed. "How about that. Guillermo was right. They fell for it."

After the sounds of scrambling footsteps died down, Melantha bowed deeply to the instructors. Black Horse opened the door, and she sprinted up the A ramp into the arena. Her coach waited for her.

Stepping into Guillermo's proud strides, they advanced to the edge of the mat. As one, they bowed to the mat and waited.

The deafening noise didn't bother her now. She blocked it out until it was only an echo. *I'm right where I'm supposed to be,* she told herself.

Another amplified voice announced, "Esteemed guests, turn your attention to Ramp D. From Indonesia on Terra, Keplar Medallist Samuel Sumatra!"

A massive human who nearly tripled her weight pounded into the arena to stand beside his trainer. Advancing, they, too, bowed to the center of the mat. The coach beside Samuel was also no tiny being.

Seemingly without cue, each competitor turned and bowed toward the panel of seven judges. Turning again, they bowed to their respective coaches before striding confidently to the center of the mat. Facing each other, they bowed stiffly.

From that moment, nothing existed for Melantha except the man whom journalists called Goliath. She'd never actually met the giant in person, although Ruiz had prepared dummy opponents to scale to prepare her. The real, deadly mass whose shoulders towered over her head was an entirely different experience. Nevertheless, with a steel expression, she waited.

Curling his lips in an obscene grin of amusement, Sumatra lunged at her. She stepped aside, almost before he moved at all, and she made it look effortless to annoy him. Once again, her uncanny ability to sense aggressive intent before it was channeled to use gave her an edge.

Repeatedly, with bull-like passion, Samuel attempted to crush her under him. Blithely, she bounced over and around him by infuriating instinct, and all the while, she was jabbing and kicking him in undefended places.

Screams of laughter from the stands added to his rage and prodded Goliath into more blind fury. But Melantha kept her cool and refused to devote any notice to diversion. Since scoring was based on blows delivered rather than the damage they achieved, dodging was her best strategy.

Eventually, though, she inflicted a flying kick that landed too close to his defenses, and he scored five deathly slams to her legs and stomach. The cheers from Sumatra's fans threatened to weaken her confidence until she heard Ruiz yell, "Conquer!"

Fighting back pain, she gulped for air and rolled away, concentrating on protecting her head and vital organs. This avoided another devastating blow when he tried to stomp on her face. Those were points she couldn't afford to give him. Sooner or later, he'd get in a few more.

Considering her options, she decided that her opponent's best hope was to hurt her so badly that she couldn't continue. She'd already seen that he didn't feel pain, and he didn't wear out. *I'll stay alive by dodging,* she told herself, *but that won't* win *the match. Think, Melantha!*

Then, she noticed that his drill suit, built to hug the body with a tough, tear-resistant canvas, had loosened at the neck after her last strike. In an instant, her brain recorded a small patch of chest hair showing. This was the opportunity she needed.

She called out, taunting him, "The ladies like that thick head of black hair, don't they? Bet they don't know it's going gray down below."

In the split second of vanity it took him to wonder exactly what part of his anatomy was exposed, she faked an attempt to stomp on his left foot, further drawing his gaze downward. He pulled back his foot and balanced on his right foot.

Simultaneously, she swept her foot across the back of his right knee. Forced to lean right, he was off balance. It was enough to make him vulnerable again.

Melantha issued a barrage of punches to his left side. Before he'd recovered and arrested his fall, she managed to deliver the last three blows to his back needed to win.

Triumphantly, she bounded away from him in backward flips. Now, only now, she heard the crowd chanting, "Scorpion!" Melantha had a new fighting alias.

COAXIS Institute, May 27, 2170

Six years had passed quickly. The day before Commencement, Melantha sat before the mirror in her dorm room. Comb in hand, she pulled at an obstinate snarl in her hair, muttering, "Your life's a mess, but don't take it out on your hair."

Since leaving Lekton, she'd enjoyed her Terran lifestyle, complete with a new, Terranized name. She'd earned unprecedented notoriety in her field by winning the Keplar after only a little more than two years of training. By the age of twenty-six, she'd won three more Keplar medals and finished a degree program. With these successes, she'd chiseled away the last of her weakness and lack of confidence.

But though her extraordinary ability made her famous, it also alienated her from everyone except her instructors. Fame definitely discouraged the attention of men, a fact that gave her satisfaction.

Her life as a loner had always made her happy until rumors started. She wasn't sure when these lies began to circulate on campus, but she knew to the day when they started to impact her life.

In January of her last year in school, vague whispers floated around campus suggesting that there was a Tserian in her graduating class. Since Tserians are shape-changers, no one could prove it. And anyway, they weren't allowed on Luna. At the Second Interworld Conference of 2121, COAXIS banned them from any member world.

To Melantha, the idea was ridiculous, since Luna ought to be the last place a Tserian would infiltrate. Nevertheless, the rumor persisted, virulent as a plague.

Then, in February, three classmates accused her of being Tserian. Despite a lack of evidence other than her habit of keeping to herself, the entire campus believed it. Even a few instructors wondered if it explained her uncanny ability in martial arts.

But it wasn't the accusation that hurt most. In March, as plans were finalized for the Commencement ceremony, the members of the class were asked to choose a partner to march with in the processional. No one would march beside Melantha. It made no difference that she was a Keplar hero or the daughter of Lekton's COAXIS Ambassador. She'd become a social outcast, and she didn't know why.

Finally, she learned why everyone avoided her. Another rumor had spread that there were two Tserian students graduating. Suddenly, everyone was afraid to go near Melantha for fear of being branded as "the other Tserian."

Now, the face looking back from the mirror was hard and unforgiving. "This is exactly why you never should have tried to fit in here. Haven't you learned yet to simply blend into the background?"

Still, her heart wanted to fight back. "It isn't fair, especially not to someone whose credo is Justice. On Lekton, offending one's credo is a punishable offense."

But she didn't live on Lekton anymore, and for the first time, she was homesick. Nothing she did helped stop the rumors, even her letter of protest posted in the campus paper. *But it did feel good to fight back,* she thought vengefully. *My final statement was pretty good.*

Sitting back, she recalled it again.

"Some have said my preference for solitude shows I'm afraid of being discovered to be a Changer. If I don't enjoy the company of other people, their vicious slander only justifies my preference. For this reason, I refuse to attend the commencement ceremony with my class."

Melantha had known that her decision would disappoint her classmates who wanted to brag about the celebrity in their midst. It would also harm the administrators who were planning a special tribute to her at the ceremony. But she didn't care, because they'd done nothing to help her fight the slander.

But that decision also hurt her father, and she did care about that. He wouldn't be coming to Luna after all, and that was a direct affront to the diplomats at the Embassy who had planned to honor him during the visit.

She looked again at her reflection. "Do you want to carry it that far?"

She went to her desk and sat down at the computer. Reluctantly scrolling through correspondence files, she found the last letter from Loris. He'd been so disappointed, especially since the Lunaran Embassy had prepared for his visit. He'd thought her decision was made solely to avoid facing him, which he found petty and immature.

That could be true, she thought. *But I think I was aiming the revenge more at my classmates.*

Then, she saw his strongest enticement. The letter said, "If you'll attend the ceremony, I promise to bring Cheelo. He's sixteen and can make his own decision about it." If Loris had arranged that with Lukeniss, it was a miracle. She wasn't comfortable about seeing her father, but she missed her brother very much. *After so many seasons away from each other,* she wondered, *could Cheelo and I ever be close again? Shouldn't we try?*

Melantha resisted reading more of her father's heartbreaking letter. His last line had been a tempting offer to pay for the ticket if she'd come to see him and Cheelo. If she read it again, she might weaken and accept that offer.

Restless, angry and bored in the tiny student apartment, Melantha decided to go for a brisk jog to exercise away the tensions that had been keeping her from sleeping well. She pulled out her running shoes. Before she'd fastened them, however, there was a knock at her door.

She called to the wall comm, "Who is it?"

A voice responded from the comm, "I'm the class president. May I talk to you?"

"Are you sure you want Melantha Chatrey?"

"I'm sure."

Hesitantly, she opened the door. The young, Terran man was tall, athletic and handsome by any standard. Pointedly, she didn't return his smile as he said, "I'm David Bellini. This is a little awkward, but could I come in? It's important."

Melantha stepped back. "Come in."

The man appraised her dorm room. "I'm surprised to see Terran furnishings. I expected no furniture and lots of pale colors."

"You came to criticize my taste?"

"No, I'm sorry. I meant no offense, it was just an observation."

She relaxed. "I'm more Terranized than most Lektonians at the Institute. Please, sit down." She sat at her desk.

He sat at the small dinette. "I wondered if you've been asked to march with anyone at Commencement."

"I don't know what you want," she said, standing. "But I won't tolerate bad manners in my home. I'm tired of this teasing. Leave, before I forget and misuse my defense training."

The man also stood. "I think you've misunderstood me. I'm asking because I want to march with you."

"Aren't you afraid of damaging your reputation by being seen with a Tserian?"

"Not a bit. You're not Tserian. I don't know why the idiots at school can't figure it out, since you have purple eyes. Tserians always have green eyes, no matter what form they take."

She studied him and decided he was sincere.

"Anyway," David continued, carefully touching her hand and retreating from the sting of her deflector, "I happen to know it's impossible for a Tserian to duplicate a deflector field. I've studied medicine, you know. Even have a degree."

Melantha admired David's courage in offering to risk his reputation to make her feel better. She answered, "Thanks for the offer, but I'm not going. Rumor has it that two Tserian students are graduating. If you're with me, people would assume you're the other one."

Without a blink, he replied, "I am."

CHAPTER 20

Fighting to control the heat rising in her, she glared at him. "Don't joke about it. I've been harassed and ridiculed for months. Believe me, it's not funny."

He looked into her eyes, carefully stating, "Melantha, I'm not joking."

Then she saw it—his eyes were an unusually dark shade of green.

Nervously, he shifted his weight from foot to foot. "I feel horrible that someone else has been taking the cruelty meant for me. As president of the graduating class, that position has protected me, but I didn't think anyone would get hurt."

Melantha knew that someone else, probably anyone else, would be frightened. But he had no reason to hurt her. Logically, he'd avoid making trouble on Luna. Like her, David had come to earn a degree. *He'll be a physician,* she thought, *and help his people.* That was noble.

But that wouldn't matter. He was violating COAXIS law, and she was a licensed COAXIS Enforcer, although an unemployed one. She should report him.

Concerned about her silence, he frowned. "I thought that if I'm seen with you at Commencement, maybe my popularity and position would make the teasing stop."

Melantha thought, *how much trouble would I be in if I don't report him, especially since my father is an Ambassador?* She replied, "It's kind of you to offer, but I wasn't planning to go."

He hung his head. "I'll understand if you don't want to be seen with me."

Is he trying to make me feel guilty for what he's been through? I didn't ban Tserians from attending the school, and it's not my responsibility to make it up to him. He's wrong if he thinks that's going to change my mind.

But then he reached for the door button, and he was in a hurry to leave. Without facing her, he said, "I didn't mean to offend you. I'll leave."

She was stunned. *Did David truly think my refusal was because of racial bias?* "Wait! I didn't mean to insult you. It's not because you're Tserian. I just don't want to reward their prejudice. You'd really want to march with me?"

His smile relieved her. "If you wouldn't mind."

Considering the trust he'd placed in her by confiding his identity to a stranger, how could she refuse? Still, one burning question remained, though she probably knew the answer. "Have you ever told anyone else on Luna where you're from?"

He whispered, "It's not safe to tell anyone as long as there's so much distrust and hatred. Knowing the harm you'd cause by telling, I think you'll be careful with the secret."

"Aren't you frightened of being here?"

"Every day. I probably shouldn't have involved you. You could get in trouble."

"Wouldn't be the first time," she laughed.

His voice grew hopeful. "So, will you march with me tomorrow? And will you attend the party with me afterward?"

She didn't hesitate. "I'd be honored. May I ask if there's another Tserian student here?"

Cautiously, he whispered, "There are several. Of course, COAXIS doesn't know that. If you want, I'll tell you more about my people."

"I'd love it!" said Melantha with genuine enthusiasm. "Learning about other worlds is my favorite hobby."

He was still wary of good fortune. "You aren't scared or offended to be with an alien?"

"On Luna, we're both aliens."

Finally relieved, he smiled, revealing what her acceptance meant to him.

"I've been an outcast, too, David."

COAXIS Institute, May 28, 2170

Melantha waited until the last possible moment before she entered the room where the graduates would line up for the processional. She felt horribly awkward wearing the regalia that seemed uncomfortably similar to an Elder's official robes of office. Mostly, she wanted to be sure David was present before she faced her classmates.

As she entered, a hush began at the door and spread through the room amid whispers of her name. Beside her, a man observed dryly, "You changed your mind about commencement. I guess our company is good enough for Tserians after all."

Attempting to maintain the placid and expressionless facade for which she was known, Melantha ignored the man who'd made that comment. She knew her face must have betrayed her relief, though, when she saw David pushing through the crowd.

"Hey, Bellini!" shouted a man across the room. "Someone with your connections ought to be able to get a human date."

Unlike Melantha, David couldn't disregard his classmate's rude behavior. "A human date? In this room? I seem to have found the only one."

Melantha ignored everyone and turned her attention to David. He was a distinguished figure and carried himself with dignity. She knew that the women at the Institute found him appealing.

Although she didn't want to admit it, she did, too. *How nice it must be,* she thought, *to be able to choose how one wanted to look.*

Suddenly, David took her hand. Without thinking, she released her deflector emission to protect him. Although she expected to dislike sensing his emotions, it wasn't so bad.

He said, "Let's claim our degrees and head to the party!"

But two hours later when Commencement ended, Melantha and David stopped outside the door of the Center City Hotel's Grand Ballroom. Hesitating, she told him, "This party isn't that important to me."

His eyes were dark behind glistening, black lashes. Melantha realized that he felt responsible for her hurt feelings.

She reflected upon the danger he faced by being on Luna. This party seemed like the last place they should be. She asked him, "Do you mind if we skip it? We could go for a walk."

"My very idea. Let's leave."

The night air was still and warm, one of a variety of programmed environments that were, for the most part, enjoyable. Randomly, the city's programmers threw in a storm or two to simulate life on Terra.

But on this night, the weather was perfect. Melantha followed David as he strolled casually through campus. She resisted holding his hand, though, and he didn't mind. Soon, the silence became oppressive, compelling her to fill it. She said, "Terrans say that if you've seen Luna, you've seen Terra, but I don't believe it."

"You're right. Here, the air is carefully manufactured to eliminate impurities, and real weather doesn't exist. I've heard about the violent storms on Terra that cropped up in the last century, but we have nothing like that here."

"But I wish I could see snow," she commented. "I've never been to Lekton's high ranges, but I understand there's snow there."

Again, the conversation lapsed. She thought, *this is my chance to learn about Tserians, and all I can do is bring up weather?*

David led her to a park at the center of campus. He stopped and faced her, as if something important had occurred to him. Quietly, he confided, "The Terrans love greenery, don't they? It's supposed to comfort them while they're away from home. It does nothing for me."

She snorted in derisive agreement. "No kidding. But I have to admit that, sometimes, I wouldn't mind seeing a lavender sky or a blue bush around here."

They walked on, comfortable at last without words until they reached a fountain. In its center, water trickled gently down a granite symbol of the Confederation. She admired how the drops sparkled in a pool below. At the fountain's base, lights reflected on the water like glittering jewels, and spotlights illuminated the inscribed words of the COAXIS Motto. She read it aloud:

"We are the Confederated Orders of Anthropoid/Xyloids in Interstellar Service. We seek the universal good. We employ understanding through a common foundation. Let it be peace which unites us in strength, in leadership and in brotherhood."

David moved close behind her. She expected it when his hands rested on her shoulders. It was that same, mysterious feeling she got right before an opponent attacked her.

She questioned her reaction. *Why did that happen? He isn't hurting me.*

"Some brotherhood," he whispered. "I appreciate being able to say this to someone who understands it: This place is so... alien! Why do Terrans love parks so much?"

His touch made her uncomfortable, as touching always did. Casually, she moved away and sat on the rim of the fountain. "I can appreciate the principle of creating a place to get away from people so I can relax and think."

He squinted his eyes, and her evasion confused him. He opened another subject and moved closer to her again. "Not me. On my world, it would be a crime to waste moisture as a form of art or recreation. And we don't cherish time alone or away from others, either. The very concept horrifies me."

She wondered if that was why he kept moving nearer whenever she backed off.

"I can't conceive of individuality or of being a unit whole and entire within oneself. You see, we're born in pairs, and we have a symbiotic link to our birthmates. Together, Ru-Mena and I are one being. When I began my studies in biology, I was surprised to learn that my species seems to be the only one of its kind."

"So far," she corrected.

He smiled and conceded the point. "I guess Xylonia could eventually find others like us."

Realizing what he'd said, she froze. "You thought other people changed their shapes?"

"Not only that. There are other differences. For example, humanoids are born without a mate and have to find someone to unite with in order to conceive offspring. How efficient is that? And then, after they locate a partner, only half the pair is involved in the actual birth."

Melantha laughed. "Well, yes."

"You laugh, but that even sounds strange to me. Why be born singly if it requires two beings to continue the species? But then, why require two to mate when only one is required to bear the young? It's crazy!"

She shook her head. "Sounds right to me."

"It's different, that's all. At birth, we're already mated and in an immediate reproductive state. Once in our lifetime, our cycle will mature, and we'll bear a litter, anywhere from one to four pairs of children. Both Tserian partners are needed to participate in the actual birth."

"Really? This is hard to grasp." It wasn't the topic but his proximity that bothered her.

Concerned by her avoidance, he stood. "You must find this repulsive. Don't worry. Racial bias is understandable."

Analyzing that statement, she decided that her behavior was being misunderstood. She stood with him, feeling ashamed. "No, I want to understand. Explain more to me."

"Why?" He turned away and looked up at a reproduced grid of holographic stars.

Of all people, she understood his reluctance to believe that anyone would accept him. Walking slowly away, she waved to him to follow.

Inhaling deeply, he followed her. "Why do you want to know?"

"Since I was young, I've always been fascinated by the cultures of other worlds. That's why I came to school here. Very little is taught about Tserian culture."

"What is taught is mostly wrong," he admitted as he joined her for a walk. "Please remember, though, that nothing can be repeated."

She pretended offense. "Of course not! I happen to be a bonded Security Agent, sworn to keep privileged information to myself. Even have a degree."

Looking around him to assure himself they were alone, he told her, "I trust you with my secrets. Someday, I may need to trust you with my life. If I do, I want someone to know…"

"Are you in trouble?"

"COAXIS doesn't allow Tserians to live here, Melantha. We're all in trouble."

She glared suspiciously when he avoided her eyes. She demanded an explanation. "That's not what you meant. Tell me."

"All right, I'll tell you, then. Our world is in trouble, and Emperor Dur wanted help from COAXIS. Since they'd never willingly help us, he decided to steal the knowledge. He chose the most talented young men of his family to attend the Institute on Luna."

"Why Luna?"

He seemed embarrassed. "Luna has lenient admission standards, so it was easy to falsify student records and identification documents. We've been sent here to get an education and to take that knowledge home."

"Why shouldn't Tserias benefit from COAXIS membership?"

"Exactly. It's a noble quest, but I don't think it's the only reason. Emperor Dur has another motive for doing this. He chose only men of the royal House. Why? Don't get me wrong; we were eager to have this chance. When it was presented to us, we agreed to the plan. But even though we agreed to go, Dur took our birth-mates hostage until we return."

Melantha shrieked, "Hostage?"

He glared, urging her to lower her voice. "They're being held in prison cells, but who knows why? It wasn't as if we needed an incentive to keep our existence on Luna a secret."

"True. I think you're right—there must be another reason."

"I believe there's something Dur will ask us to do with our new knowledge, and he'll need bargaining power to ask it."

"Maybe he just wants to help his people and thinks you won't come back without a reason."

David laughed, a sound of pain rather than humor. "Don't think that some things you've heard about us aren't true. We aren't known for honesty, not even with each other."

"I'll bet you could change that," she said confidently.

"Now that I've learned ethical values, maybe so. But I won't get that chance."

Tears fell from his eyes, and his sorrow touched her. Gently, she asked, "Why did you agree to come here if you knew the Emperor would hold your mates hostage?"

"We didn't know before we left, and we wanted the education. After we arrived here, he took our property and captured our mates."

"And you're sure about that?"

"I knew exactly when it happened. Remember what I said about our symbiotic relationship? Ru-Mena is my mate, but there's also a level of our minds on which we exist together and communicate directly."

Not too unlike a Lektonian relationship during joining, thought Melantha. "That sounds wonderful." Spontaneously, she wrapped an arm around his shoulder and continued walking.

The contact relieved his loneliness right away. "I knew you'd listen."

"You rescued me, so I owe you."

Suddenly, he stopped, grabbed her arms and whispered harshly, "I can't see you after this. No one must suspect that I've enlisted your help, not even other Tserians! There are a hundred princes of the royal House here, as well as a squad of the Emperor's Infiltrators. They're like secret agents sent to spy on us. That's part of Dur's strategy: We can't know whom to trust."

Melantha looked squarely into David's frightened, green eyes and solemnly promised him, "All right. I'll stay away, but if you call, I'll help you."

David left Melantha at her dorm and watched the night sky in silence. Inwardly, he called out to Ru-Mena. *Did I hurt you tonight by being with her, my love?*

He heard his mate's familiar voice whisper in his mind. *Da-Meed, I know your heart. I don't mind that you were with her, but was it wise to confide in her?*

She's the only person I can trust.

I don't trust anyone. Be careful!

Tserias, 10th of Rhag, Year of Dead Trees (May 28, 2170 TSE)

Emperor Ja-Ebra ab Durab reclined on sumptuous, pink satin pillows that supported his overly abundant abdomen. He disregarded the contempt his comfort caused the guards who stood in every corner of the Imperial Hall. They had no such luxuries, because they weren't heirs of the royal House of Dur, ruler of all Tserias!

Settling back on four of his eight tentacles, he sighed with pleasure and patted his royal chins. A gleeful chortle escaped him as they jiggled, mumbling to himself, "Some privileges I refuse to give up because of the famine."

Two skinny servant girls entered the Hall. Their translucent, membranous skin was covered with dust in the reverential form. Each was overburdened with a huge tray of food balanced upon their heads. Sitting back on their rumps before the Emperor, they presented the meal using all eight limbs. They were also ogling the contents of their trays.

"Have you stolen any?" growled Ja-Ebra.

"No, Great Dur!" they cried in unison. With pincers shaking, they laid the food on the table near their Emperor.

"I'll find out if you do!"

Whimpering in fear, they reverently folded their many appendages over their eyes. Humbly, they scurried backward and out the doorway.

With eager gluttony, Ja-Ebra sampled the tempting delicacies. "I'll hold a different tidbit in each pincer!" He smiled at the wanton waste of using the planet's dwindling growing fields for his private feasts. Because the guards and staff at his palace feared him, they'd never tell his secret. If they did, they knew he would stop giving them enough food to feed their families. The people of Tserias wouldn't find out that the Emperor of the House of Dur grew fat on precious foodstuffs while, around him, his people died of starvation.

"Would it matter if they knew," he exclaimed defiantly? "I am Emperor!"

He closed his eyes and devoured a sweet fruit. It amused him when the juices clung in sticky droplets to his rippling chins.

Hearing a sound, he turned. Ba-Rendo, the High Inquisitor humbly waited at the door for an audience with the Emperor.

Ja-Ebra saw him but purposely let him wait. After a few more well enjoyed bites, he grumbled, "Do you plan to watch while I digest it, too? What is it, and be quick. You're disturbing my meal!"

Ba-Rendo stumbled over three of his unusually long tentacles in his haste to prostrate himself before the throne. "Great Dur, your Infiltrators on Luna who watch the royal princes report that they despair for their birth-mates. Some are making trouble."

"Kill them, then," he answered casually.

"As you command, Great Dur. However, if I may be permitted ..."

"Don't question me! Could you use that ugly face of yours without a mouth?"

"I would not question the Royal Son, Ja-Ebra ab Dur!"

"Durab!" corrected the Emperor. "I'm of the House of Dur, but I'm the oldest heir, so don't forget the suffix."

Ba-Rendo hid his eyes in shame. "I beg forgiveness. I'm only your humble advisor. I thought you'd wish to know that the noblemen on Luna are your loyal servants. They're eager to bring back to you their stolen learning. They simply fear for their mates."

"As well they should. And my cousin of the House of Belne, is he also in such distress?" Of all men, Ja-Ebra knew that Da-Meed, the next oldest of his line would be the greatest threat to keeping his throne.

"It was reported that he's quite unhappy, but he fears you."

"Good. He's caused me too much trouble over the years. I only need one excuse to keep his Ru-Mena from him. Da-Meed will obey me, or Ru-Mena will die."

"Does the Great Dur still wish to have the noblemen killed if they disapprove of their lands and mates being assigned to you? If you do, I will personally..."

"No, no. Keep them alive. I want their knowledge brought back when they finish their education. Besides, my littermates would give me no end of grief for harming their children. No, I want that knowledge. I'll make COAXIS regret banishing us. We'll take their knowledge and start our own school!"

"Yes, Great Dur!" cheered Ba-Rendo. He assumed an informal posture. Shortening two of his tentacles and resting them on the ground before him, he leaned forward.

But the Emperor said no more. Dismissing himself with his remaining limbs carefully folded across his eyes, Ba-Rendo left the Imperial Hall. He had status enough in the palace to withdraw at a more dignified pace than the serving girls had.

Ja-Ebra belched, sighed with satisfaction and then reclined again on his plump pillows. His emerald eyes danced with visions of his revenge. "The Confederation will pay!"

Unexpectedly, his tortured mind heard the moaning wail of his dead mate, the voice he'd so loved. She cried, "Ja-Ebra, don't let me die of this disease!"

Since the moment the mysterious sickness took her, Jo-Eena had haunted his mind with these unrelenting ghost whispers.

The Emperor collapsed, holding his head with four tentacles. "Jo-Eena!"

He never knew he'd spoken aloud. His own plaintive reply startled him. He looked around him, but couldn't see her. "Jo-Eena? I had no medicines or doctors to save you."

A delightful idea suddenly occurred to Ja-Ebra, and his demeanor changed completely. "I could watch myself digest! I was joking with Ba-Rendo, but what a purely sinful way to enjoy my private banquet even more!"

Excited now, he balanced on three limbs extended behind him and stared through the gelatinous, gray membrane of skin at the food moving through his system.

"How very fun this is!"

For a few blissful moments, Ja-Ebra ab Durab forgot his dead mate. When this folly grew dull, he'd invent another one. He'd occupy his mind and keep out Jo-Eena's reproachful haunting.

Luna, COAXIS Institute, June 2, 2170

Five days after she graduated, Melantha sat in the office of the Defense Director, Commander Blake O'Connell, but no longer as a student. Her Specialty degree also ended her amateur status in martial arts. As a confirmed martial arts master, she waited now for her first job interview.

But she had nothing to prove to her professor, who had asked her to apply. That gave her confidence, but she worried about the wisdom of taking a permanent job on Luna. Her heart almost ached to see Cheelo again.

It also didn't help her anxiety that O'Connell was late for the interview. Her imagination tried to conjure up Tserian plots to keep her from staying on Luna. *But that's silly,* she told herself.

In the intervening days since meeting David, she'd been exceptionally paranoid. She thought Tserian Infiltrators were spying on her.

No, she declared firmly to herself. *More likely, O'Connell's delaying on purpose to rattle me and test my resistance to stress. Such tests are nothing to watching out for shape changers.*

The door opened and her professor rushed in, his thin, auburn hair flying. "I'm sorry, Melantha. I got caught in a meeting."

She noted that he'd apparently adjusted well to the stress of schedule interruptions, because he grabbed up her resume and went right to work. After only glancing at the page, he laughed at himself, tossing it on his desk. "Why do I need to read this?"

She laughed with him. "Especially since every qualification on there is what you and your staff taught me. Thank you, by the way."

Smiling, he sat back and clasped large, toughened hands over his chest. "A most rewarding job. We should be thanking you. Each time you won a medal, the Security Instructors got a raise. Coaching you will secure a Command degree for Guillermo, too."

Humbly, she blushed. "He deserves it." She never liked discussing her achievements and routinely denied her over-inflated reputation.

Abruptly, the Commander sat up straight and slapped his hands flat on the desk and his mood became professional once more. "Well, your letter stated that you want to take a job and support yourself. But what do you want to do with your training in the long run?"

Taking his cue, Melantha switched to a professional mode. "I've enjoyed teaching the new defense students. I'd be pleased to make it a career."

"If so, I recommend that you continue your education toward a Command degree."

"I've already registered to start in September. My internship with Galactic Enforcement convinced me I'm not made to be a GEA Enforcer."

He nodded, smirking at her remark. During her internship, he'd received continuous complaints from the Unit Commander about her inability to take orders.

He told her, "In your defense, I can tell you that anyone with a positive, independent self-image doesn't fare well with that bunch. You have other options. What about private agencies, like Security Central? Or, if you want to move back home, Lektonian Security often hires Defenders who are COAXIS trained."

"I've considered both of those agencies. I keep returning to how much I enjoy teaching."

He nodded. "Well, you can take some time to decide long term plans while you work on your Command degree, right? Meanwhile, this position as Instructor will start in two months. You'd be teaching physical fitness training to non-majors and first-year Defense to majors. You'd monitor your share of evening drill sessions for the public, too. As you know, the martial arts have a big following on Luna. And of course, as a Keplar medallist, you can take private coaching clients if you want, and I hope you do."

"It wouldn't offend Guillermo … I mean Master Ruiz?"

"First names are appropriate if you're a member of the staff. And I think Guillermo will have plenty of continuing clients without fighting over them."

"Sounds good to me."

Clapping his hands and rubbing them together enthusiastically, he declared, "That's what I want to hear! The job is yours. I ask only that you take a long, restful vacation on Lekton before you start work."

The thought of returning home and having to avoid Loris bothered her. She shook her head and smiled, "That's not necessary."

"I think it is," he said with a shrewd wink. In his strongest Gaelic accent, he told her, "That's me terms, lass."

She gave it thought. *After facing the fiercest opponents in the Confederation, why is it so hard to face Loris again? Meeting David wasn't this frightening. I overcame slanderous rumors and rejection by my classmates, but I'm afraid to face one old man?*

But helping her new friend had also brought up a few of her own emotional issues, and she realized how much she needed to see Cheelo.

And although she'd never expected to miss Lekton, David's longing to go home had infected her. So, she decided to accept her father's offer to pay for her passage to Lekton. His diplomatic status would rate her an expedited trip through the Xylonian Doorway and have her home in four days.

And lucky for me, after a visit, this job on Luna gives me a valid excuse to leave again.

The commander reminded her, "Your body needs the rest. Remember that you'll be facing continued training for your degree. To maintain your security bonding, you'll also have to attend a two-hour drill one evening a week. And don't forget the early morning runs you'll lead for your daily Fitness class."

"Maybe rest isn't such a bad idea," she admitted. "I'll take the job. If you need me sooner, you can reach me on Lekton. Thank you, Commander."

Grinning, he extended his hand and told her, "Call me Blake."

CHAPTER 21

San Durg, 27 Breel, 2170 (June 7 TSE)

On a clear, Half-light morning, the ICT set down at the Soloto Skyport in San Durg. After carefully scrutinizing every passenger disembarking at Lekton to be sure no one had green eyes, Melantha relaxed and stepped onto the gray soil of home. Regardless of her feelings about the planet's laws, it was home, and coming home was a good feeling. Bittersweet memories swarmed over her with every breeze, it seemed, and she cherished the familiar, pungent-sweet fragrance. She smiled at the pale, purple sky and orchid hues casting around her. She'd stopped squinting since there was none of the glare she was used to on Luna.

And thanks to her fit condition, the increased gravity didn't bother her at all. How different Lekton was from the effusively green environment of Luna! Suddenly, her homesickness made more sense to her. *Lekton's always been good to me. It was people who mistreated me, and people who created the Laws that allowed it. But I love Lekton.*

From behind her came a familiar voice, one she'd dreaded. "Welcome back."

Taking a mental deep breath, she turned to greet Loris. But she wasn't prepared for what she saw. His impressive figure was noticeably older and not so imposingly tall. The lightning spark that had earned Loris a formidable career in politics was missing from his eyes. The weariness in those pale, blue eyes stung her conscience, for she knew she'd put it there.

She asked, "What's happened to you, Loris? Are you ill?"

"It's not important. I've missed you." Against her will, he took her hands and murmured, "You've changed, too."

Behind him, she saw his light blue shuttle. Using that excuse to pull her hands away, she went to the craft and gave the hull a fond pat. "We've seen a few Regions in this, haven't we?"

With effort, Loris pretended he wasn't hurt and tried to be glad he could see her at all.

She said, "I wanted to thank you for sending fresh vegetables and fruits from your garden. I don't like relying on pills for the Lektonian vitamins and minerals I need."

"It's your garden, too, Melenta." Purposely, he used that name, expecting her objection.

Politely, she stated, "I prefer to be called Melantha now."

"Melenta is who you are, despite what you call yourself."

She stiffened at the inevitability of a disagreement. "But it's what I want to be called, even if it isn't who you think I am."

He slowed his strides. "Why is this name special to you?"

Melantha froze in place and faced him. "It just is."

Loris looked into her beautiful, lavender eyes that were so like Kamira's. Standing tall, he called upon reserves of self-pride to renew him. "Then, please recognize my feelings and call me Father, even if it isn't who you think I am. That name is special to me."

As he'd hoped, his logic stunned her. When she didn't reply, he knew it was time to settle the old disagreement. Loris said, "Will this heartache continue? I love you, and my health is too frail to endure more strain. I've never understood exactly what hurt you. I wronged Lukeniss by my intrusion in his marriage. I brought about your birth, which caused my brother to mistreat you. I withheld the truth from you. My shame is just punishment. But I cannot allow dishonor to my name that isn't justified."

She interrupted, "This isn't the time to talk about it."

He ignored her. "But I've also done a few good things. I fought for you and protected you. I loved you and provided for your needs, including your education. For that, don't I deserve at least the honorary title of Father?"

Her body was tense in rigid denial, but her eyes were lowered; not in denees, but because she didn't want him to see the shame she was starting to feel. In her heart she knew he was right, but she was too stubborn and proud to tell him.

Hesitantly, he continued, "Of course, I'd prefer to be called Father because you return my love." Again, he reached out. This time, he only extended his hands and waited.

She stared at her father's hands. His invitation to join and renew their affection felt threatening. She blurted out, "You knew why Lukeniss hated me, but you didn't tell me! For nineteen seasons, you let me believe that I wasn't worth loving."

Loris lowered his eyes thoughtfully, but without guilt. Instead, his brow was furrowed in confused concentration. "I never realized that was what you thought. Believe me, dear, if I'd known that you blamed yourself for his behavior, I'd have told you sooner. I thought protecting your mother's honor was the right thing to do."

Astonished, she thought, *he really didn't know! He wasn't trying to protect himself; he was trying to protect Maata.*

Old and bitter resentments evaporated inside her as she confirmed, "Protecting her was the right thing to do, and I appreciate that."

He shook his head in disbelief. "To me, your honor was never in question. I thought you believed that Lukeniss hated you because he's a hateful person."

His sincerity convicted her. Melantha was ashamed of how she'd treated this kind man who'd never intentionally hurt her. *All these seasons of being angry … it was for this? Why didn't I let him explain?*

Self-consciously, she wiped away a torrent of tears and replied, "He really is hateful, isn't he?" They both laughed.

Accepting her part in the misunderstanding, she clasped her father's hands and lowered her deflector. Gratefully, both released every inhibition. They blended their emotions until the force of it, even borne together, overwhelmed them. They sank to the ground beside their shuttle and clung to each other.

In Kaanotok Township

Melantha was pleased to find her sleep chamber hadn't changed. She ran a finger along the garland of gold and white twine flowers that framed the door. More than anything, she was glad she'd learned to duplicate her mother's craftwork. It cheered her now.

The walls had been freshly painted in the same muted mauve she'd picked out long ago. Even the soft, gray fur she'd slept on was where she'd left it, although a new layer of padding had been added beneath it. The fur-bed was inviting, but she had other plans.

Finding her father in the garden, she told him, "I'm going to take a run around the estate." She started her stretches.

He warned, "You've been away six seasons. I've heard it isn't easy to switch back to a higher gravity."

"I'll take it easy. Have you spoken to Cheelo? Do you think he'll see me?"

"I called him once I knew you were coming. He'd like to see you."

That relieved her mind. She wasn't at all sure how her little brother felt about her.

When her stretches drifted into martial arts drill forms, she discovered that the elevated gravity did have an effect on her speed and the fluidity of movement. And while the air had a more pleasant odor, it wasn't quite as free of pollutants as she was used to on Luna.

Puzzled about her workout, her father commented, "That's an unusual kind of exercise."

"This is only the beginning. The rest is much more vigorous. Drills like these helped me learn fighting skills."

He winced. He'd made it clear when she started Defense classes that he was uncomfortable with his daughter participating in fights.

She put her arms around his neck and touched her forehead to his. "I told you not to worry about me. I'm a very good Defender."

He sighed heavily. "If you believe so, I'll try to relax."

She stroked the back of his head lovingly and backed away. "Father, while I go for a run, could you please contact my brother? Ask him if I can meet him in San Durg tomorrow, and tell him I want to spend two moons with him."

He agreed, and Melantha started her run.

Circling the manor, she headed for the carved, black iron gate, the only entrance in the two-meter high, stone wall.

She enjoyed an exhilarating run. As much as she didn't want to admit it, though, she returned exhausted. At First-rest, she added two cycles more to her normal four cycles of sleep.

To be kind, her father said nothing.

San Durg, 29 Breel, 2170

Very early the next morning, Melenta and her father flew to San Durg. At the shuttle port, he told her, "I hope you won't mind, but I'd better leave."

Melantha knew he was trying to prevent a chance meeting with Lukeniss. Ever since he'd adopted her, the brothers hadn't been on speaking terms. But she trusted Cheelo to keep Lukeniss from running into either of them, for everyone's sake.

Loris told her, "I've left word at the San Durg Inn to give you whatever you need. I'll stay with Donni while you're visiting Cheelo. Whenever you're ready to go home, call my pocket comm."

"Greet Donni for me."

"Greet him yourself. I've invited him to Late-meal when we get home."

She bristled, showing that she was afraid to see his old friend, and yet she also wanted to.

They parted company, and Melantha headed for the port's lounge to meet her brother.

The lounge was a spacious, softly lit area filled with cushions and benches. On this day, it was crowded. *Will I be able to recognize Cheelo*, she wondered? The last time she'd seen him, he was a little boy. He'd be sixteen, now—grown and most likely attending an upper school. She earnestly hoped he lived on his own, rather than with Lukeniss.

And then, across the room, she barely recognized his slim, tall figure. She remembered a five-year-old Cheelo running joyfully into her arms as she walked in from school. Now, the man walking slowly toward her was distinguished and reserved. *Lukeniss certainly has taught him to preserve Dignity*, she thought dryly. Bowing, he greeted her with the gesture taama J'len, and said politely, "Mel, it's been so long! I'd begun to wonder if I'd ever see you again."

She longed to embrace him, but she couldn't seem to move. *A formal greeting*, she thought, *between us? It has been too long.* Straining to reduce the awkward ceremony, she answered, "I wouldn't let that happen. You've grown so much! I think you're as tall as I am."

She thought, *who is this? I was gone when he entered sklensonn. That growth stage made him a different person, almost grown to maturity. He's much blonder than I remember, and his body looks strong and rugged. Even his voice is totally different.*

She knew it wouldn't be long before Cheelo declared a credo and become a Familyhead. Would he risk offending Lukeniss by picking a credo other than Dignity?

Cheelo thought, *who is this? She's lived with Terrans so long that she looks and acts like one. She's lost weight, but she looks muscled and strong. Why isn't she wearing her hair the right way? It's twisted behind her back in some kind of braid like Mother's twine crafts. Even her eyes look alert, as if she's scrutinizing everything around her. Apparently, living among Terrans taught her to be on her guard at all times.*

His heart pounded in his ears as he came closer. "You've really changed, too. Would you like to sit down? Get a meal?"

He gestured gleenay to ask her to follow. They entered a small diner down the street. Sitting across from Cheelo, she clasped her hands on the table and stared at them. She said, "I've missed so much of your life. Fill me in on everything you've done."

"You won't like it," he warned.

Now, she looked into his eyes. "Are you still in trouble with your mentor?"

Cocking his head to one side, he asked suspiciously, "You know about that?"

"Elder Chonaira kept Father advised about a few things."

He gave a bemused laugh. "No, that problem was handled long ago. He was dismissed, and I got a new mentor."

"I see. Lukeniss certainly likes that method of dealing with mentors, doesn't he?"

He frowned, thinking, *apparently, Terrans don't practice good manners, either. Has she totally forgotten how to honor Tradition? She might think Father is a monster, but she ought to know that I don't.*

Then, she seemed to realize how spiteful she'd been. *On Luna, people are given the freedom to say what they please, but they still try to be considerate about it.* Gesturing gaaro, she told him, "I ask pardon. I won't say anything against your father again."

I should probably walk out on her, he told himself. *But after waiting so long to be with her, I couldn't do it.* With a silent request to The All Wise for more tolerance, Cheelo let it go. To show he wouldn't take offense, he placed a hand on his chest and gave a slight bow, the gesture leertu. Then he said, "If you don't mind, I chartered a shuttle and brought along supplies to go camping. Is that all right?"

"That's great!" she responded. "I didn't know you liked camping. Do you do any mountain climbing?"

"Yes, I love it! Do you?"

"There's always a first time."

They smiled, enjoying the dawning awareness that the difference in their ages was no longer a barrier between them. Having interests in common was the break their struggling relationship needed.

For Cheelo, it provided hope to get his sister back. He thought, *now that I'm past the age of first majority, Father can't keep me from seeing her. Once she's settled on Lekton again, we'll get reacquainted. I'll teach her to forget her Terran ways and properly honor Tradition. That won't be easy. Father couldn't do it, and obviously, Uncle Loris has no influence over her. But I'm her brother. She'll listen to me.*

In San Durg

Standing outside the Council building, Loris checked the time on his comm. Council wouldn't have begun First Session yet, so he made the call. Having finally convinced Donni to get a pocket comm, he looked forward to being the first person to make him use it.

Hearing Donni's timid greeting, Loris laughed. "Fairday, my friend! Didn't you see it was me?"

He replied quietly, "I wasn't sure I'd answered it properly."

Loris laughed in good-natured fun. "I felt that way for a while. Remember, I told you that I'd programmed it to respond only to your fingerprint when you lift it?"

"I remember," Donni teased back. "But I wasn't sure about these COAXIS devices. It's hard to beat Lektonian craftsmanship."

Claiming offense as any good COAXIS Ambassador should, Loris said, "I don't hear you doubting the shuttle you fly." After a pause, he asked seriously, "Would you mind a house guest tonight? Melenta is visiting with Cheelo, and in case it doesn't go well, I need to be nearby to pick her up."

"Of course. You're always welcome."

"Oh, and she's expecting you for Late-meal at our manor during tenday break."

Suspiciously, he asked, "You aren't surprising her with my visit, are you?"

"No, no. She knows about it. Wait till you taste what she's cooking for you!"

In the Sumer Mountains

In the morning stillness, their hired shuttle took Melantha and Cheelo to the foothills, where they hiked up the southern slope of Great Peak. Purposely, they kept to well-worn paths so that their muscles were challenged but not over-burdened.

At first, awkwardness drenched them in silence, and they went to great lengths not to touch each other. Melantha hoped no words were needed. Still, she suspected that his shyness was due to her announcement that she wasn't moving back to Lekton. He also didn't like her insistence that he use her new name.

But when the sun began to send whiter streaks toward the horizon, it became necessary to finally communicate. They stopped to make camp and prepare for First-rest. A charming lake tucked behind a ridge seemed to welcome them. In fact, Melantha could almost sense a benevolent presence nearby, as if The All Wise had joined their hike.

While she built a fire to cook, Cheelo set up a tent to shield them from the rising sun. He asked, "Why do you have to get your Command degree on Luna? The Institute here would be better, since you wouldn't have to make so many adjustments."

She'd never say so aloud, but her adopted, Terran lifestyle was hard on her body. Being on Lekton had put everything right, both physically as well as mentally.

But David's counting on me, a consideration I can't explain to my brother. She responded, "I almost came home many times at the beginning, but I'm glad I didn't. Luna's Institute has a better martial arts program. How about you? You're in excellent physical condition, and you've kept up with me through this entire climb. Is there an athletic program in your studies?"

"No. Father says I have enough boundless energy. Could you teach me self-defense? I think I'd be good at it."

"I'd love to, but not here in the mountains. You could come with me to Kaanotok, and I'll show you how to begin."

He seems pleased, she thought. *With Cheelo, it's hard to tell.* He didn't display his feelings, a side effect of being raised under the credo, "Dignity."

Sheltered in the tent that Cheelo had judiciously located below an outcropping of rock, they ate a meal together and then settled down to sleep.

Four cycles later at sunset, they resumed their upward climb until they happened on the remnants of a famous pass. Though now closed, it had once been a land bridge that linked their continent, Kolair, to Lekton's only other continent called Koleeth.

The A'laan tu Vuee people lived on Koleeth long ago. They were a pale, white-haired and blue-eyed race who struggled with their land's rugged mountains and harsh weather. One day, thirty families crossed the land bridge in search of a more favorable habitat. They were stranded on Kolair after volcanoes and land quakes destroyed Koleeth. Having no other choice, they made a home among the Barmaaj.

Those Travelers were Melantha and Cheelo's ancestors. As they stood on the historic spot, Cheelo asked, "Can you believe so much of our life on Lekton began at this very location?"

"True."

"I mean, when you think about it, everything important in our world came from the Old Ones—the credo system, the ethnic restrictions that protect our pure lineage and the Council of Elders. Why, even the creation of the Law of Tradition started with our ancestors and spread throughout Lekton as the Barmaaj migrated south."

Melantha thought, *migrated? They were forced out of their homes and pushed south so that our ancestors could keep their pure lineage!* She was disturbed that her brother counted the enforcement of Tradition as the finest contribution made by the Old Ones. Lukeniss had thoroughly instilled his views in his son.

Before the first moon set, they returned to the same, enchanting lake where they'd camped before and rested again. Cheelo's attention seemed to be riveted on the quiet water that was so dulled by the presence of mucurum. He said, "Let's make camp at the water's edge."

Seeing his preoccupation with the lake, she wondered if she could turn his interest to her love of other worlds. "Did you know that mucurum is unique to Lekton? Here, it's in our water, but on Terra, water has a reflective quality, like a mirror."

Cheelo only stared at her. Whether he was disinterested or confused, she couldn't tell. She thought of a Lektonian reference. "On Luna, there's a magnificent fountain. When light hits the water's surface, it glitters as if it were full of clear tra'adeen gems." He'd be familiar with the rare crystal mined in Soloto Valley. It was one of Lekton's most lucrative exports because of its clarity and variety of colors.

But he didn't share her enthusiasm. "This is far more beautiful and serene," he said, indicating the still lake.

She didn't try again. They sat in silence, letting the serenity speak to them in phantom whispers. Unlike some visitors to the mountains, they saw no hostile visions or felt any threatening vibrations. Instead, they felt welcomed by every ripple of water and every ancient tree. It was as if the overpowering presence of some guarding force refused to allow anything to disturb the mountain serenity.

I like it here, thought Melantha.

Annoyed, Cheelo rose and built their fire. To himself, he thought, *she doesn't care how sad I am that she's not coming home. She has no idea how it hurts me to see her deny her Lektonian heritage. She's obsessed with Terrans!*

While she cooked a meal, he stared into the fire, mesmerized. He wanted to enjoy the solitude and his sister's company, but it was hard to overlook her strange behavior.

She asked him, "What are you thinking about?"

He met her eyes—lavender, like his own. The resemblance they shared made him smile. "I was thinking about Father. I wish he knew you like I do. He thinks you're a bad influence on me. But Destiny's disgrace on anyone who disagrees with him! If only you and Father had salvaged enough of a relationship to at least talk to each other, things would be better. Do you ever miss him?"

Her face went pale. He realized, too late, that he shouldn't have brought up this subject. He thought, *this might spoil everything but, gretchit, we have to work this out!*

CHAPTER 22

Suddenly, her heart raced. Her palms perspired. Tactfully, she answered, "There's a lot you may not have heard about my relationship with Lukeniss. I'm not saying he'd lie about it, but maybe there are things that hurt him too much to discuss."

"Don't think losing you didn't hurt him, Mel."

Not likely, she thought to herself. *How much would it hurt you, though, if you ever discovered that Loris actually fathered me? But thank The All Wise, Lukeniss doesn't know. Obviously, he'd never disclosed that disgrace to his son, not the man whose credo is Dignity.*

She told Cheelo, "It wasn't pleasant for either of us, but we're both happier in separate worlds."

Without warning, Cheelo fell into her arms, hugging her desperately. He said, "I missed you so much when you left. Couldn't you have said good-bye to me?"

Although Melantha almost never cried, heartsick tears blurred her vision. "Believe me, I wanted to, but the Elder wouldn't allow it. It was terrible, losing you, losing the manor where I'd known our mother and Linnori. Mother would be happy that we're together, even though a lot of bitterness came between us."

"There's no bitterness between us," he assured her. Lovingly, he offered his cupped hand to join with her.

That willing offer startled her. Apparently, he didn't fear it as she did. Looking at his cupped fingers, she sobbed. This was the relationship she'd treasured when he was young, and it was the intimacy she'd needed over the seasons. Almost without realizing it, she lowered her deflector and returned the gesture to blend their emotions.

But now, she could tell that Cheelo had also been deprived of joining as he grew up. It must have been J'Mii who'd nurtured his youth. Someone else had given him the experience in accepting and giving love that families were meant to provide.

If we were together, Cheelo could give me that experience, too. This inspired an idea.

Carefully, she asked, "You're attending a kaamestaat in San Durg, aren't you?"

"Yes. Father pushed me to get private lessons, so I've finished over two seasons of credit."

It angered her to think that he hadn't forced his son to attend the school in Remuel Cove. "Computer degree?" she inquired needlessly.

"What else?" he laughed.

"And does the Soloto Valley Regional Kaamestaat challenge you enough?"

He shrugged. "They try, I guess, but I don't exactly fit the profile of a beginner. Once I entered school at five, Father made me stay at his office after school. The programmers at Ronjer gave me computer games. At eight, I started corrupting the games and making them troubleshoot and repair. By ten, I was writing my own game programs, they'd mess with it and make me troubleshoot and repair. That's why I don't learn the way others do. I hate the Kaamestaat."

He couldn't have given her a better opening. She told him, "Let's sit by the fire. I'm getting cold."

He agreed and surveyed the sky. "Bella seems as dim as the smaller moon tonight. When it sets, it'll get even colder. What's on your devious mind, Mel?"

"I don't play 'big sister' much anymore, but may I ask why you haven't found a more challenging school? I learned a lot from traveling around Lekton as Father's Diplomatic Aide. New experiences can recharge the brain. Maybe you could go away for school."

He smiled. "Far away, as in Luna? I couldn't even consider it." He avoided her eyes. "Father wouldn't let me go."

Bowing her head and placing a hand over her heart, she gestured non-offense in prelude to offering her opinion. "I may be overly sensitive about decisions that Lukeniss makes for you, but why wouldn't he want the best education for you?"

Tolerantly, he sighed. "We both know he'd say the best education is a Traditional program on Lekton. I rather agree with him."

Managing her temper, she allowed him his opinion. "You may both be right. But you said the Kaamestaat doesn't challenge you. I found there's an advantage to learning new points of view. It's stimulating to face life without knowing what to expect in advance."

"Sounds like 'Troubleshoot and Repair,' that game I played with Ronjer's programmers. In this case, my education would be hidden within an alien system that I have to figure out."

"You wanted a challenge. You'd also have to learn COAXIS Standard. That's not easy."

"I already did. Father asked me to learn it so that I could help him with a few of Ronjer's off-world investments."

"See? You're already ahead."

Cheelo silently dragged his finger through the sandy shoreline. After a long pause, he concluded, "It won't matter. Father wants me to stay at home and work at his firm to earn my tuition. I think he wants me to learn the value of money."

Melantha bit her lip. *How honest should I be?* Finally, she said, "If it were anyone else, I'd assume that he wants to teach his son responsibility. But I know him, too. I think it's likely that by not spending his own money, he's able to keep you at home and under his control."

She saw his jaw clench before he jumped to his feet. "I thought you weren't going to provoke me?"

"I wasn't trying to. That's just how I see it, Cheelo."

Defiantly, he stomped away from the fire and paced furiously. Melantha let him work through his anger.

At last, returning to where she sat, he looked down at her for a confrontation. "And I think it's likely that you want me to hurt him because you can't anymore."

"At the expense of your education? I think Luna could offer you new experiences to keep you challenged. A COAXIS education would also give you opportunities you can't get here. He wouldn't mind doing what's best for you. That wouldn't hurt Lukeniss unless controlling you matters more to him."

Cheelo only gave a diffident shrug. "If Father won't finance my schooling here, do you think he'd spend twice as much on a COAXIS education? And it doesn't matter why."

Without much forethought, she said, "Oh, you think it doesn't? Would he let you come to Luna if I pay your tuition and expenses?"

Studying her brother's reaction, she watched his emotions progress until he seemed to reluctantly admit she was right. His father wouldn't miss him, and the chance to save his money would appeal to Lukeniss.

To soften the blow of that realization, she stood and drew him into her arms.

Returning her embrace, he whispered, "I'll ask him. I'd like to be closer to you. I love my father, and I'll honor him, but I need someone who will bother to give me guidance."

"Now, isn't that mature," she said in genuine admiration. "Why do you think you're so in need of guidance?"

"You know how I get along with mentors. I don't know why I like to start trouble."

She knew he wanted his father's attention. "Leaving home could be good for you."

"For me to live that far away, he'd have to make you legal guardian. Is that all right?"

"Is it all right? Of course, it's all right!" She gave him an affectionate shove.

Cheelo suddenly turned away and hid his face. This abrupt change of behavior confused her, and she almost teased him until she realized that her brother was crying.

She rubbed her hand across his back to offer support.

Cheelo murmured quietly, "You know, Mel, you're more like my mother than my sister. I'll do anything to convince Father to let me go to Luna with you."

To her surprise, the young man began to sob. She didn't want to embarrass him, but his pain hurt her. Enfolding him to her, she let him release the tension and grief he'd held inside for ten seasons. Effortlessly, she lowered her deflector and comforted him.

This was the child, the "son" who'd been torn from her. That misery had never been erased from her soul.

It was there, in the Sumer Mountains that a mutual family tie forged a bond that brought a peace both needed. They were family, and they were friends, as well.

Kaanotok Township, 2 Deela, 2170

After two moons, Melantha returned to her manor very late. It was the following day before Loris saw her. When she told him about her offer to take Cheelo to Luna, he felt an overwhelming desire to shake her. But there were enough controlling fathers on their world, so he simply said, "According to Donni, the Council is often consulted about Cheelo's misbehavior. I don't agree that you're ready to take responsibility for raising him, but it's your decision."

Still, he had to try. Loris went to his desk and pulled up a correspondence stored on his computer. "Donni sent this to me two mooncycles ago." He pointed to one particular paragraph, suggesting, "You should read it."

She read aloud, "As an Elder of Cheelo's Nation and because of my feelings for Melenta, I've kept watch over him. Since he was small, the boy has demonstrated intelligence beyond his seasons, although his emotional ability to use it wisely is doubtful. The Council has received repeated complaints about Cheelo's lack of respect for the property of others. His father simply pays his son's fines. Loris, I don't think Lukeniss ever disciplines him."

She told him, "All the more reason why Cheelo needs to be with me. I just wish he'd call and tell me what Lukeniss said."

By afternoon, the call came. Loris stood nearby as she put the remote link in her ear and hit the silent respond key. Cheelo appeared on the telecomm screen with a glum expression. Obviously, his conversation with Lukeniss hadn't gone well.

She listened briefly, and Loris heard her apparently repeat Cheelo's words. "He agrees that it would be a more challenging education? Really?"

For a moment, Loris was afraid his brother had agreed. But Melantha said, "Well, yes, I guess the rules are stricter there. You'll stay out of trouble. But he still doesn't want you to go? Did you tell him I'd pay for it?"

Loris stiffened. *Melantha didn't tell me that part.*

But it sounded like Cheelo hadn't mentioned that to his father. Melenta insisted, "I think it would. Tell him and call me back."

Loris looked into his daughter's eyes and saw her despair. *I think I've underestimated how important this is to her. She's looking desperate.*

"If you want, I'll talk to him." The moment she'd said it, she winced. Loris reached out to her, as if he might take back her words. It was a terrible idea.

And from the horrified look on Cheelo's face, he agreed.

Loris sighed. He'd had enough of listening to only one side of the conversation. His daughter was losing her temper, and nothing good would come of that. He thought, *it's apparent that my daughter didn't inherit my ability for patient arbitration.*

Catching Melantha's eyes, he indicated the ear link and asked to help. "Taan J'preen?"

She told Cheelo, "My father wants to speak to you." She gave him the comm.

Loris whispered to her, "Take a walk and calm down, dear." She hesitated, but saw the wisdom in that and went into the garden.

Loris inserted the link over his ear and turned back to the tele-comm. He noted that Cheelo also used an ear link. "Hello, Cheelo!" he said pleasantly. "How are you?"

But his uncle's cheery voice had no positive effect on the young man's mood. "I'm fine," he said tonelessly.

Loris called on his best diplomatic training. "I'd like to help negotiate this. There's no reason for this conversation to be so unsettling for everyone. Is your father near you right now?"

"Yes, but…"

"You'll need to relay our messages. It will make everyone more comfortable. Please explain to him what you're going to do."

Cheelo closed the audio on his end and stepped off screen. Loris grinned. Apparently, Cheelo didn't trust his father's diplomacy.

Loris imagined the scene at the Cha'atre manor in San Durg. Unbidden, a memory of his childhood came to Loris.

As boys, Loris always pleased their father, but Lukeniss, who was three seasons younger, rarely did. Loris had resented the rift this created between him and his brother.

He recalled a day when the boys had been helping their father work on the farm. Loris asked, "Father, why are you so critical of Lukeniss? You don't treat me that way."

Ruel Cha'atre answered, "Because he needs to be pushed into working, and you don't."

"But don't you love him as much as you love me?"

Tenderly, his father had replied, "Of course, I love both my sons. You're both highly intelligent and capable of succeeding in this world. Lukeniss believes that entitles him to be respected, while you're willing to work hard to earn respect. I'm making Lukeniss work for my respect."

The daydream was interrupted when Melantha returned to the office. Alarmed, she asked, "Did Cheelo close link?"

"No. He's talking to Lukeniss. If you don't mind, I'm going to negotiate this discussion. My diplomatic training and my understanding of my brother's ego might get some results."

She hugged his neck affectionately. "Thank you. I thought you didn't like the idea of Cheelo coming with me to Luna?"

He imagined the outcome if Lukeniss continued to ignore Cheelo's misbehavior, if he accepted his son only when he earned it. "I've decided that getting away from Lukeniss would be good for that boy."

Abruptly, he turned back to the screen when Cheelo returned. Through the ear link, Loris heard Cheelo say, "Uncle Loris, Father says to tell you that this negotiation will be of no benefit unless I'm allowed to make my own decisions."

"That's fine, Cheelo. We agree to that."

"Agree to what?" asked Melenta desperately. She couldn't hear the conversation.

Apologizing to her, Loris told Cheelo, "I'll open the link on this end so that Melantha can hear you, too." Loris removed the ear link and touched the audio respond key. The hum of the open link filled the room and reassured Melantha.

Loris said, catching up the conversation for her, "We've agreed to let Cheelo make his own decisions."

"Absolutely!" Melantha concurred.

"One more thing," said Cheelo. "I'll end the conversation if a feud starts. I honor my father, and I'll allow no one to be disrespectful to him."

Loris said proudly, "I wouldn't have it any other way."

Aside to Lukeniss, they heard Cheelo say, "That applies to you, too, Father. I love Melantha. Please don't be unkind to her."

Cheelo still had his telecomm set to silent respond, but Lukeniss must have agreed, because Cheelo smiled.

Loris said, "You should know that, in spite of our differences of opinion, I don't dislike my brother. Please notify Lukeniss that I have said so."

After relaying the message in faithful detail, Cheelo replied, "He appreciates your attitude, Uncle Loris." Loris caught the fact that appreciating it didn't necessarily mean the sentiment was reciprocated.

Cheelo continued, "I've told Father that Melantha offered to be my legal guardian and to pay for my education and living expenses." He paused as Lukeniss made a comment. "He's concerned that her non-Traditional views will corrupt me." His blunt message proved the young man intended to properly relay his father's words.

Loris asked calmly, "Could that happen?" He smiled at Melantha's offended glare.

Confidently, Cheelo stated, "I have my own values, and I don't want to change them. They're my beliefs, even though Father's views are the same." He looked aside, listening to something Lukeniss was saying.

Loris interrupted. "Is he worried about Melantha's views, or is it the fact that the instructors at the Institute are off-worlders?"

"He withdrew that objection," said Cheelo.

Loris smiled. He'd managed to get Cheelo to say the right things to relieve his father's worry. "Good. You're doing fine, Cheelo. He's concerned that you're not thinking this through. Sometimes, others can sway one's views. But more often, I find that listening to the views of others clarifies my reasons for my beliefs."

"That's what Father said, too. He thinks I'll be stronger for seeing what life is like outside Soloto, and that I'll appreciate Tradition more after seeing the way Melantha lives."

Insulted, Melantha cleared her throat, but seemed to see the logic.

Cheelo asked her, "Do I have to change my habits to fit their culture?"

This time, the message relayed had the ring of paraphrase, thought Loris. Hearing a soft click over the comm link, he suspected Cheelo had enabled the audio for Lukeniss to hear her answer. Loris shot a cautioning look at his daughter, unsure if she'd heard it.

Carefully, she replied, "No. If you request it, the Institute will place you with a Lektonian roommate. There are quite a few Lektonians there who maintain their family's standards. I promise not to ask you to accept my values, and I won't influence you against your father's teaching."

Cheelo looked very relieved. "Thank you, Mel."

Loris thought the matter would probably be settled, now. He longed for this conversation to end peacefully.

Or maybe not, he thought. *Melantha has that look on her face, the one that means she won't back down from a fight.*

Before he could control the situation, she said, "Cheelo, I want us to be together. If it would help, I'll apologize to Lukeniss and admit I wronged him when he was my Familyhead."

Loris turned his back to the screen, frowning at her. He knew she hadn't meant that apology. Then, he heard another click. When he turned back, Cheelo had muted audio and left the screen.

As they waited for Lukeniss to make a decision, Loris also muted the audio and addressed Melantha sternly. "Let me manipulate this my way!"

She shrugged, gesturing an apology.

Cheelo returned to the screen, reporting happily, "Father says we can try a temporary agreement. He'll grant you custody for one term. If it works out, he'll extend it a term at a time until I earn a Specialty degree."

Loris beamed his pride and sighed in relief.

But Melantha wasn't celebrating. She stated firmly, "You'll have to hear my ground rules and agree to them."

"I'll do what you ask. I'll honor you as I would my father."

"No more trouble at school, understand? If you have a problem with an Instructor, be respectful. Then talk to me, and I'll deal with it. Agreed?"

"Agreed. I'll call you later. Thank you, Uncle Loris."

When Loris closed the link, Melantha danced around the office. But then, she suddenly collapsed on a floor pillow. "I'm scared," she told him.

"You have reason to be scared. How will you support him while you're also in school? It's important to me that you get your Command degree and upgrade your status in COAXIS. The Quiet Revolution needs you."

Until now, it hadn't occurred to Melantha that her father still expected her to move back home and pick up her work with the Lawbenders again. Once, she'd believed that, too, especially when she thought she'd be The MenD'lee. But she didn't see the sense in living on Lekton anymore.

"Father, don't you realize that my Command degree will be in Security Defense? I'm not sure how law enforcement serves any need for the Lawbenders."

"Why not?" he replied incredulously. "That would put you in a prime position to hear about injustices that can't be handled by Lektonian Security."

She thought, *it wouldn't be a bad cover for The MenD'lee, either. I haven't thought about that in six seasons.*

She told him, "Right now, I want to concentrate on showing Cheelo there are other views besides Tradition. I'll work and support us, but eventually, I'll continue my education."

As if to convince himself not to worry, he told her, "Maybe you'll counteract the Traditional propaganda Lukeniss likes to spread. You never know, Cheelo could turn out to be The MenD'lee."

Startled, she stared at him, wondering if he knew about her dreams—wondering if he was right and someone else had been chosen. *Is that why nothing I tried made any difference? And here I was thinking Time sabotaged it for me.*

"I'll tell you one thing," her father continued without noticing her reaction. "Donni isn't going to like this. I'm sure he'll share some history with you so that you know exactly the kind of trouble your brother's been to Lukeniss."

"Donni?" she said uncertainly.

"He's coming to Late-meal tonight." Loris left the room, allowing no argument.

CHAPTER 23

That evening, Melantha paced the garden in restless fury. Any moment now, Donni would arrive. Inside the manor, the meal was ready and the wine was chilling. Loris patiently cleaned his latest crop of vegetables from the garden, oblivious to his daughter's nervous fretting.

Then in the distance, Melantha heard the sound of an approaching shuttle. Before the Elder's personal shuttle touched down on the pad outside the estate walls, she'd imagined several ways their reunion might go.

Will he rush eagerly to me, desperate to embrace me, but unsure if I'd allow it? No, he's probably been hurt by my rejection, so he'll be cold and aloof and ask me, "Demolished any other hearts lately?"

Firmly, she denied those thoughts and whispered, "Donni would never disgrace his credo to be callous or cloying. You'll be the one who acts like a fool."

From the kitchen, Loris called, "Mel? Do you want to meet Donni at the gate?" When she didn't answer, she saw him wipe his hands dry on a cloth and walk to the door of the manor.

But Melantha, feeling every bit a fool for hiding, headed to the garden as if she faced execution rather than a reunion with her dearest friend in the world. Through the window, she saw them enter the kitchen. They spoke so softly that she couldn't understand.

Just when she thought she was prepared enough to join them in the kitchen, her father sent Donni alone to the garden, and Melantha muttered an oath no Elder should hear.

Opening the door, he stood for a moment, scanning the area until their eyes locked. Instantly, his face brightened in delight. Closing the door, he took long strides toward her.

At his approach, every fear melted into memories, and the affection she'd hidden from even herself glowed within her. It surprised her to realize how she'd missed him. Words effortlessly came to her mind, "It's good to see you."

Smiling warmly, he strode purposefully to her. But when she extended her arm to offer a Comrade's Grip, he paused in awkward confusion. "Oh, I don't think that will do." He threw his arms around her shoulders and hugged her soundly, lifting her off the ground in his enthusiasm.

Embarrassed, she pulled back, caught by his eyes as he analyzed her features.

He said appreciatively, "You've grown more beautiful than ever."

But she was thinking, *he looks exactly the same, as if six seasons hasn't changed him at all.* The difference in their ages no longer seemed so obvious.

"Melenta, I couldn't wait to see you again."

She stiffened at the use of her Lektonian name, and wondered why that bothered her. "I use Melantha now."

At last sensing her tension, he didn't pursue the intimacy further. "I knew that, and I meant to use Melantha. I ask pardon." Walking to the marble table and benches, he called, "Come and sit down. Tell me how you're doing."

Relieved beyond words, she let the conversation drift to impersonal trivialities while Loris brought the meal to the table.

While they ate, there was no talk of other worlds and occupations far from home. She could almost believe no time had passed since the three of them had last enjoyed a meal together in this garden. But when they'd finished eating and settled onto lawn pillows with another glass of trillin wine, Donni turned to topics of important business.

"Has Loris been telling you about the increasing violence on Lekton?"

Loris interjected, "I've left her out of Lawbender business, Donni. She's not involved anymore."

But the subject had captured her attention, so she asked, "What do you mean by violence?" Her mind told her he must mean some innocuous explosion of temper or unprovoked vandalism.

"For the past several seasons, violent crimes of various kinds have increased. Lately, it seems like I hardly hear anyone attempt peaceful settlements to disputes."

This disturbed her. "Do you mean they actually hurt each other?"

"Oh, yes," her father agreed.

This made no sense to her. As long as she could remember, she'd been taught that every Nation was founded upon a pledge of peace. Lektonians had always been gentle people who respected life so much that violence was abhorrent to them.

She asked, "Where is this happening? Surely not Soloto."

Donni shook his head sadly. "Soloto and every other Nation. Last mooncycle, a merchant in Selli Oasis had his business burned down because he'd accidentally sold a defective food processor. A food processor! Remember that, Loris?"

Her father's expression was grave, and he avoided answering.

Donni continued, "You may not have heard yet. Two moons ago, a Lawbender in Sarazan was killed. He voiced objection to the Law of Tradition and a neighbor killed him for it. I tell you, Melantha, there's no better time to have someone with your training as a Defender to rejoin the Movement. Something must be done to protect the Lawbenders, especially the Messengers."

Oh, grechit, she thought. *Doesn't he know I'm staying on Luna?* Uncomfortably, she stared at her lap. "I'm afraid I can't help, Donni."

Loris added, "She isn't moving back here."

Donni blinked several times, as if they'd lapsed into an unknown language. "It doesn't have to be Kaanotok. Wherever you settle, your help will be needed. Perhaps in San Durg, to be near Cheelo?" His suggestion sounded hopeful, for he lived there, too.

Loris started to explain, but Melantha cut him off. She should deliver the news herself. "I'm staying on Luna. I'm only here for a visit."

Donni's puzzled expression tore at her conscience. His confusion changed to disbelief and then settled into defiance. "Why?" he demanded.

"I've accepted a job as a Defense Instructor at the Institute."

Angrily, his glare turned on Loris, accusing him for not convincing her otherwise. Stubbornly, he insisted, "You said that she needed to know the trouble that Cheelo's been in so that she could help him!"

"And I do need to know. Cheelo will be moving to Luna to attend the Institute. I'll be his guardian."

Donni put down his glass and sat up. "Does Lukeniss know about this?"

"Of course," she said with more insult than she'd meant. "I wouldn't ask Cheelo to run away, Donni."

He jumped to his feet, staring down at her and shaking his head in disbelief. Suddenly, he turned his back to her. Running a hand through his hair, he uttered a frustrated oath under his breath. This was very uncharacteristic of her friend, but doubly improper behavior for an Elder.

Melantha stood, too. "I'm sorry to disappoint you."

He whirled around, exclaiming, "The Lawbenders need you! I need you!"

She didn't look away but bore his angry stare, letting the silence fill the moment. She was glad her father stayed seated and didn't interfere. There ought to be something she could say to comfort Donni, but words eluded her.

"So, you'll never come home again?"

"I plan to, one day. For now, I'm going to do whatever it takes to show Cheelo an alternative to Tradition. I won't get a better chance than this."

Bitterly and reluctantly, he agreed. "Well, that's certainly true. Lukeniss is one of Reform's greatest enemies. At least if you won't help stop Lukeniss, you may stop the man Lukeniss is grooming to replace him. But Cheelo is one man. One man amid so many!"

She'd conceded that preventing her brother from following in his father's political footsteps seemed minor in comparison to stopping murder and violence. How could she explain? She told Donni, "Yes, he's only one man, but he's the one most important to me. If that sounds selfish…"

"No," sighed Donni as he gave up his anger and tension. "No, I understand that. Our first responsibility must be to save our families."

Loris felt he could now add a comment. "It's possible that Cheelo won't like it there, or that Lukeniss won't let him stay longer than one semester."

Donni looked at her. "And if he comes home to Lekton?"

"I'll probably come with him. He needs me."

She saw the earnest longing in his eyes. It didn't take words to know that Donni also needed her. She hoped he'd understand that, regretfully, she must decline his expectations… again.

COAXIS Institute, August 23, 2170

Melantha entered her apartment in faculty housing and heard the familiar beep that meant she had messages waiting. She begged, "One at a time, Dearest All Wise. That's all I ask. Let the problems come one at a time."

She and Cheelo had been on Luna only two weeks, and Cheelo was already bored. But classes would begin soon. She'd be a Defense Instructor then, although for now she'd already taken a few private coaching jobs.

Tossing her running shoes into a closet, she glared at the wall comm. *What if one of those messages is a problem with Cheelo again? Or all of them?*

She began a mental inventory of her best accomplishments. She'd need that to defend a battered ego when she had to admit at last that she couldn't handle him. "And let's not forget, you've successfully stayed free of men! I'm satisfied with my life. I wish Cheelo was, too."

But that wasn't true. He seemed determined to dislike the environment, his dorm and the cafeteria food. His Lektonian roommates didn't meet his standards, as well. Lukeniss, no doubt, would demand a private room for him, but she wouldn't do that. He also resented the vitamin supplements he had to take since laneeg and teerush weren't present in human vegetables and fruits. She shared the supplies her father sent from his garden but doubted Cheelo appreciated his uncle's sacrifice. How spoiled Lukeniss had allowed him to become!

Most of all, her brother criticized his curriculum. When his credits transferred from Lekton, he was told he'd have to repeat two courses because the Kaamestaat didn't include lessons about Luna's computer systems. When the Registrar told him he'd have to take two remedial courses, Cheelo talked the Instructors into allowing him to test out of them. He passed the tests and told Melantha, "I know more about computers than any four of them."

Steeling her nerves, she listened to the three messages. The first was Blake's assistant informing her of a department meeting tomorrow. The second was Cheelo's dorm supervisor who was calling to inform her that a private room had opened, and for the sake of all concerned, would he please take it.

She gave an ironic laugh. "Well, you little sneak, you got your way anyhow, didn't you?"

Holding her breath, she played the third message. It was another student asking to hire her as a private coach. With a grateful sigh for hearing no bad news, she returned that call and took the extra work.

But just when her nerves had settled, the wall comm buzzed. She was afraid to look at the I.D. "One at a time. That's all I ask." She answered, "Melantha Chatrey."

A deep, male voice said in Standard, "Miss Chatrey? At your earliest convenience, will you please come to Security Central? It isn't serious, but your brother was brought in for questioning."

"About what?"

"Well, it's a bit sensitive, I'm afraid. Cheelo was caught tampering, well I shouldn't say tampering, exactly..."

She knew he was trying to be kind. "I'll be right there."

She didn't miss the irony as Melantha Chatrey, a bonded Security Enforcer, entered the halls of Security Central Enforcement Agency to bail out her little brother. Approaching an officer at the desk, she explained, "I'm here to see Cheelo Cha'atre."

The Enforcer smiled at her. "Don't be too hard on him, Miss." It was the same, deep voice from earlier. "He didn't do any harm, and Mr. Danforth doesn't intend to press charges."

"Danforth?" gasped Melantha. "As in Danforth Computer Systems?"

A quiet voice behind her called, "Miss Chatrey?"

She turned to see an elderly man in an elegant suit. He said, "I'm Noah Danforth. I'm sorry for frightening you. I told the officer to stress to you that this isn't serious."

His kind manner and cultured British accent softened her reaction. She told him, "I worry about my brother. He's been hard to handle lately."

"Really?" said Danforth in surprise. "Seems like such an intelligent lad. Miss Chatrey, can we talk?"

"If Cheelo damaged anything, I'll pay for it." She winced at finding that, like Lukeniss, she was willing to pay his way out of trouble.

"Nothing was damaged. On the contrary, he repaired something. Apparently, as he passed one of the bank's computerized tellers, he noticed something was wrong with the machine. I assure you; we service our CTM's often, but the ones on campus tend to get more abuse than use. Anyway, Cheelo saw a customer make an account transfer to pay a debt, but the computer didn't exit the transaction. Cheelo said he's worked on computers at a bank on Lekton and was rather good at troubleshooting and repair. He decided to repair the computer."

Melantha struggled to listen, afraid to hear more.

Danforth said, "Of course, to the Enforcer who saw him, it appeared your brother was robbing the CTM. One of my technicians double-checked his story and discovered a serious program malfunction. Cheelo was interrupted prior to his final repair, but I have no doubt that he knew how to do it. He's undoubtedly gifted."

"Then, he didn't do anything wrong?"

"Not as far as I'm concerned. As a matter of fact, I'd like to hire him for my repair service. I can give him a few hours a week, and we can work around his school schedule. We need bright, honest workers like your brother."

In spite of her embarrassment, Melantha was very impressed.

As Cheelo left Security Central with his sister, he laughed and thought, *I'll never be bored again!* He told Melantha, "I told Mr. Danforth I'd take the part-time job. Is that all right?"

"Sure," she agreed enthusiastically, but then finished flatly, "You can use it to pay for the extra dorm fees you've incurred for a private room."

Her glare showed him that she knew he'd arranged to get kicked out.

Gesturing gaaro, he attempted a humbled look while contemplating his good fortune. *I'll be working for the company that services every computer on Luna. Think of it! I'll be given maintenance codes that give me access to any Danforth computer. Unlimited un-boredom!*

He'd like to think that his sister wouldn't have been as easy to fool as the Enforcer who arrested him. *Someday,* he thought, *when I won't get in trouble for it, I'll tell Melantha how predictable Enforcers are. The man caught me repairing the machine but never suspected that I'd programmed the error in the first place.*

COAXIS Institute, August 31, 2170

After her usual early morning run, Melantha returned home to find a special courier waiting to deliver a letter from Commander O'Connell. Reading it as she entered the apartment, she exclaimed in delight, "Time, you ill-mannered offspring of The All Wise, are you slipping? You let me have a raise."

Guillermo Ruiz was going on leave this year in order to complete his Command degree. In his absence, he'd recommended Melantha to move up to Keplar Director.

As the letter instructed, Melantha went to the gym to see her newly furnished office. Using the code provided in the letter, she opened the door and almost screamed. "What generous good deed did I do to deserve this special blessing?"

Looking behind her as she entered her new office, she had to wonder. Had she unknowingly met the Herald of The All Wise? Would he even come to Luna to check on the behavior of Lektonians living so far away? Although she hadn't always accepted the legend, she said a silent thank you to the universe.

Maybe, she thought suddenly, *that's who has been following me for the last few days.* It wasn't an intangible someone, but a real presence that watched her. *Better the Herald than Tserian Infiltrators.*

One look in her office and she was embarrassed for anyone to follow her there. The office was much too spacious for her meager instructor's job. It was equipped with expensive furniture and every kind of clerical equipment she could ever need.

Then, she saw the real reason for the special treatment. Over the desk, four golden Keplar medals gleamed in a lighted display case that was mounted on pastel, purple walls.

Again, Melantha looked behind her. Boasting made her uncomfortable. To her, it was shamefully flagrant to take credit for a natural ability.

However, the administration at the Institute didn't agree. Despite her obstinate refusal, they'd required her awards to be displayed somewhere on campus. To comply, she had displayed them in the bathroom of her apartment.

Who brought them here? And when? This morning, they were in my apartment when I left, weren't they?

On closer inspection, though, she saw that these weren't her medals but the duplicate set given to the Institute.

With a groan of resignation, she grabbed a schedule from the printer on her desk and looked at the public drill sessions held at the gym each evening. Once again, she'd been given the preferential time slots to monitor drills. With effort, she reminded herself that this job paid the bills and kept Cheelo in school here.

Resentment gnawing at her, she posted the schedule outside the office and closed the office after her. She listened for the hum of the lock and then turned her attention to the student who waited in the gym for his lesson.

Since she'd returned from Lekton, Melantha had been coaching him every day for the preliminaries of the Keplar competition. John Mark McCarthy was bewildering. The twenty-year-old young man from Scotland was proficient, but not particularly talented in martial arts, and his Specialty field was Biotechnology. She suspected that he had other motives for hiring her, something involving a crush.

It took a moment to find John. He stood at a far door of the gym talking with two men who wore black drill suits. One of the men she didn't know, but the other was a Master who regularly attended the public drills in the evening.

Melantha called, "John, are you ready?"

John jumped and glanced nervously at her. Too casually, he shook hands with each man, and his dark hair flew with the halting movements of pushing them toward the door of the gym.

This made her more curious about her mysterious student's motives for hiring her. Determined to investigate, she called to him, "That's all right. You can take a few more minutes to talk. I remembered something I have to do."

Confidently, she approached the three men, glancing at each to memorize their features and to analyze their body language. The door where John seemed intent upon sending them led to the lobby. She wondered, *does John specifically want them in the lobby for a reason, or only away from my scrutiny?*

Passing John, she walked, then, between the two strangers, deliberately parting them. Suddenly, her suspicion was confirmed.

She sensed a threat from John's two companions, something that her mind interpreted as a readiness to fight.

Her mind was saying, *it's ridiculous to draw that kind of assumption from a feeling.* Yet, trusting her instincts, she acted on them. Pivoting fluidly, she faced them, demanding, "What's this about?"

Abruptly, every threatening vibration ceased. The men exchanged astonished looks.

The man she'd never seen before, a tall, overly thin blond who seemed slightly older than her, said to John, "You've got our support, Johnny, but remember, we're only going to back you. You have to do the work."

Having her pupil named in this apparent conspiracy added to her anxiety. She knew John's ability for spontaneity. One moment, he could be a docile little house pet. Then, without warning, he'd snap his entire being into a tiger-like aggression. He'd caught his coach off guard a few times by this ability. *Not this time, John,* she said inwardly.

Although her student showed no intention to fight, she moved clear of him and backed further into the lobby.

Following her, John held the gym door open, watching her.

She studied the tall blond, who still waited inside the gym. He'd relaxed to an observation stance. By all visible indications, his intentions weren't hostile.

So, why can't I dismiss the apprehension?

Then shifting her attention, she studied the other man. He was Oriental, had broad shoulders and a moustache. His feet were set to balance his weight to the center of his body. Melantha recognized him from public drills and knew he was her equal in mastery. For sure, he was more experienced because she'd seen him in master's competitions when she was a novice in the field.

She glared at John until he cautiously stepped back, allowing her to re-enter the gym. Spreading her feet, she nodded at the dark young man, signaling her readiness for a confrontation.

Unexpectedly, the man bowed and placed his hands behind his back. Aside to his companion, he said, "Hill, I think she's misunderstanding." Both men backed away.

But unconcerned, John came toward her. "I'm sorry to worry you, Master Chatrey, but it was the only way they'd believe me."

She took a menacing step closer, looming over him.

"Take it easy!" he yelled quickly. "I wanted to prove a theory. I told them that you could recognize aggressive intent without using your senses."

This caught her attention. She recalled that she'd already passed between the men and was beyond them before receiving the impression of danger.

She scolded John. "Senses are always used to recognize aggressive intent."

The two men behind John approached again, but the threatening feelings had vanished.

Provoking her, John said, "If you don't believe me, let's test it. Turn your back and don't look behind you. Most importantly, don't lower your deflector emission. One of us will attack, and I think you'll anticipate where to defend before it happens."

She narrowed her gaze, thinking, *he seems sincere.* "You really believe this?"

"Yes! You might as well know that I've been making a study of you as my final thesis in Biotechnology."

"Why in the great galaxy would you do that? That thesis is required to complete your degree!"

"It's a viable study," he defended. "I don't think your ability for quick response comes from exceptional reflexes. It's almost like you sense your opponent's intention before he acts."

"This is your specialty field, John! You can't afford to play around with it."

"Who's playing around? They believe me." He pointed to the men behind him. "They've seen it demonstrated. You're the one who's not taking this seriously. Wasn't your Specialty field thesis about recognition of aggressive intent? Wouldn't you like to know why you're such an authority on that subject?"

She shook her head.

John fired at her, "Or do you assume a non-major couldn't understand self-defense?"

"I never said that. Why would I develop such a skill when other Lektonians don't?"

"I'm not sure," he stammered in embarrassment. "In most species, adaptations serve a rational purpose. Maybe it gives you added protection against being touched."

I wouldn't doubt that for a second. I hate to be touched. But she still wasn't convinced. She challenged him with another question. "Where do you think I get this ability?"

"As I see it, you're sensitive to all forms of energy, so you know the exact moment that potential energy is converted to a kinetic form. That lets you instantly block an attack."

"But how?"

With a reluctant sigh, John committed himself to announce his theory. "This is probably an inherent feature of your deflector."

"You think my deflector can sense energy?"

"Sounds like a decent theory," called the tall blond behind her.

Ignoring the comment, she told John, "You know that Lektonians aren't allowed to use deflectors during training. How could my deflector sense energy when it isn't emitting a field?"

His face lit up. "Don't you see? That's why you haven't been aware of this ability before now. During training matches, you release your deflector, so your field wouldn't be emitting by the time aggression is aimed at you."

"Think about it," called the Oriental. "You were allowed to use your deflector as a natural defense during the Keplar competitions."

And he was right. Her eyes widened. "I guess that's true."

Encouraged, he gushed out his next point. "Suppose someone planned a sneak attack against you, like these guys did earlier? Your field was at full emission to deflect, or to be accurate, repel their emotional vibrations. Right? And you knew they planned to attack you."

Tentatively, she said, "My deflector senses energy?"

"Or it attracts energy. I don't know why, but I know it isn't something common to the Lektonoid species. Want me to prove it?"

Melantha didn't know what to think. Sure, maybe she had sensed danger when she passed them, but that could also be a reaction to the suspicious behavior of strangers. "Prove it how?"

"When you passed my friends, I'd told them to think of aggressive action as if planning to do it. They were careful not to move in any way that would show you what they planned."

"They 'thought' danger at me? I'm not sure I believe this."

From behind John, a man's voice said, "Then, let's demonstrate this again."

She refused to look, knowing it was the Oriental who spoke. It was too obvious where this was leading, and she didn't care to credit this idea enough to pursue it. "I don't think so."

"I promise not to hurt you," he sneered.

She stood a little taller. Her glance at John's excited expression told her that everyone knew how that remark would rankle her. *I refuse to be baited,* she thought, and she turned her back on him.

An amused laugh resulted from her silence. "En guard, Miss Chatrey!"

"What does that mean?" She turned to look. The dark young man stared directly into her eyes and grinned. His hand slipped seductively to the belt of his drill suit and triggered the button that prepared his apparel for combat. Helpless to ignore it, she watched the material contract to fit snugly against his body, highlighting his muscles. The sleeves slowly retracted up his arms to bare spectacular biceps.

Melantha only stared. *This man is calculating his moves to seduce me. Just look away*, she told herself without success.

He raised his hands behind his head and, lifting a leather, cord necklace, caught his long, black hair to tie it back. With a smooth, practiced motion, the cord was knotted and he lowered his hands slowly to rest on his hips. Giving her a superior grin, he waited.

A challenge is a challenge.

CHAPTER 24

She fingered the retractor button at the belt of her own suit. The familiar hug of the material intensified the thrill of her mental preparation to fight. She had no physical attributes to flaunt that would distract her opponent, but perhaps that showed him how contemptible his display had been.

John backed away, warning, "Remember to keep your deflector at full emission."

She turned her back to her opponent, ignoring the spark of excitement she'd noticed in his unusual, brown eyes. Looking straight ahead and clearing her mind, she waited.

Melantha used every sense at her disposal to anticipate his intentions. She neither heard nor felt any displacement of air around her. She saw no shadows and smelled no change in the air. This was a master, not an amateur who attended drill as a hobby.

She received no warning from her senses as he approached, and yet she whirled unexpectedly around to find his hands reaching for her shoulders and pushing his weight forward to upset her balance.

But her defense was already in place. Rather than try to back up or twist away from him, she slipped her arm to his wrist and shifted her weight. He wasn't able to follow through on his intended move. She used his momentum against him, and the leverage in her throw sent the man flying through the air until he took a careful fall on the mat.

Melantha's instincts told her that he ought to try another attack. After all, one lucky throw wouldn't prove she had any unconscious advantage in the match. However, something else convinced her.

Displaying his prowess for an unexpected attack, John leaped toward her from behind. Losing no time in deciding where he'd begin the offensive move, he simply moved. A person with flawless telepathy wouldn't have had enough warning.

She reacted automatically to the attack from behind her. Pivoting without knowing why, her hands came up to her shoulder. John's flying kick in mid-air was aimed exactly at the place she defended. In the split second it took for his foot to make contact, one of her hands was already deflecting his ankle away from her and turning his body off balance in mid-air. Her other hand was automatically positioned to catch his shoulder while she supported the deflected leg.

Pivoting gracefully with the momentum of the attack, she held John in a balanced position like a small child. Then, effortlessly, she gently lowered him to the mat. He was in a helpless position, lying on his side at her feet.

By this time, the Oriental man had stood. Once he'd signaled that he wouldn't attack again, she asked John, "Are you all right?"

"I'm fine."

Instinctively, she felt the dark-featured man move very close behind her. He commented, "That's what you call a perfect execution, using an opponent's strength and energy against him."

Turning, she saw his hand extend to shake hers. She usually didn't practice this Terran custom because, after living and working among Terrans so long, protecting them from deflector shock had become instinct. But this time, she didn't want to cause offense. Unconsciously lowering her deflector, she shook his hand.

As expected, she felt the man's emotions. He was proud of her. There was also a sense of relief. Apparently, during their brief contact, her deflector had caused him discomfort.

But then, she also felt a sudden sweep of wonder and awe that she couldn't account for within her own thoughts. Following that, a stimulating, sensual thrill surged to the surface, and its intensity surprised her. She hastily examined that emotion to decide if it originated from him, or if it had been her own feeling.

Admit it, she told herself. *He's an alluring man. Did I pay him more attention at those drill sessions than I'd realized?*

By instinct, her deflector returned to repel the uncomfortable, intruding emotions. She pulled her hand out of his, although he resisted letting her go. *Had the allurement been on his part,* she wondered?

The blond man named Hill said, "Congratulations, Johnny! What a remarkable discovery! You'll win a scholarship to Command school with this thesis."

Melantha asked Hill, "I don't understand. What is your interest in this?"

"If you're willing to undergo testing of this ability, I'd like to sponsor the research. Also, if this ability is as useful as it seems to be, I'd like to offer you an opportunity to serve Security Central as a sideline job."

She studied the man's proud manner. Physically, he wasn't very imposing. *He works for Security Central? Could he truly have the influence he claims to have?*

Turning to the darker man, she asked, "And where do you fit into this?"

He glanced at John before answering, "It looks like I'm your practice opponent for the experiments."

His stare didn't distract her from noticing his suggestive grin. Meter for meter, she matched him, but beyond doubt, he had a broader and more solid build. Both of them knew that this had little to do with assessing which of them would defeat the other in a match. But his confidence and his easy acceptance of the challenge made him a threatening adversary.

And although she'd never lacked self-confidence, and it didn't particularly bother her to be challenged by an equally self-confident Master, his smile disturbed her.

Remembering the pain he communicated to her through their handshake, she asked, "Are you sure you really want to help with these experiments? Remember what happened to Goliath."

He wasn't intimidated. "I'm sure, but if you're not, why don't we go somewhere and talk it over?" There was no mistaking the sexual implication in his voice and his smile.

"That's a good idea," said Hill. "Miss Chatrey, I'll talk to you soon about that private security work. Until then, Mr. Toshimoto, I'm assigning you to introduce her to us. That is, if you'll refrain from too thorough an introduction to yourself."

Toshimoto smiled shyly, looking at the floor. "Don't give her the wrong impression. Most of my reputation is fabricated for the sake of my cover."

"Most?" laughed John.

"Cover?" questioned Melantha.

"I do some private security work, too." Then he glared at John, saying, "I'm really not that bad."

Hill chortled under his breath. "Of course not. How bad could you be at J. Paul's for doughnuts and coffee?"

"I think he's trying to tell you something, Toshi," teased John.

Toshi swatted him on the arm. "Go practice your drill forms, kid." Leaning against the wall, he looked into her eyes and awaited a response to his flirting.

Resolved that responding was something she'd never do, she stared intently back at him, giving him no impression of her thoughts.

He reacted to her blank stare as if it had been a slap. He stood straight and corrected his conduct. "I've misjudged you, and I ask pardon. I'd be pleased to meet you at J. Paul's for doughnuts and coffee, if you still want to go."

Good, thought Melantha. *He left the opportunity open for me to decline. Maybe he's not as arrogant as I thought.*

She told him, "Since you ask that way, I'll meet you there after I finish John's lesson. That is," she turned to John and finished, "unless hiring me to coach you was only a ploy to meet me. Do you really want to better your fighting skills?"

Hill interjected, "Uh, yes. He needs it."

She nodded at Hill and prepared to work with John. But it occurred to her that she'd better get control of her involvement with Toshimoto. She couldn't allow his flirtatious teasing to continue. So, she turned back to call, "Is your name Toshi or Toshimoto?"

"My name is Toshimoto. I'm called Toshi."

"People call you Toshi Toshimoto?"

"They do if they like the present arrangement of their features. I never use my first name, only the nickname."

Suddenly, it struck her that he was the person who had been following her for the past few days. Without showing any emotion, she replied, "How interesting. I guess I'll have to find out your real name."

She left without waiting for his reaction, but she knew that she'd managed to annoy him.

"Better men have tried!" he yelled.

Toshi hoped his "last word" had sounded more imposing to her than it had to him. He thought, *our first meeting went according to plan. She's even more exciting than I'd imagined!*

At the COAXIS Institute Campus

By 11:00, Melantha stood outside the door of a small pastry shop on campus. J. Paul's was a popular place with students and Embassy staff alike, and at any time of day, it was crowded. She paused outside and considered going home. But her sense of adventure had been tantalized, and she was too intrigued to back out. Gathering her courage, she entered the shop.

She didn't see the man named Toshi. *I'm sure I'd recognize him,* she thought. *Maybe he's running late.*

Once she'd ordered, she took her doughnut and juice to a table and sat alone in a corner. She was about to conclude that this was a joke when, from nowhere, a voice said, "May I sit here? There don't seem to be any tables left."

Melantha looked up, prepared to refuse, and Toshi was standing beside her. She told him, "Go ahead."

As he took a chair across from her, she glanced around the room. *Where had he been waiting? The man's a shadow. No wonder I haven't caught him following me. Is he in disguise or something?*

As a matter of fact, he did look different without the drill suit. He wore the same COAXIS Diplomat's field uniform that she'd once worn when she worked as an aide for her father. The jacket was gold with maroon piping at the edges, and his slacks and boots were black. Thinking about it, that would be a good disguise since Embassy staff could be seen anywhere.

He gave her a reassuring smile and said, "You almost didn't come in. Why?"

"I have this habit: I don't trust people who behave in a suspicious manner."

"A good habit to have." He took a bite of pie.

Melantha thought to herself, *there's something very different about him now. His attitude is more dignified, less arrogant. Maybe it's the jacket.*

She said coldly, "You aren't going to any trouble to make me trust you. Who are you, really? Why have you been following me?"

His eyebrows lifted. "You knew about that? When did you figure it out?"

"Three days ago," she replied smugly.

"Oh." He hid a sly smile by taking another bite.

"All right, then. How long have you been snooping into my life?" Her hands twitched on the table.

"When did you start coaching John?"

"About a month ago."

"About then. It takes time to investigate someone for a top security clearance."

"I never authorized that. Maybe invasion of privacy is common where you come from, but where I'm from, privacy is considered sacred. And I think it's in poor taste to use a diplomat's office as a disguise to carry out illegal activity."

Toshi looked up with a start. "You mean this?" He pointed to the triangular patch on his shoulder that indicated Embassy employment. On a dark blue background, a silver COAXIS logo was superimposed over a field of stars.

Her reply was haughty. "I certainly do. Anyone given that emblem ought to have to earn it." Her hands dropped to her lap.

Over the table, Toshi proudly extended his right hand toward her, displaying a class ring that bore an opal, the stone of Luna's Institute.

"So, you have a degree from Luna. I do, too."

But his stare was persistent, and he didn't lower his hand. He wanted her to look at it again. Suddenly, she realized why. To each side of the stone, the specialty field and rank of the degree would be indicated.

Timidly, she looked. He twisted the ring to show that one side bore the emblem of the Diplomatic Services Order. Twisting it again, she saw that Toshi had a Command Diplomat degree.

Embarrassed, she lowered her eyes. "I apologize, then. It was still rude to invade my privacy."

"You don't owe me an apology, Melantha. I was rude when we met this morning. I ask your pardon. I hope that when you've heard the reason for my invasion, you'll approve."

She examined the sincerity in his eyes and thought, *that's exactly what Father might have said at that moment.* Pretending that she wasn't familiar with those manipulative communication techniques, she replied coolly, "Even if I approve, how can I trust what you'd do with the information?"

"Oh, I'm a highly ethical person."

"Right."

"I live by strict codes of conduct that were designed for Japanese warriors over fifteen centuries ago."

"That's comforting."

"So, how do you feel about investigation? Like it?" He took another bite of pie.

Her mind said, *I caught the switch of mood, you ludjit, and the assumption that I'd accepted your apology.* But she answered, " I've been trained for it, but I don't care much for investigation."

Although the pastry shop was crowded and no one paid attention to them, he whispered, "If you'd like to try your hand at it, there's a Private Security team who could use your skills. Earlier, we couldn't explain why we were watching you because it's a secret organization. But Hill is satisfied with your security clearance and impressed by your defense qualifications. He said I can tell you a few details, if you want."

"This is incredible! Are you serious?"

He smiled at her, and that suggestive, threatening flirtation was back. He seemed unable or unwilling to control it. Then, mimicking a famous woman-chaser in Terra's cinematic history, Toshi twirled his moustache and said, "Quite serious, my dear. Trust me."

Melantha stiffened and glared.

Abruptly, as if finally realizing her displeasure, he continued in his own voice. "Of course, since it's a secret, I can't tell you too much detail."

Chills climbed her spine. *What am I getting into? I chose a Defense degree in order to avoid investigating. No, I don't need other options. I couldn't even consider it.*

Could I?

He asked, "Well? If you're interested, tell me now."

He was pushing her into an awkward position. She'd just learned about this opportunity, and he wanted an immediate agreement? She shook her head. "I'm honored that you trust me, but I don't want to be responsible for knowing this."

As if she'd agreed to join them, he launched into a description of their work. "The job lets us travel, even off-world, sometimes, since we have our own shuttle."

"Wouldn't that take a long time to travel between worlds?"

"We get authorization to use the Xylonian Doorway. Hill is very influential. We use makeup, costumes, whatever is necessary to keep a cover. We bring back suspects, along with the evidence to convict them. After that, the case is turned over to Hill and his partner at Security Central, and we're out of it. Are you sure you don't like investigating?"

"It's attractive, I admit. So, the story about John's thesis research is only a cover story?"

"No, it's real. Everyone on the team has a primary job or is in school."

To Melantha, this story seemed ridiculous. "You investigate in your spare time?"

"Well, I'd say it's more than a hobby. Would you like to meet other members of the team?"

She leaned forward, whispering, "Are you supposed to reveal their identities?"

Toshi fell back against his chair and gave a loud, good-natured laugh. It so broke the mood of secrecy she'd formed in her mind that Melantha longed to clap a hand over his mouth. *Am I being teased? Ridiculed? Humiliated?*

He said, "I'm not sinking any ships by loose conversation." He grinned at her confusion. "What I mean is that Hill wouldn't so much as say hello to you without getting a complete clearance on you. We trust you to keep this secret."

To her, this meeting was a serious matter. She hoped he wasn't making fun of her. With icy formality, she told him, "Commander Toshimoto, my concern was to keep you out of trouble. I also don't want to force information from you that I'd become liable for knowing."

All at once, he stopped laughing, although one errant snicker slipped out before his face sobered. Pulling another communication trick from his repertoire, he put her on the defensive by assuming a martyred pose.

She was stunned—entirely confused.

Toshi raised his brows above closed eyes. As his eyes slowly opened, he stated in a flat whisper, "Don't do that."

With a reflexive response that made her feel like a fool, she turned completely around, thinking that he must have been speaking to someone else. Finding no one there, she figured out what he'd meant: Toshi was asking her not to address him by rank.

Swallowing her embarrassment, she turned back to face him, prepared to apologize for offending him. She was immediately caught in the grasp of his intense, brown eyes. He was staring at her.

Politely, she apologized. "I beg your pardon."

But to her dismay, he didn't flinch, not even to blink. She thought, *my apology isn't adequate? What does he want?*

And then, she got it. She said, "I beg your pardon, Toshi."

But once again, he detoured the subject while still, his brown, almond eyes maintained a disciplined stare. His jaw remained firm, and even his moustache never quivered to betray a smile. Apparently, Toshi had his share of non-expressive expressions, too.

At last, she asked him, "What's the matter? I said I'm sorry."

"They're purple."

"What are purple?"

"Your eyes—they're purple. I mean, I knew they were, but …"

Now, Melantha burst into laughter. "That's right, and my blood really has a phosphorescent glow in the dark, too."

She knew what he'd done. By his innocent surprise about her different racial features Toshi had turned the laughter on himself and eased the tension between them. After that, their meeting became less formal.

However, it also produced one dangerous consequence: While she sat in a corner with Toshi, chatting and laughing, her brother came into J. Paul's.

Cheelo often asked her to be more forward with men, but with Lektonian men. Seeing her laughing and enjoying herself with a Terran man had obviously distressed him. Melantha knew that might mean trouble.

She thought, *what should I do? If I don't look at him, maybe he'll assume I don't want to be interrupted. Later, I'll make up something to explain.*

That was her first mistake.

Cheelo approached boldly. "Hello, Melantha. Excuse me if I'm interrupting."

She grumbled to herself, *if it had been polite, you'd have taken a seat to be sure you interrupted.* She tried not to panic, tried to sound conversational. "Hi, Cheelo. What are you doing here?"

He gave her a glare. "I'm eating, of course. Who is he?"

Assuming that she shouldn't disclose Toshi's name, she tried to stall. "Cheelo, don't be rude," she scolded him.

Toshi rescued the situation. "That's quite all right, Miss Chatrey. You must be her brother. You look a lot alike—same eyes." Standing, Toshi placed his hands behind his back in the Lektonian posture of a greeting of honor. In Lektonese (flawless, she observed,) he said formally, "Fairday. I'm Toshimoto. I am pleased to be presented."

Cheelo hesitated in confusion, but his Traditional training took over. "Cheelo Cha'atre. I am honored."

Showering her brother with respect, Toshi's pleasant treatment took away the younger man's right to be upset. Toshi said, "I was telling your sister that her personal knowledge of Ambassador Cha'atre would be most helpful to my work. I'm a Diplomatic Interpreter at the Embassy, and I'm drafting a document for him."

Still suspicious, Cheelo returned an uncertain smile.

Toshi told Melantha, "I need to go back to work. Can you meet me tonight to finish my interview? Would the campus library be all right, let's say at 19:00?"

Relieved to get out of her blunder, she replied, "That's fine. I'm happy to help."

Nodding a bow, he left the shop.

Cheelo glared at her and demanded, "Are you really going to see him?"

"Cheelo, what's your problem? You heard him say this is Embassy business. Even if it wasn't, I thought I was supposed to be your guardian."

Offended, he screamed, "But he's Terran!"

She frowned at his outburst. Lowering her voice menacingly, she said, "I noticed. Father works with Terrans. He's a COAXIS Ambassador, remember?"

"I refuse to let you ruin your life!" With that impassioned declaration, he stormed away.

Cheelo left J. Paul's and broke into a run, forcing people to step off sidewalks to avoid him. The memory of his sister's laughter and the familiarity she'd displayed with the Terran burned in his mind. He was beyond angry and rapidly approaching a decision to do something he shouldn't do.

While working at Danforth, he'd found a maintenance code that was used to repair the computers at Security Central. For days after that, he'd wondered how to make use of that knowledge, and now he knew.

Security Central keeps a personal file on every citizen on Luna. I'll look up the file on Toshimoto and make sure Mel isn't involved with someone dangerous.

CHAPTER 25

That evening, Melantha made her way to the Institute's library through unlikely routes, watching to see if Cheelo had followed her. She never saw him, but finding Toshi was no problem. As soon as she entered the three-story building, he dropped a stack of vid disks. The clatter of plastic hitting the floor caught her attention.

Once he'd made eye contact, though, he didn't speak to her directly. For a moment, she wondered again if this was some kind of elaborate prank. *Is he trying not to talk to me? Maybe I'm supposed to approach him.*

But before she could move, he walked away. *Very well,* she complained to herself. *I guess I'm supposed to follow him.*

Casually, she followed him to an adjoining reading room, where he paused before a bank of three elevators. When she was beside him, he bent over a water fountain and pretended to drink. She heard him whisper, "When the elevator on the right arrives, take it to the third floor."

Shortly, the elevator on the left arrived. It was on its way down. He entered and paid no attention to her as the door closed.

Signing in frustration, she muttered to herself, "Is this necessary?" Obedient to his directions, though, she waited for the elevator on the right, entered it and pushed a button for third floor.

When it delivered her, she realized that this would be a good location to talk privately. This floor housed only offices and conference rooms and wasn't used during the evening. She called out, "Hello?"

Toshi came around a corner from a stairway. Without explanation, he took out his pocket comm and pressed a memory code. *Who is he calling, and why at this moment?*

But instead of speaking to someone, he aimed his comm at the bank of elevators. The middle car opened in response, and he gestured for her to enter.

By this time, Melantha was beyond confused and well on the way to impatient. *What's he doing now? One of the conference rooms on this floor would have been private enough to talk, but he's going back into the elevator? Why didn't we take the same elevator while we were downstairs?*

She demanded, "What are you trying to pull?"

"Please?"

Though annoyed at the subterfuge, she did as he asked and entered the open elevator. Soon, she regretted it. When the door closed, he pushed the pause-stop and held the car. She expected an alarm to sound, but nothing happened.

Suspiciously, she began a mental checklist of available resources to fight.

Sensing her fear, he smiled. "Don't you trust me?"

"Should I?"

"Of course. Bushido only allows me to be respectful."

"Your warrior's code?"

"Exactly. I'll need you to tell me now if you aren't interested in taking the job with our team." His dark eyes surveyed her with interest.

"You mean, right now?"

"Hill is waiting to talk to you, but I can't take you to him unless you're accepting the position."

She imagined Hill sitting in one of the conference rooms. "I expected more time to think about it."

"You need more time? I can hold the elevator forever, you know." A sly grin insinuated that he wouldn't mind being stuck in the elevator with her.

"Spare me and get on with it."

"You're going to join our team, then?"

To Melantha, the only consideration was the extra income she needed to support Cheelo. She was about to agree until the excitement in the Terran's eyes alarmed her. What motive did he have for wanting her on the team?

Nevertheless, she answered, "Looks as though I am."

As he released the pause, she prepared to follow him to a conference room, but he didn't open the door. "What are you doing, Toshimoto?"

Grinning, he held up his comm. "Taking you to Hill. This is the only way the middle elevator works. Going down."

Confusion warred with irritation in her mind, but anger was gaining ground. She growled, "We're leaving the library? What was the point of coming here if we're going right back where we started?"

"We aren't leaving the library. We're going to Hill's office on another floor. First, I'm going to create a code that will let you operate the middle elevator using your pocket comm."

"Hill has an office in the library? I thought he works for Security Central?"

"He does and he does. You'll understand in a minute. Get ready to record a vocal passcode. Use your first name and a description, something like, Melantha of Lekton."

"But you'll know my passcode."

Scowling, he rolled his eyes. "You want me to flash my top secret clearance, and security bonding I.D.?"

"Would you, please?" she asked sweetly.

Sighing, he activated his comm's recorder and said, "Identify Toshimoto." Again the elevator beeped in response. "Program vocal access code for a new member." Faint, musical sounds were followed by another beep. Holding the comm near her, he nodded.

It was customary for Lektonians to identify themselves by using their father's name. She bent the custom and said, "Melantha, daughter of Kaantina'a."

His eyes widened, but he pressed another button on the comm to accept the recording. "I've never heard a Lektonian use a mother's name as identification."

"How do you know it's my mother?"

"I worked your background check."

She attempted to hide her concern about that. "You know a lot about Lekton."

"I'm a Linguistics Specialist, remember? Lekton was my primary field. There's nothing wrong with using that code as long as you remember it. We can go now. You're in for a real surprise. It's not a typical office."

She gawked at him. *This has to be a joke, a prank meant to humiliate me. Is this some revenge about the Tserian rumor? There must be a camera somewhere recording how foolishly I do whatever I'm told to do.*

But then again, Toshi had said that joining this team required the highest security clearance. This could be for real. Knowing the library had archive storage in the basement, she wondered, *wouldn't Hill want a private office to be less accessible?*

Facing forward, he spoke into his pocket comm, giving his own vocal passcode, which she guessed was in Japanese. As the elevator descended, he stepped behind her and waited.

At the basement, she watched the door and prepared to exit. She heard the sound of a door open, but it wasn't the one she faced. Turning around, she discovered that Toshi had disappeared.

The back elevator wall had opened. Beyond, she glimpsed what appeared to be the living room of someone's home, but not any home she'd ever imagined before. This home existed in a previous century. *Did I go back in time,* she wondered?

Suddenly, Toshi stepped into her line of view, laughing like a demented child who was playing a trick on a sibling. "Welcome to Headquarters. This way, my dear," he said, sweeping his hand in a gallant bow.

She refused to move and didn't bother to cover her anger. "Enjoyed that, did you, making me feel foolish?"

He snickered again. "I was having a little fun. I do it to every new recruit. Follow me, please."

Hesitating, she asked, "Headquarters for what?"

"The Special Investigation Team. It's easier to call it the S.I.T."

Peeking out of the elevator and looking around her, Melantha was filled with confused awe. The room was decorated to represent a Nineteenth Century American living room. Then, stepping boldly inside, she inquired, "I assume the Library Director doesn't know about this addition to the basement?"

"Nope, and neither does Security Central. This part of the base-ment isn't on the original blueprints for the library, except for…"

But she'd quit listening. Her jaw dropped in reaction to what she was seeing. Smiling, he continued patiently, "… except for the elevators."

"Who built this place?"

"Hill did. The first time I saw it, I thought I'd stepped into another dimension."

She could see why. The suite was devoid of any modern decora-tion and furnished entirely in antiques. To her left, she saw an adjoining room with an old-fashioned dining table. Peering around a corner, she found a small kitchen with a cooking stove and refrigerator.

Toshi called out, "As you've noticed, this part isn't the office. The suite is also used as a residence."

"Hill lives … here? With his obvious means, he could live anywhere. Why do without modern conveniences?"

"Hey, it would make sense if Hill lived here! I'd understand why he's spends so much money to decorate it. Two of our Investigators live here. Hill only uses one of the upstairs bedrooms as an extra office during the daytime. Nobody knows where he lives."

"More mysteries!" she teased, at last looking at him. "You never reveal your first name, and Hill never reveals his residence. Has it occurred to you that by creating curiosity about yourselves, you're inviting others to snoop?"

He shrugged. "It's not hard to find out why I don't use my first name."

"It isn't that easy," she confessed, letting him catch her meaning—she'd tried.

Although he kept a polite smile and showed no concern, she noticed that he swallowed hard. If he were as devious as she suspected, his next move would be to divert the topic of conversation. That's how the Lawbenders would keep control. She quoted to herself, *confuse the issue, pretend indifference, divert attention, or shift blame.*

Taunting her, he said, "I'm sure you must have some secrets of your own. For example, why don't you ever date anyone? Should I see what I can find out?"

More Lawbender techniques—make an offensive strike, shift priority, and maintain momentum in an opposite direction.

She didn't give away what she knew and dropped the subject. "Where's Hill?"

To his credit, he didn't show any pleasure at so skillfully manipulating her. "Hill's upstairs." He pointed across the room.

Wooden-railed banisters that were polished to a deep, mahogany shine rose to a second story landing where four doors were visible. Toshi wandered toward a framed oil painting on the wall of the dining area, anticipation shining in his expression. Once he was sure that she watched, he pushed the picture to one side on its hook.

Melantha gasped. Behind the picture was a highly advanced communication system. *What an odd sight among antiques!*

He pressed a button and said, "We're downstairs, Hill."

"Come up," came a cheerful response.

Allowing the picture to return to its place, he walked to the stairs. But pulling the frame aside again to inspect the system, she asked, "This doubles as a security system, doesn't it?"

"Yes, and it controls our use of the library's middle elevator."

She examined the control panel. "I'd think someone would wonder why they never see the middle elevator work and try to repair it."

Toshi was amused by her enthusiastic interest in technical gadgetry. "Most people aren't very observant. You're an instinctive investigator." Rejoining her at the panel, he tapped her shoulder and turned her to face him. He thought to himself, *since she didn't clobber me for touching her, I'll find more excuses to do it again.*

He said, "Hill wants us upstairs."

"Oh, sorry. It's such a fascinating system!"

He smiled tolerantly. "Occupational hazard. Security agents tend to be gadget hounds."

That got her attention. "Hounds?"

"Fanatics?" She still looked puzzled. "Never mind."

As she climbed the stairs, he watched her hand slide along the smooth, cool wood of the railing. She looked down at her feet as if listening to their unfamiliar tap on wood. *Who'd have thought stairways would be an experience to savor?*

Leading her to a door at the top of the stairs, he waited, knowing she'd look for a thumb lock or some standard wall device. Her eyes searched the seams of the door for a remote sensor.

Toshi chuckled, enjoying her confusion. "This is rich! It opens by a door knob."

She glanced down. "A... door... knob? I've seen this in Terran history texts, but I've never actually used one. This place is strange. Why did he do this?"

Rapping lightly on the door, he whispered, "He wanted a replica of an early American homestead. He traded convenience for authenticity."

From behind the door, Hill called, "Come in."

He allowed Melantha the pleasure of turning the doorknob. She shivered, and he laughed at her curious reaction.

As soon as the door opened, Melantha froze to appreciate the delightful room. Hill's voice startled her. "Come in, Melantha."

Hill sat on a wine-colored, overstuffed sofa of taffeta. A matching, high-back wing chair sat in a corner with intricately carved, wooden tables presiding to each side. A plant cascaded over one table, and on the other, two brass statuettes held leather-bound books between them.

Hill said, "Welcome to Headquarters. This is my office away from the chaos of Security Central. I come here for a break. For me, it's like a walk in the woods. Time slows down, and my blood pressure goes back to normal."

Toshi could tell that Hill was also enjoying her reaction as she scanned the rest of the room. It looked more like a living area except for a large, wooden desk that sat prominently in the center of the room.

The floors were hardwood, but a large area rug in muted beige and green covered most of the surface. On the walls, reprints of famous paintings, all pastoral scenes, were framed in simple, wooden elegance.

She mumbled, "The rich textures combined with common shapes is a Lektonian style."

Hill didn't understand. "Excuse me?"

Toshi saw a chance to show off for her. "I think it masters bold texture interwoven with subtle color enhancement."

She stared at him and then nodded.

Hill asked, "What are you talking about?"

Toshi explained, "Lektonians define aesthetic appreciation by the methods in which different concepts are contrasted. To me, this is the best example of complementary contrast I've seen, other than on Lekton."

"You've been to Lekton?" she asked in surprise.

"I have, yes." There was no reason to explain that for one season during 2156 and 2157, he'd lived there while completing a practicum for his Linguistics degree. A little more mystery, he decided, would keep her interested.

She said, "Hill, this room is truly magnificent! I can't imagine how it was done, but that only makes it more impressive."

Toshi couldn't wait to show her the feature of Hill's suite that he liked best. He pointed to one wall. She saw a window where sunlight and breezes entered, despite the fact it was a basement room! Starched, sun-drenched, white draperies flapped at the window in pleasant rhythm to the tick of a grandfather clock standing in a nearby corner.

Enthralled, she wandered to the window. As Toshi pointed outside, his other hand gently cradled her shoulder. He was in luck—she didn't realize it.

They saw cows grazing in a pasture beyond a whitewashed, wooden fence. Just outside the window was a tree with a bird's nest perched on a limb. The nest held baby birds that chirped urgently, hungry for their meal.

Melantha said under her breath, "The window must be an illusion."

"Is it?" Toshi reached toward the window as if to snatch a birdling in his hand. A mother bird returned instantly to the nest and screeched a warning.

Hill told Melantha, "I saved the best for last." Standing, he moved from the sofa to his desk and opened a drawer. He exposed a complex control panel and pushed a button.

Warm gusts of a summer breeze touched her face. The crisp, white curtains whipped gently against her hair. As Toshi expected, she sighed and smiled. He knew the thrill of that first introduction to Hill's simulation window.

Melantha was lost in thought, staring out the window as she felt the tension in her shoulders ease. She tried to forget that Toshimoto was standing closer than she liked. In the future, she'd remember to keep her distance from him. He had the most infuriating habit of touching her when he thought he had an excuse.

Hill called, "Melantha, please have a seat. There are a few things I need to go over." He sat at the oak desk and picked up a pipe, puffing at it in a philosophical pose. Melantha thought that was carrying his old-fashioned theme a bit far, and presumed it wasn't real.

But to her surprise, circles of cherry-scented smoke soon ringed his head. She'd smelled the mentholated scent before which was used by people with breathing problems. *It must be the only equivalent available that he could put in a pipe,* she thought.

Melantha crossed to a rocker across from the desk. She followed Hill's stare to Toshi, who was still at the window and gazing across the field.

Hill quietly called, "Toshi?"

"Yeah?" he returned absently. The tranquil scene had mesmerized him.

Addressing a tiny fleck on the desktop, Hill asked, "What happened at J. Paul's?"

Toshi turned around, asking innocently, "What are you talking about?"

By the way Hill inspected it, the tiny particle on the desktop held great interest for him. But she knew that his full attention was on them.

Hill answered, "You've been followed most of the afternoon, Toshi."

Laughing, Toshi scoffed at that. "I don't think so."

"And someone's been asking questions about you and getting answers."

"I did nothing to break my cover!"

In Melantha's estimation, Toshi's reaction was overplayed, unless he really was hiding some sinister secret about himself.

Hill looked at her. "It's your brother."

"Cheelo?" A chill tingled at the back of her neck.

Hill studied her. "He's digging up every fact he can find about Toshi. I'd like your opinion about why he'd do that."

Hill's tone was even and firm, but she couldn't tell if he was angry. "I don't know," she answered truthfully. "He happened to walk into J. Paul's and saw me with Toshi. For some reason, he was suspicious. I'm afraid I didn't handle his questions very well, so I probably made the situation worse."

Hill looked at Toshi for confirmation. Toshi shook his head. "She didn't do anything wrong that I noticed, except for avoiding answers to a direct question. Maybe he knows his sister well enough to read more into her reaction than I did. But I think my answer reassured him."

Melantha thought, *I'm going to show him the consequences of lying.* "Looks like he didn't believe you. You should have known he'd check out your story."

"That's why I told him what I did. If he was looking for proof that I lied, he found out otherwise."

She didn't believe him.

Hill instructed her, "Quickly and truthfully answering a direct question creates trust. You know that's the first lesson in keeping a cover. If you're caught in a lie, your word won't be credible after that."

Dejectedly, Toshi plopped down on the sofa.

Melantha still had doubts. "You're saying that was true? You're a Diplomatic Aide at the Embassy?"

"More than an aide," Hill chided.

She asked sheepishly, "Then you really interpret the documents that COAXIS sends to my father?"

"That's part of my job. I could say something, but I won't risk making you angry."

Hill added solemnly, "Toshi doesn't lie. His standards won't permit it."

She laughed. "Don't tell me: He follows an ancient, Japanese code of conduct?"

Hill's expression was calm. "Bushido, yes. You can believe him. Too bad Cheelo didn't. He not only verified Toshi's employment, but also learned his current assignments. Then, he began an investigation of his personal background. I wish I knew why."

She dropped her head. "I'm sorry if it endangered your cover, Toshi. Cheelo has been pushing me to get acquainted with men. Maybe that's what he thought I was doing."

Ignoring her, Toshi interrogated Hill. "What personal information did he get?"

Despite his annoyance, Hill continued to speak to her. "Obviously, your brother thinks he should check out your relationships. You've got to put a stop to his probing right away."

Toshi who hadn't gotten an answer, scowled fiercely.

Hill held up a hand, asking him to wait and then told her, "The S.I.T. has clear-cut rules in our organization. When you see teammates in public, don't acknowledge acquaintance. That way, if an Investigator loses a cover, the others won't be compromised. Is that understood?" It was a courteous request for confirmation.

"Yes, sir. I understand. But what will I tell Cheelo if he sees Toshi working with me on John's experiments? I'm with my brother often since I'm teaching him martial arts."

"It will be my responsibility to see that no one observes you. I'll arrange a private location for Johnny to carry out his experiments. Be careful that Cheelo never sees the two of you together again."

Toshi could take no more. He leaned over the desk and pressed his face very near Hill's. "What personal information did Cheelo get?"

Hill chuckled. "I didn't mean to ignore you, Toshi. I was getting to it. You were right about the need to change your birth records to remove your first name. Somehow, he found that record. But of course, I'd changed it to read only Toshimoto."

Toshi paced the room, pounding his fist into his hand. "Didn't I tell you someone would try that? How did you find out I was followed when I didn't know?"

Melantha remarked, "Cheelo can be resourceful when he wants something."

Hill told her, "Correction: He knows how to carry out a deep background investigation. I'd say he's accomplished too much by his probes into Toshi's private life. I wish I knew what he was trying to find out."

"So do I!" Toshi's aimless pacing became directed as he went behind her and pressed his body threateningly against the back of the rocker.

She decided to take a cue from Hill about handling Toshi's intimidation. Shrugging, she glanced up at him. "I suppose he wants to find out how close I am to you. Cheelo's a talented young man. Even though he's young, he'd make a good contribution to your team."

"I'm considering it," Hill replied.

Toshi did a double-take. "You're impressed with this kid because I didn't catch him tailing me?"

"No, not entirely. I didn't think he did such a terrific job of that since Bonnie spotted him doing it. And when she started tailing him, he never knew it."

Standing abruptly, Hill hurried to the window and obviously avoided them. His hair blew in the gentle breeze, sending his long, blond bangs into his eyes. Absently, he swept them away from his eyes.

Toshi appeared to be fascinated by Hill's reaction. "What was it that impressed you? Did he learn something about me you didn't already know?"

Hill turned, demanding menacingly, "Is there something about you I don't already know, Toshimoto?"

"No, no," Toshi replied swiftly, waving his hand at Hill to calm him.

After pacing a few more minutes, Hill finally confided, "It's only that this sixteen-year-old boy found out everything he wanted to know so easily, but I couldn't find out his sources! It's like he picked it right out of city computers!"

"Nonsense! That's a locked file!"

A sick feeling drifted through her mind. "Don't underestimate him. His first toys were computers."

Awed, Toshi exclaimed, "It isn't often someone gets past Hill's sources."

Having recovered his dignity, Hill returned to his desk. "I'll consider processing a security clearance on him. Meanwhile, Melantha, let's get you oriented. Would you mind moving to a vacant apartment here? You could use Headquarters most of the time for Johnny's experiments. It's a nice apartment, rent-free, naturally."

She thought of the savings she'd achieve by moving out of faculty housing. She told him, "I'd like that, but is it part of the salary? Raising my brother isn't cheap."

"No, it's not. I think you'll find I'm generous. If I put you on the payroll as a Consultant, you'll be paid regardless of the amount of time you spend on assignments. If you prefer, I'll pay you by the job at a Defense Specialist's wage. That pays more."

He scribbled something on a memo sheet from his desk and handed it to her.

Melantha nearly choked. The Consultant's monthly salary was equivalent to her salary at the Institute, but the Specialist's pay was twice that amount. Either way, this income would be an enormous help. She told him, "I'll accept either position, whatever helps you most."

"Good. I'll make you a Specialist, then, since I have Toshi available, too. I'll call a meeting for 07:00 tomorrow morning. Every member of the team will be here to meet you, and I'll go over policies and procedures with you then."

Hill escorted them to the door. "Toshi, you'd better ask Bonnie to meet Melantha at the faculty house after curfew to oversee her move to Headquarters." He told her, "She's an Enforcer. In uniform, it would appear like she's assisting a citizen. I'll see you both tomorrow."

The door closed softly behind them as she and Toshi descended the stairs to the living area. Toshi showed her how to call the elevator to the basement so that she could use her pocket comm from now on.

As the elevator door opened, he told her, "You can start packing and I'll have Bonnie meet you after student curfew."

She nodded and entered the elevator, waiting for him.

He shook his head. "We leave the library separately. I'm glad you're on the team."

After the elevator door had closed, she remembered his excitement when she told him she was joining the team. She whispered to herself, "And you never lie, do you, Toshimoto? What is your agenda?"

CHAPTER 26

Melantha was packed and waiting for Bonnie to arrive. The knock at the door was aggressive, anything but an action of stealth. She jumped. *I wonder if I'll ever reprogram myself to the S.I.T.'s style of security?*

When she opened the door, she expected the uniformed Enforcer, but she was wrong. A petite redhead in jeans and a sweater smiled at her warmly, but with equal surprise, asking, "You're Melantha?"

"That's right."

"Do you always open your door after curfew without knowing who it is?"

Melantha had become more cautions since she'd learned there were Tserians on Luna. But she couldn't explain that. So, she laughed, thinking of the unfortunate person who would dare attack her. "I'm not worried. And who are you?"

"I'm Bonnie Gorishek. I was told you'd need an escort after curfew?"

"And I was told you'd be in uniform."

"I decided it was safer not to broadcast the fact that I can defend myself. In the uniform, anyone knows I'm at least a first-degree black belt."

"Yes," she agreed hesitantly. "But wouldn't that deter someone from thinking you're easy prey?"

"Unless he's a second degree belt." She lifted her eyebrows.

Melantha surveyed this cocky woman carefully. *Her short, slim physique doesn't look lethal,* she thought. *There's a lot of cunning, though, in those bright, green eyes…* Warnings went off in her mind. *What if she's a Tserian instead of the Enforcer I was told to expect?*

But not wanting her suspicion known, Melantha said, "And I suppose you're not a first-degree belt, right?"

"Negative. Fourth. And you? What am I thinking? Defense is your Specialty degree. You must be about…"

How odd that anyone on Luna wouldn't know about my Keplar fame. She replied bashfully, "Eighth."

She looked suddenly abashed. "You're the Lektonian woman who won all those Keplar medals, right? And I'm here to defend you… why?"

Melantha stepped back, allowing her to enter. She liked the confident young woman, despite doubts about her identity. "I haven't a clue. Frankly, from what Toshi and Hill said, I expected a gorilla."

Her quiet giggle was pleasant. "I was thinking the same thing about you. It's hard to convince men that size isn't everything."

Together, they gathered the four suitcases containing her belongings. Bonnie asked, "What brought you to Luna?"

Melantha had assumed that the entire team would have been privy to her security check. "I wanted to attend this Institute. I decided to stay here and teach, and now, I'm putting my brother through school."

"That's terrific. My family's so far away that we never see each other. Don't you have more boxes?"

Melantha pulled a pack onto her back. "This is everything. Between the two of us, we can move everything in one trip. I don't keep many material things."

"I should say not! I couldn't move my bathroom cabinet in one trip."

Melantha laughed. Bonnie's refreshing sense of humor put her at ease. She told herself, *I doubt a Tserian would go to the trouble of befriending me if she were going to capture me for interrogation. I have to quit worrying about this.*

Outside, the night was still and pleasantly cool as they left the Faculty House. Though dark, security lighting along sidewalks was bright. Melantha turned in the direction of the library.

Bonnie stopped. Her voice echoed on the street. "We're taking a different route."

Trying to curb her anxiety, she followed.

Bonnie led the way to a park beyond the campus and soon found herself watching every shadow, wondering why she'd suddenly developed a case of nerves. Finally, she had to ask, "Why are we going so far from the library?"

"Shhh!" Bonnie set the two suitcases on the ground in order to pull a pocket comm from beneath her sweater. She hit a program key. "Nobody around. Let's keep going."

Melantha stopped dead. "How do you know there's nobody around?"

"I just checked. Come on!" Bonnie whispered again, taking up her load.

Sighing, Melantha followed once more. "If we're alone, why are we whispering?"

Bonnie glared at her. "Because I don't trust gadgets."

"Then, why did you check?"

"Do you have to ask so many questions?"

Melantha fought the nagging suspicions growing in her head by the minute. After all, Hill had said to expect a woman in uniform, and Melantha hadn't met Bonnie before. Abruptly, she stopped and stared at the woman.

Her escort stopped, too, and turned back to gape at her. "What's wrong?"

"Only an officer's duty comm would have sensor equipment to track the proximity of life signs. I know a pocket comm from a duty comm, and that was a pocket comm."

Bonnie went nearer, whispering, "I knew you were sharp. You're right; this is a pocket comm. But the link is open, and the person on the other end does have a duty comm—my duty comm. He signaled me that we're clear to make it to the back door of Headquarters."

This didn't settle her questions.

Bonnie turned and went on. "Are you coming?"

A half-kilometer from the library, they arrived at their destination. A stairway down into the underground shopping district illuminated the surrounding night. To Melantha's dread, that was where Bonnie led her.

In the dead of night, we're going to tramp through one of the most notoriously crime-ridden areas of the quadrant?

"Nervous, Melantha?" teased Bonnie.

"Ha! I can handle myself. Who's going to protect you?"

The steps glowed white with recessed lighting as they descended below street level. At the bottom of the stairs, Melantha laughed at the presence of an automated flower shop. "I don't imagine a flower shop gets much business in this neighborhood. Who would open a shop here?"

"Hill owns it. What doesn't sell is donated to the hospital. Most decent folk don't come here after hours. Those who do aren't interested in flowers, let me tell you. Guard behind you if you use this back way into Headquarters."

Suddenly, the door to the shop opened. Toshi, holding a duty comm, waited inside. Melantha locked onto the welcome sight of his brown eyes, unaware until this moment that she'd still harbored a suspicion that she was being kidnapped by Tserians.

"Hi," Toshi called to her. "How do you like our 'crime and intrigue' act?"

"I don't! I hope I won't have to use this entrance often."

"You shouldn't use it unless you have to. Tonight, we couldn't exactly break into the library to use the elevator."

Smiling, she let her frayed nerves rest and followed them into the tiny shop. There was nothing here except six, automated flower displays. For a moment, Bonnie and Melantha set down their bags and rested.

Once more, Toshi glanced at Bonnie's duty comm to make sure they weren't observed. Then, he directed Melantha to take out her pocket comm, point it at the largest flower vault, and give her vocal passcode. When she did so, they heard a faint click and then the entire vault swung open on a hinge.

Beyond the vault was a tunnel. Its walls weren't tall or wide, but the corridor was painted pale yellow and had pastel green carpeting.

Carrying suitcases in both hands, the two women entered the vault, followed by Toshi. He aimed the duty comm at the vault and issued the code to close the door. At the last second, he reached through the door and snatched one flower from a vase.

Turning to Melantha, he took one of her suitcases from her, offering her the flower.

Confused, she took the pale, pink flower and gently caressed its delicate petals. "What's this for?"

He smiled. "A gift—the first decoration for your new apartment."

He handed Bonnie's duty comm to her, taking one of her suitcases, as well. Without another word, he moved through the tunnel.

The tunnel twisted occasionally, revealing only a segment of their course at a time, and each was varied in color. Soon, Melantha realized that each new twist in the way showed a shorter stretch ahead, which relieved the mind from worry that the journey in close quarters would never end.

When Toshi had moved farther ahead, Melantha showed the flower to Bonnie and whispered, "Why?"

She whispered back in amazement, "Haven't you ever had a guy give you flowers?"

"I guess I haven't. Is there a significance I should understand?"

Bonnie frowned. "You bet there is. I'll explain it later."

At last, with a final, brief bend in the corridor, they faced a dead end. Her mind might have panicked to reach the end and see she was trapped, but painted on the wall were the words, "This is a door."

Bonnie said, "The library is directly above us."

And as expected, when Toshi told Melantha to use her pocket comm again, it triggered a response. The entire wall before them lifted into the ceiling.

Melantha recognized a hallway of the library's basement. Mere steps away, she saw the bank of three elevators. She ducked back into the tunnel, asking Bonnie, "What if someone happened to be working late in the archives? Isn't this a little risky?"

"Not a bit. There are security sensors guarding the wall. If anyone is close by, the door won't be triggered. The same goes for the middle elevator. You can't call it if anyone is near enough to see you."

Cautiously, they entered the library. Melantha asked, "Wouldn't this door be noticeable from this side?"

"Take a look," Toshi answered, indicating behind them. The wall fell, hiding the tunnel, and once closed, it seemed like only a wall. *Evidently,* she reflected, *no expense was spared to hide this private suite, and that somehow disturbs me.*

Absently, she followed Toshi and Bonnie into the middle elevator and through the back wall of it into S.I.T. Headquarters. It was secure and warm, even on second viewing. She appreciated the unique and stimulating décor that was alien in both culture and era to anything she'd experienced before.

Toshi handed off the two suitcases he'd carried. "I have to get some sleep. Welcome home!" He returned to the elevator, and the door closed.

"This way," Bonnie prompted as she guided Melantha upstairs.

At the top of the stairs, the door to Hill's office was closed. To the right of that, the doors of two other apartments were also closed. But a door to the left of the stairs, adjoining Hill's office, was ajar. Bonnie nodded toward it, and Melantha went inside.

At her entry, light from diffused ceiling panels brightened the barren and simple room's off-white walls and beige carpets. "I can decorate it myself?"

"Sure." Bonnie crossed the room, turning away to set the suitcases on the floor. She seemed distracted as she wandered back to the door.

"Thank you for helping."

"No problem." She seemed about to say more, but decided against it.

"You were going to explain about the flower?"

She sighed. "I should warn you that when a man gives flowers to a woman, it's sometimes a symbol of affection. If that's what he meant, watch out. Hill won't like it."

"I doubt a Terran man would feel that way about me."

"Think what you want, but I've seen Toshi flirt with just about every woman on Luna. That doesn't mean anything because it's part of his cover. It makes people shy away from him. But when he starts to treat a woman respectfully, he cares about her."

"Thanks for the warning. I assume that Hill doesn't want his investigators to be entangled in distracting relationships."

"That's an understatement." She looked at her feet.

"He has a point. It's a common policy in security agencies."

Her head shot up, looking intently at Melantha to declare, "No. Hill goes beyond that. His policy is almost neurotic. Don't let Toshi get you in trouble with Hill, or he'll fire both of you."

Melantha sneered at the thought of any man daring to flirt with her. "I had a feeling that he can't be trusted. He told me some line about following a strict, Japanese code of conduct."

"Oh, that's no line. Bushido is notorious around here. He teaches it to anyone who'll listen. He's so disciplined in it that you can depend on whatever he says."

"And what he does?"

Bonnie reacted as if she'd been overheard. "He's harmless. Well, I'd better go." Excusing herself, she left.

Melantha reflected on her new home and her new job. The vague, disquieting alarm she felt as she learned more about the S.I.T. was beginning to concern her. The intricacy and depth of the team's cover (not to mention the money expended) struck her as odd for a simple, Private Security organization.

What if Hill used these consultants for more than solving local crimes?

Thoughtfully, she went over what she knew. She'd met some of the team members: John, Hill, Toshi, and now Bonnie. "I should have asked how many others are on the team."

At the moment, though, she'd find no answers. Grateful for her simple life, she unpacked her fur-bed, spread it out over a few clothes for padding and laid down to rest.

During the last moments of consciousness, it came to her what had changed about her life. *Once more, I feel like I have a sense of purpose. I'll be able to afford to keep Cheelo in school and, hopefully, teach him to think for himself where Tradition was concerned.*

And even if I'm not meant to be The MenD'lee and rescue Lekton, at least I'll help keep Luna free of crime. Maybe I'll even be able to help David free Tserias from a tyrannical government. Under the right lead-

ership, it might be time to give Tserias a second chance at enjoying the fruits of COAXIS membership.

Yes, life is good, she thought.

But as sleep claimed her, she dreamed of battling monsters and demons of every sort. They wanted to make her fall in love. Strangely enough, they were all Japanese.

EPILOGUE

San Durg Township, 30 Lairees, 2170 (September 1 TSE)

Elder Donni Chonaira trembled with fright. Aside to Elder Garthrik, he said, "Please excuse me from the Bench, Jonik."

Without asking for an explanation, Donni was dismissed, but he could tell that the Council Leader was confused by his reaction to this case.

Once he was away from everyone's hearing, Donni whispered, "What am I doing? I've never been overly sensitive about any case before. Get this under control before you draw too much attention."

Hurrying to his inner office, he said nothing to his assistant and closed his office door. Quickly, he took out his pocket comm and accessed Loris' private number.

His friend greeted him with curiosity, for Donni was supposed to be in session.

"Not exactly," Donni said cryptically. "Did you hear the news?"

Hesitating to admit that he'd understood the code, Loris answered, "I've been traveling. I arrived at the Embassy only a quarter-cycle ago. What happened?"

Donni collapsed against the wall and whispered urgently, "Alert your friends to keep out of public view. A family in San Durg was murdered last night."

Horror and disbelief in his voice, Loris whispered back, "Did you say murdered? That's terrible! Was it ... someone we know?" He was asking if it was a Lawbender.

"Yes. Jiiram Gresh and his family were high in my regard." Although that code indicated the family was down-chain to Donni, someone he'd recruited, it could also mean that he'd respected Jiiram. The father had been a very important Lawbender contact, though, and Loris would know that.

"Does anyone know why this happened?"

As quietly as he could, Donnie relayed the story of a dispute between neighbors. Gresh had been too vehement in his criticism of the Law of Tradition.

"Loris, we have citizens who expect the Council to vindicate the neighbor who committed the murders."

"Dearest All Wise! They don't want him punished?"

"Quite the opposite. His friends think he should be commended for defending the Law."

Loris found it hard to speak, too. "The case has been brought to the Council, I hope."

"Yes. We've exiled him to the asteroid mines on Pandeera Station, of course. His family is causing us strife over it. But it surely bodes disaster when someone kills a man over political differences. Loris, no one will be safe!"

But his friend's steady voice reassured him. "The All Wise will protect us. Instead of hiding, we need to be stirring up outrage against strict Traditionists."

"I don't know about that, Loris." Although The All Wise had always protected the Quiet Revolution, Donni was afraid of retaliation if they fought back. Trying to keep his voice from quivering, he answered, "I'll get some sound advice first." Translated, that meant he'd send a message up-chain and get instructions.

Loris didn't seem satisfied, but he finally said, "I guess that's wise. I'll pass the word to my friends to be careful."

"There's been such peace and progress recently that I'd assumed The MenD'lee was at work."

Loris groaned, "If so, The MenD'lee must be on holiday now."

Luna, Center City Hospital, September 1, 2170

At 06:30, a beep from his wrist chrono warned Dr. David Bellini that his shift was about to start. Hastily, he swallowed one more bite of his breakfast, washed it down with the last of his milk, and stood. Already, he looked forward to the first break. After three months of his internship, he felt like he lived at the hospital.

For the benefit of any of the Emperor's Infiltrators who might be watching him, he stretched his tall frame and yawned. Tserians didn't yawn, but during his indoctrination to come here, that was one of the suggestions he'd been told would make him seem more Terran-like. Sneezing was another suggestion, but he'd discovered that wasn't a good idea for hospital employees.

Taking his tray to the recycle slot, he smiled at a pretty brunette nurse who noticed him in passing. He knew that he'd attract more attention by not noticing her.

He walked on, inwardly communing with the mind of his mate. *Ru-Mena, love, I hope you understand what I go through in this body.*

Immediately, her calm, loving thoughts filled him. *It's your own fault, Da-Meed, for choosing to be a what did you call it?*

Sex symbol, dear. And yes, you're right. Bad move, he agreed.

He turned into the Pediatrics hallway, his current rotation assignment. With growing unease, he knew he was being followed. Ever since graduation, he'd been watched carefully. Actually, since meeting Melantha, he realized. *I hope I haven't brought suspicion on her.*

A Tserian Infiltrator entered the hospital. His day was beginning like every other day, laboring to undo the mistake he'd made. Shortly after arriving on Luna in 2162 with the last group of Tserian students, Ke-Resh al Dubir had been the guard on duty when one of those princes, Ge-Ralt ab Belne disappeared into thin air. His student alias, Gerald Davies, never appeared on class rosters, and Ke-Resh was to blame.

Today, as every day, he set out to correct that shame on his record. Years ago, the Emperor had lost faith in him and had sent one of his elite Inquisitors named Bu-Rhat al Gekk to take over the investigation. Ke-Resh was determined to fix his own problem, though, and find Ge-Ralt before Bu-Rhat did.

Today, he'd decided to find out if Da-Meed was in contact with the missing prince, as they were direct cousins. Disguised as a middle-aged man in the uniform of a city maintenance worker, Ke-Resh fell into step behind David.

For days, he'd followed the activities of Prince Da-Meed, even though Bu-Rhat said David was already cleared. Something about the prince bothered him. Quietly, the Infiltrator promised, "You're out there somewhere, Ge-Ralt. You can change your alias all you want, but I'll track you down and kill you myself."

When David began to sense he was being followed, the maintenance worker pushed open the door of the men's room and entered. Moments later, a young man of twenty walked briskly out of the same door and headed away from Pediatrics.

Then, his pocket comm buzzed, and the young man put it to his ear. "Yes, I know what you said, but I'd rather check it for myself."

He sidestepped a woman trying to steer a hyperactive toddler through the hospital corridors. Again Ke-Resh replied into his comm, "Yeah, I heard you're the one who can recognize him! So what? I lost him, and I'll find him again. Just because the Em... the boss sent you here doesn't mean I can't hunt for him."

Following a long tirade, the young man pounded a nearby wall with exaggerated frustration. Sighing, he answered, "Fine. Yes, I will. Look, I said I'd drop it and leave Da-Meed alone." He pocketed the device again with a sturdy curse. More determined than ever, he resumed the search.

Wasn't there one more lead I was going to try? What about Melantha Chatrey, that new instructor at the Institute who went to Commencement with Da-Meed? I heard they were very chummy that night. Maybe those rumors about her had some validity. Bu-Rhat ordered me to leave David alone, but she didn't say anything about the teacher, right?

"Look out, Melantha Chatrey. I'm coming after you."

The End

APPENDIX

Lektonian Gestures

Acknowledgment: *dendee saal*

To show agreement or understanding, nod once. The Lektonian nod uses the entire upper body in a slight, bowing gesture.

Affection: *jhaarteel*

To offer, use the back of the fingers to stroke the jaw line. Note: Using an open palm against the face is considered disrespectful and implies domination.

Apology: *gaaro*

To offer, touch tip of index finger to forehead. Add other gestures to denote sincerity, remorse or humility.

Assistance: *maykair*

To either request or offer emotional help, extend clasped hands outward.

Come or Follow: *gleenay*

To request, nod head twice, dipping chin without moving the body.

Comradeship: *ra'a K'jhon*

"Comrade's Grip" To exchange, each person extends right arms and grasps the other's forearm, lingering in a brief squeeze. This is ordinarily exchanged between equals of station or title. Thus, it implies equality and is a special honor.

Concern or Worry: *teepaa*

Express by touching the first two fingers of both hands together.

Friendship: *J'la'a*

To offer, clasp hands behind your back at waist level. This gesture of goodwill demonstrates no touch will be offered without permission.

Gratitude: *alay*

To offer, tap a hand on your chest. Adding a bow denotes sincerity.

Greeting of Honor: *taama J'len*

To offer, bow with eyes lowered, hands outstretched, palm upward. This is a formal greeting.

Honesty Oath: *kaalsoto*

To request, extend crossed wrists, palms upward. To swear honesty, extend crossed wrists, palms downward. Speaking falsely under this gesture dishonors one's self and family.

Honesty Doubted: *paan kaalsoto*

Requested for hostile or untrustworthy testimony. To request, ask for kaalsoto with fingers curved upward to invite joining. To answer, offer kaalsoto and curl fingers into the offered cup. Lower deflector and allow a union of emotions.

Indecision: *merikos*

To denote no preference, extend closed fist, palm downward and then open fist, "dropping the choice." Opening the fist in a throwing gesture adds negativity, "despising the choice." The depth of displeasure is expressed in the violence of the throw.

Interruption: *preen daam*

To request, raise a hand in the air. Note: One of only a few gestures common to both Lekton and Terra.

Intimate Love: *Taam skla'a Kai*

"Salute of Trust" To request, extend a cupped hand, palm upward. To answer, extend a hand, palm downward over the cup, curling fingers together into a link. Lower deflectors and join emotions. The depth of the union is discretionary.

Mercy: *J'lek seen*

To request, cover face with crossed wrists, palm outward. To offer, pull wrists away from the requestor's face. Note: Mercy is granted only if requested. It is honorable to allow one to feel remorse and learn from it.

No or Decline :   *kos*

To express, wave a hand up and down. It is similar to the Terran gesture for, "goodbye."

Non-Offence: *leertu*

To show no offense intended, give half-bow with hand over your heart.

To show no offense taken, gesture is repeated back.

Petition: *lesin*

To make legal request of an Elder, kneel on one knee before stating a request. Once answer is given, it is permissible to rise. If unable to kneel, it is permitted to bow deeply to petition.

Remorse: *shel gaaro*

To express, hold palm on the forehead.

Respect: *denees*

To express, lower eyes to avoid direct eye contact. This is expected of children when speaking to adults and of adults when addressing someone of higher social station or authority.

Silence: *keesla*

To request, hold index finger in the air.

Wait: *beknees*

To request, hold four fingers in the air.

Yes or Accept: *bays*

To express, wave hand from side-to-side. It is similar to the Terran gesture, "shoo-a-fly."